2003/7

10/11

WISH COME TRUE

ALSO BY EILEEN GOUDGE

Taste of Honey

Stranger in Paradise

The Second Silence

One Last Dance

Thorns of Truth

Trail of Secrets

Blessing in Disguise

Such Devoted Sisters

Garden of Lies

EILEEN GOUDGE

WISH
COME TRUE

A CARSON SPRINGS NOVEL

DOUBLEDAY LARGE PRINT HOME LIBRARY EDITION
VIKING

This Large Print Edition, prepared especially for Doubleday Large Print Home Library, contains the complete, unabridged text of the original Publisher's Edition.

VIKING
Published by the Penguin Group
Penguin Group (USA) Inc., 375 Hudson Street,
New York, New York 10014, U.S.A.
Penguin Books Ltd, 80 Strand, London WC2R 0RL, England
Penguin Books Australia Ltd, 250 Camberwell Road, Camberwell,
Victoria 3124, Australia
Penguin Books Canada Ltd, 10 Alcorn Avenue,
Toronto, Ontario, Canada M4V 3B2
Penguin Books India (P) Ltd, 11 Community Centre, Panchsheel Park,
New Delhi - 110 017, India
Penguin Books (N.Z.) Ltd, Cnr Rosedale and Airborne Roads, Albany,
Auckland, New Zealand
Penguin Books (South Africa) (Pty) Ltd, 24 Sturdee Avenue,
Rosebank, Johannesburg 2196, South Africa
Penguin Books Ltd, Registered Offices:
80 Strand, London WC2R 0RL, England

Publisher's Note
This is a work of fiction. Names, characters, places, and incidents either are the product of the author's imagination or are used fictitiously, and any resemblance to actual persons, living or dead, business establishments, events, or locales is entirely coincidental.

ISBN 0-7394-3580-9

Printed in the United States of America

For

Susan Ginsburg:

friend and agent, from beginning to end.

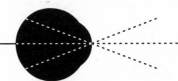

This Large Print Book carries the
Seal of Approval of N.A.V.H.

Be careful what you wish for.
—CHINESE PROVERB

Just as she was stepping into the carriage, the good fairy said, "Mind, whatever you do, don't be later than twelve," and warned her, that if she did not leave in time, her carriage would turn back into a pumpkin, her horses to mice, her coachman to a rat, her footmen to lizards, and her dress to rags . . .
—CINDERELLA (*McLoughlin Bros., New York, 1897*)

WISH COME TRUE

CHAPTER ONE

Anna Vincenzi had never seen so many reporters. Not even in the days when her sister's every move was gobbled up by millions hungry for the smallest scrap—or in the aftermath of the accident that had left Monica paralyzed from the waist down. They swarmed like insects at the end of the drive, where it emptied onto Old Sorrento Road, jockeying for position, Minicams and boom mikes poised to strike. Lining the road were interchangeable white panel trucks sprouting satellite dishes and antennae nearly as tall as the surrounding sycamores. A blond female anchor decorously holding a microphone to her glossy lips stood with her back to the hedge in the glare of a handheld reflector while a scruffy-looking cameraman filmed her stand-up. For a disoriented instant, as the patrol car bumped its way down the potholed drive amid a boiling cloud of dust, Anna felt as though she were watching it all on TV. Then someone shouted, "It's her!" and all hell broke loose.

Panic sluiced through her in an icy wave as bodies surged around the car, slowing it to a crawl. Knuckles rapped against her window and faces loomed into view, distorted by the sun's glare glancing off the dust-streaked glass. A man's voice bellowed, "Anna! Can you comment on your arrest?" Another one rasped, "Did ya do it? Did you kill her, Anna?" The cop behind the wheel, a heavyset middle-aged man with pale creases on the back of his tanned neck, swore. "Christ. Don't they feed these animals?" Anna wanted to shout, *I'm innocent! This is all a mistake!* But when she reached for the button to roll her window down she once more became aware of the handcuffs holding her shackled at the wrists, and stopped short.

That was when it sank in: She was under arrest. Which was why, on this sunny day in April, with the daylilies in bloom and the acacia snowing yellow blossoms over the mailbox—which leaned drunkenly, a legacy from when Finch had been learning to drive—she was on her way downtown to be booked.

A wave of dizziness spiraled up and the world went pale and grainy, like the snowy reception on the old black-and-white Zenith in her mother's bedroom. She thought, *This isn't happening.* In fact, the past few days had been nothing short of surreal—starting early Friday morning with the hysterical call from Arcela. Even with all that had happened since, it still hadn't sunk in. How could her sister be *dead*? It was like trying to grasp that the planet had spun off its axis.

It was 70 degrees outside but Anna was chilled to the bone. With some difficulty— the handcuffs made even the slightest movement ungainly—she drew about her a sweater that she'd grabbed from the closet on her way out the door and that was several sizes too big. She must have forgotten to pack it up with the rest of her fat clothes. Her mouth flickered in a small ironic smile. And she'd thought being overweight was her biggest worry.

The patrol car slowed to a near standstill. Vic Purdy, in the passenger seat, a veteran cop with more than thirty years under his belt—one that over time had had to be let out a few notches to accommodate his ever-expanding girth—rolled his window down to bark, "Move it along, folks! You'll all get your chance down at the court-house!"

A set of meaty fingers hooked over Vic's partially lowered window and a face loomed into view, only its upper half visible: a pair of beady eyes peering from under an australo-pithecine brow. "Anna! Did ya do it for the money? Your sister must've left you a bun-dle." The fingers were snatched back just in time to keep them from being caught in the window as it whirred up. The cop behind the wheel muttered another curse and gunned the engine. They jerked forward, the throng fanning out on either side, then with a final lurch over the worst of the pot-holes, in which every spring at least one hapless motorist became mired, they were on the road.

Hearing her name spoken—no, shouted— had had the effect of cold water being dashed over her. Ever since she could remember, it had been Monica in the spotlight, Monica they clamored for. Few had even noticed Monica's mousy nobody of a sister—whose last name was Vincenzi, not Vincent—standing quietly off to the side. Anna might have found it exciting, that *she* was the center of attention now, if the circumstances that had placed her there hadn't been so ghastly.

The patrol car picked up speed as it headed toward town, a pale scarf of dust twisting in its wake. Anna sat rigidly in her seat, staring out the window at the fields and pastures scrolling past. They rattled over cattle grids and jounced over potholes. Cows and horses, peacefully grazing, flashed by like storybook images from a period in her life long past. The cop seated beside her, a young Hispanic woman, asked if she wanted the air conditioner turned down. Anna, who hadn't realized she was shivering, turned toward her, noticing her for the first time. IRMA RODRIGUEZ, her nameplate read. She had glossy black hair pulled back in a braid and would have been pretty if not for the acne that had ravaged her face. Anna found herself mentally counseling: *Eat plenty of leafy green vegetables, stay away from saturated fats, and cleanse with a good exfoliative.* But Irma Rodriguez wasn't one of Monica's fans seeking advice.

Anna recalled the last e-mail to which she'd replied, just hours before word came of Monica's death.

To: Mamabear@earthlink.com
From: monica@monicavincent.com
Subject: RE: What now?

Dear Jolene,
What's going to be different this time?
From what you've told me, he's
begged your forgiveness before. If he
were really sincere, he'd get help. But
if he won't, that shouldn't stop you
from doing so. If not for yourself, then
for your kids. Do you want them
growing up this way? Do you think the
fact that he hasn't hit them—yet—is
any reason to keep from leaving him?
There are other ways to damage a
child, believe me.

Now she would never know how it had all turned out. Not just for Jolene, but for the countless others to whom she'd doled out big sisterly advice, everything from beauty tips to safe sex. What if they found out she had been posing as Monica? Would they feel betrayed, thinking it some sort of cruel joke, not something she'd fallen into almost by accident, the result of Monica's indifference to her fans? The thought brought a sharp stab to the pit of her stomach. Would she get the chance to tell them she'd had only their best interests at heart?

Irma offered her a stick of gum. Anna sensed she was nervous, like someone on a first date. Crimes of this sort were almost unknown in Carson Springs. There'd been the nun murders the year before last, but Sister Beatrice was now safely locked away in an institution for the criminally insane. Other than that, the most that ever happened were Waldo Squires's overnight detentions for being drunk and disorderly. Now, with Monica's death, cops whose public exposure had been limited to addressing the town council about such matters as the need for more parking meters downtown found themselves thrust into the glare of the limelight.

It seemed suddenly essential to Anna that she have at least one ally. "I was home that night." She spoke in a near whisper. "Watching TV."

Irma's expression remained impassive. Anna's panic mounted. Should she have said instead that she'd loved Monica, that she wouldn't have lifted a finger against her? Was that even true? At one time it might have been, but toward the end she *had* imagined how much easier her life would be without her sister.

"You got a lawyer?" Irma chewed her gum placidly, her jaw rotating like those of the cows in the fields.

Anna shook her head. "I didn't know I'd need one."

"You do now."

Irma regarded her curiously. Anna knew she didn't look anything like the usual murder suspect. In her navy skirt and pale blue top, the gold studs in her ears and small gold cross about her neck her only adornments, she might have been on her way to a job interview.

They turned onto the highway, where the blacktop smoothed and pastures gave way to row upon row of trees laden with oranges so perfectly round and bright that from a distance they appeared artificial, like a child's crayon drawing of an orange grove. Here and there amid the dappled shade, fat white geese, fiercer than dogs in guarding against trespassers, strutted like pompous little generals. Amid the Technicolor landscape, they might have been creatures in an animated Disney film.

Farther off in the distance, a sprawl of green hills rose to meet the snow-capped mountains beyond, sparkling jewellike in the overturned bowl of sky that washed their valley in sunlight nearly year round. Her eyes watered with their brilliance, and she wished she'd thought to grab her sunglasses on the way out. *Always pack a hat, sunglasses, and sun block when going on a trip. You can never be too careful.* How many times had she dispensed that particular pearl of wisdom?

It occurred to her that where she was going she wouldn't be needing any of those things. But before panic could once more take hold, she told herself, *As soon as we get there, it'll all be straightened out.* They'd see it was a mistake, that she wasn't guilty of anything worse than the overdue fine for a parking ticket she'd neglected to pay. But minutes later her pulse was still racing and her palms sweating as they turned off Mariposa onto the palm-lined drive fronting the municipal building that housed the police station and courthouse.

A Victorian white elephant, originally the home of the Mendoza family—descendants of the valley's early Spanish settlers, known as the *gente de razón*—it stood four stories, with enough in the way of gables and gingerbread to employ every painter in town. It was graced with an impressive array of stained glass said to be actual Tiffany, yet as they cruised up the drive, Anna's eyes were on the reporters clustered on the steps outside. The same ones as at the house, or was this a whole new bunch? God, how many *were* there?

The car rolled to a stop, and Irma took firm hold of her elbow as they emerged into the open. Anna instinctively ducked her head, bringing her hands up to shield her face from view. Voices shouted her name. Camera flashes sizzled between cupped fingers. She caught the mingled odors of sweat, cigarette smoke, and perfume. The heat of all those bodies crushing in sent a bolt of terror slamming through her. Her knees buckled, but strong arms held her up on either side. Before she knew it, she was inside, being hustled down a fluorescent-lit hallway.

Police headquarters, such as it was, consisted of several rows of Eisenhower-era desks crowded into what had once been a ground-floor parlor. On the high ceiling, plaster rosettes were still visible in places not covered in Sheetrock and acoustical tiles. Beige metal filing cabinets lined the wall at one end and at the other sat the dispatch sergeant at his station. She caught a whiff of fried coffee and something else, a smell she associated with institutions— schools and hospitals and standing in line at the DMV. Everyone stopped what they were doing to look up at her, and Anna had the sense of time stopping, like in a movie freeze frame.

She fought the urge to smile in greeting. Several of the faces were familiar. She recognized burly Tony Ochoa and lanky, red-haired Gordon Ledbetter; they were the ones who'd retrieved her mother the time she'd wandered off in Los Reyes Plaza. And Benny Dickerson, who walked with a limp, a casualty of his gun discharging while still in its holster. He'd been the one to respond to her frantic call the night she'd woken up to find Betty's bed empty. Benny had found her in the field between her house and Laura's, shivering in her nightgown with no idea how she'd gotten there.

He approached Anna now, favoring his bad leg, a slope-shouldered man just shy of retirement with mutton chop sideburns that had been fashionable in the seventies but now, white with age, seemed to frame his bassett hound face like a pair of drooping ears. "Hey, Anna." He spoke in a low voice, his eyes not quite meeting hers.

"Hi, Benny."

"You okay?"

How could I possibly be okay? she felt like screaming. Instead, she shrugged. "I've had better days."

"This won't take long." For a brief, euphoric instant she mistook his meaning, but he was only referring to the booking process. "Can I get you something to drink?"

Not the sharpest pencil in the pack, as Monica would have said, but right now Anna could've hugged him. "Water would be nice," she replied. Her throat was so parched she could hear a clicking sound in her ears when she swallowed.

He touched her arm. "This whole thing . . . it could all blow over by tomorrow."

She could have held out in the face of indifference or even cruelty. But not sympathy. She choked back the sob that rose. The compassion in Benny's drooping brown eyes was almost more than she could bear.

The following minutes passed in a blur. She was fingerprinted, then taken into a small room that doubled as a utility closet—paper towels and toilet paper were stacked at one end—where she posed for mug shots against a wall smudged from all the heads that had pressed against it through the years. Throughout it all, no one would meet her eyes. It wasn't that they were coldhearted, more that they were fearful of letting their inexperience show. She didn't know how she knew, she just did. Years of living in Monica's shadow had left her skills of observation finely honed, for it was in those moments when people didn't know they were being observed that they were the most transparent. She could see what made them tick. She often knew what they wanted before they did. The only thing she hadn't seen was what made *her* tick. And she might never have known had it not been for Marc.

The thought of him plowed into her like a fist. She doubled over on the bench where she'd been temporarily parked. She wanted desperately to phone him, but he was miles away and even if he agreed to come, it wouldn't be fair. He'd become involved in this mess, maybe even implicated. She shuddered at the prospect.

She looked up to find a middle-aged man in khakis and a blazer standing over her. She took in the ruddiness of his cheeks and web of broken blood vessels across his nose, like a map of every bar he'd been in— the same unrepentant bloom her dad had worn toward the end. He smiled, if you could call it that, revealing a row of smallish teeth below an expanse of gum. His pale blue eyes were cold.

"Miss Vincenzi? I'm Detective Burch. If you'll come this way." He gestured down the hallway; clearly he meant to interrogate her.

Anna was surprised to hear herself say, "Not without my lawyer." A line from every cop show she'd ever seen. She didn't even *have* a lawyer.

"Suit yourself." He shrugged, but she could see he was annoyed. He dug into his pocket, tossing her a pair of quarters with a contemptuous flick of his wrist. He pointed toward the pay phone on the wall before striding off down the hall.

Anna clutched the change, hesitating. The only lawyer she knew was Monica's, but somehow she couldn't envision Gardener Stevens, with his burnished silver hair and monogrammed cuffs, being anything but irritated at being bothered on Sunday. She recalled Monica's party last Christmas, the way he'd looked right through her because she hadn't been the one taking his coat at the door, as usual.

Liz might know someone, but that would mean wasting her one call on the person she could count on the least. These past few days, while she'd been braving the storm unleashed by Monica's death, where had her younger sister been? Hiding out, that's where. Not that she blamed Liz. Wouldn't she have done the same if she could?

Anna rose from the bench on legs of

foam rubber, every eye on her now as she walked to the phone and punched in the one number besides her own and Monica's that she knew by heart. Laura. Hadn't she always been there for her? Stopping by at least once a week to see if she needed anything, seldom empty-handed. Usually it was something small she brought—a loaf of bread just out of the oven; a tool to replace one of the broken ones in Anna's shed; and one time, a cat for the mice that had invaded her pantry. Look up *neighbor* in the dictionary, Anna thought, and you'd see Laura's picture.

The phone was picked up on the fourth ring. "Kiley's Feed and Seed," Laura answered merrily, sounding out of breath, as if she'd dashed in from outside. Anna pictured her in what Laura called her "uniform"—sweatshirt and jeans, a pair of toe-sprung cowboy boots.

"It's me. Anna." She kept her voice low, a hand cupped over the receiver.

"Anna! Thank God. I've been trying to reach you. One of those damn reporters was at the door a little bit ago, wanting to know if I could comment on your arrest." Laura sounded disgusted, as if at a cruel practical joke. Clearly she couldn't conceive of its being true. "Don't worry, Hector chased him off. Where *are* you?"

"At the police station."

"You mean—?"

"I'm afraid so."

"Oh, God. How—?"

"They seem to think *I* killed her."

"What on *earth*—?"

"I don't know much more than that."

"It's an outrage! You're no more a murderer than . . . than . . ." She broke off, maybe remembering Sister Beatrice.

"Apparently, they have other ideas."

"Okay. First things first. You'll need a lawyer." Suddenly Laura was all business. "Let's see . . . where is that number?" Anna could hear the rustling of pages at the other end. "Okay . . . here it is. We'll get this straightened out, don't worry. Hang tight, okay? I'll be there as soon as I can." She hung up.

Anna lowered the receiver into its cradle with infinite care. Worry? She was beyond worry—light years from anything she might have experienced in her previous life. What she felt now was a kind of numbness, like she'd had just after the anesthesia for her root canal wore off and the pain came thundering in like a herd of elephants.

She returned to the bench, dropping her head into her hands. Not, as those looking on no doubt assumed, because she was overcome with despair, but because of the hysterical laughter she was stifling. How ironic: She'd once believed shedding her old, fat self would be the answer to her prayers when, in fact, it had been her undoing.

CHAPTER TWO

SIX MONTHS EARLIER

Anna frowned at her computer screen, biting her lip to keep from talking back, a habit
that had once prompted Arcela, in her room
down the hall, to poke her head in to see
what all the fuss was about. Normally it was
Monica who ranted and raved and Anna
who absorbed it all in silence.

Now she typed furiously:

*From: monica@monicavincent.com
To: kssnkrys@aol.com
Subject: RE: This sucks!*

*Dear Krystal,
What a creep! Your boss is lucky you're*

not suing him for sexual harassment. In my opinion, he did you a favor by firing you. The last thing you need is to work for someone like him.

You'll find something else, I'm sure. Don't give up hope. Look how far you've come! Anyone else would've given up. The worst is behind you—I sincerely believe that. You've cleaned up your act and gotten your kids back. Finding another job is the least of your worries.

Let me know how it goes. Remember, I'm here if you need me.

Love,
Monica

She hit the Send button and sat back. Answering Monica's e-mail was the one part of her job that made it tolerable: For a few hours each day she got to be someone other than Anna Vincenzi. It wasn't just knowing there were women out there more desperate than she was; it was the chance to slip out of her skin and into the persona she'd created—a Monica ennobled by the tragedy that had left her wheelchair-bound, who was kind and compassionate, whose heart of gold shone brighter than her star on Hollywood's Walk of Fame. Never mind it was as far from reality as Venus from Earth. While answering those e-mails, Anna sincerely believed it. Just as she believed in the women whose lives had been derailed by circumstances or men or both and who clung to the hope that it would get better someday. *You don't know your own strength,* she would write. *You'll get through this; just keep the faith.* Advice she might well have taken herself.

She often wondered what they would think if they knew. Would they feel duped? Or worse, would they laugh at the idea of plain, plump Anna Vincenzi posing as her famous sister, as if she had the slightest idea what it was like to be dumped (for which you had to be with a man to begin with), sexually harassed, or pregnant for the fourth time in as many years? If they could see her, would they laugh even harder at the ludicrousness of her giving out fashion and beauty tips—on everything from shinier hair (don't dye it, ever) to face-lifts (you'll look good for your age but not a day younger) to what to wear on a budget (invest in quality accessories; cheap shoes and belts are dead giveaways)? Dieting was the only thing she knew from personal experience. She could have written several volumes on what not to eat, and when and how not to eat it.

Anna caught a glimpse of herself in the full-length mirror on the closet door—a holdover from when her tiny office had been a maid's room—and frowned. If she had no illusions about Monica, she had even fewer about herself. All her life, long before whole floors in department stores were given over to plus sizes, she'd been buying clothes designed to hide a multitude of sins. She was careful to avoid every no-no—horizontal stripes and splashy prints, skirts above the knee, slacks that stretched across the front to form "kitty whiskers." The predominant color in her closet was black. The problem was that nothing ever disguised the simple fact that she was fat.

Growing up, her mother's friends had tactfully referred to her as pleasantly plump, but over the years she'd found there was nothing remotely pleasant about being plump. These days those same ladies shook their heads and clucked in dismay, wanting to know why a nice girl like her wasn't married. "You're not getting any younger!" Mrs. Higgins, down the road, had remarked just the other day. As if Anna needed reminding. She was thirty-six and without a single prospect on the horizon. Wasn't that reminder enough? Nevertheless, she'd learned to smile enigmatically, hinting that there might be a mystery man in the wings. They didn't have to know her cat Boots was the only male with whom she shared her bed.

Anna smoothed back a stray wisp. Her hair was the plain brown wrapper in which she'd been delivered into this world and she wore it shoulder length, parted on one side and clipped back with a barrette. If she had to choose one feature that was her best, it would be her eyes—not the startling cobalt of her older sister's, but the pale, hopeful blue of airmail envelopes and for-get-me-nots.

She brought her gaze back to the computer screen, scrolling down to the last of today's messages—Mary Lou from Tennessee, who was thinking about having her breasts enlarged and wanted to know what Monica thought. From its tone and plethora of exclamation points, Anna guessed her to be in her teens. She wrote back:

To: songbird988@aol.com
From: monica@monicavincent.com
Subject: RE: Flatchested in Fayetteville

Dear Mary Lou,
It's a huge step. Before you take it, you should be clear about your reasons. Do you think bigger breasts will fix everything that's wrong with your life? Because nothing on the outside will change how you feel on the inside. I urge you to talk this over with a counselor or therapist first. You might be surprised to know that many of us adults haven't forgotten what it's like to be your age.

Best of luck,
Monica

She was printing out a batch of e-mails Monica might or might not look at, depending on her mood, when the intercom buzzed. "Anna? What's taking you so long?" Monica's voice carried a hint of exasperation, as if Anna were up here playing solitaire.

"Be right down." She spoke with forced cheer. "I'm just finishing up."

"Well, *hurry!*"

Anna stifled a sigh. With Monica, it was always urgent. But usually by the time she'd raced down three flights to see what the big emergency was, Anna would find it to be no big deal. One time Monica had forgotten altogether why she'd summoned her.

"I'm coming, I'm coming." Anna injected a note of bemusement, as if Monica were an adorable, if somewhat spoiled, child she indulged.

She took a deep breath and forced herself to count to ten. Still fresh in her mind was the time she'd twisted an ankle in her rush to get downstairs—all because Monica needed more ice in her drink—and she was determined to maintain both her well-being and self-respect. If she were to fall and break her neck, let it at least be something worth dying for. Anna didn't want it in her obituary that she'd perished rushing to replace the batteries in the TV remote control.

She took her time clearing off her desk. It was half past four. As soon as she'd tended to Queen Monica she could head home, where dinner, a hot bath, and the latest Anne Tyler novel awaited her. But first there'd be her mother to feed and bathe and put to bed. She prayed it would go smoothly tonight. This morning Betty had seemed almost like her old self, but Anna knew not to count on its lasting until she got home. Betty slipped in and out of her fog like a ship lost at sea.

She glanced about the office as she was leaving. Since a maid's comfort was the least of her employer's concerns, particularly in the 1930s when LoreiLinda had been built, by real estate magnate Henry "Huff" Huffington, the room faced north and got almost no sunlight. It was also cramped: If one walked toe to heel, it measured roughly eight by twelve feet, with a sloping ceiling to which Anna, who was five feet eight, had thumbtacked a tree-shaped air freshener that had the dual purpose of reminding her to duck and masking the mildew odor from the corner of the roof that leaked.

She headed down the back stairs, which were narrow and poorly lit compared to the

majestic marble sweep of the main stair-
case, and exited into the laundry room,
where she found Arcela ironing Monica's
340-thread-count Egyptian cotton sheets.

Arcela didn't wait for her to ask where
Monica was. "She outside." She nodded toward the doorway that opened onto the
kitchen, where the sliding glass door to the
patio stood open.

"Everything okay?" Code for whether
Monica had had too much to drink.

The housekeeper shrugged, a small
brown fist of a woman in perpetual motion—Anna had never seen her still, much
less sitting down—and brought the iron
down with a thump, as if to make clear she
wanted no part of whatever Monica might
be up to. It wasn't that Arcela was un-
friendly, but between her limited English
and keeping up with her work—enough for
a staff of five—their exchanges tended to
be brief.

"Well, I guess I should go see what she
wants." Anna hesitated nonetheless. It
wouldn't hurt Monica to cool her heels.
"Heard from Cherry lately?"

Arcela's dark eyes lit up at the mention of
her daughter in the Philippines. "I show

you." From an apron pocket she fished out a photo of a pretty, smiling girl in a starched nurse's cap and uniform, proudly presenting it to Anna. Cherry, short for Concepción (the double meaning was lost on Arcela), had just graduated from nursing school.

"You must be so proud," Anna told her.

"She good girl." Arcela tucked the photo back in her pocket with a wistful look. She hadn't seen either of her children, Cherry or her sixteen-year-old son, Eddie, in almost three years.

"If she's looking for work, I know a few people." Cherry was planning to move to Carson Springs to be near her mother, and Anna had thought of Dr. Steinberg, a close friend of Maude's.

Arcela's eyes shone. "You good lady, Miss Anna." Anna had requested repeatedly that she drop the *Miss,* but Arcela stubbornly refused to comply. "I talk to Miss Monica, but . . ." The light in her eyes dimmed. Anna had no trouble guessing Monica's response. She would have agreed to help, perhaps even to sponsor Cherry for her green card, then had forgotten all about it.

"I'll get on it first thing tomorrow," Anna

promised, patting Arcela's shoulder as she sidled past.

She stepped into the sunny black-and-white tiled kitchen, with its rows of gleaming copper pots and pans that were mostly for show: Monica didn't eat enough to warrant hiring a chef. Four years earlier, when the house had been remodeled, the decorator had wisely left most of the kitchen's original fixtures intact—the old porcelain sink, glass-front cupboards, and built-in breakfront—choosing instead to update the appliances and install a thirties dinette from an antique dealer who specialized in art deco. It had cost a small fortune and was nearly an exact replica of the one they'd eaten at as children, the one that still sat in the kitchen at home.

Anna crossed the room and pushed open the sliding door screen. At that end, the patio was sheltered by a cabana, where at the moment Monica lay stretched on a chaise longue, gazing out at the pool, her wheelchair parked a few feet away. If she'd been a portrait, Anna thought, it would have been titled *Study in Blue.* The dark blue robe draped over her shoulders showed off her creamy skin and pale, slender limbs. A scarf the same deep indigo as her eyes was tied about her head, from which auburn tresses cascaded over the perfect half moons of breast swelling from her lilac bikini top.

"Well, you certainly took your sweet time. I could have been lying here dead, for all you knew." In one hand was a crystal tumbler in which amber liquid sloshed amid melting ice.

Anna's heart sank. There'd be no getting away early today. When Monica got like this, the only hope was that she'd pass out. "Obviously rumors of your death were greatly exaggerated." She struck a light tone. "What's the big emergency?"

"You can freshen this to start with." She handed Anna her glass. "Honestly, where *is* that woman when you need her?" Meaning Arcela, of course. But even with Monica's eyes hidden behind a pair of Jackie O sunglasses, Anna could see that she was more bored than annoyed. "I think she only cleans when she knows I'm watching. God only knows what she does the rest of the day."

Anna held her tongue. Past experience had taught her that sticking up for Arcela did no good. In fact, it often made it worse.

"The usual?" she asked with only a slight lifting of her brow.

Monica didn't reply, which meant the answer should have been obvious. Anna went back into the kitchen, returning moments later with a refill—scotch and soda, light on the soda. Going easy on the scotch never worked; past experience had taught her that, too.

"Thanks, sweetie." Monica was suddenly all smiles. "Listen, I just got off the phone with Glenn. He's on his way over. You'll see him in, won't you?" Her agent, Glenn Lefevour, was the only regular visitor permitted these days.

Anna glanced pointedly at her watch. "I'm leaving in a minute, but I'll let Arcela know."

"I don't trust her." Monica's lower lip edged out. "Remember what happened last time."

She was referring to the occasion on which Glenn had been left idling at the gate. Anna had been out running errands and Arcela vacuuming, so only Monica had heard him buzz. By the time she'd managed to get to the intercom, it was too late. He'd turned back, thinking no one was home. "I'll tell her to listen for the gate." Anna was quick to add, "I'd stay, but I have to get home to Mom."

Monica blew out an exasperated breath. "Isn't that what I pay Edna for? Anyway, it's not like Mom even knows what day of the week it is, much less what time you get home."

"She knows more than you think." But Monica, who hadn't visited in months and wouldn't dream of inviting their mother here, had no way of knowing that Betty grew fretful when Anna was late.

"Well, it won't hurt her to wait. I feel like a swim." Her unsmiling mouth let Anna know it wasn't a request.

Anna's sinking heart touched bottom. Monica would need help getting in and out of the pool, and even if she weren't handicapped, she couldn't be trusted in the water—not after several scotches. She glanced again at her watch. "Now?" Joyce, the physical therapist, would be here tomorrow, and she spent most of the time doing exercises with Monica in the pool. Why couldn't her sister wait until then? "I promised Edna . . ." She faltered, the look on

Monica's face telling her she wouldn't be leaving anytime soon.

"I'm sure Edna will understand." Monica spoke slowly, drawing out every syllable.

"I don't—"

"How would *you* like it if you had to depend on other people for every little thing?" Monica's voice wavered. "Don't you think I'd like to be able to get in and out of the pool on my own?"

"It's not that I don't sympathize." *Just that I've heard it all before.*

"Sympathize? You haven't the faintest idea. Every morning I wake up thinking . . . then I remember." She gulped back a sob, pressing a hand to her forehead in a gesture so theatrical it was all Anna could do not to groan.

Anna lived with it every day, too: The photo shoot for *Vanity Fair* up at Monica's Tahoe cabin. Hadn't it been *her* idea that they get some shots of Monica on her Sea Breeze? As if she could've known that the boat would hit a log and flip over, and that her sister would be left paralyzed from the waist down. Monica didn't hold her responsible, or so she said—often enough for Anna to suspect otherwise. For months, years even, Anna had also blamed herself, but enough was enough.

"Look, I know it's hard for you, but—"

"You don't know a *thing*." Monica's mouth trembled.

All right, you win. Anna sighed in defeat. "I'll go change."

Trudging off to the pool house, she felt as if she were already in up to her eyeballs, being slowly dragged under. All at once she was catapulted back to the sixth grade, hearing the gym teacher's whistle shrilling and seeing everyone scrambling out of the pool. But she'd been too fat to pull herself over the edge. Amid the jeers and snickers of her classmates, she'd kicked and strained until finally Miss Babcock, with a look of disgust, had roughly seized her by the arm and hauled her onto dry land. Her nickname from that day on had been Moby, as in Moby Dick.

All these years later, Anna's cheeks burned at the memory. The mere thought of being seen in a swimsuit was enough to bring it all back, even though there was no one but Monica to witness her humiliation. She eyed the pool, twinkling like shards of glass in the late afternoon sun. If she hadn't been filled with trepidation, she might have appreciated its charms. The same vintage as the house, its mosaic tiles and a decorative border gave it an opulent, old-world feel. Trees planted in Huff Huffington's day—jacaranda and tulip and Paraguayan nightshade—cast a lacy shade over the patio and louvered pool house beyond. As she neared it, her gaze was drawn to the built-in barbecue off to the right, a reminder of the lavish parties Monica had been known for— parties to which she and Liz were occasionally invited—and of how different life had been since the accident that had divided it into Before and After.

Minutes later she emerged from the pool house clad in a one-piece suit that might have been stylish in her grandmother's day, a towel knotted about her waist. As she made her way across the patio, she was aware of Monica's eyes on her, noting every jiggle. Shouldn't it have been the other way around, Monica ashamed to be seen half naked? Except no one who didn't know better would have guessed she was anything less than whole. If anything, Monica looked even more beautiful than before the accident.

Anna puffed and wheezed as she dragged the chaise on which Monica lay to the edge of the pool. She was bent over, her arms about her sister's waist and Monica's wound tightly about her neck, when she felt something in her lower back give way. Gritting her teeth against the pain, she lowered Monica into the water. Moments later Anna joined her, holding a hand pressed to the throbbing small of her back.

"Oooo. It's cold!" Monica maintained a tight grip on the coping.

Anna opened her mouth to disagree—the water, warmed by daytime temps that even in November seldom dropped below seventy, was quite comfortable—but thought better of it. With all her blubber the Arctic ocean would seem warm. As she pushed away from the edge, the old panic closed in. For a moment she couldn't find her breath, and the water seemed to drag at her arms and legs. But she managed to stay afloat . . . barely. "Do you want the kickboard? You'll warm up faster."

Monica shook her head, teeth chattering. "N-n-no. I'm fine." She clung to the edge, her legs, pale as water lilies, floating lifelessly below the shimmering surface. It wasn't until Anna was stroking her way into the deep end to retrieve the kickboard that her sister called out, "We should do this more often. The exercise wouldn't hurt either of us."

Holding on to the Styrofoam board, Anna kicked her way back to Monica. "You're right, we should." She struck an even, noncommittal tone. Monica knew perfectly well she loathed being anywhere near the water. Anna waited for the other shoe to drop.

"You might even lose a few pounds."

Anna felt her stomach clench. "I'd have to swim all the way to Hawaii and back for that," she replied with a laugh. She'd learned early on that the best defense was a joke at her own expense. "Here." She nudged the raft toward Monica. "Your turn."

Monica ignored it. "The only reason I mention it is because I care. I don't have to remind you of the statistics."

"Thanks, I appreciate your concern." Anna injected the right note of cynicism into her voice. Yes, she could stand to lose a few pounds—okay, more than a few—but she didn't exactly qualify as a "statistic."

"If you'd only—"

"Grab hold and I'll push you."

"You're not—"

"Come on. I promise I won't go too deep."

"If you'd just listen to what I'm trying to—"

Anna abruptly released the raft and went splashing off into the deep end. She came up gasping for air, her hair plastered to her head and water streaming down her face, to hear Monica trill in greeting, "Glenn, darling!" Anna, pushing clumps of wet hair out of her eyes, squinted up at Monica's agent poised beside the pool. *Oh, God.* There was no way out without his seeing her in all her naked glory.

Monica held out her arms to him, the dying swan in her final pas de deux. "Just in time. I'm freezing." The plaintive note in her voice left the impression that she was being ignored while Anna selfishly went off in pursuit of her own fun.

"My pleasure." He waved to Anna. "Hey, gorgeous."

Anna gritted her teeth as she waved back. She knew it wasn't a put-down; in his own way he was only being nice. Maybe there was still a way, while he was occupied with Monica, to slip out and into the pool house without his seeing her.

The slim hope was dashed when Monica called out, "Anna, sweetie, I'm sure Glenn could use a hand."

Had the shallow end been shark infested, Anna couldn't have swum toward it more reluctantly. She paused when she reached the steps, blinking up at him through the water trickling into her eyes. He stood with his back to the sun, but even with his face engulfed in shadow, no one could have missed how handsome he was—if you liked the type. Glenn could have been a movie star himself, though strictly the action variety. There was nothing subtle about him, from his swarthy skin and *mano-a-mano* build to the wavy black hair expertly gelled to look as if he'd just tumbled out of the surf . . . or bed.

Glenn seemed to be making a point *not* to stare at her as she climbed dripping out of the pool (she imagined water pouring off her in sheets as if from a surfacing submarine). She trudged over to retrieve her towel, the fifteen feet or so to the chair over which it was draped seeming more like a mile. With each step she felt her thighs jiggle and heard childish voices in her head jeering, *Moby, Moby two-by-four can't get through the bathroom door.* She burned all over as if she'd been baking in the sun for hours.

She snatched up her towel, hastily tying it around her waist. Now it was her breasts on display, jouncing like—an old taunt came to mind—two pigs in a sack as she walked back toward Glenn. *Please, God, let this end soon.* Hadn't she suffered enough for one day?

Together, she and Glenn managed to haul Monica out of the pool and onto the chaise. Anna was patting her sister's legs dry when her own towel slipped off. Glenn quickly averted his eyes, *too* quickly it seemed. She was awash with shame, tears prickling behind her eyes as she hurried off to the pool house to change.

When she emerged, clothed once more in her wraparound denim skirt and blouse, Glenn and Monica were seated in the shade, laughing over some long ago exploit of Monica's. "I'll never forget the look on that man's face! You'd have thought I'd offered to sleep with him instead of telling him to fuck off." She adopted a playful look. "Maybe I *should* have . . . just to tweak him." And who knew better the many and varied ways to torment any man foolish enough to fall into her trap?

"Are you sure you didn't?" he teased. A reference to her drinking, no doubt.

Monica eyed him narrowly before letting loose another throaty laugh. He was the only one allowed to tease her like that, probably because it meant that she wasn't someone to be tiptoed around and that his dropping by could just as easily be to offer her the latest hot script as to relive old times. There'd been a time Anna had wondered if Glenn and her sister were lovers. But if that had ever been the case, which, knowing Monica, was entirely possible, the relationship was now more eternal flame than old flame.

"Well . . . I'm off." Anna forced a smile.

They glanced up as if surprised to see her standing there.

"So soon?" Glenn put on a bereft look.

If he'd been poking fun at her, or even if he were the typical sleazy Hollywood agent, she'd have been less forgiving. But despite his rough edges, Glenn wasn't a bad guy. His only fault, if you could call it that, was that he did everything he could to disguise the fact that he'd come up the hard way, down to the preppie khakis and polo shirt he was wearing. The result was that he seemed to have dropped from nowhere; even his speech had the modulated, unaccented tone of a radio announcer's. While it didn't make sense to Anna—in Hollywood the scramblers were kings and queens of the heap—it was what he and Monica had in common: They'd both reinvented themselves.

"I should get home," she told him. "My mom's expecting me." She realized too late she'd said "my" instead of "our." But in some ways it did feel as if she were an only child.

Glenn brought a hand to his chest. "Sis, you break my heart every time."

Anna turned quickly so he wouldn't see the tears in her eyes. However benign, his teasing was that of a kindly uncle humoring a fat kid he felt sorry for. He wouldn't have joked that way if there'd been the slightest chance she'd take it seriously.

She was almost out of earshot when she heard them laughing. Blood rushed to her cheeks. That was the thing about being fat, she thought. There was no safe place.

When you heard people laughing, you always assumed it was at you.

It was almost six, the sun riding the shoulders of the distant mountains, when she let herself out onto the columned front porch. When she'd called home to say she'd be late, Edna had grumbled a bit, which didn't bode well. Betty was acting up again; Anna could hear it in Edna's tired voice. There would be no warm bath or book to curl up with tonight. She'd be lucky if she could grab a bite to eat.

Anna drove slowly nonetheless, nosing her ancient blue Corolla through the tall, wrought-iron gates that guarded the entrance to the estate—the most impressive in Carson Springs, with its twenty pristine acres that included a lily pond, an orchid house, and a rose garden to rival the White House's. No sense taking unnecessary risks, she thought as she wound her way down the steep canyon road toward the valley below. What would become of Betty if she were incapacitated in some way?

She knew what people thought: that they'd both be better off with Betty in a nursing home. But had they seen some of those places? Did they know what went on there? And it wasn't as simple as finding the right one. Medicare didn't cover extended care, so she'd be forced to sell Betty's house—the only home Anna had ever known.

It'd be useless asking Monica to pitch in. She'd made it clear that the extent of her responsibility, as she saw it, was footing Edna's salary and the portion of Betty's doctor's bills that weren't covered by insurance. Not that she couldn't afford to do more, but what would be the fun if they weren't dancing like marionettes on her purse strings? With each penny squeezed from her, Anna had to jump a little higher . . . and button her lip a little tighter. As for their mother, it was almost as if Monica were punishing her in some way. Probably because in her mind Betty hadn't done enough to protect them when they were growing up. As if anyone could've gone up against their dad.

A memory surfaced: She must have been six, seven—small enough to fit under the bed. All she could see from where she lay pressed against the floor were two pairs of feet, one in low-heeled black pumps worn to a slant at the heels and the other, her dad's, in scuffed brown work boots. They'd seemed unconnected somehow to the loud voices overhead. She watched in fear as the boots advanced . . . and the pumps retreated. There was a scuffle, her mother's voice pleading, "No, Joey . . . please . . . the children . . ." Then came the awful choking sounds, Betty's strangled cries twisting about Anna's throat as she lay motionless, a fist stuffed into her mouth to keep from screaming.

It was months before she'd been able to sleep through the night.

They'd all suffered. Liz, too. What made Monica so unique?

As she made her way past the Carpenter's sleek trilevel, its glass and steel expanses afire in the lowering sun, she thought of Alice and Wes, which in turn reminded her of Laura and Hector. If she had it rough in some ways, at least she was blessed with caring neighbors. That included Finch. Adopting her was the best thing Laura had ever done besides marrying Hector. Finch, who was sixteen going on forty and no stranger to life's travails, had taken Anna under her wing instead of the other way around, stopping by several times a week to help with Betty.

The road flattened, oaks and sycamores taking the place of manzanite and scrub pine. Even after a lifetime Anna never failed to be captivated by the scenery, shifting from one extreme to the next like postcards in a revolving rack. To the east lay a forested lake and to the west chaparral-scrawled hills, with orchards and orange groves in between. All of it nestled within a ring of snow-capped mountains. If she lived to be a hundred, Anna would never take all this for granted. Though if a landscape could be too bucolic, such was Carson Springs. Where was the grain of sand to chafe at her dull and at times desperate existence? What pearl would ever come of this rut she'd trodden for herself?

Evening shadows stretched across Old Sorrento Road as she neared home. She rattled over the cattle grids and bumped over the potholes. There was a time when this stretch of country road had been nothing but grazing land. Not much had changed except that there were more houses and fewer animals. At night her headlights still picked out the gleam of feral eyes—possums and raccoons, and the occasional bear or bobcat that had wandered down from the hills.

Before long she was pulling into the driveway of the modest frame house where she'd lived the better part of thirty-six years. It beckoned from the dusk that hid its peeling paint and the shingles missing from its roof, the glow from its windows making her feel all at once hopeful that things would turn out okay.

Her optimism vanished as soon as she climbed from her car. Even from this distance she could hear her mother's screams—like those of a scalded cat. Her stomach clenched. As she trudged up the walk, the house came into focus, its long-dead nasturtiums clinging in brown squiggles to the porch lattice that framed the sagging steps; the blisters on the clapboard siding, which Hector had repeatedly offered to repaint—as if he hadn't done enough already—and which looked like an advanced case of leprosy. There were days, like this one, when she imagined herself to be like this house, growing spongy with dry rot while she settled on her foundation. Would she ever be free or, God forbid, end up like Betty?

Anna walked in the door to find Edna locked in mortal combat with her mother. It might have been a comical sight, an old woman, no more than ninety-eight pounds soaking wet, kicking and thrashing while her paid companion, twenty years her junior and broad across the shoulders from a lifetime of working with horses, struggled to subdue her. "Nooooooo! Legooooo! You son of a bitch!" Betty wailed, hammering at Edna with her fists. "I'll call the cops. *I mean it this time!*"

Anna dropped her purse and rushed to Edna's aid. "It's okay, Mom. No one's going to hurt you." She grabbed hold of a flailing arm, and after a moment Betty quieted, allowing Edna to release her. "Dad's gone. Remember?"

Betty's pale blue eyes stopped their panicked rolling and fixed on Anna. The tension slowly drained from her limbs. "Anna, honey? Is that you?" It always took her a moment or two to adjust to that fact that Anna was grown; in Betty's mind, her children would be forever small. "I thought you were in school."

"No, Mom. I have a job, remember?"

"Yes. Yes, of course." Betty was hoarse from screaming. Her hair floated about her head like smoke from a doused fire, patches of pink scalp showing through.

Anna exhaled wearily. "Have you eaten yet?" Edna shook her head just as wearily, as if to say, *What do you expect?* Keeping Betty out of mischief was a full-time job in itself.

Betty was getting that wild-eyed look again. "What time is it? Where's my coat? The bus will be here any minute!"

Anna seized her by the shoulders, forcing Betty to meet her gaze. She could feel the hard knobs of bones beneath the skin that encased them like tissue paper. Her mother had always been petite, but now there was almost nothing left of her. "Calm down, Mom. There's no school today. It's . . . it's a holiday."

"Oh." Betty's shoulders sagged.

"Why don't you watch TV while I fix you something to eat?" She guided her mother to the old, seat-sprung recliner, reaching for the remote while mentally scrambling to recall what was on this time of day. *People's Court*? *Sally Jessy Raphael*? *I Love Lucy* reruns? For some unfathomable reason her mother loved *Jerry Springer,* though in her right mind she'd actively loathed such programs. Probably because she'd had enough screaming in her own life.

"I need a cigarette," Edna said with a sigh when they were alone in the kitchen. Smoking wasn't permitted in the house, but Anna didn't say anything as Edna fished a pack of cigarettes from the pocket of her oversize corduroy jacket.

"Has she been like this all day?" Anna spoke in a low voice, though her mother, happily absorbed in a *Cheers* rerun, couldn't hear. From the living room came a hollow burst of canned laughter—to Anna's mind the loneliest sound in the world—and her mother's faint cackling in response.

"Ever since the PG&E guy came to read the meter." Edna lit her cigarette and took a long drag. She was ruggedly built, with graying hair plaited in a braid as thick as a horse's tail, her leathery skin so creased it resembled the old chopping block out back.

"Pete?"

"She kept calling him Joe."

They exchanged a knowing look.

"I'm sorry, Edna." It seemed she'd been apologizing all her life for things she'd had no control over. "I know how tough it is. You're worth twice what I pay you."

"In that case, I wouldn't say no to a raise." Edna squinted against the smoke rising in a lazy wreath about her head, her brown eyes gentle despite the hard set of her jaw. She knew who the real boss was. When she bitched to Anna, it was as one co-worker to another.

"I'll speak to Monica about it."

Edna snorted. "While you're at it, have her throw in a new set of tires for my truck." They both knew Monica would see Betty out on the sidewalk rather than part with another nickel toward her upkeep.

Anna sighed. "I'm sure if I explain to her—"

"Look, it's none of my beeswax," Edna cut her off, "but you oughta give some thought to what we talked about. Or the next thing you know it'll be the men in the white coats carting *you* off."

Anna gave in to a wry smile. "It'd be the closest I'd ever get to a vacation." She was in no mood to go over the same tired ground. Edna meant well, she knew, but

Anna wasn't ready to ship her mother off to a nursing home. Betty wasn't *that* far gone. She had her good days as well as her bad days.

"I could use one myself." Edna glanced about in search of an ashtray before tapping a long ash into the leathery cup of her palm. She carried it to the sink, where she stubbed out her cigarette with a wet sizzle and tossed it into the garbage. "Okay, I'm off." She reached for her quilted barn jacket on a hook by the back door. "There's macaroni and cheese in the oven. I didn't get a chance to heat it up." She tossed a meaningful glance toward the living room. "Good luck."

I'll need it. As Edna was putting her jacket on, Anna caught a glimpse of the purple mottling on her wrist. With a grim smile, she pulled back her own sleeve to reveal the bruises that ranged from ocher to violet. "Look. We're a matched set."

"You wouldn't know it to look at her, but she's strong as a horse." Edna gave a half-admiring snort. "Stubborn, too. Once she gets it into her head that . . ." Her expression turned grim. "Your dad did a real number on her."

It was on the tip of Anna's tongue to defend him, but what would've been the point? He'd been dead for years. Besides, everyone knew what he'd been like. Joe Vincenzi, the meanest drunk around. That he'd been nice when sober didn't count because few ever saw him when he wasn't three sheets to the wind.

"Well, I'm off," Edna announced for the second time. She paused as she was stepping out the door, looking at Anna as if there was something else she wanted to say. But whatever it was, she apparently decided against it. "See you in the morning."

Morning? Anna didn't know how she was going to survive the night.

Minutes later, the table set and the macaroni and cheese bubbling in the oven, she was on her way to fetch Betty when laughter, not canned, rang out in the next room. She froze. It couldn't have been her mother; she hadn't laughed like that in years. It was what Anna missed most, her mother's laugh—the one thing Joe hadn't been able to beat out of her. That, and her sense of fun. Anna remembered coming home from school one day to the unexpected treat of a cake with candles and a pile of tissue-wrapped presents. Betty had decided to throw them an *un*-birthday party. The presents weren't expensive—a pink plastic hairbrush and a comb set for her, nail polish and the current issue of *Mademoiselle* for Monica, a nightgown for Liz—but the occasion stood out in memory more than any real birthday.

Remembering helped, but it made her sad, too, in the same way that photos of her dad, grinning into the camera with a little girl on each knee, made her feel as if she'd had two different fathers. These days her mother was like a whole other person from the one she'd known, with Anna the grown-up and Betty the child.

In the living room, she found Laura's adopted daughter, Finch, seated on the sofa, chattering away while Betty smiled in delight as if an exotic bird had flown in through the window.

Finch caught Anna's eye and smiled. "The door was open," she said. "I guess you didn't hear me knock."

"Perfect timing," Anna told her. "I was just putting supper on the table."

"I can't stay. I just dropped by to give this

to your mom." She dug into the pocket of her jean jacket, producing a key chain with a penlight attached. "I thought she'd like it." She thumbed its button, and it was as if a light had been switched on in Betty as well. Her eyes glowed like a child's on Christmas morning.

Anna's own eyes unexpectedly filled with tears. When Finch dropped by, it was always with some little trinket for Betty, or to return a book she'd borrowed, never leaving Anna to feel like some sort of charity case. Her years in foster care had left her far more sensitive than most to the sting of handouts.

Finch rose to her feet with a graceful little dipping motion as she swung her long dark hair over her shoulder. It fell in a rippling sheet down her back, and Anna was struck anew by how she'd blossomed in the past year. In her jeans and UCLA sweatshirt, she looked like any normal teenager, the hollow-eyed runaway of last summer already a distant memory.

"Sure you can't stay? There's more than enough," she urged.

Finch hesitated. "I'll have to check with Laura."

She went into the bedroom to use the phone, returning moments later to say it was okay. Anna knew that it had probably been the plan all along, and tonight she was too tired to refuse when after they'd eaten Finch offered to put Betty to bed.

Finch coaxed Betty to her feet, saying gently, "Come on, Mrs. Vincenzi. Wait 'til you see how cool this looks in the dark."

She reached to pry the penlight from her grasp—Betty had held on to it throughout supper—but Betty balked. "Mine! Monica gave it to me," she cried.

Finch smiled at Anna. "I'll take that as a compliment."

If Betty had mistaken her for Monica it was because there was a certain resemblance. In the framed photo over the fireplace, taken when she was Finch's age, Monica was a fresh-faced beauty as yet unspoiled.

When she was alone, Anna turned to the dirty dishes in the sink, which included those from breakfast—Edna wasn't much when it came to housekeeping, and Anna wasn't in a position to complain. Fifteen minutes later, with the last dish stacked in the drainer, she tiptoed down the hall to check up on her mother. She found Betty tucked in bed, Finch reading aloud to her from a storybook.

" 'One day the two sisters received an invitation to the ball that was to be made at the palace of the King, in honor of his son the Prince. . . .' "

The tears she'd been holding back all evening spilled down her cheeks as she hovered in the doorway. Finch was so patient with her mother, almost as if she understood her in a way Anna couldn't. Maybe because she knew what it was like not to fit in. One day she might tell Anna what it had been like, all those foster homes, the last one so bad she'd run away, but for now Anna was simply grateful for her kindness.

Anna retreated down the hall and was straightening up in the living room when she heard the door to her mother's room click shut. Finch appeared a moment later, saying in a hushed voice, "She's asleep."

"You're so good with her." Anna had muted the TV and now there was only its flickery glow, casting the furniture in shadowy relief. She didn't dare say more; she might get choked up again.

Finch shrugged nonchalantly, as if it weren't a school night and she didn't have better things to do. "I like her. She's more like a little kid than someone Maude's age." Laura's eighty-two-year-old housemate, who was like a member of the family, might be forgetful at times, but she had all her marbles.

Anna knew what she meant: just as with a child, everything was up-front with Betty. "I wish you could've known my Gramma Nini," she said. "It was like that nursery rhyme about Jack Spratt and his wife—she was as big as a house and Grandpa Eddie as skinny as a beanpole." She smiled, re-membering the meals at her grandmother's groaning table. *No wonder I'm so fat.* "I guess it's pretty obvious which one I take after."

"Why do you do that?" Finch frowned.

"Do what?"

"Put yourself down like that."

Anna chuckled to hide her embarrass-ment. "I'm just stating a fact."

"Well, it's also a fact that you're pretty and smart."

Anna's smile faded. "I've been hearing that all my life," she said with a sigh. "Such a pretty face. It's just another way of saying it's a shame you're fat."

"I didn't mean it like that."

"I know you didn't."

She braced herself for what inevitably came next: the helpful suggestions about dieting and exercise. She'd heard them all. Even Laura, who'd rather bite her tongue until it bled than offend someone, had invited her more than once to go horseback riding.

But Finch only said, "I should be getting back. I have homework." She rolled her eyes, but Anna knew she liked school. This past semester she'd even made the honor roll.

Anna followed her out onto the porch. The temperature was falling rapidly; it was at least ten degrees cooler than when she'd arrived home. The only sounds were the cheeping of crickets and nightjars. She hugged Finch, a bit too tightly perhaps, wondering what it would be like to have a daughter of her own. Then Finch was bounding down the path, disappearing into the darkness. A moment later came the roar of Hector's old pickup.

Shivering, Anna retreated inside. If the

outside of the house showed its age, the interior was virtually unchanged from when she was growing up. The old Motorola stereo cabinet was where it had always been, never mind the CD player that had made it obsolete. Surrounding it were the clunky old breakfront that had been her grandmother's, the worn plush chairs, and the brocade sofa with its granny-square afghan that her mother had crocheted to cover the burns from her father's cigarettes. It might have been only yesterday that Anna had been summoned home from college for his funeral. Sixteen years—had it really been that long? The week or two she'd planned to stay before returning to Cal State had spun out into months, then years.

At first it had been to help her mother to adjust. Amazingly, after nearly thirty years of being beaten and bullied, Betty missed the old man; she'd drifted about in a daze like a boat that had come unmoored. When it became clear that the daze was more than just grief, Anna had felt obliged to stay just to make sure she didn't set the house on fire or do herself bodily harm.

She'd been there ever since.

Now she wondered if her reasons for

staying had as much to do with her own fears as with Betty. One day she'd woken up to the realization that her friends all had careers, or were married with children, or both. A kind of panic had set in. Where would she go? What would she do? A woman in her thirties without a bachelor's degree who wasn't qualified for anything more than minimum wage. It had seemed the answer to her prayers when, shortly after the accident that had left her a paraplegic, Monica tearfully begged Anna to come work for her at LoreiLinda, where she'd taken up permanent residence. Monica claimed to need her desperately, offering to hire a companion for their mother, and at the time it had seemed like the answer to both their prayers—the insurance money from their dad's death had run out just as Betty's condition was worsening, making it impossible for Anna to hold down even a part-time job without outside help. It wasn't until too late that Anna saw she'd only become more deeply mired.

Her cat came slinking out from under the sofa to wind in and out between her legs, purring loudly. Anna bent down to scoop him up. "It's just you and me, pardner." She stroked his silky black head. "What'll it be, Rocky Road or butter pecan?"

Boots, named after his three white socks, was the cat Laura had brought over on loan from Lost Paws the year before last to cut down the mice population in her pantry. He'd been with her ever since, her feline counterpart. Neither had intended to stay, but there they were nonetheless. When she put him down, he followed her into the kitchen, meowing piteously as if it'd been days, not hours, since he'd been fed. Anna dropped a spoonful of Rocky Road into his bowl before helping herself to three large scoops.

She was settling into the recliner to watch TV when she caught her reflection in the breakfront's glass doors, distorted like in a funhouse mirror: a huge head atop the blob that was her body. She was filled with self-loathing and had a vision of herself ten years from now, seated in the same chair, digging into the same heaping bowl of ice cream. With each passing day she'd become that much more helpless to combat Monica's will. Glenn and the others would eye her more pityingly, until it edged over into disgust.

Just as her own disgust was now creeping over into horror. Had she seen this coming when her father died, she'd have run for the hills.

Only once before had Anna experienced an epiphany on this scale. As a child she'd suffered her father's beatings in choked silence until one day something in her had snapped. She'd looked up at him as he towered over her with his hand raised and blood in his eye—she couldn't have been more than ten or eleven—giving him a look of such intense hatred he'd immediately lowered his arm. She'd sensed somehow that in the same way a bomb needs to be detonated in order to explode, he had to see fear for his rage to be released. At that moment she had stopped being afraid. He never raised his hand to her again.

With the same clarity, she knew it was now or never. If she didn't act quickly, the moment would pass and with it any chance of a future. Trembling all over, she rose to her feet, the bowl in her hands cradled like something sharp that might cut her. She hurried into the kitchen, where she dumped the ice cream into the sink. Watching it disappear down the drain in a muddy swirl, little white clumps of marshmallow clinging to the lip, she felt a flicker of hope, the first in months, maybe years.

I can do this, she thought. *I can change.*

CHAPTER THREE

"New dress?" Laura asked as Anna climbed into the backseat, squeezing in next to Maude and Finch. This morning when Anna's car wouldn't start, Laura had offered her a ride to church.

"I haven't worn it in a while." Anna didn't add that the flowered dress she had on was from her Atkins phase, when she'd been fifteen pounds thinner. This was the first time she'd been able to fit into it since then—at least three years.

"Well, it looks nice on you." Laura went on eyeing her as Hector backed the Explorer out of the driveway. "No, it's not just the dress," she said. "You've lost weight."

"A few pounds." Anna didn't want to make a big deal of it. She'd been on so many diets through the years, she was like the boy who cried "wolf," except that in her case she'd eaten like one. "You look nice, too," she said, eager to change the subject. Laura, who practically lived in jeans, except at work where she wore slacks, had on a stylish ecru dress and high heels.

"It's my brother's christening. I figured I'd better dress up."

"Jack won't recognize us," Finch said.

"I hardly recognize myself," grumbled Hector, looking uncomfortable in his suit. He'd been to the barber, too; his shiny black hair stood up in spikes except where slicked down around his collar. The one maverick touch was the bola tie from his and Laura's hilltop wedding earlier in the year.

"Well, I, for one, am celebrating the fact that there's even going to *be* a christening." Maude peered out from under the cartwheel hat that matched her vintage polka-dot dress. "When I think how it might have ended . . ." Her voice trailed off, her blue eyes, bright as buttons sewn onto the soft little pillow of her face, momentarily clouding over.

A silence fell, everyone remembering the

car accident the previous spring that had nearly claimed Sam's life along with that of her unborn baby—the climax of the soap opera that had begun with Laura's widowed mother falling in love with Ian, fifteen years her junior. That he was her younger daughter's stepson to boot had only heightened the drama.

But now it was November and no one in the extended Kiley-Delarosa clan could remember what life had been like before Jack. Sam was like any new mother besotted with her baby, never mind she was old enough to be his grandmother. Laura and Alice, who'd been horrified by their mother's pregnancy, doted on him. Finch would have baby-sat for free if Sam hadn't insisted on paying her. And Maude, named an honorary grandmother in the absence of any real ones, knitted little sweaters and booties as fast as Jack grew out of them.

They arrived at the church to find it packed. Luckily, Sam and Ian had saved seats up front. Sliding into her pew, Anna said a silent little prayer of thanks that Edna hadn't given her a hard time about putting in the extra hours. She wouldn't have wanted to miss this, and much as she hated to admit it, her mother would have spoiled it for her.

The joyous pealing of the *campanario* bells gave way to the organ's full-throated baritone. Anna rose for the opening hymn. Those used to seeing her at mass every Sunday might have been surprised to know she didn't consider herself especially devout. Oh, she believed in God and found comfort in the Bible, but the main reason she kept on coming year after year was because it was here, at St. Xavier's, that for a few hours each week she was lifted up to become a part of something larger than her tiny sphere.

Much of it had to do with the church itself. She looked about at the adobe walls as thick as a fortress's and the high, stained-glass windows through which sunlight slanted to form jeweled mosaics on the scuffed oak floor. Carved devotional statues gazed serenely from the niches lining the nave, and the reredos over the altar, with its gilded carvings worthy of a cathedral, glowed honeylike in the soft light. When Anna was growing up, the mission on Calle de Navidad had been the one place she'd felt utterly and completely safe, and even now it seemed to embrace her as tenderly as the statue of Mary cradling the infant Jesus.

She glanced over at Finch. She wore a formfitting suit in a flattering shade of green that made her look more mature than her years, an effect offset by the half dozen earrings in each ear and the small butterfly tattoo above her right ankle. Finch caught her eye and smiled.

Laura's younger sister, Alice, sat with her husband to Anna's left, Wes looking every inch the proud grandfather. Anna was struck, as always, by the contrast in the two sisters. Laura, earthy and olive skinned, with arms brown and muscular from the outdoors and hair that wouldn't stay put, and sleek, coolly blond Alice, who looked as though she'd stepped from the pages of *Vogue.* Yet no two sisters could have been more devoted. Anna wished she were as close to her own.

There were more hymns and prayers, then a reading from Timothy, followed by the sermon, which was mercifully brief. Before long Father Reardon was motioning to Sam and Ian. They rose in unison, baby Jack nestled asleep in his father's arms, every eye on them as they made their way to the stone font in the baptistery off the nave. Sam and Ian shared a small, secret smile over their baby's head as the amber light streaming down from overhead seemed to anoint the three of them. Anna felt a wave of longing sweep over her: Would she ever stand there with a baby of her own?

Watching Father Reardon perform the ritual, she was reminded of the crush she'd had on him in junior high. She hadn't been alone—every other girl in her catechism class had been in love with him. Even now that he was a bit thicker about the waist and his curly black hair shot with silver, he was still the handsomest man around, with Irish eyes and a smile that could brighten a rainy Monday.

Jack woke with an outraged cry as Father Reardon poured water over his head. Sam looked pained, as if she couldn't bear seeing him in any kind of discomfort. But Jack, in a pint-size sailor suit, quickly recovered and by the end was his usual sunny self. Anna couldn't help noting, too, how slim Sam was; you'd never have guessed she'd recently given birth, much less that she was the mother of two grown daughters. She felt a pang of envy watching Ian slip an arm about her waist as they headed back to their pew.

Out of the corner of her eye she saw Alice and Wes exchange a look. Clearly it wasn't lost on them, the irony of Wes's mother-in-law giving him his only grandchild. Anna recalled that Alice was on the fence about having kids of her own, and wondered if they would ever make the leap. Looking at Wes, as robust as his son, it wasn't hard to imagine.

To the swelling chords of "Lord Dismiss Us with Thy Blessing," the congregation rose and began making its way outside. Moments later Anna stood on the sun-washed steps, watching Sam and Ian hold court with the baby. It seemed everyone was stopping to coo at Jack, even that battle-ax Marguerite Moore, who'd been so hateful to Sam last year. By the time Anna had rejoined Laura and Hector, it was lunchtime and her stomach was grumbling. It didn't help that they were on their way to Tea & Sympathy for the party in Jack's honor. She knew she'd have to be extra vigilant.

It had been six months since her last diet—a grape juice fast that had lasted all of four days before she'd fainted from hunger. She'd made up her mind then and there: no more. Hadn't she tried every diet known to mankind? There'd been Atkins, Scarsdale, Beverly Hills, and Pritikin; low carb, no carb, all the fat you can eat, macrobiotic, and more recently *The Zone* and *Eat Right for Your Type.* That didn't include Weight Watchers, Jenny Craig, Nutri/System, and Richard Simmons, or the gallons of Slim-Fast she'd downed through the years.

What was different this time? Nothing . . . and everything. For one thing, she refused to label it a diet, which would have been the kiss of death. Instead of denying herself, she ate what she liked, the only catch being that she limited herself to tiny portions of the fattening stuff. The French ate cheese, why couldn't she? A cookie? Fine, but just one. Cake? As long as she could see through it to the plate underneath. Amazingly, she'd found that given the choice, she often preferred fruit over gooey desserts and chicken over cheeseburgers. As a result, the pounds were melting off.

She'd even taken up jogging. The first week she could barely make it to the end of her driveway without collapsing, but now she could easily jog the half mile to Laura's and back. She knew it'd had a positive effect when, halfway to Tea & Sympathy, she wasn't even out of breath.

It was such a beautiful Indian summer day, the sky so crisp and blue it seemed to crackle, that when Hector had suggested they leave the car where it was parked and go on foot, Anna had readily agreed. Finch had gone on ahead with Andie, and Maude had caught a ride with her friend Mavis, so it was just the three of them. They took their time strolling along Old Mission. The shops were closed except for Lickety-Split, with its usual traffic jam of strollers stretching out onto the terra-cotta-roofed arcade. Anna's mouth watered at the thought of a scoop of Brandy Alexander fudge.

A block from the arcade, they passed the bougainvillea-draped arch to Delarosa Plaza, with its tiered fountain and Spanish-style storefronts, the largest of which was Delarosa's. A general store in the days of the Gold Rush, it had been in Laura's family for generations and had recently passed into her hands when Sam's pregnancy forced her to retire.

Across the street stood the Depression-era post office, with its Moorish bell tower that was featured on postcards and in guidebooks. Glancing up as she passed it, Anna wondered if the deep sense of connectedness she felt walking these streets was partly to blame for the rut she was in. What incentive was there to leave? Where could she go that would be better than Carson Springs? Never mind it was a gilded cage in some respects.

At the light, they turned the corner onto Orange Avenue and after several blocks Tea & Sympathy came into view: a quaint shingled cottage with pink fairy roses climbing up the front. Though only open six months, it was already a local institution. Anna's stomach rumbled anew at the thought of all the mouth-watering treats inside.

A number of the guests had gathered on the porch. Through the open door she could see more milling about inside. "Mom had to book *months* in advance," Laura told her as they started up the marigold-lined path. "It's one of the reasons she put off the christening until now."

Anna didn't doubt it. From what she'd heard, booking Tea & Sympathy for an event was the toughest reservation in town, though she also knew that Claire would've found a way to accommodate her mother's oldest friend even with a few weeks' notice.

"I thought maybe it was because she wanted to get married first," she said.

Laura paused to pluck a dead nasturtium from the trellis alongside the porch. "I thought so, too. God only knows when they'll get around to it. Mom says things are great as they are, so why rock the boat? But I think it's because she wasn't all that happy with my dad."

"Marriage," Hector grumbled good-naturedly, "is Sunday afternoon in a tearoom with a bunch of ladies from church." Left to his own devices he'd have been tinkering with his pickup or puttering about the ranch.

"I don't see that it's hurt *you* any." Laura grinned, poking him with her elbow.

Anna watched them with envy. She didn't begrudge Laura her happiness, especially after what she'd been through all those years—first trying to get pregnant, then her husband leaving her. She only wished someone would look at *her* the way Hector was looking at Laura now—as if she were the sun, moon, and stars all wrapped up in one.

They stepped inside to find the sunny room crowded with friends and family, the air awash with heavenly scents. With the man of the hour down for his nap, Sam and Ian were busy greeting their guests, stopping to kiss a cheek here and squeeze a hand there. Sam enveloped Anna in a warm hug.

"I'm sorry your mother couldn't join us," she said, making it sound as if Betty had had a more pressing engagement.

It was the same sensitivity Anna had come to expect from Laura. *The apple doesn't fall far from the tree,* she thought. She looked over at Jack, sound asleep in his carrier. "I can't believe how big he's gotten."

"I'll be ready for a hip replacement by the time he's walking." Sam gave a mock groan, though from the way she carried herself, Anna guessed it would be years before she'd have such worries. "I hope you're hungry. Can you believe all this food?" She gestured toward the buffet table laden with plates of finger sandwiches and sweets.

"It all looks wonderful," Anna said, her mouth watering.

"Help yourself, there's plenty more where this came from." Claire was making the rounds with a tray of sticky buns fresh from the oven. Willowy, with a cloud of pre-Raphaelite hair and cheekbones to die for, she didn't look like someone who spent her days in the kitchen. With so much to tempt her, how did she stay so thin?

It took a supreme effort—however firm her resolve, Anna's taste buds had a mind of their own—but she managed to resist. "Thanks, I think I'll wait a bit," she murmured, wandering over to the table, where she helped herself to a finger sandwich and single cookie instead.

She was looking for a place to sit down when Gerry Fitzgerald beckoned her over to the table she and her husband were sitting at. "You're just in time," she said, scooting over to make room. "We can't decide which is better—the apple cake or raspberry-almond tart." She pushed her plate toward Anna, who took a tiny taste of each to be polite.

"This one." She pointed to the tart, though it was a close call.

"My sentiments exactly," Aubrey pronounced.

Gerry looked as proud as if she'd baked it herself. "He's only saying that because it's my recipe. Well, not mine exactly." She'd be the first to tell you she was the world's worst cook. "I clipped it out of *Gourmet*." She gave a mock sigh. "The extent of my culinary skills." As if someone who looked like an Italian film star, with a sexy wardrobe to match, needed to add cooking to her credits.

Claire paused at their table, resting a hand on Gerry's shoulder. "Don't listen to her," she said with a laugh. "She does more than two people around here." Anna marveled anew at how much alike they were, mother and daughter. Not so much in terms of looks as in their sparkle, and the ready laugh that could fill a room. It seemed incredible that less than a year ago they'd been total strangers. If Gerry hadn't decided to search for her, they'd never have met. Claire would still be a lawyer up north, engaged to the guy she'd been with before Matt. The thought brought renewed hope. If

Claire could reinvent herself, why couldn't she?

"She's only saying that to be nice," Gerry said, though Anna could see she was pleased. "Anyway, I only help out on weekends." Her full-time job as lay manager of Blessed Bee, the local convent's honey operation, kept her busy the rest of the time. "And with all the plates and cups I've chipped, I'm not sure if she's coming out ahead."

"I'll take it out of your Christmas bonus," Claire teased before moving on.

Gerry's eyes followed her, filled with pride . . . and something more—incredulity perhaps. If Anna sometimes wondered whether there was such a thing as miracles, she need look no further than Gerry's.

Her gaze fell on a small drab woman seated by herself at a table against the wall. Martha Elliston. Anna knew her from church. Wasn't she on some committee with Sam? Though not much older than Anna, Martha had the look of an old lady in the making, the shapeless dress she wore doing nothing to alter that impression. As far as Anna knew, she'd never been married or even had a boyfriend. She lived with her elderly mother, who must be either widowed or divorced—Anna had never heard any mention of a husband. With a small shock, Anna realized the description would have fit *her.* She shuddered at the idea.

She turned to find Aubrey eyeing her. "You're looking exceptionally well, my dear," he said, his European accent matched by his cosmopolitan look. It was as though he'd read her mind and knew exactly what she'd needed to hear just then. "A good advertisement for country living." As if Old Sorrento Road were the boonies, which to a man like Aubrey she supposed it was.

Anna felt her cheeks grow warm. "Thanks," she mumbled. Coming from Gerry's husband, who had once been Carson Springs's most eligible bachelor in addition to being a world-renowned celebrity, it was a true compliment. It also hardened her resolve to resist the plates of mouthwatering treats making their way around the room.

"How's your mom these days?" Gerry dropped her voice. People always asked after her mother as if Betty were at death's door. Though Anna supposed that to many, a grave illness was preferable to missing most of your marbles.

"She has her good days and her bad days." Anna shrugged. No sense bending her ear.

"And your sister?" From the forced politeness of Gerry's tone, it was obvious she meant Monica, who hadn't exactly endeared herself to the locals, whom she referred to as the "natives." Never mind that Monica herself had been born and raised in Carson Springs.

"She's fine." Anna didn't want to come across as rude, but if she said another word, or even *thought* too much about Monica, it would spoil her mood. She was still angry from yesterday when Monica refused to let her have the afternoon off—as if *her* needs were far more pressing than anything Anna could possibly have to do.

Talk turned to other things. Aubrey spoke of his upcoming tour, one that Gerry would accompany him on. "Sort of a delayed honeymoon," she explained, turning to him with a small secretive smile. Anna hadn't been at their wedding last June—only a handful of family and close friends were invited—but she could see that theirs was a match made

in heaven. Gerry had even traded her sub-
urban ranch house for Isla Verde, the beautiful old estate Aubrey leased from Sam.

The green-eyed monster reared its ugly
head once more.

"First stop, Albert Hall," Aubrey was saying. "I'm told the prime minister will be
there. The queen, too." He didn't sound the
least bit intimidated at the prospect, which
probably came from being famous in his
own right. With his dignified bearing and
imposing crest of silver hair, he could easily
have passed for royalty.

"I'm afraid I'll have to settle for the CD."
London might have been the Emerald City
as far as Anna was concerned. The only
time she'd seen Aubrey conduct was at last
summer's music festival, which, come to
think of it, was where he and Gerry had
met.

Gerry glanced at Anna's plate. "Is that all
you're having?"

The difference between Gerry and Sam in
a nutshell, Anna thought. Sam wouldn't
have put her on the spot while Gerry was
well known for what she herself jokingly referred to as her foot-in-mouth disease.
Anna recalled the church committee they'd

served on together last year, and how Gerry had mistakenly had the bulletin printed to read, "For all those who wish to become Little Mothers, please see Father Reardon at the parish house." It had generated more than a few snickers, particularly in light of the fact that it had been Gerry's long-ago affair with a priest, when she was a novice at Our Lady of the Wayside, that had resulted in Claire's birth.

"I'm not all that hungry," Anna lied.

"In that case, you should take some home with you."

"Leave the poor girl alone." Aubrey patted Gerry's hand, on which sparkled a diamond the size of a sugar cube. "You mothers are all alike, forever trying to fatten people up."

Never mind that Anna was fat enough as it was.

She excused herself as soon as she could and said her good-byes. No one asked why she was leaving so early; they were used to Anna dashing home to her mother. She was on her way out the door when Finch caught up with her, asking, "We still on for Thursday?"

Anna drew a blank, then remembered the

film festival. Every year, the Park Rio showed back-to-back classics the second week of November. *Stranger in Paradise* was on Thursday night's bill. Filmed on location in Carson Springs in the fifties, it was known locally as The Movie. Anna must've seen it a dozen times, though never on the big screen. It had seemed like a good idea when Finch first mentioned it, but now she shook her head, saying regretfully, "I'm not sure I'll be able to make it."

"We'll save you a seat just in case."

"You'll be with your friends. What do you want with an old lady like me?" Anna joked.

The crease between Finch's dark brows deepened—what Anna thought of as her don't-try-to-pull-one-over-on-me look. "For one thing, you're not old. Besides, no one knows more about movies."

That much was true. If there was one advantage to being home every night, it was that Anna had seen nearly every movie ever made. "I really will try," she promised. It would depend on Edna.

Anna caught a ride home with Hector, who was leaving early to meet with Doc Henry back at the ranch—something to do with one of the horses. The two were companionably silent throughout most of the drive—a relief after all the people at the party, most of whom it seemed were attached. Hector was the only person she knew who didn't feel the need to talk just for conversation's sake. By the time he dropped her off she was feeling a little less blue about the prospect of being shut inside with her mother the rest of the day.

She walked in to find her answering machine blinking. Six messages, more than she usually got in a week. A sinking feeling told her to wait until Edna had gone home before playing them back—instincts that proved correct. No sooner had Anna punched the Play button when Monica's wheedling voice filled the room.

"Hi . . . it's me. Are you there? Pick up . . ." Sigh. "Okay, I'll try you later."

Click.

"Me again. Where ARE you? It's two o'clock, you couldn't possibly still be at church. All right . . . all right . . . call me when you get this. I'll be in ALL DAY."

Click.

"I don't effing BELIEVE it. Are you purposely not picking up? CALL ME, okay?"

Click.

"This is getting old." Deep sigh. "What? Did you suddenly take up scuba diving? Is that where you've been all this time? Listen, it's important. Call me."

Click.

"Oh, for Chrissakes. Are you still mad about yesterday? I'm sorry, okay? But it's not like I ask that much of you. Do you know how many people would *kill* to have your job?"

Click.

"All right, I really *am* sorry. Is that what you wanted to hear? I should have given you the afternoon off. You know I *would* have if I could have managed on my own . . ." Her voice trailed off piteously. "Look, I feel like an idiot talking to this machine. I'll wait until you call back."

Click.

With a sigh, Anna picked up the receiver and punched in the number for Monica's private line. Her sister answered with a breathless, "Hello?" as if she'd been waiting by the phone.

"I just walked in."

"Where were you? I was worried." Monica affected a concerned tone.

As if she didn't know perfectly well that

Anna would've phoned in the event of an emergency—or would even give a damn if their mother had suffered a heart attack or fallen and broken her hip. "It was Jack's christening," Anna replied as evenly as she could with her blood pressure mounting. "There was a party afterward."

"Jack who?"

"Sam and Ian's baby."

"Do I know them?"

"Sam Kiley, from Delarosa's." Monica should know; she shopped there often enough. Just before Sam retired she'd bought a beautiful handblown vase as a wedding gift for her friend Candace.

"Oh, yes, I remember." Like she had a clue. "Listen, about yesterday, I really *am* sorry. I was in a lousy mood, but I shouldn't have taken it out on you. I want to make it up to you."

Monica apologizing? Anna was speechless.

"I know," Monica went on, mistaking her silence for acquiescence. "Why don't you treat yourself to a manicure? You can charge it to my account."

"That's big of you." Anna couldn't keep the sarcasm from her voice. The account

Monica referred to was at May's Beauty Shoppe, with its turquoise plastic chairs and fifties dryers, where Anna took their mother twice a month to have her hair washed and set. The only reason Monica picked up the tab was so she could rub it in even more about everything she did.

But as far as Monica was concerned, it was settled. "Listen, while I've got you, I'll need you first thing tomorrow. I want to make sure we're all set for Thierry."

Anna felt her anger burst through its fire wall. Monica hadn't phoned to apologize. *She's just making sure I'll be there for the shoot.* "He's not coming until eleven," she reminded her sister coolly. She felt as if she'd swallowed a live coal.

"I know. I want the house to look perfect."

Anna sighed. Thierry LaRoche, an old producer friend, had cajoled Monica into letting him shoot some footage of Lorei-Linda—a segment on celebrity homes for *Entertainment Tonight.* Which would mean that in addition to her usual duties, Anna would have to be on hand to keep the hysteria to a minimum.

"I . . ." *Say it. Tell her to shove her effing apology, and while she's at it, shove the job, too.* But the words stuck in her throat like a dry-swallowed aspirin. Even if she could find another job that paid as well, how would she afford Edna? And if she had to stay home and take care of her mother full time, she'd go crazy herself. Her only other choice would be to put Betty in a nursing home, which would mean selling the house—leaving her homeless in addition to jobless. "I'll see you in the morning," she forced through lips numb with suppressed fury.

"Okay, then. Bright and early," Monica chirped. "Oops, there's my other line. Bye!"

Anna's hand was trembling as she hung up. It took several attempts before she was able to fit the receiver into its cradle. She eyed her mother, seated at the card table by the window, absorbed in her jigsaw puzzle—never mind that most of the pieces ended up in her pockets or on the floor. Betty glanced up, taking note of Anna's unhappy face. "Is something wrong, dear?" she asked with such genuine concern that Anna felt even worse. How could she even *think* of putting Betty in a home?

"Everything's fine," she lied. "Have you had lunch yet?"

Betty shook her head. "Don't go to any trouble, dear. I'm fixing myself an egg. It should be ready any minute."

An alarm bell went off in Anna's head. She raced into the kitchen to find a pan smoking ominously on the stove. It had boiled dry, the egg a gummy mess at the bottom. Unthinkingly, Anna grabbed the handle and a bolt of pain shot up her arm. "Damn!" She dropped it with a clatter, clutching her wrist, bits of exploded egg and shell scattering like shrapnel.

Moments later she sat slumped at the table, her throbbing hand submerged in ice water while she dug into a bag of Oreos with the other, tears running down her cheeks.

"To the left . . . a little more . . . yes, that's it." Monica wheeled back to survey the newly rearranged mantel.

Anna had moved the Staffordshire dogs to the end, repositioning her sister's Oscar, for her Best Supporting role in *Wild Lilies,* so that it was directly below her portrait. The effect was Monica times two. She said, "You don't think it's overkill?"

Monica gave her a withering look. "Why don't we let Thierry be the judge?" As if he'd dare suggest moving so much as a knickknack. If Monica didn't approve of the finished piece, it would be a waste of his time and money.

"Good idea." What difference did it make in the end?

"Well, then, I guess it's showtime." Monica's gaze swept the living room and she let out a satisfied sigh. The stage was set to perfection. In addition to Anna going over it with a fine-tooth comb, it looked as if Arcela had been up all night cleaning. The grand piano and Chinese lacquer cabinets had been polished to a high gloss and the carpet swirled into meringue by the vacuum cleaner except where crisscrossed by wheelchair tracks. Even the floor-to-ceiling windows sparkled, their postcard view of the valley below unimpeded by so much as a fly speck.

"The only thing missing is the orchestra," Anna remarked dryly.

Monica must've caught the edge in her voice, for she shot her a cool look. "I suppose you think this is some kind of ego trip. Well, it's not. I'm only doing it for Thierry."

Anna kept her thoughts to herself. She was saving her energy for the little speech she planned to give later on. Last night, after the binge that had left her wallowing in self-loathing, she'd decided it was time to stop fixating on losing weight and start concentrating on what she needed to *gain,* starting with a spine.

There will have be some changes around here if I'm to go on working for you, she would say. *Starting with my hours. I want the* entire *weekend off, not just Sunday. And no more coming in early and staying late without overtime. If you expect me to—*

"Anna? Are you listening?"

Anna tuned in to find her sister eyeing her impatiently. "Sorry. You were saying?"

"Make sure Arcela understands she's not to say a *word* to Thierry or his crew except Please and Thank you and May I take your coat. Even if it's off the record."

"I'll tell her." *God forbid your fans should find out how little you pay her.*

Monica glanced at her watch and gasped. "My God! They'll be here any minute."

It was ten-fifteen, which left her forty-five minutes to get dressed and made up, but that was barely enough time as far as Monica was concerned. They rode up in the elevator to the second floor. Six years before, when her sister purchased the estate, it had seemed an added bonus along with the private screening room, sauna, and temperature-controlled wine vault, but now Anna viewed the elevator installed by Huff Huffington after his stroke as an eerie foreshadowing of her sister's accident. Listening to the creaking of its cables she felt a slight chill, the way she always did.

Moments later she was wheeling Monica into her palatial bedroom, tastefully done up in art deco style with lots of buttery wood and mirrored surfaces. Anna resisted the urge to tiptoe as she entered the inner sanctum—a dressing room the size of the entire misses clothing department at Rusk's—that felt more like a tomb.

An entire wall was devoted to dresses and evening gowns, carefully preserved in plastic shrouds like bodies in a morgue. Each one bore an index card taped to its plastic sheath, on which were neatly printed the dates and occasions when it had been worn. Along the opposite wall, slacks and blouses were hung according to color, the lighter shades graduating like paint strips to the darker hues. Wheelchair-accessible drawers contained everything from lingerie and stockings to shoes and scarves. Anna wondered if Monica had ever considered the irony of owning so many pairs of shoes when the ability to walk was the one thing she couldn't buy.

"Now, let's see . . ." Monica pursed her mouth. "The Moschino? No, the stripes won't work on camera." She fingered a sleeve. "This one maybe? It's a little bold, but the color is good on me."

A dozen outfits later she wheeled herself over to the three-way mirror wearing a sleeveless cashmere top that was light as a whisper and matching peach trousers. "Perfect," she pronounced. "Now for the finishing touches." She gestured toward her jewelry chest but Anna was one step ahead of her, pulling out a velvet-lined drawer. Monica indicated a filigreed gold pendant. "What do you think?" she said when Anna held it up to her neck.

"Nice," Anna said. "But I think the pearls might work better."

Monica ignored her. She always asked Anna's advice but seldom took it. After nixing all of her suggestions, she chose a simple gold choker and sapphire earrings that matched her eyes. The overall effect was stunning. Monica's behavior might leave something to be desired, but when it came to her appearance, there was never a false move.

Back downstairs, Anna helped her sister onto the living room sofa, rearranging the pillows at her back until Monica was satisfied that she'd be shown off to her best advantage. She stepped back to study the effect. "I don't know about the throw . . ." Draped over Monica's legs, it was a touch too, well, Deborah Kerr in *An Affair to Remember.* Though she supposed that was the idea. "It might look as if you have something to hide," she said.

"You're right. I hadn't thought of that." Monica threw it off as if it were crawling with lice. Before the accident she'd been famous for her legs, and the idea that her fans might imagine them to be withered and ugly was intolerable. Now she turned her attention to Anna, eyeing her critically. "Is that what you're wearing?"

Anna felt suddenly conspicuous in the navy skirt and pin-striped blouse she'd worn precisely because it would help her blend into the background. "What's wrong with it?" Even as she spoke, she saw the answer in her sister's disapproving gaze.

"Nothing. Except . . ." Monica frowned. "It looks like something Mom would wear. Also, it's too baggy." She studied her more closely. "Have you lost weight?"

So it's taken you this long to notice? "A little." Anna dropped her gaze.

She looked up to find Monica smiling her patronizing little smile that made Anna feel as if she were biting down on tinfoil. "Which one is it this time? All the rice you can eat— or the one with all the eggs and butter but no bread? Please tell me it's not the fruit juice fast again. You'll be running back and forth to the bathroom all day."

"I'm not on a diet. I just decided to cut back." Anna spoke quietly.

"Well, it's working. You look great." Anna listened for the condescension in Monica's voice, but she seemed sincere enough. "When you get to your goal, we'll celebrate with a shopping spree. Rodeo Drive, the works. A whole new wardrobe, my treat."

"That's nice of you, but . . ." Anna didn't want to get her hopes up. Monica was famous for making promises she didn't keep, though you were supposed to fall all over yourself thanking her regardless. "I was thinking of bringing Mom's sewing machine down from the attic."

"That old thing? I didn't know she still had it." Monica's expression turned wistful. "God, all those matching dresses she used to make us. One Easter she had us in these little blue pinafores with daisies on the bibs. You were probably too young to remember . . ." She gazed off into the distance, something dark flitting across her face. Then her smile switched on again. "Those were the days," she said with a bitter laugh.

"They're probably in a box somewhere." Betty had saved every little memento, including the clothes they'd outgrown. She'd look for them in the attic while she was up there.

"Along with Dad's things." Monica's mouth curled in disgust. "I can't believe she didn't throw out all that stuff after he died." She cast a scornful glance at the framed eight-by-ten of their parents on the mantel, taken just before Joe was diagnosed with cancer. It was the sole photograph of them on display in the house, and the only reason it was there was because an absence of family photos might have looked strange.

Anna shrugged. "Sentimental value, I guess."

"Yes, who wouldn't want to cherish the memory of being beaten to a pulp?"

"He wasn't like that *all* the time," Anna felt compelled to remind her.

"Go on, defend him. Isn't that your job?" Monica turned her hard gaze on Anna. She looked about to unload, then seemed to think better of it and sighed wearily instead. "Never mind. Why don't you mix me a drink? It'll calm my nerves."

Anna glanced pointedly at her watch. Usually Monica held out until lunch. If she got started this early, well, God only knew what she'd be like by the end of the day.

Her worries were in vain, as it turned out. Monica was at her best, regaling Thierry, a short balding man with an annoying habit of drumming on his knees, with stories of her days as Hollywood's reigning queen. He and the crew lunched on sandwiches provided by Arcela, and were given free rein to roam about setting up shots. Monica didn't make so much as a peep when one of the men bumped up against the wall with his camera, leaving a scratch in the wallpaper.

It was nearly four o'clock by the time they had all cleared out. Anna was exhausted— she'd been on her feet all day—but Monica's eyes glowed like the sapphires in her ears—and not just from being the center of attention. There'd been something more than soda in those Diet Cokes she'd been sipping all afternoon. As Anna helped her off the sofa, a glance into the carryall hooked over an arm of the wheelchair confirmed her suspicion when a silver flask, half hidden by a box of tissues, winked up at her.

"I just hope I don't live to regret this." Monica's voice was more than a little slurred. "I wasn't *too*-too, was I?" In other words, had they noticed she was drunk?

"You were fine." Anna spoke more curtly than usual.

Monica eyed her with reproach. "Looks like someone took a grumpy pill." Their mother's expression, which sounded strange coming from her sister.

"I'm just tired, that's all." Anna ran a hand through her hair. This was probably the worst possible moment, but she *had* to get it off her chest. Or risk a repeat of last night's binge. She cleared her throat. "Listen, there's something I've been meaning to talk to you about."

Monica's eyes narrowed. "I'm all ears."

"It's too much, looking after you *and* Mom. I need to cut back on my hours."

"Go on."

The flatness of her sister's tone should have signaled her to stop there, but she plowed on. "I'd like Saturdays off, for one thing. And . . . and half days on Thursdays." What the hell. Why not shoot for the moon? "Also, I don't think it's appropriate for me to be washing your lingerie and clipping your toenails."

Monica was silent for so long that Anna was momentarily lulled into thinking she'd pulled it off. Then the storm hit. "Appropriate? Christ Almighty. Who do you think I am, Steve Fucking Forbes? I'm stuck in this thing twenty-four seven," she banged her fists against the arms of her wheelchair, "and you're yammering about what's *appropriate*?"

Anna had opened Pandora's box and now it was too late to close it. She stood her ground even so. "It's no good playing the sympathy card," she shot back in a surprisingly calm voice. "I've heard it all before."

"Oh, really?" Monica gave her a look that would have cut glass.

"Frankly, I think you're being selfish."

"*Selfish?*" Monica hissed. "Is that how you see me? Well, if I am it's because of *this.*" She glared at her wheelchair as she might have at iron shackles imprisoning her.

Anna closed her eyes, but couldn't shut out the memory. She was once more hearing the collective gasp that had gone up on shore. And seeing the boat in pieces, bobbing in the distance like a toy smashed by a capricious giant. It had happened in a heartbeat; one minute it was skimming over the surface, the next flipping up into the air. If the boat with the photographer and his crew hadn't come to the rescue within moments, her sister would surely have drowned. Anna sometimes wondered what her life would be like now if Monica *had.* If instead of the ghastly days and weeks that had followed, shuttling back and forth from the hospital and then the rehab center, there'd been a funeral that would have allowed Anna to mourn, then move on. But such thoughts always brought a flood of shame. The difference was she no longer felt she was to blame just because it had been her idea—the one time Monica had listened to her—that the photographer snap some shots of Monica on her boat.

If anyone, Monica should blame herself for pushing to go at top speed. Even as a child she'd loved going fast, the faster the better. Speeding downhill on her bike, then later in muscle cars with boys eager to show off for the prettiest girl in school. Anna recalled a procession of Band-Aids, ice packs, Ace bandages, and casts. The wheelchair was only the last in a long line.

"Come on, Monica," she cajoled. "It's not like I'm asking for the moon."

"And if I don't give you what you want?"

Blood surged into Anna's cheeks. She'd hoped it wouldn't come to this. "That's up to you."

"You want me to fire you? You'd like that, wouldn't you? Mean old Monica, once again cast as the villainess while poor Anna rakes in all the sympathy."

"It . . . it's not like that." But Anna could already feel her resolve shrinking. In desperation she burst out, "I'm your *sister,* for

God's sake! And even if I weren't, I'd deserve to be treated with consideration. Not like some . . . some medieval serf."

"I see. So all I do for *you,* that doesn't count?"

"If you mean Edna . . ."

"Who's paying for Mom's meds? And the taxes on the house? I suppose you take it all for granted—whatever you need, just ask Monica. She's rich. She can afford it."

"That's not true, and you know it. We're grateful for . . ." Anna bit her lip. Dammit, she was *not* going to get suckered into apologizing. "She's your mother, too."

"I don't need you to remind me." Monica's tone was icy.

"Apparently, you do." Anna forced herself to meet Monica's glittering gaze. "She asks after you all the time. When is she going to see you, when are you coming to visit? Frankly, I've run out of excuses."

"Maybe you haven't noticed, but I don't get around all that well."

You do when it suits you, Anna wanted to fling back. But she kept her cool. "It wouldn't kill you to visit once in a while. You could even have her here."

"Don't be ridiculous. The minute our

backs were turned, she'd be off God knows where." Monica snatched up her glass and drained it. "Sure, let's all feel sorry for poor Mom. Don't mind me, I'm only a cripple." She was breathing heavily, an unhealthy flush rising in her cheeks.

This was Anna's cue to feel guilty. Didn't she have two legs to walk on while Monica had to depend on others for every little thing? But something rebelled in her. She wouldn't give in this time, even if it cost her her job. "Would you rather I resigned?" she asked quietly. "Would that make it easier?"

She steeled herself against the full onslaught of Monica's fury. It would be a relief in a way because it would only harden her resolve, galvanize her like a blowtorch, from which she'd emerge gleaming and new. Why hadn't she done this years ago? In her mind the future glimmered miragelike, the day she wouldn't have to drag to work as heavy inside as she was out, when she could hold her head up and know that her wants and needs mattered as much as anyone's.

But the expected blast didn't come. Instead, Monica's chin began to tremble and tears rolled down her cheeks. Not crocodile tears this time, real ones. "You wouldn't do that to me? Not really? Oh, Anna, promise you won't leave." Her voice was small and meek. "I'm sorry I was such a bitch." She was crying in earnest now, hunched over in her chair. "I didn't mean all those things I said. I don't know what gets into me sometimes. It's this . . . fucking . . . thing." She beat with her fists at the arms of her wheelchair. "I know, I know. I should've gotten past it by now, but I can't. *I can't!* Oh, God . . ." She slumped forward, covering her face with her hands.

If she'd been whacked behind the knees with a baseball bat, Anna couldn't have dropped to her haunches any quicker. Later, when she'd had a chance to reflect, she would wonder how much of it had been because of Monica and how much because of her own need to feel needed. But in that moment all she could see was her sister in pain. And wasn't it her job to take care of Monica?

"Shh . . . it's okay. I'm not going anywhere." She stroked Monica's heaving back.

"Promise?" Monica lifted her head, her

eyes red and swollen behind a tangle of damp hair.

"I promise." Anna fished a Kleenex from the carryall. "Blow."

Monica dutifully honked into the tissue. Anna was reminded of what many considered her sister's finest role, that of the blue-collar wife dumped by her cheating husband in *Roses Are Red.* Except for once Monica wasn't acting. "Do you hate me?"

Anna sighed. "No, of course not."

"I hate myself sometimes."

"You shouldn't."

"I know how I come across. I don't mean to." She managed a tremulous smile. "Remember that fairy tale Mom used to read aloud to us, about the two sisters? I'm the one with the toads jumping out of her mouth."

You didn't have any trouble being nice to Thierry and his crew, said a voice in Anna's head. "I know it's hard," she said gently. "It would be for anyone in your place."

"But not you." There was no sarcasm in her voice now. "You'd be the poster child for paraplegics. How do you do it, Anna? How do you stay so upbeat all the time?"

I eat. And eat. And eat. "I don't know." She shrugged. "I guess it's the way I'm built." *Truer words were never spoken,* she thought, picturing the old Pontiac station wagon they'd had growing up, which ran on fumes and never seemed to break down.

Monica sniffed into the balled-up tissue. "Honestly, I couldn't manage without you."

Anna took a deep breath. "You won't have to."

"Cross your heart, hope to die?"

"Stick a needle in my eye." Anna grinned, and in that instant they were sisters again. Two little girls hugging each other tightly as they cowered in the closet, listening to their father beat the living daylights out of their mother. Before Liz was born. Before Dad got sick. Before Monica ran away to Hollywood and became famous.

"Why don't you take the rest of the day off," Monica said magnanimously. "You've earned it."

As Anna rose to her full height she had the oddest feeling of sinking into the floor, like an elevator going down. She'd won, hadn't she? Why did she feel so defeated? "Thanks, I think I will."

"See you in the morning?"

"First thing."

It wasn't until she was outside, trudging toward her newly repaired Toyota, for which she was now in the hole for two hundred eighty dollars she could ill afford, that it struck Anna: She hadn't gained a thing. Not really. Monica had given in, yes, but at what price? Anna couldn't shake the feeling that the other shoe had yet to drop.

She was in her nightgown, brushing her teeth, when the phone rang.

"Miss Anna . . . you come. Hurry." It was Arcela. She sounded agitated.

Anna felt a jolt of alarm. "What is it?"

"Miss Monica, she fall down. She hurt, I think."

More like passed out cold. Anna recalled how drunk she'd been. And that was before cocktail hour, when the fun *really* started. But what if she really was hurt? "I'll call an ambulance," she told Arcela. "Just keep an eye on her until it gets there."

Punching in 911, she felt a great weariness descend on her. This wasn't the first time, nor would it be the last. She could no longer ignore the fact that her sister was an alcoholic.

Her next call was to Laura. "I know it's late," she apologized, "but something's come up. It's Monica. I'm on my way to the hospital and I was wondering—"

Laura didn't let her finish. "Finch can drive you. And don't worry about your mother; I'll look after her."

"I hate to bother you this time of night."

"Don't be silly. What are neighbors for?" As if she'd asked to borrow a cup of sugar. "Just stay put. We'll be there as soon as I throw something on."

Anna fought back tears. "Thanks. What would I do without you?" It was a familiar refrain, yet each time it amazed her that someone who didn't owe her a thing could be so giving.

Minutes later she heard a knock at the door. Laura let herself in before Anna had a chance to answer it. She wore a jacket over her flannel nightgown, a pair of cowboy boots peeking from under the ruffled hem. "Take all the time you need," she said, as Anna was leaving. "I just hope it isn't serious." Something in her tone caused Anna to go cold inside: Laura knew. Which meant it was even worse than she'd thought. There'd be no sweeping it under the rug this time.

CHAPTER FOUR

"Is she awake?" Liz asked nervously.

Anna shook her head. "Out like a light."

"Do you guys, uh, want some coffee or something?" Finch piped.

They stood in a tense huddle in the hallway outside Monica's room on the third floor at Dominican, Finch hovering a few feet away from Anna and Liz. She felt as though she were butting in on private family business.

"I could use some." Liz looked put out, as if she'd been dragged there for no reason. She dug into her purse and handed Finch a crumpled bill. "Milk, no sugar."

Finch could see the resemblance to Anna in her heart-shaped face with its wide-set blue eyes that crinkled at the corners. The difference was that Liz took better care of herself. Her brown hair was stylishly cut and streaked with subtle highlights; her body that of someone who worked out regularly. And no wonder. Liz managed the spa at the hot springs, where Alice was always threatening to drag Laura one of these days.

"I'm good, thanks." Anna flashed Finch a weary smile. She wore sneakers and rumpled sweats, and in one corner of her mouth was a tiny smear of toothpaste.

Finch felt a rush of protectiveness, which was odd given that Anna was more than twice her age. Probably because they were alike in some ways; neither had had it easy. Finch saw it in the shyness with which Anna greeted new people, as if experience had taught her that not everyone with a hand out meant well, and in her reluctance to step to the head of the line, as if to do so would make her a target. It wasn't until you got to know Anna that you realized how amazing she was—strong in the way that trees are, quietly enduring each storm.

Like now, with Monica. Some might see Anna as subservient to her famous sister, but Finch knew the truth: Anna was the glue that held Monica together. But even she had her limits. Everyone in town knew that Monica was a drunk. Anna could only hold it together for so long.

Finch was on her way back from the cafeteria, walking carefully to keep the Styrofoam container of coffee from spilling over, when she saw the two sisters still huddled in conversation. And from the looks they wore it wasn't the weather they were discussing. She slowed her steps, their voices drifting toward her.

"Are you sure it's as bad as all that?" Liz was saying. "I mean, just because she drinks a little too much—"

"It's not a little; it's a lot. And it's getting worse." Anna wasn't backing down. Good for her. "You don't want to be around when she's been drinking, believe me."

"I don't want to be around her, period." Liz gave a dry little laugh. "I deal with enough celebrities at the spa. The worst? The ones who come across sweet as pie in public. You should see how they treat my staff."

"Ever heard of Pathways?"

"Isn't it one of those religious cults?"

"It's a rehab facility. A lot of famous people go there."

"Oh yeah, it's coming back to me. Isn't that where what's-his-name went to get off drugs?"

Anna nodded. "That's what made me think of it. Anyway, I put in a call." This wasn't news to Finch; Anna had phoned from the car—someone named Rita. It sounded as if they'd spoken before.

"And?" Liz arched a brow.

"They're sending someone to evaluate her."

Liz made a face. "I wouldn't want to be that person."

"Well, the thing is . . ." Anna became suddenly absorbed in rubbing at a spot on her sleeve. "We'll have to be there, too. Sort of like an intervention."

"Sort of? There's no such thing as *sort of.*" Liz took a step back, glancing about wildly as if in search of the nearest fire escape. But she must have realized she was stuck, for she moaned and slumped back against the wall. "Oh, God, I should've known."

In a quiet but firm voice, Anna said, "I can't do this alone. I need you, Liz."

"Why should I? What has she done for *me* lately? She barely gives me the time of day. And Dylan? The last time we were up at the house, she took a nap while he splashed around in the pool. I'm surprised she even remembers his birthday."

"Well, it's something at least."

The telltale flush in Anna's cheeks was the tip-off. Liz's eyes narrowed. "It was *you,* wasn't it? *You're* the one who sends those gifts."

Anna looked as if she were going to deny it, then shrugged. "I charge it to her card, so technically they're from her."

Liz sighed in defeat. "Okay. I'll do it for you. But that's the *only* reason."

Anna looked relieved. "Great. Meet me here tomorrow morning at eight."

"Why so early?"

"Supposedly it's better if we do it first thing—before she knows what hit her."

Liz sighed again, looking even more put upon. "I'll have to find someone to cover for me at work. Janelle's out sick and I've been filling in at the front desk. But I suppose I could spare an hour."

"Actually, it's a little more involved than that." Anna suddenly had trouble meeting her gaze. "There's also family week."

"You're kidding, right?"

"It's not for a couple of weeks, until she's had a chance to settle in, but it's important that we both come. Not just for Monica's sake. For ours too."

"No way." Liz was shaking her head like a child ordered to eat something that would make her gag. "No fucking way am I rearranging my entire life for that . . . that . . ." She couldn't bring herself to say it. Whatever Monica might be, she was still her sister. In a sullen voice, she added, "She wouldn't do it for either of us."

"Probably not," Anna admitted, looking more sad than angry. "But isn't that all the more reason? God knows it can't get any worse. And maybe it'll get better. For *all* of us."

Finch chose that moment to step forward. She handed Liz her coffee, saying, "Sorry, I didn't mean to interrupt. I'll be down the hall if you need me." She'd started off in the direction of the lounge when Anna grabbed her gently by the elbow.

"You're not interrupting anything." She gave her a look that said, *You're family, too.*

A warm glow stole over Finch. For most of her sixteen years she'd been on the outside looking in. Fourteen foster homes in as many years, never in any one long enough to call it home. It was only in the past year or so, since she'd come to live with Laura, that she'd felt as though she belonged. And now here was Anna making room as well.

Liz smiled. "The more, the merrier."

"Is she going to be okay?" Finch asked with a glance into Monica's room, where she slumbered on, oblivious to what was about to hit her.

Liz snorted. "Depends on what you mean by okay."

Finch had heard the rumors. She'd also been around enough drunks to know one when she saw one. Once, when waiting on Monica in Delarosa's, she'd smelled booze on her breath.

"I'm just glad she wasn't hurt," Anna said.

"How the hell do you fall out of a wheel-chair? I mean, even drunk it's quite a stunt." Liz glanced about, as if afraid someone might overhear. "By the way, what's the *official* story?"

Anna smiled grimly. "That she was taken suddenly ill. Pneumonia probably. It sounds more glamorous than a bump on the head."

Finch shuddered, a memory rushing in.

She was eight years old, in the emergency ward at King's County, her arm being set into a cast. She was crying, not just because it hurt or because she was in an unfamiliar place, but because the nice doctor fixing her arm had wanted to know how she broke it and she didn't know what to say. If she told the truth, her foster dad might hurt her even worse, as he'd threatened. So she lied instead, telling the doctor she'd fallen off a jungle gym.

From inside Monica's room came a soft moan. Finch peered in to see her stirring awake. She didn't look so glamorous right now. Her face was pale, with dark circles under her eyes, her hair snarled. A few years ago, Finch had torn a photo of Monica from a magazine and taped it to her bedroom wall. She'd dreamed of one day being rich and famous like her, but now she wouldn't have traded places with Monica for all the money in the world.

While Liz and Anna hung back, each waiting for the other to go first, Finch found herself drifting into the room. "Hi," she said, lifting her hand in a little wave.

"Who are you?" Monica squinted groggily up at her.

"A friend of Anna's." Clearly, Monica didn't remember her from Delarosa's.

Monica looked past her, calling sharply to Anna and Liz, "Will someone please tell me what's going on?"

Anna stepped up beside Finch. "You took a little tumble back at the house." Her voice was matter-of-fact.

Monica frowned. "Funny. I don't remember."

"Hey, Sis." Liz planted a little peck on Monica's cheek. "You look a little under the weather."

"I feel like shit." The dark circles under Monica's eyes looked as if they'd been drawn on with a Magic Marker. "Where's Dr. Berger?"

"He's not here," Anna said.

"Where the hell is he? Why haven't you called him?"

She struggled to sit up, but Anna gently pushed her back. "It can wait until morning. No sense disturbing him tonight."

"All right, if you won't call him, *I* will." Monica reached for the phone by the bed, but Liz snatched it out of reach.

"You're not exactly in a position to be calling any shots," she said.

Monica looked stunned. Clearly, she wasn't used to being talked to this way. "What's going on?" Her eyes narrowed. "There's something you're not telling me. Don't deny it; it's written all over your faces."

"We might as well tell her. She'll know soon enough." Liz cast a meaningful look at Anna before turning back to Monica. "The doctor says you have six months to live."

"Go to hell," Monica shot back.

Finch fought the urge to giggle.

"We'll be back in the morning," Anna said. "We can talk about it then."

Liz glanced at her watch, then lowered the phone onto the floor.

"So that's it—you're abandoning me?" Monica gazed up at them piteously. Finch was reminded of the movie in which she'd played a woman dying of cancer. Finch had cried the whole way through, but now she looked on dry-eyed.

"Looks that way." Liz cast her a last unsympathetic look as she headed for the door, Anna and Finch behind her. "If you get lonely, you can always watch yourself on TV." There was usually a Monica Vincent movie on some channel or other.

They were stepping out the door when something went flying past them to land with a thud against the jamb—a Gideon Bible, Finch saw. It appeared Monica was recovering nicely.

"Shh . . . it's starting."

Andie snuggled down in her seat, passing the popcorn box to Simon. He helped himself before handing it to Finch. The credits were rolling over the opening shot: a car winding its way down a familiar mountain road.

"Studebaker," Simon muttered.

"What?" Finch whispered back.

"The car." He turned toward her, tiny twin images of the Studebaker flashing across the lenses of his Clark Kent glasses. Andie's boyfriend was the worst kind of know-it-all, the kind who was always right. If he hadn't been so nice, Finch could easily have hated him.

Turning her attention back to the screen, she quickly became caught up in the movie. It was a scratchy print, its colors dulled by age, but *Stranger in Paradise,* the story of a man on the run from the law who takes a wrong turn and ends up in a town that turns out to be heaven, held her captive from start to finish. By the final scene, when the hero realizes he's in love with the woman he was falsely accused of murdering and has to choose between staying with her and going back to his life on earth, she was sniffing surreptitiously into the tissue balled in her fist. Glancing at Andie out of the corner of her eye, she saw that her friend was doing the same.

They should pass out Kleenex at the door, she thought. Even Simon had taken his glasses off and was wiping them on his shirttail. And he was nothing if not cynical.

Andie reached across him to nudge Finch. "Look." She pointed at the closing credits rolling down the screen. The name Lorraine Wells jumped out at Finch. Before she'd become a Kiley, her name had been Wells—Bethany Lorraine Wells. Andie arched a brow, as if to suggest that there was a connection.

But Finch only shrugged, as if to say, *What of it?*

"You could be related," Andie said as

they gathered up their things. "You never know."

"It's a common name," Finch said.

"Still."

"It's a stretch." Simon tugged his backpack out from under his seat. He didn't go anywhere without it; inside was his notebook and pen, Nikon and minirecorder. You never knew when you'd come across a lead, he'd often said.

"Yeah, well, maybe it's fate. Did you ever think that there's a reason you ended up in Carson Springs?" Andie could be like a dog with a bone even when debating something she didn't necessarily believe in. Whatever the consensus, you'd generally find her on the opposing side. "I remember you telling me that it felt like you'd been here before."

"Maybe in another life," Finch joked. They were making their way down the aisle, its carpet littered with popcorn and candy wrappers.

"Don't you believe in destiny?"

"Sure—as in Destiny's Child," Finch cracked.

A tiny seed had taken root nonetheless. What if it was true? Stranger things had been known to happen. And getting off the bus that first day, Finch *had* felt as if she were coming home. Suppose in some weird way it was connected to Lorraine Wells?

By the time they reached the lobby, she'd decided that it was only the movie putting such ideas into her head—all that stuff about the hereafter and souls finding their mates. Like after watching *Salem's Lot,* when she'd seen a vampire in every shadow.

Glancing about, she saw a number of bloodshot eyes—it seemed she wasn't the only sucker for a tearjerker—though everyone appeared to be having a good time. Myrna McBride, the red-headed owner of The Last Word, was chatting with the elderly Miller twins, Olive and Rose, dressed in identical seersucker shirtwaists and clutching matching straw purses. And over by the vintage popcorn machine, burly, tattooed Herman Tyzzer from the Den of Cyn was regaling the small group gathered around him with little-known facts about the film. Herman was one of the festival's organizers. He also knew more about movies than anyone.

She waved hello to Dawn and Eve Parrish, Rose's identical twin granddaughters, a pair of towheads. Dawn sat next to her in bio, and had once brought in a marijuana leaf as part of a project on medicinal herbs. She wouldn't say where she'd gotten it, but everyone knew her dopehead parents grew it in their backyard. Luckily for her, their teacher hadn't reported it.

Finch was sorry that Anna couldn't be there, and she hoped things would get better now that Monica was in rehab. Between her mother and her sister, Anna had her hands full.

They made their way outside, where a light breeze had kicked up. The leaves of the mock orange trees in tubs along the curb rustled as they strolled along the sidewalk. Like the Park Rio, most of downtown Carson Springs was in a time warp. The post office bell tower chimed the hour just as it had for the past seventy years, competing with church bells on Sunday. The fountain at Parson's Drugs, with its red vinyl stools, still served cream sodas and malteds. And the Tree House Café had been guarding its recipe for cream of chili soup since David Ryback's grandfather ran it. The only real change, Laura had said, was that a scoop of ice cream at Lickety-Split that used to cost fifty cents was now a dollar fifty.

They were passing Between the Covers, the bookstore owned by Myrna's ex-husband Peter—the two were bitter rivals—when Andie pointed across the street at The Last Word, the only shop on the arcade with its lights blazing. It was normally closed at this hour; Myrna must have kept it open late because of the festival. "Let's go in," Andie said, grabbing Simon's hand and setting off across the street. They made an odd couple—Andie petite and bouncy, Simon lanky and bookish—yet they worked somehow.

Hurrying to catch up with them, Finch felt unreasonably left out. However much they bent over backward to make her feel included, there was no getting around the fact that she was a third wheel. Not that she hadn't gotten her share of interest, just that the guys she'd met seemed immature.

At the coffee bar, Andie treated them to lattes and slices of lemon meringue pie. It was a school night, but they were in no hurry to get home—maybe because they never ran out of things to talk about. Simon and Andie were the only ones besides her family and Anna with whom Finch could totally be herself. They didn't judge her for being behind in some ways and older than her years in others. In her former life, she'd never been in one place long enough to make real friends. Now she had two she could count on through thick and thin.

They were on their way out when a display of books on film caught her eye. She picked up a slim volume titled *On Location: The Making of Stranger in Paradise,* a sticker on the front identifying its author as local. Before she knew it, she was thumbing through the index. If Lorraine Wells was listed anywhere, it would be here.

Andie peered over her shoulder. "I knew it."

Finch whirled about, embarrassed. "What?"

"You're curious. Admit it."

"Okay, I admit it." With Andie, it was sometimes easier just to give in. "But that doesn't mean I think you're right."

Simon picked up another copy of the same book and began flipping through it. "I see Orson Welles, but no Lorraine."

"So that's it? We just give up?" Andie said.

He shrugged, returning the book to the stack. "Either way, it's probably a moot point. Chances are she's dead—or too old to remember much."

Andie glared at him. "You don't know that."

"Why are you making such a big deal of this?" Finch wanted to know.

"*I* believe in fate, even if you don't." She snatched the book out of Finch's hand and marched over to the register. "Like with my grandparents."

"What about them?" Finch asked.

"When they met, and Grandma found out his name was Fitzgerald, the same as hers, she knew then and there that they were meant for each other."

"A name as common as Smith among the Irish," Simon pointed out, looking bemused. He was used to her flights of fancy—like the time she'd dragged him to a fortune-teller, who'd told him his future included lots of children (which was how he knew she was a fake, because playing dad to his five younger brothers and sisters had made him vow to remain childless). When Andie shot him a dirty look, he was quick to add, "Though I'm sure fate had something to do with it."

"Look, I know it's a needle in a haystack, but why don't we look for her anyway?" Andie said as she took out her wallet and paid for the book.

"Your grandmother?" Simon teased.

"No, dummy. *Lorraine.*" This time she giggled.

Finch sighed. "All right. But I want it on record that I'm not expecting anything to come of it." The less you expected, she'd found, the less disappointed you were.

She didn't dare reveal the truth, not to her best friend: that she longed to know where she'd come from. All her life she'd wondered about her parents—if they were married to other people, if she had sisters or brothers. The thought that she could pass them on the street and not know them nagged at her constantly.

Was Lorraine Wells some long-lost relation? The chances were a million to one. But that didn't stop her from wondering . . . and wishing.

Simon volunteered to do a little poking around on his own first. "I'll talk to this guy, see if he can give us any leads," he said, seizing hold of the book.

"Have I told you lately that I love you?" Andie flashed him her most dazzling smile. Poor Simon. How could he resist?

On the way back to their cars, Andie talked about her mother and stepfather's upcoming trip to Europe, and how absolutely amazing it was that she'd been entrusted to look after her little brother while they were away. Since going to her dad's was out of the question after her disastrous stay earlier in the year, her mom had decided she was old enough to be left in charge. Finch didn't want to burst her bubble by telling her that being on your own wasn't all it was cracked up to be.

Talk turned to the new kid who'd transferred from some prep school back east. Finch hadn't yet met him, but according to Andie he was just her type—brooding and mysterious. Like Andie would know her type. More to the point, like she had the slightest interest in hooking up with him or *any* guy. Never mind the rumors going around school that she was frigid, or maybe even a lesbian. Let people think what they liked. Would it be better if they knew the truth—that she'd slept with more guys than Madonna?

"I'd better get going. I have to study for a test," she said as she was hurrying toward Hector's pickup parked in the municipal lot. "Like there's any reason you'd ever need to know about the Peloponnesian Wars." She rolled her eyes.

"Ask Andie; she was probably there in another life." Simon grinned.

"Bite me," Andie said sweetly.

"Why is it that in past lives, people always claim to have been someone famous, like Cleopatra or Napoleon?" Finch paused, reaching into her purse for her keys. "Aren't ordinary people ever reincarnated?"

"One of these days we'll find out," Simon said with a wink.

Finch laughed as she waved good-bye, but deep down she wondered uneasily if her own past life might come back to haunt her.

"Hey, faggot!"

"Dude, are you, like, deaf or something?"

"Are all preppies faggots, or is it just you?"

There were two of them, a pair of hulking Neanderthals. Yet the new kid—at least that's who she assumed he was—remained a picture in studied disinterest as he stood slouched against the bus shelter, squinting off into the distance, his dark shoulder-length hair tucked behind his ears and a tattered paperback of *Catcher in the Rye* under one arm. Finch watched as the two Neanderthals—she didn't know their names but had seen them around school—began circling their prey. The larger of the two was built like a meat locker, with a buzz cut and beady eyes that brought to mind Bluto from *Popeye*; his shorter bulletheaded sidekick had such bad acne, his face resembled a fully loaded pizza. When they were practically on top of him, the new kid turned at last to look at them with mild interest.

"I'm sorry." He spoke pleasantly. "Do I know you?"

Finch saw a flicker of uncertainty in Bullethead's stupid eyes as he turned to his friend. But Bluto only leaned closer to the kid, his jaw thrust forward. "I don't hang with faggots." His gaze slithered down the front of the navy blazer the kid wore over his T-shirt. It bore a school crest, she saw.

"Really?" A corner of the kid's mouth curled up. "Because you seem pretty interested in the subject."

"Dude, you callin' my friend a faggot?" Bullethead, all jacked up on adrenaline and maybe something more, jive-stepped to within inches of the kid, thrusting his pimply jaw forward in an unintentionally comic imitation of his friend.

The kid shrugged. "Hey, it's cool. Everybody's entitled to his own thing."

The smirk dropped from Bluto's face and a flush crept up the sides of his Neanderthal neck. "One more word outta you, asshole," he growled, "and I'll rearrange your fucking face."

Those waiting for the bus just stood there gaping, except Courtney Russo, who was too busy yakking on her cell phone to notice what was going on. But Finch had seen enough. She stalked over. "What's the matter with you two? You get off on this shit?" She rocked forward on the balls of her feet so that she was eye to eye with Bluto, her heels lifting off the packed dirt littered with cigarette butts and gum wrappers. "Where I come from guys like you get eaten for breakfast."

"Yeah, and where would that be—the gutter?" Bluto smirked at her. "I heard about you. I heard you were in trouble with the cops before you came here."

Bullethead let loose a shrill, hyena laugh. He reminded Finch of a toy she'd once had, a clown on a stick with arms and legs that flopped up and down when you pulled a string. "Yeah, I bet it was for turning tricks," he sputtered.

"How much for a blow job?" Bluto's smirk had taken on a menacing slant.

She trembled in fury. All her life she'd been dealing with assholes like these— guys with brains the size of their dicks and girls that could've taught Lady Macbeth a thing or two. "First," she said, speaking loudly enough for the others to hear, "I'd have to find it."

"Fuck you, bitch!" Bluto flicked her shoulder hard enough to throw her off balance. She stumbled and caught her foot against a tree root, reeling backward to land on her rear end. A hard jolt traveled up her spine, and the world went a little fuzzy. When the kid stepped between her and Bluto, it seemed to take place in slow motion.

"Back off," he ordered.

"Yeah, and who's gonna make me?" Bluto gave him a hard shove that caused him to stagger.

The kid just stared at Bluto. That's when Finch noticed his eyes: They were blue-black, the color of dreams she'd had of falling endlessly in space.

As if some silent signal had been given, the onlookers gathered into a huddle. On the other side of the parking lot, the American flag over the lawn whipped smartly in the breeze, the hollow clanking of its pulley against the pole like an alarm being sounded.

Bullethead flicked an uncertain glance at his sidekick, braying with a patently false bravado, "Watch it, Dude. Me and Dink, we'll fucking an-i-uh-late your ass."

The kid ignored him to eye Bluto, who was advancing on him like a one-man commando division. "You heard me." His voice was low and unafraid. "I said back off."

Bluto either wasn't listening or didn't care. He charged, head lowered and fists cocked, swinging his arm in a clumsy roundhouse blow. But the kid was quicker, landing a hard uppercut to his belly. Finch heard a *huhhnh* of escaping breath and saw Bluto lurch backward, his face flooding with color. The look of utter astonishment he wore might have been comical if she hadn't seen what was coming next: Bullethead getting ready to jump the kid from the rear.

"Watch out!" she cried.

The kid wheeled around, and Bluto took advantage of his being momentarily off guard, clipping him on the jaw. He staggered and nearly fell, but managed to stay on his feet. "Had enough, faggot?" Bluto sneered as he and his friend circled in for the kill.

Bullethead lashed out with a kick that would have caught the kid in the groin if he hadn't caught hold of the foot, giving it a hard wrench that sent Bullethead flipping back onto the pavement with a high, girlish squeal. He began to thrash about, clutching his ankle and howling, "Oooooowwwwww. Fuck, man, I think it's broken!"

Serves you right, Finch would have said if she'd been able to unglue her tongue from the roof of her mouth. But she stood rooted to the spot like the others, looking on in disbelief. It wasn't until Courtney Russo pulled her cell phone away from her ear to cry petulantly, "Cut it *out,* you guys!"—they might have been disrupting her enjoyment of the latest episode of *Dawson's Creek*—that Finch was jolted into action. She grabbed her backpack and hurled it at Bluto with all her might. It struck him square in the chest, halting him in midcharge and throwing him off balance just long enough for the kid to wrestle him to the ground.

"Leggo! That hurts!" Bluto's arm was pinned behind his back, his contorted face the color of raw hamburger.

After a moment that seemed to stretch on forever, the kid released his grip. Bluto lurched to his feet, scuttling out of reach. "What the fuck, man. Can't you take a joke?" he muttered in a desperate attempt to salvage what little dignity he could.

"Looks like the joke's on you." The kid eyed him with cool disdain.

Bluto, wearing the look of the injured party, stalked over to haul his howling buddy to his feet, snarling, "Shut the fuck up, you pussy." He gave Bullethead a little shove that sent him hopping backward on one foot, then grabbed him roughly by the arm and steered him off toward the parking lot as fast as he could limp.

Finch walked over to the kid. "You're bleeding." She touched the hand cradled against his side.

"It's nothing." He slid his hand into his pocket.

He'd dropped his book in the scuffle. She saw it in the dirt a few feet away, and stooped to retrieve it. Handing it to him, she muttered, "Come on, let's get out of here." While Courtney and the others stood gaping as if at a circus act, Finch snatched up her backpack, motioning for him to follow her. They were halfway across the parking lot before she said, "By the way, I'm Finch."

"Lucien Jeffers." He started to put out his hand, then winced and slipped it back into his pocket.

"You're new, aren't you?"

"How'd you guess?" He grinned.

Her gaze dropped to the front of his blazer, streaked with dirt now and missing a button.

"I transferred from Buckley," he explained.

She'd heard of it, one of those rich kids'

schools. "Look, no offense, but if I were you, I wouldn't advertise it."

He cocked his head, regarding her with interest. "You're not from around here either."

"No shit, Sherlock." Anyone could see that.

They exchanged a smile.

Lucien cocked his head, tucking his hair behind his ear. "I wasn't kicked out, if that's what you're thinking."

"I wasn't thinking anything."

He eyed her curiously. "You weren't scared back there. How come?"

She shrugged. "I've been up against worse."

They'd reached the quad, where a scattering of students sat waiting for rides or just shooting the shit. If she didn't hurry, she'd miss the last bus. Yet all at once she wasn't in any rush.

Finch ducked into the nearest bathroom, which happened to be a boys', pulling Lucien in with her. Noting the surprised look he wore, she told him, "There's nothing in here I haven't seen." Growing up in houses with doors that didn't always lock and people who didn't always knock, she'd had an early education.

"Coast is clear," he said, scanning the rows of urinals and stalls.

She held his bleeding hand under a tap, gently removing the embedded bits of gravel. She was pushing his sleeve back to keep it from getting wet when he abruptly jerked away.

"Was I hurting you?" she asked.

He shook his head. "Nah. Listen, why don't you run on ahead? You can probably still catch the bus."

"I'm almost done." She reached for his hand, but he folded his arms over his chest, leaning back against the sink.

"You're from New York. I can tell from your accent," he said in an obvious attempt to distract her.

"Brooklyn, actually," she told him.

"That explains it." He smiled, and she saw that he was actually pretty cute up close. "You're the first person I've met so far who doesn't look at me like I have two heads. What brought you here?"

"It's a long story." She didn't like talking about those days. "You?"

"My parents got divorced. Then last year

my dad decided to move out west . . ." He shrugged. "And here I am."

"You live with your dad?"

"It's a long story." He grinned.

"Fair enough. Here—" She reached once more for his hand.

He hesitated before relinquishing it, and when his sleeve fell back to reveal the angry purple scar on his wrist, she understood. So that's what he hadn't wanted her to see. She felt an odd tingling deep inside. Almost as if they'd kissed.

Their eyes met in the mirror over the sinks (which, she made a mental note to tell Andie, was every bit as big as the one in the girls'). He had a beautiful, slow-breaking smile, the kind that sneaked up on you rather than hitting you over the head. She'd have to watch out for this guy.

Lucien was the first to break the silence. "Listen, do you, uh, want to get together sometime?"

She shrugged noncommittally.

"Do you like to swim? There's a pool at my house." He tried again.

"So it's, like, one of those fancy houses on the hill?" She'd meant to sound flip, but it came out sarcastic. Blood rushed up into her cheeks. God. Why did she have to act this way?

"Would it make a difference?" He didn't seem offended.

"You tell me." She'd been down this road before. If she wasn't good enough for his dad and his rich friends, she'd rather know now and save herself the grief.

But what she saw in Lucien's depthless blue-black eyes sent a delicious shudder through her. What mattered most, she could see, was what she thought of *him.*

"What are you doing this weekend?" he asked softly.

She wanted desperately to tell him she had no special plans. But something made her hold back. She wasn't ready to trust him. "I don't know yet. Can I get back to you?"

"More potatoes, anyone?"

The bowl Laura was passing to Hector collided with Maude's elbow as she was reaching for the salt shaker. Knocked from her grasp, it rolled off the table onto the floor, which brought Rocky scampering over to investigate, ears pricked, while Pearl only lifted her gray muzzle from her box by the stove to delicately sniff the air. Laura and Maude bent in unison to retrieve it, bumping heads. They straightened, laughing.

Dinner as usual in our house, Finch thought, smiling to herself. If they weren't reaching over one another, they were all talking at once. But though chaotic at times, it was different from the kind she'd known in her other life, which had been about everyone scrambling to get their share. At this table, no one ever went hungry—Maude made sure of that—and the mood was one of happy confusion rather than frantic jockeying, all of them eager to share tidbits of their day.

"That shipment from Mexico finally came in," Laura was saying. "I had some trouble getting it through Customs. Apparently, Santa Maria is near an airstrip used by drug smugglers." She helped herself to some broccoli. "They wouldn't sign off on it until they'd inspected every pot."

"I hope nothing got broken," Maude said. Though Laura had once described her as a walking flea market, today she was more conservatively dressed than usual in a striped cotton dress and Adidas running shoes.

"Not so much as a crack. The patron saint of shopkeepers must be watching out for me." Laura made the sign of the cross.

Remembering Lucien, Finch cleared her throat. "Um, I was wondering. Will you be needing me this weekend?" She only worked on weekends when there was a big shipment to uncrate.

"You and Andie have something planned?" Hector smiled at her across the table. He was the most easygoing of the three. Where Maude tended to be flighty and Laura to fuss like a mother hen, Hector was a rock: always there in an unobtrusive way.

"Uh, no. Me and another friend." Finch ducked her head, sawing at her chicken breast with new vigor. She hadn't made up her mind to go, but just in case . . .

"Anyone we know?"

She looked up to find Maude regarding her with bright anticipation, blue eyes shining in her scrunched little pillow of a face, the bundle of snowy hair atop her head listing to one side. She felt a surge of affection, remembering when she'd first arrived, how Maude had welcomed her with open arms, even offering to share her room. If she occasionally got the salt and pepper mixed up, or forgot to put water in the kettle before setting it on to boil, her heart was in the right place.

"A kid from school," Finch answered as casually as she could. "He's new, so I'm sort of showing him around."

Laura glanced at Hector, then at Maude. The only sounds were the clinking forks and Rocky rooting around under the table. Finch felt herself grow warm.

Laura was dying to know more—it was written all over her face—but all she said was "That's nice of you. Sure, go ahead."

"You can borrow the truck. I won't be needing it," Hector said.

"I could pack you a picnic lunch," Maude offered hopefully.

Finch set down her knife and fork, eyeing them sternly. "Why don't we put out a bulletin? Let the whole town know I'm not gay or frigid or—" She broke off with a laugh. "Don't take it the wrong way, guys. I know you mean well, but back off, okay?"

Seeing the startled looks around the

table, Finch immediately regretted her outburst. She was grateful when Laura piped, "Do I smell something burning?"

All eyes went to Maude, who clapped a hand to her mouth. "Oh, dear. I *knew* there was something I forgot." She excused herself and hurried over to pull a pan of smoking biscuits from the oven.

Finch looked about the big old-fashioned kitchen with its walk-in pantry and hutch filled with mismatched crockery from at least three different sets. The old pipes shuddered when you turned on the tap and the floor sagged in spots. The scuffed linoleum by the back door was a collage of muddy paw and boot prints. But no other place on earth, she was sure, could better embody the words of the cross-stitched sampler on the wall: NO MATTER WHERE I PUT MY GUESTS, THEY ALWAYS LIKE MY KITCHEN BEST.

By the time the biscuits had been doused in the sink and Maude once more settled in her chair, the subject of Finch's mystery date had given way to the latest gossip.

"Anna tells me that Monica's in rehab," Laura remarked.

"The poor dear," Maude clucked, quick to add, "Anna, I mean. When I think of what she's been through." She shook her head. "Is there anything we can do?"

"She said to include them in our prayers. Though, if you ask me, it's Monica who should be praying—for forgiveness."

Finch was surprised by the unaccustomed sharpness of Laura's voice. She usually bent over backward to give people the benefit of the doubt. Alice was always saying that if her sister had a fault, it was that she had a hard time finding it in others.

"I'll be feeding Boots while she's away," Finch told them.

Maude perked up. "Is Anna going somewhere?"

"Family week," Finch explained.

Maude looked confused, and it occurred to Finch that to someone who hadn't grown up on the likes of *Oprah* and *Sally Jessy Raphael,* family week meant Christmas on Walton's Mountain, or a *Brady Bunch* reunion.

"It's something they do in rehab." Laura sounded a little vague herself.

"Oh, yes . . . my friend Lillian went through that with her son." Maude helped herself to more potatoes. "Which reminds me, did I tell you what we decided at our last meeting?" She was referring to her sewing circle, which met every Thursday. "It was Lillian's idea, actually. She'd heard about this ladies' club in England that raised money for cancer research by putting out a nude calendar."

"I read about it in *People,*" Laura said, nodding. "All very tasteful, of course."

"Lillian said she didn't see why we couldn't do the same," Maude went on. "Well, you could've heard a pin drop, but once we got used to the idea . . ." She smiled her sweet smile. "I mean, at our age it's not as if we'd be putting *Playboy* out of business."

When it sank in that Maude would be posing *nude,* everyone froze with their forks in midair. Even the normally unflappable Hector suddenly had trouble keeping his mouth closed. Laura was the first to break the silence. "Did I just hear what I thought I heard?"

"Isn't it wonderful?" Maude brought her hands together in a soundless little clap. "Dorothy's daughter is going to photograph us. She's a professional, you know."

"A professional what?" Hector teased.

Finch grinned. "Maude, you rock."

"Thank you, dear." She looked uncertain as to whether or not it was a compliment, but smiled anyway and sat up straighter. "You're looking at Miss January of 2003."

Laura gaped at her in speechless wonderment, then began to laugh. Soon they were all joining in, dabbing with their napkins at the tears rolling down their cheeks. Even old Pearl waddled over to see what the commotion was about.

What, Finch wondered, would this family dream up next?

WISHCOME TRUE

CHAPTER FIVE

"I haven't dreaded anything this much since Dad's funeral," Anna said.

"Monica's the one who should be scared," Liz said darkly. Her gaze was fixed on the road ahead, her eyes hidden by sunglasses that didn't mask her grim expression. She was gripping the steering wheel so tightly her knuckles stood out like bleached knots on a rope.

"There's more at stake here than just her cleaning up her act. I wouldn't put it past her to cut Mom off without a cent."

They'd crested the hill and were approaching the turnoff for Highway 1. In the distance fog lay smudged along the horizon, like something haphazardly erased, a slice of glittering ocean visible below. There was a hint of coolness in the air as Anna rolled down her window, letting the breeze wash over her. If it'd been anything but family week, she'd have been excited at the prospect of five days in Malibu. Instead her stomach was in knots.

"I doubt she'd go that far," Liz said. "It's more fun keeping you on a tight leash." Her voice was as hard and unforgiving as the sunlight backfiring off the hood of her sporty red Miata. "Why do you think she pays you just enough to get by?"

"Well, yes, but there's Edna. Without her—" Anna broke off. Liz was right. Monica's motives were self-serving even when Anna benefited in some way.

Liz shot her a glance. "It's not your job to stick up for her."

"I know. It's just . . ." Anna sighed. "Well, she's not *all* bad."

"That's our Anna, always looking for the good in everyone." Liz's voice was laced with sarcasm. She slowed as they neared the junction, flicking on her turn signal.

Anna wondered if they should've taken her car instead: There was a better chance of its breaking down, and then they'd have had a legitimate excuse to turn back. "You make it sound like there's something wrong with that."

"There isn't." Some of the tension went out of Liz's face, and she reached over to pat Anna's knee. "Sorry, I don't mean to take it out on you. It's just that it was a real bitch getting out the door. Dylan threw a major fit. And the girl who was supposed to fill in at the front desk didn't show up—half the help at the spa is out sick with some flu that I'll probably come down with next—and to top it off—" She broke off. "Never mind."

Something was up—Liz had been acting weird all week, and Anna didn't think it was strictly due to Monica. "Okay, who is he? Out with it." Anna knew her sister too well. It didn't take a crystal ball to guess that there was a new man in her life. "That new masseur, the one the ladies at the spa are all drooling over?" Liz had dated some since her divorce last year, but no one special. Was it serious this time?

"What makes you think I'm seeing someone?" Liz's expression was elaborately nonchalant.

"Probably because I have no life of my

own. I live vicariously through others." Anna gave a rueful little laugh.

"I wish you wouldn't do that."

"What?"

"Put yourself down like that."

Hadn't Finch said the exact same thing? She winced, protesting weakly, "I was only kidding."

"You know what Freud says: There are no jokes." Liz pushed a button and the windows whirred up, sealing out the ocean breeze. She switched on the air conditioner. "You're far too young to be talking like an old lady in a rocking chair."

"You left out the part about how pretty I'd be if I lost weight."

"Well, you *are* pretty." Liz cast her a sidelong glance. "And speaking of weight, I can't remember ever seeing you this thin. How much *have* you lost?"

Thin? Compared to what she used to weigh, maybe, but she wouldn't be modeling for *Vogue* any time soon. Anna shrugged. "I don't know. I stopped weighing myself last year, after a nice little old lady in Safeway asked me when I was due."

"Ouch." Liz winced in sympathy. "Well,

whatever you're doing, it's working. You look great."

Anna glowed, for a fleeting moment allowing herself to bask in Liz's praise. "I'm down a couple of sizes." She was wearing a pair of jeans that hadn't seen the light of day since Pritikin, when she'd starved herself down to size twelve.

"It shows. Hey, I know. How about a day at the spa—my treat? You deserve a reward." Liz flashed her a smile, her first genuine one of the day. "Believe me, you haven't lived until you've had one of Enrico's Peruvian hot rocks massages."

"Hot rocks?"

"You don't know the half of it." Liz laughed. Enrico was the spa's flavor of the moment. Was he also sharing her bed?

Anna remembered when they'd been teenagers together giggling over boys. The difference was that Liz had never lacked for male interest while Anna had spent her Saturday nights with girlfriends or watching TV.

"I appreciate the offer." She realized how much she'd missed Liz. It was hard making time to get together; they were both so busy. And Monica didn't exactly make it any easier. The last time the three of them had met for lunch, Liz had vowed never again.

All at once Anna became aware of how close they were to the silver Mazda in front of them, just inches from its bumper, and she found herself pressing down on an invisible brake. But she refrained from commenting because getting her sister to slow down was like trying to rein in a Santa Ana wind. Like Monica, she had a reckless streak.

She wondered again about Liz's mystery man, which in turn led to thoughts of her own nonexistent love life. Anna had had her share of crushes through the years—most notably Father Reardon—but her only real boyfriend had been Gary Kingman, in college. All these years later her cheeks still burned at the memory. The words of love he'd whispered in her ear, the tenderness with which he'd soothed her afterward, only to discover days later that he'd—

"I just hope we're not going to be opening a can of worms." Liz's voice broke into her thoughts.

Anna knew that hers wasn't the only stomach in knots. It was clear from the literature Pathways had sent that alcoholism wasn't the only issue they'd be dealing with, which would mean airing the Vincenzis' dirty linen.

Anna wondered if this was such a good idea. What would she gain in the end? If she told how she really felt, she'd pay the price. It might not be right away, but Monica would casually announce one day that she was going to need her to work on Saturdays after all, or that she no longer felt it was *her* responsibility to pay their mother's bills.

She recalled the ghastly scene at the hospital the other morning—the way Monica had glared at her. If looks could kill, Anna would be on her way to her own funeral now instead of family week. Even with Liz at her side and the counselor from Pathways, a woman with twenty years of sobriety, she'd felt like crawling under the bed. Yet she'd stuck to her guns, calmly explaining to Monica why she thought this was best for her.

"I see," Monica said when she was finished, her expression dangerously flat. "Feel better now that you've gotten that off your chest? *I* certainly do. It makes such a difference when you know your loved ones care." Her voice had all the warmth of battery acid.

Anna's stomach twisted, but she forced herself to meet Monica's gaze. "I'm not saying it to be mean. I . . . I *do* care about you." She faltered, wondering if it was still true. "If you don't stop drinking, I really will quit."

"To hell with you. I don't need you. I don't need anyone." Vivid slashes of color stood out on Monica's pale cheeks, and her eyes glittered with tears. "Who the fuck are you, anyway, telling *me* what to do?" Her gaze settled on Rita as if she were a large pile of manure that'd been dumped at the foot of her bed.

Rita went on smiling, seeming not the least bit ruffled. She'd clearly seen and heard it all before. "Liz?" she prompted. "Is there something you want to say?"

Liz cleared her throat, looking as if she'd rather be in the OR having her appendix out. "She's right, Sis. I've noticed it, too. That time we all had lunch? You were drunk as a skunk. You kept knocking things over, then yelled at the waiter as if it were his fault. I've never been so embarrassed."

"I don't suppose it could've had anything to do with the fact that your ex probably slept with half the women there," Monica lashed out. "Before you start telling me how fucked up *my* life is, try taking a look at your own. You couldn't even hang on to your own husband."

Liz went white as the sheet she looked as if she'd have liked to twist about Monica's neck.

"Your sisters aren't here to beat up on you," Rita said.

Monica's head whipped around to face her. "Is this how you get your kicks, picking on paraplegics when they're down? What kind of sick puppy *are* you?"

Anna could hear a patient wailing down the hall. "Nurse! Nurse! Where the hell is everybody? Oh, God, it hurts. Oh. Oh. Oooooaaaaaahhhhhhhhhhhhhhh . . ."

"No one can force you to do anything," Rita went on in the same measured tone. "What your sisters are saying is that they have choices, too. One of which is not to stick around watching you drink yourself to death."

Monica turned toward the wall. Then abruptly she burst into tears. "Oh, what's the use? You're ah-ah all against m-me," she sobbed, her chest heaving. "I m-might just as well puh-put a gun to my head." She lifted a tear-streaked face to Anna. "All right, I'll go . . . but not because I think I have a problem. I'm only doing it for *you.* If this will make you happy . . ." She broke off, turning her face into the pillow in a performance worthy of an Oscar.

Happy? Anna wondered now how long it had been since she'd felt anything more than glimmers of contentment here and there. No, this wasn't about being happy; it was about hanging on for dear life. If she didn't go through with this, her own sanity would be at stake.

After a fitful night at the motel, they set off the following morning bright and early. Guided by the map that had been sent with the other material, they found the turn-off and wound their way up a steep tree-lined drive. Minutes later they were stepping out onto a windswept rise where a cluster of low redwood buildings connected by paths looked out on a billion-dollar ocean view. It might have been a posh hideaway hotel if not for the discreet sign that read INVITED GUESTS ONLY. They joined the other family

members, forty or so in all, who were strag-
gling into the cafeteria, where they sipped
coffee and nibbled on bagels before heading off, armed with booklets and badges, to
the orientation lecture in LH2 next door.

The lecture hall, with its rows of folding
chairs facing a standing blackboard and
podium, was about half filled by the time
they took their seats. The families seated in
clusters, marked by empty chairs at either
end, looked no happier to be there than
Anna and Liz. Anna eyed the one she had
mentally labeled the Country Mice: a patri-
arch with a long white beard and bib overalls and his Minnie Pearl look-alike wife and
four strapping sons. Behind them sat Mr.
and Mrs. Got-Rocks, both dressed to the
nines, the wife glancing about apprehensively as if at fellow survivors of a shipwreck
with whom she'd been stranded, while their
teenaged daughters looked as though being shipwrecked would be a preferable al-
ternative. Next to Anna and Liz sat an Indian couple murmuring softly to each other,
the woman's sari a welcome splash of color
in the sea of beige folding chairs. A family in
back—a portly florid-faced older man conversing loudly in a Southern drawl, his wisp

of a wife whose sassafras curls fluttered about her neck as she sat fanning herself with a booklet, and assorted motley members of their clan—might have been plucked from a Tennessee Williams play.

Anna glanced over at her sister. Liz was dressed for the mercurial Malibu weather— foggy one minute, sunny the next—in a pair of off-white chinos and an open-collared turquoise shirt, a cotton sweater draped over her shoulders. They exchanged a look, and Anna was reminded of the silly game they'd played as kids: Would you rather . . . be ugly with brains or beautiful but dumb, walk naked in broad daylight or fully clothed down a dark alley at night, marry an ugly rich man or a handsome pauper? If they were playing it now, the choice would be a root canal or this. Anna didn't have to ask to know which one her sister would pick.

Liz had an aversion to digging up old bones. No, make that an allergy. Whenever the subject of their childhood came up, her face would grow blotchy and she'd start to itch. If seated, she'd repeatedly cross and uncross her legs while playing with her hair, which for Anna was as nerve-racking as sitting next to a fidgety six-year-old.

But at least they wouldn't have Monica to cope with for the time being. This morning's lecture would be followed by a group therapy session. They wouldn't meet with patients until after lunch.

All heads turned toward the attractive thirtyish woman breezing in through the door. She had a friendly face and shiny dark hair that swung at her shoulders as she strode toward the podium. "Hi, everyone. I'm Dr. Meadows," she said, leaning into the mike. "I want to thank you all for being here. I know many of you have traveled some distance and gone to great lengths to carve out the time. You've also shown tremendous courage. Whatever your differences, you all share a common experience—a family member whose addiction has strained your patience and at times even your love. Your being open to new possibilities and paths is the key to the journey you'll be taking." She cast her gaze about, smiling warmly.

Liz began to fidget as Dr. Meadows went on, stressing the need to break old patterns and form new ones. Addiction was a disease, she said, not a moral weakness. "Addicts don't wake up in the morning thinking about how they're going to hurt their families and wreck their lives," though she was quick to add that it didn't make a person any less accountable for his or her actions. It was up to family and friends to draw the line. "As long as you keep putting up with bad behavior and picking up after them, why should they admit they have a problem or do anything to change it?" She asked for examples of the ways family members unwittingly enable.

A male voice in back called out disgustedly, "Hauling her ass into bed every night."

Dr. Meadows smiled knowingly.

A thin, dark-haired woman raised her hand. "Making excuses to his boss."

"Buying her a new car when she smashes up the old one," piped Mrs. Got-Rocks, shooting an accusatory look at her husband, who shifted uncomfortably in his seat.

The speaker nodded. "Okay, let's talk about boundaries."

"What are those?" someone joked, prompting a wave of laughter.

Dr. Meadows drew a pair of stick figures several inches apart on the blackboard, saying, "This is what a healthy person's boundaries look like." Below, she drew a second pair, spaced more closely together, one figure larger than the other. She pointed at the smaller of the two. "That's you, the codependent. You don't see yourself as an equal. You allow yourself to be bullied. At the same time, you feel it's your job to fix what's wrong with everything and everyone around you. You may even ignore it when you're ill, or make yourself sick running around trying to please everyone but yourself. A lot of you get injured, too, your heads so crammed with concerns about others you literally don't look where you're going."

A shudder of recognition went through Anna. It was as though the woman were talking directly to her. The time she'd burned her hand snatching the pan off the stove: Hadn't she been fretting over her mother? And last winter, that flu she'd had that turned into pneumonia because she'd been too busy shuttling back and forth between Monica and her mother to stay in bed. *No wonder I'm so miserable.*

Out of the corner of her eye, she saw heads nodding in silent acknowledgment. Apparently, she wasn't alone. And what had all that frenzied effort accomplished? In her case, nothing. Monica was no better off, and she certainly wasn't. Betty was the only one who benefited, but at what price?

Even Liz seemed to be taking it all in. She'd stopped fidgeting, her gaze fixed on the speaker. At the end, as everyone was shuffling to their feet, she muttered, "Mom's life story."

It was true. All those years of putting up with their dad, years that had worn Betty down like shoes treading the same tired ground day after day. How different all their lives might have been if she'd stood up to him instead. "I guess there are some advantages to losing your marbles," she said dryly. Betty wouldn't spend the rest of her life agonizing over the choices she'd made.

They'd each been assigned a color group—Anna and Liz were in the Green Group—but as they wandered outside, blinking in the sunlight that had burned off most of the fog, Anna was in no hurry to get to their classroom. They strolled past the smoking area, a gazebo where a handful of die-hard smokers, presumably patients, stood huddled, greedily puffing away. Her gaze was drawn to a spiky-haired kid in a faded denim jacket. He looked vaguely familiar.

Liz nudged her. "Isn't that—?"

Anna remembered where she knew him from. "Gabe Talbott," she whispered back. The star of the popular sitcom *Boys Will Be Boys.* Who would it be next, Captain Kangaroo? "I didn't know he was a—" She bit her tongue; she was in no position to judge.

They walked into their assigned room to find a dozen chairs arranged in a circle. Noting the box of Kleenex strategically placed beside each one, Anna felt her stomach clench. *Please, don't let me cry.* She always felt like such a fool when she cried in public. No one felt sorry for you when you were fat; you just looked pathetic.

The other members of the Green Group included Mr. and Mrs. Got-Rocks, a poodle-haired older woman and her meek middle-aged son, a shy young woman in a long Indian cotton skirt and Birkenstocks, a man with dark circles under his eyes who could easily have been mistaken for a patient, and three generations of women from the same family, all with the same easy smiles and outgoing manner. They looked the least likely to break down, so it surprised Anna when the youngest, who looked to be about her age, had no sooner settled into her seat than she was reaching for a tissue.

Their group leader was a strikingly attractive man with clipped dark hair graying at the temples and eyes the deep marine of the ocean visible through the window at his back. Anna might have been intimidated, but his expression was so warm as he surveyed the room, she was immediately put at ease.

His badge identified him as Dr. Marcus Raboy, though he introduced himself as Marc. When the woman sniffling into a Kleenex raised her head with a sheepish look, he said in a kind voice, "We'll be talking about stuff that's painful. It might cause some feelings to come up, but what goes on in this room stays in this room. Understood?" He looked about the circle, his gaze lingering on Anna. Or was she just imagining it?

Oh, God. Why did he have to be so good-looking? She thought of nice old Dr. Fredericks, their family practitioner when she was little, who'd told elephant jokes and given out lollipops. That would've been less distracting. Now all week she'd be concentrating on this Mel Gibson look-alike instead of the business at hand.

They went around the circle, introducing themselves and telling a little bit about why they were there. When it was Anna's turn, she hesitated, tongue-tied all of a sudden. "I'm Anna . . . and I'm here for my sister Monica. I guess you could say that things have . . . gotten out of hand. With her drinking, I mean. I work for her, you see . . ." She paused, acutely aware of Marc's gaze on her. "So I'm around her a lot. More than normal, I mean. That is, more than I would be otherwise . . ." Her voice trailed off, and heat climbed into her cheeks. "So, anyway, that's why I'm here."

Liz was next. "I'm not sure why I'm here." She sat with her legs crossed and her arms tightly folded over her chest, a faint line creasing her brow. "Monica and I were never that close. After she became famous, it was as if she didn't even know me. Even so, I'd like to see her get sober. If not for her sake, then for Anna's."

Marc's expression was mild and considering. Anna was sure he'd heard tales far worse than any she or Liz could tell. They seemed to have plenty of company in the

Drunk and Disorderly Family Members Department. She relaxed a bit. Maybe this wouldn't be so bad after all.

They spent the first half hour talking about what they hoped to get out of the week. Then Marc passed out sketch pads and crayons. "I want you each to draw a childhood memory," he instructed. "But here's the catch: You have to do it with your left hand."

It seemed a pointless exercise, but Anna was willing to go along. At first, all she could manage were squiggles, but gradually a little girl all alone in the backseat of a car began to emerge. She looked unhappy—no, more than that, miserable. Anna frowned, catching her lower lip in her teeth. Where had *that* come from? It was so long ago she barely remembered it.

One by one, they shared the stories behind their drawings. Mrs. Got-Rock's was of a dog on a leash being dragged away from a sobbing little girl. "His name was Teddy," she said in a voice so soft Anna had to strain to hear. "I'd been begging my parents for a dog, so they finally broke down and gave me one for my birthday. I just loved him. He was so cute, with these big brown eyes and Dumbo ears. The only bad thing was that he peed all over the carpet and chewed up everything in sight. It wasn't his fault. He was just a puppy. But Mother . . . well, she wasn't too happy about it." Her voice cracked. "The worst of it was they didn't even tell me. This man came one day and took him away."

Her husband stared blankly ahead as if to show emotion would be a sign of weakness. His drawing was of a little boy building sand castles on the beach that could have been an ad for Sea & Ski.

The shy woman in the long skirt and Birkenstocks, whose name was Sophie, burst into tears before she could get a word out. Marc told her not to worry; they could talk later on in private. Sophie nodded, hunched over with her head buried in her hands. However traumatic the memory, it wasn't to be found in her portrait of a smiling family gathered around the dinner table.

Then suddenly all eyes were on Anna. She took a deep breath. Her father had taken them out for root beer floats that day, she began. But on their way downtown she'd done something that made him mad—she couldn't remember what—so he'd punished her by making her wait in the car.

"What were you feeling?" Marc prodded gently.

"Disappointed, I guess." It was so long ago. Who remembered?

"Not upset?"

"Well, yes . . . I suppose so."

"You must have been angry."

She shrugged. "I was a pretty easygoing kid."

"Is that you talking or your parents?"

She thought for a moment. "I don't know. I've heard so many different versions of my childhood that I'm not sure anymore which is mine. Is that normal?"

"Define normal."

"Normal," she said with a rueful smile, "is everyone but you."

He smiled back. "That's one way of looking at it." She thought she saw a glint of something in his eyes, and remembered the poster on the wall in the cafeteria with its slogan FAKE IT TILL YOU MAKE IT. Did Marc have demons of his own?

They moved on to Liz, with her crude drawing of a baby falling out of a high chair, presumably her. But Anna found she couldn't concentrate on the story. Instead she thought of Marc, unable to shake the feeling that his empathy came from personal experience. He was married, she could see from the gold band he wore, yet she sensed a loss of some kind. Even odder, she found herself wanting to reach over and give his hand a reassuring squeeze. She blushed at the thought, and wondered if she was on her way to becoming as peculiar as old Miss Finley from church, who talked obsessively about the love of her life who'd been killed in World War II and who, according to Althea Wormley, she'd barely known.

When they broke for lunch, it was with a collective sigh of relief. This was twice as hard as any work they'd ever done. In the cafeteria Anna helped herself to a salad and small bowl of fruit with cottage cheese, while Liz, who could eat anything and not gain an ounce, heaped her plate with lasagna. The weather was mild, so they carried their trays outside and sat at one of the picnic tables on the sheltered patio that faced the lawn. Surprisingly, the fear Anna had felt on the way here seemed to have faded. Maybe it had something to do with

Marc, who, in addition to being their group leader, was Monica's primary therapist. Her sister might have every other man in the universe wrapped around her little finger, but Anna couldn't imagine Marc falling under her spell. Which meant there was hope that when Monica was sent home in two weeks she'd be considerably humbled and maybe even likable.

Her mind must have wandered because the next thing she knew Liz was waving a hand in front of her face, calling, "Yoo-hoo. Anyone home?"

Anna blinked, and her sister's face came into focus. "Sorry. You were saying?"

"It's certainly not what I expected." Liz looked out over the lawn, where people sat quietly conversing or simply basking in the sun. "I thought it'd be just about Monica, but it's not, is it? We're all in this together in a way."

Anna nodded. "Apples from the same tree."

"With a few rotten ones mixed in," Liz replied with a mirthless laugh.

"I'm sorry I didn't remember about the high chair." Anna shot her sister an apologetic look.

"It wasn't *your* fault. You weren't even there." Liz sounded annoyed for some reason.

"I know, but—"

Liz turned on her. "Will you cut it out! You're always so damn nice, I end up feeling like shit."

"Why?"

"Because you're the one doing all the heavy lifting."

"You mean with Mom."

"Among other things." Her gaze cut away.

Anna surprised herself by saying, "If you feel that way, then maybe it's time you did your share."

Liz looked on the verge of defending herself but broke into a sheepish grin instead. "*That's* more like it." Then she frowned, muttering, "I'm not as bad as Monica, at least. And let's not forget I have a child."

"I wish I could say the same." Anna sighed.

Now it was Liz's turn to apologize. "I'm sorry. I know I shouldn't complain."

"It's okay," Anna said.

"That day with Dad? I remember it as if it were yesterday." Liz was staring off into the distance, the food growing cold on her plate. "You were supposed to keep an eye on me, and when I wouldn't quiet down, he took it out on you instead. Do you know how that made me feel?" Liz turned to her, and Anna was surprised to see her eyes brimming with tears. "On the way home I threw up all over the backseat."

Anna had forgotten that part. "Funny, we all grew up under the same roof, but it's as if we had different childhoods."

Their attention was drawn to a man and a boy seated side by side on the lawn. The boy was bawling openly, the man had an arm about his shoulders in an attempt to comfort him. Liz quickly averted her gaze. She'd obviously had her fill of family angst for one day. "So what do you think of Marc?" she asked.

Anna thought of the laugh lines that radiated from the corners of his eyes, eyes that had seemed to *see* her where to others she was invisible, good old dependable Anna, like a faithful dog at their feet. She sidestepped the question by asking, "What did *you* think of him?"

"Tall, dark, and handsome." Liz's lips curled up in a sly smile.

Anna blushed. "I didn't mean *that* way."

"I can't help it that he's sexy. Don't tell me you didn't notice?"

Anna's blush deepened. "He *is* good-looking." That much was fact.

"Maybe he's up for grabs."

"He's not." Anna spoke more sharply than she'd intended, feeling a surprising flash of envy at the thought of Liz's making a play for him. At the same time, a voice in her head mocked, *Face it, he wouldn't be interested in you even if he was single.*

"What makes you so sure?"

"The ring on his finger. Besides," she ventured cautiously, "I thought you were seeing someone."

"What's that got to do with anything?"

"You mean—"

"I was talking about *you.*"

"Me?" Anna squeaked. Okay, the same thought had occurred to her, but she also daydreamed about winning the lottery and waking up one morning magically slim.

"You don't see it, do you?"

"See what?"

"How pretty you are. You always were, but now that you're thinner it's even more . . ." She searched for the word. "Dramatic."

"I guess Hollywood discovered the wrong sister." Anna gave a dry laugh but was secretly pleased. Especially since Liz wasn't known for giving out false compliments.

"Joke about it all you like. Someday you'll be swept off your feet, and I'll say, 'I told you so.' "

Anna nibbled on her salad, thinking, *That'll be the day.* "What about you? Is it serious with this guy?"

Liz shrugged, tearing bits of crust from her bread and tossing them to the sparrows. "Who said I was seeing anyone?"

Something in her expression raised a red flag, or maybe it was all the talk about Marc. "Don't tell me he's married," she said with a groan.

A guilty flush rose in Liz's cheeks, and Anna thought, *Oh, dear.*

"It's not what you think." Liz was quick to defend herself.

"I'm not thinking anything. I just don't want to see you get hurt."

"I'm a big girl."

"Does Dylan know?"

"God, no." Liz looked aghast at the idea. "It's only the nights he's at his dad's."

"What about the wife?"

"His marriage is over. He's only staying because of—" Liz broke off, frowning. "It's complicated." She looked so unhappy, Anna couldn't imagine its being anything more than a garden variety affair—sneaking around, lies, promises that never materialized. You had only to watch *Oprah* to know it would end in tears.

What made Liz think her situation was so unique? Did she imagine she was so different from the countless other women who'd been down that road? Was she that deluded?

Anna refrained from putting in her two cents. She had larger concerns at the moment. Like Monica. What would she be like after two weeks in this place? Humbled—or chafing at the bit? Marc had instructed them to prepare a list of confrontations, which they'd have a chance to air later in the week. Hers would be a mile long, but would she find the courage to risk Monica's wrath? Undo thirty-six years in just four days? Yesterday she wouldn't have be lieved it possible, but now she found herself wondering if pounds weren't the only thing she was dropping.

"All right, who wants to go first?" Marc glanced about the circle of patients and family members, a knowing little smile on his lips. It was the final day of family week, and the moment they'd all been dreading had arrived. He might as well have asked who wanted to be the first to face a firing squad.

No one's hand went up. They were four days and several boxes of Kleenex into it, their workbooks grubby and souls stripped bare. They now knew more about each other than did many of their closest friends. Anna had heard stories that would curl even Oprah's hair, and had wept for the innocent children these men and women had been. Sophie, who'd been molested by her uncle as a little girl. And Scott, with the dark circles under his eyes, whose parents had disowned him when they found out he was gay. Not surprisingly, Mrs. Got-Rocks, whose real name was Lindsay, turned out to have been the classic poor little rich girl, raised by a succession of nannies who were fired as soon as she grew too attached to them.

Even Liz had crept out of her shell. She'd talked candidly about their father, and Anna had been surprised to learn that she'd been wrong in believing that Liz, as the youngest, had been spared to some extent. Listening to her speak about those years, how on nights when she'd wet the bed she'd lie awake for hours, soaked in urine, afraid to make so much as a peep for fear that their father would hit her if he found out, Anna had found herself swallowing back tears.

But most surprising was the change in Monica. The first day, Anna had expected to find her snarling like a caged tiger, but she'd been remarkably subdued. Maybe it was the meds she was on, but she seemed fragile almost. More bruised than rotten. When she'd opened up about her drinking and how hard it was to give it up, despite knowing what it was doing to her and everyone around her, it was obvious she was sincere. No one was that good an actress, not even Monica.

Anna had found anger and resentment giving way to pity at times. Yet she'd secretly applauded when Marc had busted Monica for blaming it all on the accident, and forced her to admit she was an alcoholic. Anna had been right about him. He *was* the only man in the universe her sister couldn't wrap around her little finger.

Now she looked over at Monica, scarcely recognizable as the goddess immortalized in countless magazines and movie posters. Her famous face was scrubbed of makeup and her auburn hair loosely pulled back in a ponytail fastened with a rubber band. In her oversize T-shirt and baggy drawstring trousers, clothes that two weeks ago she wouldn't have been caught dead in even at home, Anna was reminded of the teenage Monica, before she'd dropped Vincenzi in favor of Vincent and become the superstar known to millions worldwide.

Monica didn't raise her hand, and shot a warning look at her sisters, lest they volunteer. That's what did it. Suddenly Anna was remembering all the times she'd swallowed her feelings along with her pride so as not to rock the boat. Her hand shot up seemingly of its own volition.

"I'll go first." Her stomach fluttered and her heart began to knock in her chest, but she was rewarded by the warmly encouraging smile Marc directed at her.

Monica cast her a baleful look before slowly wheeling into the center of the circle. Anna dragged her chair over, planting it opposite Monica. A dozen times the night before she'd gone over her list of confrontations, rehearsing each one with Liz so she wouldn't screw up, or worse, wimp out. But face-to-face was an entirely different matter.

"Is that a comfortable distance for you?" asked Dr. Meadows, the pretty dark-haired woman who'd lectured that first day, a day that seemed to have taken place in another lifetime. She was cochairing this afternoon's group.

Anna waited for Monica to reply before remembering that she had a say in it as well. "Fine by me," she said, thinking the distance from here to Pittsburgh would be more like it.

Monica gave a nearly imperceptible nod.

"Remember, this isn't about proving a point," Marc said, reminding Anna of the guidelines, which they'd gone over in yesterday's group. "Stick with what happened to you, not some other family member, and how it affected you." He shifted his gaze to Monica. "You'll get a chance to respond later on, but for now I'll ask you to just listen. All right?"

"Do I have a choice?" she quipped feebly.

Anna opened her workbook and withdrew a sheet of dog-eared paper covered in her neat, precise handwriting. Her hands were clammy and her head hummed like a receiver off the hook. Monica's expression was flat; it was like looking into the windows of a stretch limousine where all you saw was your own reflection.

She started with the most recent event. "When you passed out on the bathroom floor, and ended up in the hospital, I felt . . ." She struggled to recall the correct phrasing. "Fear and . . . and anger," she stammered, glancing at the chart on the wall on which, printed in large block letters, were all the emotions she was feeling now, jumbled together in a steaming stew: ANGER. FEAR. PAIN. GUILT. SHAME. JOY. LOVE. Except joy, that is. There was no joy in any of this as far as she could see.

Oddly enough, Monica's silence didn't help. Anna would have found it easier in some ways if she'd been able to talk back. At least she'd have known what to expect.

She glanced once more at her notes. "That time you screamed at me in front of Glenn over that stupid necktie, I felt anger, pain, and shame." It all came rushing back. Christmas of last year, when she'd mistakenly wrapped the wrong present for Glenn—though he'd have been none the wiser if Monica hadn't lit into her, cursing a blue streak. She'd been drunk, of course. Anna's cheeks burned at the memory.

She caught a glint of something in her sister's eyes. Remorse? Or surprise that she was still upset after all this time? Anna looked down to find her hands trembling.

"The party I was supposed to be a guest at, when you had me take coats at the door, did you ever stop to think how humiliating it was? There I was, in my best dress . . ." Tears threatened, and she quickly blinked them back.

"Stick with your feelings." Marc's gentle voice brought her back on track.

Anna nodded fiercely, sucking in a breath. "I felt shame," she said in a small voice. This was so hard, and Monica's stony expression was making it harder. What was going on behind those eyes? What price would Anna have to pay?

There are worse things than losing your home, she told herself.

She sat up straighter. "That time I had the flu, and you kept saying that the best thing for a cold was to stay on your feet, only because you didn't want me to take the time off. I felt . . ." She faltered, overcome by the enormity of her rage. Before she knew it, she was shouting, *"Dammit, I ended up with pneumonia because of you!"* Anna sat back, shocked by her outburst. Though she thought she saw Marc out of the corner of her eye nod faintly in approval.

Monica's mouth dropped open. Not in shock at her audacity, Anna could see, but in bewilderment. *She doesn't even remember!* She could have died, and it wasn't even on Monica's radar screen. Suddenly it was all too much. Earlier on, Liz had jokingly referred to the chair now facing Monica's as Old Sparky, and Anna experienced a physical jolt as years of unleashed fury surged through her. With a sob, she jumped up and bolted from the room.

When Marc found her, she was huddled

on the lawn, sobbing her heart out. "The world didn't come to an end, at least." His voice was mild but not unsympathetic.

She lifted her head to find him regarding her with a mixture of admiration and empathy. She gulped in a breath. "I'm sorry. I didn't mean to—"

"You did just fine." His eyes were gentle and smiling, the lines at their corners curving to meet his silvering temples. He seemed taller, too, or maybe it was because he was standing over her.

She knuckled away her tears. "And I thought I was here for Monica."

"Would you have come if you'd thought otherwise?"

"Probably not." A small laugh escaped her.

"You're not alone."

"Does that make us cowards?"

"Far from it." His expression turned serious. "What counts is that you stuck it out. There are those who'd sooner risk their necks in battle."

"It's not so different, is it?" If this were a battle, they'd all have earned Purple Hearts.

He nodded, lowering himself onto the grass. "In some ways it's even harder."

The lawn glistened in the fog that had rolled in. She watched the resident cat slink out from under a bush with what looked to be a lizard in its mouth. As it headed up the path to the main building, which housed the offices and dispensary, she thought of how helpless she'd felt until now—as helpless as that lizard.

She turned to Marc, propping her chin on her knees. "Why do I get the feeling this battle is far from over?"

"I wouldn't rule out a peace treaty."

"You don't know Monica."

"You'd be surprised. We like to think of ourselves as special—in AA we call it terminally unique—but we're not." She was reminded that he, too, was an alcoholic, ten years sober. "When you've sat in on a hundred meetings and heard a hundred people tell your story, it can be pretty humbling."

"Humble" wasn't a word that came to mind with Monica. "I guess we were all fooling ourselves one way or another." She sighed. As the cat disappeared under another bush, she saw that the lizard in its jaws was no longer wriggling.

"Change can be scary."

"But there's no going back, is there?"

Right now she longed for the relative safety of her cocoon. Just as it had been easier for her sister to use the accident as an excuse to drink, it had been convenient for Anna to blame everything on Monica.

He arched a brow. "Would you want to?"

She thought of the life that awaited her back home and shook her head. No, what she wanted was to be free—without the struggle and heartache of getting there. "I just . . . I didn't expect it to be so hard," she said.

"I wish I knew an easier way." He stretched his legs out on the grass, and she noticed that he was wearing navy socks with brown loafers. She found it oddly endearing, and couldn't help wondering why his wife hadn't said something.

"I thought you guys had all the answers," she said lightly.

He laughed, throwing his head back, a wonderful deep laugh that was like a gulp of warm, sweet tea. "Don't I wish. The truth is, a lot of the time we stumble around in the dark like everyone else."

"What made you decide to become a therapist?"

"I got sober."

"What did you do before that?"

"Believe it or not, I used to be a pilot."

"Seriously?" She hugged the knowledge to her like a found coin, certain she was the only one in their group in whom he'd confided. "I mean, it's not the kind of thing you think someone would give up."

"It wasn't voluntary—the FAA yanked my license after I crash-landed in the desert with six pharmacists who were on their way to a convention in Vegas."

"How awful. Was anyone hurt?"

"Luckily, no. But when it came out in the investigation that I'd been drinking that day, I was pretty much washed up. I spent a year or so just getting sober before I decided to go back to school for my degree."

"At least no one could accuse you of having a boring life."

"Define boring." His gaze fixed on her, as if he'd known she was thinking of her own dull existence.

"I dropped out of college after my dad died," she told him. All he knew from their groups was that she lived with her mom, not what had led to that decision—if you could call it that. "It wasn't something I planned on. After the funeral I was only going to stay for a few weeks to help out. But Mom . . . well, she wasn't herself. She'd go off on an errand and then get lost, stuff like that. At first I thought it was because she was grieving, but then we found out she had Alzheimer's." Anna found it easier to talk about this with Marc than with her sisters. Monica seemed to think Betty was only getting what she deserved, and Liz avoided the topic out of guilt. "You want to know something awful? Sometimes I hate her for it." As if it were her life savings Betty had lost through foolish investments, not her mind. "Does that make me a bad person?"

"No, just human."

I could fall in love with you. The thought came swooping down out of the blue. She'd had crushes before this, but none that had come on so quickly or with such force. *Was* she becoming like Miss Finley, or was it just that the circumstances had made her more vulnerable? She'd read somewhere that it was normal in situations like these.

It was on the tip of her tongue to ask about his wife, but she didn't want him to think she had an ulterior motive, so she asked instead, "Shouldn't we be getting back?" No one would miss her, but there was a roomful of people waiting on him.

"Beth can handle it," he said, referring to Dr. Meadows. "I wanted to make sure you were okay."

A lightness in her belly spread until her whole body felt buoyant. Didn't that prove she was special? Then the voice in her head scoffed, *Don't be ridiculous. He's only doing his job.* Ignoring it, Anna turned to him. "Define okay."

"Okay," he said, smiling in a way that let her know she wasn't alone, "is what you pretend to be until you can start to believe it."

CHAPTER SIX

From: kssnkrys@aol.com
To: monica@monicavincent.com
Subject: Guess What?

Dear Monica,
I got a job!!!! Its just cleaning rooms at
a motel but like my ma always said it
beats a poke in the eye with a sharp
stick. I admit i didn't believe it when
you told me it would happen but i
didn't give up. When i get down i think
about how a famous person like you
cared enuf to write back and i think
maybe i can do this after all. Yesterday
at the early bird AA meeting, i got my 3
mo. chip. It felt good even tho I still
have a long way to go. My parole

*officer says if i stay out of trouble
there's a good chance I can get my
kids back soon. I miss them so
much!!!!! Brianna's birthday is next
week. Thanx for the gift certificate.
When i give her the Barbie bake shop
I'll tell her it's from both of us.*

*Bye for now,
Krystal*

*From: monica@monicavincent.com
To: kssnkrys@aol.com
Subject: RE: Guess What?*

*Dear Krystal,
Hooray! That's great news about your
job. But the main thing is you're clean
and sober. That's the best gift you can
give your kids (though I'm sure Brianna
will love the Barbie bake shop!). I'm
sorry it took so long to answer your last
e-mail. There's a lot going on right
now. Most of it good but, like with you,
it's not always smooth sailing.*

*I'm praying that this job will lead to
bigger and better things. And that soon*

you'll have your kids back. Believe me, that's a way bigger deal than being famous.

Love,
Monica

It had taken Anna the better part of a week to weed through the letters and e-mails that had piled up while she was away. She'd lugged home the computer from her office and made a makeshift desk of the kitchen table, where she sat now, smiling at Krystal's news. It seemed a good omen somehow, for in many ways her struggle mirrored Anna's.

In the ten days since family week Anna had lost five more pounds. Even the "thin" pants in her closet were baggy. More important, her eyes had been opened to the ways in which she'd allowed herself to be victimized. The day before yesterday, when Althea Wormley called to urge her to join the altar guild, she'd replied, "Thanks for thinking of me, Althea, but I really don't have the time." Whereas not so long ago, she'd have given in, or at the very least promised to consider joining. There'd been a long silence at the other end—Anna didn't know who had been more taken aback, her or Althea—but after she'd hung up she began to laugh giddily. *That wasn't so hard,* she'd thought. No one had died, and she wasn't going to hell (though Althea might have other ideas).

Anna turned her attention to the message that had popped up on her screen—another of Monica's regulars, whom she knew only as Hairy Cary. He e-mailed several times a week wanting such personal information as Monica's shoe size (a foot fetishist?), her favorite foods, and what kind of perfume she wore. As she scanned the latest, Anna felt goose bumps swarm up the back of her neck.

To: monica@monicavincent.com
From: HairyCary@aol.com
Subject: A word to the wise

I worry about you, my dear. Walls aren't enough to keep people out. You of all people should know that. Look what happened to John Lennon, and that actress, I forget her name, whose face was all cut up. If you want those of us who CARE about you to sleep better at night, please, PLEASE, watch out. There's a lot of nuts out there.

YOUR BIGGEST FAN

How had he known that the security system wasn't foolproof? Intruders occasionally sneaked onto the grounds, but as far as she knew those incidents had never been publicized. The last one to make the newspapers was several years ago when a man had been apprehended as he was climbing through an unlocked window, clutching a gift for Monica—a diamond engagement ring, as it turned out. Because crime in Carson Springs was almost unheard of and her fans mostly harmless, Monica didn't let it worry her too much. Anna would speak to her about it when she got back. The gardener, Esteban, had seen signs of a trespasser not too long ago. Hairy Cary? Or a kid on a dare, like the Sullivan boy, who a few months before had sprained his ankle scaling the wall. Either way, there wasn't enough for Anna to go to the police.

When she glanced up at the clock, it was half past eleven. She jumped up, and moments later was waving good-bye to Edna and her mom on her way out the door. If she didn't hurry, she'd be late for her appointment at Shear Delight.

It had been Laura's idea; she'd put an end to Anna's excuses by giving her a coupon for a free haircut. Supposedly it was a birthday gift, though Anna's birthday wasn't until March. But Anna was grateful nonetheless. If nothing else, it was nice just to get out. The sun was shining, and as she rattled her way along Old Sorrento Road, leaves drifted from the white oaks overhead. The surrounding fields that in recent months had been saffron and purple with goldenrod and lupine were now tawny with the onset of winter. The air blowing in through the window was cool against her face, its grassy scent reminding her of when she used to wander these fields as a child gathering wild blackberries and eating most of them on the way home. It occurred to her that until just recently she'd have felt guilty leaving her mother with Edna to do something that didn't involve work or chores, something that was just for herself. But now all she felt was a warm glow of anticipation.

Edna's right. We'd all be better off with Mom in a home.

Last week's scare had been the final straw. They'd been shopping in Safeway; Anna hadn't turned her back for more than thirty seconds, and when she looked around, Betty was gone. After several frantic minutes Anna had found her wandering about the parking lot, none the worse for the wear. Even so it was becoming increasingly clear that her mother was more than she, or even Edna, could handle.

What had once been unthinkable was beginning to seem like the only reasonable course of action. They'd been lucky so far, but the next time Betty could be hit by a car or fall down and break a hip. Even at home, you had to watch her like a hawk to make sure she didn't burn the house down or electrocute herself.

You have your own selfish reasons; admit it.

Anna frowned. *Okay, what of it? Don't I deserve to be happy too?* She'd spent half her life looking after her mother; when was it going to be her turn?

She began to shiver, and rolled up the window. It was a moot point. Nothing would change unless Monica agreed to foot the bill. And that was a tall order.

Liz had been right about one thing: Monica kept her on a tight leash, which would be harder for her to do with their mother in a nursing home, where all Betty's needs would be met. It would take some convincing, or browbeating if necessary, to get her sister to do the right thing.

Anna was reminded that by this time next week she'd be on her way to pick up Monica. What would she find—the lady or the tiger? Only the thought of seeing Marc again kept her from dreading it too much.

Anna hadn't stopped thinking about him. She'd hoped the feelings she'd had at family week would fade, that the bond she'd felt was merely that of someone drowning toward her rescuer. But this . . . *thing,* whatever it was, had a life of its own. At odd times throughout the day, she'd find herself wondering what he was doing, if he was wearing the wrong color socks, or drinking coffee out of that silly cow-shaped mug. She knew it was too much to hope that he thought of her apart from the sea of family members who washed in and out like a tide, leaving the flotsam of their angst and fears, but in daydreams anything was possible.

Well, at least those fantasies weren't as pathetic as they might once have been. Lately, she'd noticed men giving her the eye. And the other day in Orchard Hardware, when she'd been hunting for a hinge to replace the broken one on the screen door, which Hector had volunteered to fix, she'd realized that the clerk who was being so attentive was actually flirting with her. He wasn't in Marc's league, of course, but it was nice to be noticed.

She arrived at Shear Delight with minutes to spare, pulling into the driveway of a neat white-frame house shaded by a large chestnut tree several doors down from Tea & Sympathy. Even if she hadn't seen the sign, she'd have known she was in the right place from Laura's mud-streaked green Explorer parked behind Sam's red Honda. Clearly, her friends weren't leaving anything to chance.

Anna mounted the steps to the porch, where wind chimes tinkled and a cat napped on a cushioned wicker chair. The door was open a crack, and she stepped into a narrow foyer that smelled of hairspray. To the right was an archway onto the living room, which had been converted into a salon. All she could see from where she stood was a pair of crimson-nailed feet in cork-heeled espadrilles propped on a footrest. They belonged to Gerry Fitzgerald she saw when she rounded the corner; she lay tilted back with her head in the sink while a pretty, light-skinned black woman washed her hair.

"We thought you could use some company," Laura said, rising from one of the easy chairs along the wall.

"In other words, she was afraid you'd chicken out," Sam said with a laugh. She sat with her feet in a tub of soapy water in preparation for a pedicure, the latest issue of *Parents* magazine open on her lap.

Norma Devane, dabbing dye onto a foil-wrapped head from which clumps of wet hair trailed like spaghetti, turned to smile at her. Anna recognized the head under all that goop as Gayle Warrington's. She and her husband owned Up and Away Travel, with its posters of the exotic locales that always made Anna slow her steps when walking past. "Watch out," Gayle warned. "Norma's a hair Nazi—she won't take no for an answer. What *she* wants is what you get."

"I have my reputation to think of. Can't have you walking out of here looking like somebody else's warmed-over mistake." Norma snorted, giving Gayle a playful nudge before toddling over in her spike heels, which, along with her sheer rhinestone-studded black blouse over a black bustier and skintight capris, gave her the look of an overage gun moll. Lifting the hair off Anna's shoulders as if it were a dead mouse, she said, "Honey, no offense, but I oughta be performing last rites. When's the last time you did anything with this hair?"

Anna gave a self-conscious laugh. "Honestly? I can't remember."

"Never mind, sweetie. When I'm through with you, you won't recognize yourself."

If anyone could transform her, it was Norma. To hear people talk, she was a miracle worker. Though looking at her, Anna didn't feel much confidence. At fifty plus, Norma was growing old disgracefully, as she liked to say. Her punk hair, the dark red of rooster feathers, stood up in spikes all over her head, and a pair of silver earrings the size of teaspoons swung from her ears.

She wore enough makeup to singlehand-edly keep Revlon in business.

"If it weren't for Norma, I'd look like a sock just out of the dryer," Laura said, touching the ends of her hair, feathered in a stylish cut that suited her face perfectly.

"Anything would be an improvement with me," Anna said.

"Relax, ladies. It's not a boob job." Gerry was sitting up now, her head wrapped in a towel that made her look like a sultana on her throne.

"Which *you* certainly don't need." Sam's gaze dropped pointedly to Gerry's chest. It was the kind of teasing only old friends could get away with. And Gerry, with her stretchy top that showed off more than an inch of cleavage, wasn't exactly hiding her assets.

It was hard to believe that years before, Gerry had been a nun. There were those, like Althea, who saw her as an affront to the church, with her sexy clothes and string of former lovers, but Anna admired her for having the courage to shed her old skin. It wasn't as easy as changing professions or, in her case, losing weight.

"Have a seat. Be with you in a sec."

Norma gestured toward the easy chair next to Sam's. On the table beside it were thermoses of coffee and tea, and a plate of bite-size muffins.

The other stylist must have noticed her eyeing them, for she called out, "Help yourself."

Anna was tempted, but shook her head. "I'd better not."

"I envy your willpower," Gerry said. "With all the time I spend at Tea and Sympathy, it's a battle keeping what's left of my waistline." She seldom missed an opportunity to remind people that it was her daughter behind all those mouthwatering baked goods.

"Don't rub it in." Gayle groaned, patting her flat stomach. Anna remembered Sam's telling her that in high school Gayle had been a cheerleader. She still looked as if she could show the current squad at Portola High a thing or two.

Anna lowered herself into the chair. This was nothing like May's Beauty Shoppe, where twice a month she took Betty to have her hair washed and set, with its old-fashioned hair dryers that always made her think of Elsa Lanchester in *The Bride of Frankenstein.* Norma's place was homey, with knickknacks scattered about and a pair of thirties mirrored vanities serving as styling stations.

"Make me beautiful for when I meet the queen," Gerry told the stylist, whose own hair was in cornrows strung with beads that clacked softly as she bent to retrieve her scissors from a drawer.

"Are you practicing your curtsy?" Laura wanted to know.

"I thought I had it down the other day— until I lost my balance and landed on my ass." Gerry let loose a throaty laugh. "Think her royal highness will mind having to bend over so I can kiss her hand?"

Everyone in town had to know by now that she was to be presented at the royal court in London, the first stop on Aubrey's European tour. It was all she'd been talking about for weeks.

"Why don't you bring her a jar of honey? That ought to sweeten her up," Laura suggested with a laugh. Gerry seldom missed an opportunity to give out free samples of Blessed Bee. You knew her friends by the jars of honey lining their kitchen cupboards.

"It'll take more than honey to sweeten up that old bag." Norma slathered more goop onto Gayle's head. "Though don't go telling her I said so."

Gerry snorted. "Are you kidding? I'll be lucky to get two words in."

"Sure you don't need a guide?" Gayle offered, only half jokingly. Her agency was known for its tours, which were advertised in the brochures Anna saw everywhere she went. A stack on the coffee table caught her eye now. Printed in bold letters across the topmost one was UP AND AWAY TAKES YOU DOWN UNDER!

"Oh, I think we can manage on our own." Gerry wore the small-cat smile of a newly-wed. "All I ask is that you guys keep an eye on the kids while we're away."

"Andie's welcome to stay with us," Laura told her.

"Believe me, she'd love nothing more . . . if it weren't for the lure of lording it over Justin."

Gayle eyed her in amazement. "If we left our girls on their own, there wouldn't be anything left of the house when we got back. You sure you know what you're doing?"

Gerry shrugged, snippets of her black curls drifting onto the floor. "They'll be at their dad's both weekends. And Claire's promised to look in on them at least once a day. Besides, I can't go on treating Andie like a baby. She's sixteen . . . as she never gets tired of reminding me." She winked at Anna. "Wait till you have kids, you'll see. Changing diapers is the least of it, believe me."

"Don't I know it." Sam rolled her eyes.

Anna felt a pang. *Would* she ever have kids? She glanced over at Laura, who was staring off into space, wearing an odd look. Anna wondered if she was thinking about the babies she would never have. Poor Laura. She'd tried so hard with Peter, and then to have him dump her for a woman who got pregnant right away . . .

Just then Laura cleared her throat and said, "While we're on the subject, ladies, you might as well be the first to know . . ." A beatific smile spread across her face, and Anna felt her heart leap thinking, *She's pregnant.* "Hector and I have decided to adopt. A baby, that is," she quickly added, no doubt in reference to Finch.

"Goodness." Gayle sat up straighter.

"Oh, Laura. That's wonderful!" Anna jumped up and threw her arms around her friend. Okay, so maybe she was a little hurt to be only just now hearing of it, but mainly she was thrilled. No one deserved this more.

"My friend Sally's daughter adopted the cutest little boy," Norma put in. "Everyone says he looks just like her."

"Ours'll look more like Hector." They were looking to adopt a baby from Mexico, Laura explained. The agency had warned that it would be a long process, but Hector's being a native would help.

"Finch must be excited," Anna said.

"You don't know the half of it," Laura said. "And Maude . . . well, she's over the moon. It's the only thing she talks about besides the calendar."

Maude wasn't the only one talking about the nude calendar put out by her sewing circle. The whole town was buzzing.

"They should've asked me to pose." Norma waggled her hips and ran a hand through her rooster-feathered hair. "I'd have given folks their money's worth."

"I was at the shoot. It was a riot," Laura told them. "You should've seen Maude— wearing nothing but a hat and pearls." She chuckled, shaking her head.

"You've got to give it to those gals. It takes guts to bare all when it's all going south." Gerry pushed up her boobs for emphasis.

"When I'm in my eighties," sniffed Gayle, "the only thing showing will be my roots."

Anna reveled in the exchange. So this was how women talked when they weren't holding back. All her life she'd been the fat girl people politely tiptoed around. No one talked about dieting, much less how they'd look naked. Even the subject of marriage and children was kept to a minimum. Had she really changed that much?

Minutes later, she was seated in front of a mirror.

Norma went to work in a flurry of snipping. No one spoke; they were too transfixed by the sight of the butterfly emerging from its cocoon. Even Gerry was silent for a change.

When Norma was done, she switched off the blow-dryer and stepped back, Botticelli unveiling the *Birth of Venus.* "Not bad, if I do say so myself."

A hush fell; then Laura said softly, "Oh, Anna. You're beautiful."

Hair that had hung limply to her shoulders now fell in breezy layers to just below her ears. Its natural curl made it look slightly windblown in a Meg Ryan-ish way. Anna turned her head this way and that, gazing at her reflection with the wonderment of encountering a long lost twin. "Hello," she mouthed silently, her eyes filling with tears. It wasn't just her hair; her double chin was gone, and cheekbones had begun to emerge where there'd been only chipmunk cheeks. It made her eyes look larger and more luminous.

"Norma, you're a genius," Gayle breathed.

Norma smiled as though she didn't need to be told. "Like I always say, why pay a fortune in Beverly Hills when you can get the same thing here for forty?"

"Her own mother wouldn't recognize her," Gerry said.

Half the time she doesn't anyway. But Anna pushed away the thought; she didn't want to spoil the moment. "I hardly recognize *myself,*" she said, unable to tear her eyes from the mirror.

Gerry dug a makeup kit from her shoulder bag and went to work. The end result wasn't as dramatic as the haircut; it only amplified the effect. There was no question that the days of being mistaken for Liz's mother, as had once happened with a near-sighted clerk—easily Anna's most embar-rassing moment in recent years—were be-hind her.

She rose from the chair feeling lighter somehow. "I can't thank you enough." She hugged Laura. "It's the best birthday pres-ent anyone's ever given me."

"For those of you who are still celebrat-ing." Gayle gave a rueful laugh.

At that moment Anna felt all of sixteen.

"Ladies, this calls for a celebration." Norma darted from the room, reappearing moments later with a bottle of chilled cham-pagne and stacks of paper cups. She poured some for everyone, including Myrna McBride, who'd strolled in just as she was popping the cork.

"To beauty in all its many manifestations," Laura toasted.

Anna lifted her cup. "To your baby."

"To a fabulous trip." Gayle glanced at Gerry.

Gerry grinned, raising her foaming cup. "God save the queen!"

The drive didn't seem as long this time. She wasn't exactly eager to see Monica, but the prospect of even a few minutes alone with Marc made her feel less anxious. Was this fixation on a man she barely knew unhealthy? Was she on the verge of becoming a bunny boiler, like in *Fatal Attraction*? Well, at least she *looked* presentable. In honor of the occasion, she'd splurged on a new pair of slacks and a cotton sweater in a shade of blue that matched her eyes.

Before she knew it, she was turning off the Coast Highway onto the steep drive that wound uphill to Pathways. She'd timed it to arrive just as the morning groups were wrapping up. Marc usually headed back to his office before lunch and she hoped they'd have a chance to talk. She grew lightheaded at the thought, a pulse leaping at the base of her throat. Her legs felt weak, as if she'd spent the past two hours pedaling uphill, as she climbed from the car and set off along the path, pausing only to smooth her hair and dry her sweating palms on her slacks.

She was nearing the main building when she spotted him heading in the same direction along a different path. He paused, as if trying to place her, before striding over to greet her. "Anna." Her hand was engulfed in his warm grasp. "I didn't recognize you at first. Your hair . . ." He seemed momentarily at a loss for words, but quickly recovered. "It looks nice."

"Thanks." She fingered the ends self-consciously, her cheeks warming.

"You're just in time. Your sister should be down any minute—she's in her room packing."

His blue eyes crinkled at the corners as he spoke. She'd forgotten just *how* attractive he was. He was wearing jeans and a white oxford shirt rolled up at the sleeves. His tan socks matched his brown bluchers, she saw.

"Actually," she said, "I was hoping to have a few words with you."

"Why don't we step into my office?" He gestured toward the main building, and as they strolled together along the path, Anna felt as if she were barely touching the ground.

They reached the entrance, and she caught her reflection in the plate glass door: an attractive woman with head held high. She thought, *Okay, so I'm not hideous. But that doesn't change the fact that he's married.*

They passed through Intake, where a nurse was distributing meds in paper cups to several patients, then turned down a carpeted hall. Marc unlocked a door at the end, and she stepped into a small book-lined office with a view of the grounds, over which an iridescent mist from the sprinklers shimmered. She lowered herself into the chair opposite his desk, a framed photo of a slender dark-haired woman astride a bike catching her eye. His wife? Anna felt a pang at seeing how pretty she was.

He sat down across from her, leaning back in his chair and propping a leg on the opposite knee. "You're probably wondering what to expect." It was a moment before she realized he meant Monica.

"Well, yes," she said, though that wasn't what she'd wanted to talk to him about.

"She's eager to get home, that much I can tell you."

"I know the feeling." She smiled, then dropped her gaze. "No offense."

He chuckled. "Family week tends to have that effect."

"Is she—is there anything I need to watch

out for? You know, like . . ." She caught her-self, realizing that was the old Anna talking, and smiled ruefully. "Sorry. Old habit."

He nodded, seeming to take it in stride. "Old habits die hard."

"Do you recommend slow starvation or a bullet to the head?"

He cocked his head, smiling. "I'm sure you'll do just fine."

She cleared her throat. "Actually, there's something else I wanted to ask you. It's about my mother. I've been thinking it's time to . . ." She faltered, guilt creeping up on her. But from the look he wore it was ob-vious he wasn't judging her. "I've called a few places," she went on, the image of her mother in some dreary institution, doped into a stupor, looming in her mind. Logically, she knew they weren't all like that, but . . . "The worst of it is, I don't even know if it's the right decision."

"I'm sure you've given it a lot of thought." His voice was gentle and reassuring.

"That doesn't change how I feel." Her gaze drifted to the window. Outside, the grass sparkled in the noonday sun, as invit-ing as one of the posters in the window of

Up and Away. She wished she could be transported to somewhere far from here.

"Which is how, exactly?" he asked like any good shrink.

"Like the world's worst daughter."

"Have you discussed it with your sisters?"

"Liz is all for it." And why not? She wouldn't have to feel so guilty about not helping out. "I don't know about Monica. I haven't talked to her about it yet."

"You don't sound too optimistic." He regarded her intently, his face illuminated by the sunlight slanting through the blinds. She noted the deep lines bracketing his mouth and the smaller ones like notches in the corners of his eyes. He'd known his share of suffering, and that made her like him all the more.

"I already know what she'll say since it'd be coming out of her pocket."

"I see." He'd clearly spent enough time with Monica to know why Anna didn't feel too optimistic.

"I was going to talk to her about it on the ride home," she said. "Unless you think it'd be better if we discussed it here—with you."

But he only smiled and said, "I think you can handle it on your own." She didn't know whether to feel complimented or mildly put in her place, as if she should have known better than to ask. "Remember, there's more than one way to skin a cat."

"Such as?"

"Be prepared to make good on any consequences."

Anna sighed. "I threatened to quit once. You can see how far it got me."

"I'm not sure that working for your sister is such a good idea to begin with."

"Are you kidding? It's a terrible idea," she said with a laugh. "Believe me, if there was a way out, I'd leave in a heartbeat. But right now I can't afford it." When Marc didn't offer any further advice, she went on, "Just in case Monica decides to cooperate, I made a list of the homes in our area. I was hoping you could give me some guidelines. You know, what to look for . . . and what to look *out* for."

He was silent for a moment, as if mulling it over. Then he surprised her by saying, "It'd probably be easier if I went with you."

Anna suddenly had trouble catching her breath. Then the enormity of what he was

offering hit her, and she stammered, "That's
. . . well, that's extremely generous of you,
but . . . I wasn't asking . . . I mean, you're
so busy and all . . . I couldn't possibly—"

He didn't give her a chance to finish. "I
have a conference in Santa Barbara next
Friday. I should be free after lunch. Is that
good for you?"

"N-no. I mean, I . . . yes, that's fine." If
Monica refused to give her the afternoon
off, she *would* quit.

"Good. I'll put it on my calendar."

All at once she felt overheated despite
the cool, ocean-laced breeze blowing in
through the window. Was he just being
nice, or was there something more to it?
She found herself blurting, "I can't believe
you're doing this."

He smiled, and once again she had the
feeling of something closely guarded miles
below his calm surface. "I know what you're
going through. It's the least I can do."

"Your mom or your dad?"

Something flickered in his depthless blue
eyes, then he shook his head, answering
softly, "My wife."

He hadn't meant for it to slip out. It was just that he couldn't think of a reason not to tell her. Which surprised him. Normally he avoided any mention of Faith. Not because it was a secret—everyone on staff knew—but because of the reaction it usually elicited: comments ranging from well meaning to insensitive to downright cruel. In general, he'd found that people approached the subject the way they might a growling dog. Even incest, thanks to *Oprah* and the like, was more openly discussed than mental illness. Paranoid schizophrenics, in particular, had all the appeal of lepers.

"I'm sorry." Anna gazed at him with those soft eyes that on more than one occasion, he was ashamed to admit, had followed him into bed. "It must be hard for you."

"I manage."

"Where is she now?"

"Thousand Oaks—it's a psychiatric hospital."

Anna's sweet face crumpled in sympathy. "Has she been there long?"

He was pleasantly surprised. Few people ever asked that; usually they dropped the subject. "Eighteen months," he told her. "The time before that—" He broke off with a shrug. "Schizophrenia is treatable, but not curable."

"But most schizophrenics aren't institutionalized."

"Hers is an extreme case. It's better this way, believe me." *She's where she can't hurt herself.* "In time, who knows?" Hope, he'd discovered, had a life of its own.

"It's ironic. I mean, you being a therapist and all." Color crept up into her cheeks. "I'm sorry, that was out of line."

"It's okay. I've thought the same thing myself . . . on more than one occasion." *You don't know the half of it.* "For the longest time I couldn't shake the feeling that it was my job to fix her." He gazed at the photo on his desk. It had been taken the summer they'd rented that farmhouse in the Dordogne, their last real vacation. Eight years ago—had it been that long?

She nodded slowly. Anna's eyes were a clear, guileless blue. For some reason just looking at her gave him hope—if not for himself, then for the human race. She said softly, "Most people don't have the slightest idea, do they? What it's like. The person you love is there . . . yet they're not. Sometimes I think death would be preferable."

The color in her cheeks crept higher, form-ing ridges along her cheekbones. "I know that sounds terrible."

"Not at all." He smiled to let her know she wasn't alone in thinking that.

"My mother was ..." She spread her hands in a helpless gesture. He knew the frustration—how to sum up in fifty words or less a person about whom volumes could have been written. "She had a wonderful sense of humor and loved to read—our house was full of books. She was good with her hands, too. For years she sewed all our clothes, all these adorable matching dresses. When we were little, people used to think Monica and I were twins." Her smile was one of such earnest sweetness, it went through him like a knife. "What's your wife like?"

Marc understood now why he felt so drawn to her. There were none of the usual artifices with Anna; what you saw was what you got. He glanced down at her hands resting lightly in her lap, their fingernails no longer chewed to the quick. Hands both soft and capable, the small opal ring she was nervously twisting their only adorn-ment. He felt something loosen a half turn in his gut, and found himself wanting to reach across the narrow space that separated them and cup a hand over hers.

"My wife . . ." He paused, finding it difficult to summon the memories he spent the bulk of his waking hours trying to suppress. "She was . . . *is* . . . a lawyer. We used to joke that the only way to end a debate in our house was for one of us to fall asleep. She was so fierce in her opinions. It was one of the reasons I fell in love with her."

He pictured Faith at the government-issue desk in her shithole of an office at WCF—Women and Children First. Not that she'd paid any attention to her surroundings; she could have been working out of a cardboard box on the curb for all she cared. The only thing that mattered were her clients—poor women, single moms mostly, for whom she'd battled tirelessly, everything from deadbeat dads to the INS. There were no lengths to which she wouldn't go, and it wasn't unusual for him, on nights when he'd arrived home late from work—usually after stopping at a bar along the way—to encounter a blanket-covered figure stretched out asleep on the sofa.

"How long has she been this way?" Anna eyed him with compassion.

"It seems like forever."

She sighed in commiseration. "I know just how you feel. The worst is how it creeps up on you. Instead of losing them all at once, you lose pieces. Sometimes I want to scream at my mom, as if it were her fault she can't remember things. Then I hate myself."

Marc found her frankness refreshing, and he let his guard down a little further. "With Faith it was nothing I could put my finger on at first," he recalled. "Just a lot of little things. Comments she made that were out of context. The way she'd look at me sometimes, as if she thought I was out to get her. Then she started obsessing about the people next door."

"What about them?"

"She was convinced they were spying on us."

She nodded. "My mom sometimes gets it into her head that my dad's after her—never mind he's been dead almost twenty years. She'll get this petrified look on her face, and I swear I have to look over my shoulder to make sure he's not there."

"The fear is real even if the demons aren't."

"The thing I hate the most is feeling so . . . so . . ." Her hands clenched and un-clenched. "It's as if I'm on the other side of a locked door, and no matter how hard I try, I can't get in. Do you ever feel that way?"

"All the time."

Did she have any idea how lovely she was? Probably not. He knew from talking to her that all *she* saw was her size, which was blown out of proportion in her mind. What made her beautiful, far more so than Monica, was a purity of heart he rarely saw except in children.

Dr. Fellows, the founder and director of Pathways, would surely look askance at his volunteering to help her choose a nursing home for her mother. He'd wonder aloud if Marc had an ulterior motive. And in the fleeting moment of indecision that had accompanied his impulse, Marc had wondered himself. But he wasn't looking to bed Anna. Aside from its being on the line professionally, he didn't want to see her get hurt. She wasn't anything like Natalie, his current lady friend, who didn't care that he was married and wouldn't have wanted more if he wasn't.

His intercom buzzed, sparing him any further thoughts along those lines. "Monica's here," announced Cindy in Intake. "Is her sister in with you?" Her voice was strained. Clearly, Monica was being her usual demanding self and Cindy was eager to be rid of the patient he'd overheard her refer to the other day as Her Royal Pain in the Ass.

"Tell her we'll be with her in a moment." He couldn't help feeling discouraged. Monica had been a tough nut to crack. Even after a month of daily groups, one-on-one sessions, and AA meetings, the progress she'd made was incremental at best.

He rose to see Anna out, and as she stood, something in the curve of her cheek, the tilt of her chin, brought to mind his mother. She didn't resemble her in the physical sense—Essie had been short and dark, with direct brown eyes and a mouth to match—but in the air of resolve she wore. His mother had come to this country with nothing, and she'd raised her fatherless brood with little help from anyone. From what he knew of Anna, she was cut from the same cloth.

She took his hand at the door. "I can't thank you enough."

"Don't mention it." He remembered how hard it had been for him when he'd been looking at facilities for Faith—and he was a doctor.

Once again, he wondered again if his impulse had been a good one. *Was* he interested in more than playing the Good Samaritan? Maybe. But nothing untoward would come of it, so what was the harm?

"Roll up your window. I'm freezing."

Anna compromised by rolling it up halfway. Was it going to be like this the whole way home? Monica seemed determined to give new meaning to that old saying, A leopard never changes its spots.

"Why don't you put your sweater on?" It lay crumpled on the seat, a cashmere cardigan the pale yellow of clotted cream that had cost more than Anna made in a week.

Monica only crossed her arms over her chest. She looked a little pale, though it might have been because she wasn't wearing makeup. "I don't know why you didn't send a limo. That's all I need, to be stranded along the road in this old heap." She glanced out at the guardrail that was the only thing standing between them and a two-hundred-foot drop into the ocean glittering below.

"I thought it'd give us a chance to talk." Anna struggled to maintain an even tone, thinking, *Let's start with the reason I can't afford anything better than this old heap.*

"Talk?" Monica snorted. "All I've done these last few weeks is talk. I'm so sick of it I don't care if I never speak to another person for the rest of my life."

Which would suit me just fine. "Well, it must have done you some good. I don't know when I've seen you looking more . . . refreshed."

"As opposed to what, exactly?"

"You know." Anna wasn't going to play this old game.

She waited for Anna to wade in deeper, and when she didn't sighed heavily. "Okay, I admit it. You were right to ship me off. Is that what you wanted to hear?"

"All I did was give you a push in the right direction." Good or bad, she didn't want this on *her* head.

"Either way, a month in the gulag would have been a breeze in comparison. Mind if I smoke?"

Anna opened her mouth to ask nicely if it couldn't wait until they stopped for gas, but realized that would have been the old Anna talking. "Actually, I do," she said.

Monica eyed her narrowly. "Well, well. Miss Assertive. I suppose next you'll be telling me to shut up."

"That's not a bad idea." The calm with which she spoke amazed her. Where had it come from? It was as if she'd been suffocating for years and all of a sudden could breathe. "Look, it's going to be a long drive and you're not making it any easier."

Monica looked as if she were going to say something nasty, then slumped back with a sigh. "Sorry. It's just . . . I'm scared, you know?" Her voice was small, almost childlike. "Back there everything was taken care of. No decisions. No—" She broke off, pulling in a shaky breath. "I'm not sure I can handle being on my own." Her eyes shimmered with tears, and she reached out to grab hold of Anna's hand. Her fingers were icy. "Forgive me?"

Anna shrugged. "There's nothing to forgive."

She felt a tug of sympathy, but resisted it. Why was it always about Monica, never anyone else? Their mother, for instance. She hadn't once asked about Betty.

Anna gathered up the courage to broach the subject. She felt stronger since her talk with Marc. And here she'd thought *she* had it bad. "Listen, there's something—"

She didn't get a chance to finish. "Just one itty-bitty little cigarette?" Monica wheedled. "I'll roll my window down."

Anna was on the verge of caving in when a snippet from a poem popped into her head: *For want of a nail . . . the kingdom was lost.* If she waffled on even something this small, she might lose her nerve . . . and ultimately the battle. "It can wait," she said briskly, and out of the corner of her eye saw Monica's jaw drop. "We need to talk."

"About what?" Monica asked sullenly.

"Mom. She's worse."

"So?" Monica didn't even pretend to care.

"So . . ." Anna took a deep breath. "It's gotten to be more than I can handle."

"Isn't that what I pay Edna for?"

"Edna isn't there all the time."

"Well then, have her work an extra hour or two a week." Monica spoke as grandly as if she were offering a million dollars.

"That's not what I had in mind."

"Come on, how bad could it be? All she does is sit in front of the TV."

Like you would know. "You have to watch her every minute. Last week she almost set the house on fire."

"What do you expect *me* to do about it?"

"I think you know."

Monica glanced at her in surprise. She wasn't used to Anna's being so direct and it had clearly taken some of the wind out of her sails. "A nursing home, you mean." Her voice was flat.

"I don't see any other choice."

"Have you talked to Liz?" Monica hedged.

"She's all for it."

"Easy for her to say." Monica didn't have to spell it out: Liz wouldn't be the one footing the bills.

A pulse in Anna's temple began to pound. If Monica didn't go along, she'd be left with no choice but to put her mother's house up for sale. And even then the money it would net wouldn't be enough for long-term care in one of the better homes. Betty would end up in one of those dreadful places that were little more than warehouses for the elderly. "Obviously, we can't do anything without you," she said as evenly as she could.

"Damn straight."

Anna slowed going into the next turn, thinking of the steep drop-off ahead. If she were to accidentally drive off a cliff, it would solve everything, wouldn't it? Then she remembered Marc . . . and Liz . . . and her dear friends Laura and Finch. The life that only weeks ago had seemed intolerable was all at once precious. "I'm not going to get down on my knees," she said sharply. "She's *your* mother, too."

"I've done more than my fair share."

Anna fought back the sharp retort on the tip of her tongue. "Look, I'm not saying you haven't been generous." Without Edna, *she'd* be in an institution.

Like Marc's wife. She'd felt a flicker of selfish joy at his revelation, but seeing the pain in his face she'd instantly been flooded with guilt. Envy, too. Would any man ever love *her* that much?

"You must think I'm made of money,"

Monica snapped. "Do you know what that little getaway set me back? Thirty grand. And it's not like I'm raking it in these days." True, her acting days might be over, but Anna calculated that the bill for a month at Pathways equaled about what her portfolio threw off in the same amount of time. She wouldn't be going to the poorhouse any-time soon.

"I'll be looking at places next week," Anna plowed on in the same measured tone. She purposely didn't mention that Marc had volunteered to go along; Monica might take it the wrong way. "I was hoping to have it settled by then."

"And if I don't agree?"

The throbbing was in both temples now. She recalled Marc's advice: *Be prepared to make good on any consequences.* Her pulse slowed, and she remembered some-thing else—the way Monica had reacted the one time Anna had threatened to quit. She might need her paycheck, but Monica needed her even more.

"Don't expect me to like it," she replied coolly.

"Meaning?"

"You might be looking to replace someone other than Edna."

"Very funny." Monica forced a laugh as false as the bravado with which she spoke. "You *wouldn't.* You promised."

"Promises can be broken."

"Is that a threat?"

Anna shrugged.

"I could just as easily fire you," Monica went on, her voice rising.

"Go ahead then, fire me."

"You don't mean that."

All at once Anna was seeing it in her mind—the accumulation of indignities, the years of kowtowing—like a vast mudslide sloughing away, leaving her mind clear. *Anything would be better,* she thought. Selling pencils on the street—or her body, if it came to that. She said firmly, "I've never been more serious in my life."

Monica glared at her. A shift had taken place. Anna detected a touch of awe in her sister's narrowed eyes. "Fine," she spat. "I'll expect your letter of resignation first thing tomorrow morning."

It sounded so much like a line from a movie that Anna giggled. "Let me guess—*Sweet*

Smell of Success?" She nudged Monica. "Come on, lighten up. I'm your *sister.*"

"Which you seem to have conveniently forgotten." Monica's lower lip was trembling.

"What do you expect? You're not leaving me any choice."

"You wouldn't dare treat me this way if—" She broke off, perhaps not wanting to overplay her hand. Instead, she said pitifully, "It's easy to take advantage of someone in a weakened state."

"You should do a telethon," Anna said with a snort. "Jerry Lewis could host it."

Monica looked stunned. Anna was a little shocked herself. Had she really said that? Anyone listening in would have thought her heartless. But dammit, she was tired of tiptoeing around. And handicapped or not, Monica wasn't exactly Camille.

"You'd really do that—leave me to fend for myself?" Monica's voice grew choked. "Why don't you just pull over now and dump me by the side of the road?"

Keep talking, and maybe I will. "I have a better idea," Anna said. "There's a burger place up ahead. Why don't we stop and talk this over like two civilized adults?"

Monica didn't say anything at first. She sat staring out the window, a forlorn look on her face. Or was she calculating her next move? At last she turned to Anna with a sigh of surrender. "As long as we sit outside where I can smoke."

Anna stifled a smile. "Fair enough."

CHAPTER SEVEN

The second to the last nursing home on the list was just down the road from Dos Palmas, with a view of its fairway. A pink Spanish-style stucco shaded by live oaks and surrounded by sweeping green baize lawns, it seemed almost too good to be true after the places they'd visited so far. Inside, it was even more impressive, everything sparkling clean and up to date, its rec rooms and visitors' lounge furnished in comfortable chairs and sofas, and hung with Impressionist prints. And best of all, it fell within the price range Monica had agreed to.

Anna waited until they were walking back to Marc's car before asking excitedly, "So what did you think?"

Marc shrugged. "A little light on staff for its size."

Her heart sank. "Maybe they're all out with the flu."

He looked unconvinced. "Did you notice anything unusual about the patients?"

"Yes. They seemed happy." Dazzled by visions of her mother eating in the chandelier-hung dining hall, or enjoying afternoon concerts like the one being given in the rec room right now—First Presbyterian's organist, Carrie Bramley, on piano—she hadn't looked too hard for negatives.

"More like doped up." They reached the end of the palm-lined driveway, where his silver Audi was parked. "Oldest trick in the book—keep them sedated so they're easier to handle."

"Are you sure?" Come to think of it, they had seemed a little *too* happy.

"Not based on what I've seen, but when something looks too good to be true, it usually is." They got in and he started the engine, backing out of the drive. "We still have one more to look at though, so don't lose hope." He flashed her a smile, which went through her like a hot drink on a cold day. It was all she could do to concentrate on the task at hand.

She watched as he navigated the twisting turns of Fox Canyon Road. She couldn't tell what he was thinking—whether he was sorry he'd volunteered for this or enjoying the afternoon away from work. "I couldn't have done this without you," she said. "Honestly, I can't thank you enough."

"Don't mention it."

He seemed uncomfortable being thanked. Gazing out at the sunsplashed hills dotted with oaks, he said, "I had no idea Carson Springs was so beautiful. It's like Shangri-La. Let me guess, you're really as old as Methuselah and if you were ever to leave—"

"I'd wither up and die," she finished with a laugh, feeling vaguely discomfited at the thought of being so deeply rooted.

"In that case, I promise not to take you past the city limits."

"There's a downside to staying in one place too long. You can rot." Avery Lewellyn was rattling toward them in his pickup, its bed piled with old furniture on the way to his antiques barn, no doubt from some estate sale. The sight depressed her for some reason—those few dusty pieces of furniture that were all there was to show for a lifetime in Carson Springs.

Marc glanced at her out of the corner of his eye. "I don't see any evidence of that."

Anna felt her cheeks warm. Was he flirting? No, it was the kind of remark Hector would have made. She had to stop reading things into every word and gesture or she *would* end up like Miss Finley, who every year on the anniversary of her beloved's death asked Father Reardon to say a special mass, seemingly unaware of the patronizing smiles and snickers it evoked.

Ten minutes later they were pulling up in front of a rambling Victorian on a small side street several blocks east of Old Mission. Over the latticed porch festooned with morning glories hung a discreet sign: THE SUNSHINE HOME. The name had struck her as implausibly cheerful, which was why, despite the woman she'd spoken to over the phone sounding so pleasant, she'd saved it for last.

"There must be bodies buried in the basement, like in *Arsenic and Old Lace*," she muttered under her breath as they made their way up the front walk shaded by huge old catalpas, their pods rattling like sabers in the breeze.

"I take it you're a fan of old movies." Marc walked with a spring in his step. Amazingly enough, he seemed almost lighthearted.

"Is there any other kind?" She hadn't been to a current release in too many months to count. Usually, by the time she'd lined up someone to watch her mother, it was more trouble than it was worth. She smiled ruefully. "Needless to say, I don't get out much."

"I have a feeling that's about to change." He took her arm as they stepped up onto the porch, and Anna tingled all over. But she knew the freedom she'd soon enjoy would come with a large heaping of guilt.

Marc rang the buzzer and after what seemed an eternity, a woman appeared at the door. Anna wondered if she was one of the residents; with her snow-white hair and forcibly erect carriage, she looked to be the right age, but that notion was dispelled when she put out a hand, saying warmly, "You must be Anna. I'm Felicia Campbell. Sorry to have kept you waiting. I was in the kitchen washing up." She had an open face, its crisscrossed lines forming a kind of basket in which her warm brown eyes and smiling mouth were nestled.

"I'm Marc. Nice to meet you." He extended his hand.

"How lovely that your husband could join you," Felicia remarked, her smile widening.

Blood rushed to Anna's face. "Oh, he's not . . ."

Marc rescued her, saying casually, "I'm just a friend."

They were ushered into a hallway lit with antique sconces and dominated by a grandfather clock that chimed the hour just then. Felicia slid open a pocket door, and they stepped into a cozy sunlit parlor furnished in vintage sofas and chairs. Half a dozen elderly men and women were scattered about, sipping tea and nibbling on sandwiches and cookies from the tiered stand on the coffee table. "We serve high tea every afternoon at three," she explained. "It's our little ritual."

"We all look forward to it," chimed a plump, henna-haired woman with her teacup held daintily aloft.

"I wouldn't go that far," grumbled a portly, bald-headed man as he brushed at the crumbs sprinkled over the front of his shirt. "But it sure as hell beats pinochle."

"Don't mind Henry," said one of the other ladies, a little bit of a thing with wispy white hair that floated about her head like a dandelion gone to seed. He doesn't like it that the boys are outnumbered three to one. If it was the other way around, believe me we'd all be smoking cigars and playing billiards."

The women tittered, and the two men exchanged looks of weary resignation.

Anna and Marc were shown into Felicia's tidy office off the stairs, which was dominated by a rolltop desk. "You're in luck," she said. "One of our residents recently passed on, so we have an opening."

"What are your requirements?" Anna didn't want to get her hopes up. From what she'd seen, she doubted the Sunshine Home was equipped to handle someone as far gone as her mother.

"We're only licensed for eight beds, so it's a little less structured than some of the other places you may have looked at." It was what she'd told Anna over the phone. "The only requirements are that our residents be ambulatory and able to feed and go to the bathroom by themselves."

"That's it?" Betty certainly qualified on those counts.

Felicia smiled, handing her a single type-written sheet rather than a glossy brochure like she'd been given at the last place. "We like to think of ourselves as a home away from home. I know that sounds trite and that nothing can replace one's own home, but we do our best. We've found a family atmosphere helps enormously in keeping the mind active. Most of our residents don't require a lot of looking after."

Anna's heart sank. "My mother isn't . . . well, she has a tendency to wander off." No use gilding the lily; it would catch up to her in the end. "I'm afraid she might be too much for you."

"Because she is for you?" Anna drew back, startled, but Felicia's voice was kind. "It's only natural for you to feel over-whelmed. Who wouldn't in your shoes? The difference is, we've *chosen* this, my hus-band and I. And besides Oren and me, there's Genevieve and Sheila—Sheila does all the cooking—and our three part-time staffers. Our guests are free to help out around the house, too, which many of them do."

"It sounds ideal," Anna said, casting an anxious glance at Marc. She couldn't tell what he was thinking. Was this another case of too good to be true?

After a brief run-down on finances, Felicia rose to her feet, bringing her hands together in a soundless little clap. "Now, shall we have a look upstairs?"

They climbed the stairs to the second floor, passing an elderly woman with a cane balanced on her lap who was being lowered on the chair lift. The moment Anna walked into the room that would be Betty's, if all went well, she knew it was the answer to her prayers. It looked out over the yard in back, and sunlight poured in through tall double-hung windows hung with ruffled sheers. There was a four-poster bed covered in a pretty flowered spread, and matching wardrobe and vanity. The only thing missing were pictures on the walls; residents were encouraged to bring their own, Felicia had explained.

"It's perfect." Anna swallowed against the lump in her throat, scarcely aware that Marc had slipped an arm about her shoulders. *Don't get your hopes up,* cautioned the voice in her head. Betty would have to be evaluated and given a complete physical. Monica would have to cut a check as well. Though she'd given her word, Anna knew how worthless it generally was. She would probably try to stall by claiming her money was tied up or coming up with a long list of bullshit conditions.

Felicia looked about in satisfaction. "I'm glad you think so," she said. "We know that this isn't an easy decision. Seeing your loved one comfortable and well cared for makes it a little less difficult."

Anna didn't think anything was going to alleviate her guilt. Hadn't she spent countless sleepless nights agonizing over her decision? It wasn't just guilt, she'd miss her mother in some ways—especially those moments Betty came to life like the parlor lamp in their living room when the sunlight hit it just so, turning its crystals into dancing prisms.

They were heading back downstairs when a tabby cat came bounding from the shadows to rub up against Felicia's leg. She scooped it up, scolding affectionately, "There you are, you naughty boy. Where have you been hiding?" She held him out for Anna to pet. "Meet Sunshine, our resident mascot. My husband told me I was silly for naming this place after a cat, but it seemed fitting. The residents all love him and Sunshine is an equal opportunity host—he never spends more than one night in the same room." A look of mild consternation crossed her face. "Your mother's not allergic to cats, I hope."

"No, she'll love him." Anna smiled, thinking of Boots.

It wasn't until they were back in Marc's car that she let out her breath. "If there's something the matter with that one, too, I don't want to hear it. Let me go on wearing my rose-colored glasses a little while longer." He gave her a mysterious smile, but remained silent as he started the engine and pulled away from the curb. It wasn't until they'd gone several blocks that she surrendered with a sigh. "Okay, you win. What's wrong with it?"

"Nothing," Marc said. "I was just thinking how nice it would be if they were all like that."

She slumped back in her seat, relief washing over her. "No kidding. I'm about ready to move in myself."

He chuckled as they cruised past Delarosa Plaza. By its bougainville-draped arch was a blue pushcart filled with buckets of cut flowers, the bright idea of Violet Kingsley, a retired florist from New York. She'd named her little stand Petal Pushers.

"For one thing," she went on, "I'd always be a spring chicken compared to everyone else."

"That's one way of looking at it."

"Plus, three meals a day."

"And high tea—let's not forget that."

"I bet they're big on old movies, too."

"Still think there are bodies in the basement?" He cast her a teasing glance.

"If there are, I'm sure they deserved whatever happened to them."

They shared a laugh, and for the first time all day Anna allowed herself to relax.

"Well, I'm glad you found it." He made a right turn at the light, heading in the direction of Old Sorrento. "I'd hate to think I came all this way for nothing."

Anna's happy mood dissolved. This wasn't a social outing. He was doing her a favor, that's all. "I couldn't have done it alone," she told him, careful to keep her voice neutral. "You really saved me."

He shrugged. "You'd have managed just

fine." Once again, she had the feeling he was uncomfortable being thanked. Had she been too effusive? It was one of the perils of being cooped up—you tended to overdo it on the rare occasions you got out.

She looked out at the sun riding the shoulders of the mountaintops. They were passing an orange grove, where shadows had gathered in pools between the neat rows of trees, spilling out onto the road. The air blowing in through the vents was noticeably cooler; she'd have to put an extra blanket on tonight.

All at once she couldn't bear the thought that she might never see him again. What should have been one of the most awful days of her life had turned out to be one of the best, and she didn't want it to end.

"Well, the least I can do is buy you dinner." She spoke lightly, her words skipping like stones over the surface of a lake.

There was a long pause, and her breath caught in her throat. Then he replied, "Sounds good, but—" She braced herself. "Only if it's Dutch treat."

She relaxed, the breath easing from her lungs. "No way. I owe you a lot more than dinner."

He hesitated just long enough to send her heart into maximum overdrive, then said, "In that case I accept."

"There's an inn out at the lake. I've never eaten there, but I've heard the food's good."

"Do we need to reserve?" He reached for his cell phone.

"This time of day? We'll have the whole place to ourselves." At Boulders Inn, the moonlight on the lake was the big draw.

What she hadn't counted on was the sunset. They pulled into the parking area just as the tangerine sky above the forested horizon was fading to violet, transforming the lake into a sheet of hammered gold. She climbed from the car, pausing to take in the view as she drew in a breath of pine-scented air. Had she ordered this up, it couldn't have been more perfect. The question was, perfect for what?

"My sisters and I used to go swimming here in the summer," she told him. "I remember the water being freezing even in August." She gazed out at the lake, where the gold was deepening to bronze. "Thousands of years ago this whole valley was under water. Every once in a while someone digs up a shark's tooth or a marine fossil. Native Americans used to trade in them before the settlers came along."

"You know a lot for someone who doesn't get out much," he observed with a bemused smile.

"As a kid I was pretty adventurous."

"They say people don't really change; they just get better at disguising their real selves."

"In that case, I've gotten so good at it I don't recognize myself."

His smile spread up into his eyes, which fixed on her for a heart-stopping moment. "Keep looking. You'll find her."

They started down the slope, toward the inn, picking their way down a path of large flat stones cantilevered to form steps. Halfway down she caught her heel and stumbled a bit. When Marc took her arm to steady her, she prayed he wouldn't notice her trembling, and if he did, that he'd chalk it up to the cool breeze whispering in the pines overhead.

"What about you?" she asked. "What were you like as a kid?"

He thought for a moment, then said, "I don't know that I was ever really a kid." She waited for him to explain. "I was the eldest of six. My mom worked two jobs, so I sort of fell into the father role. You grow up fast that way. I think that's part of why I was so dead set on to becoming a pilot—it must have been a desire to escape." He turned to her, his eyes dark amid the shadows of the trees. "Don't get me wrong. I love them, but it was a lot to handle."

Anna nodded. "I know the feeling. College couldn't come soon enough."

"Where did you go to school?"

"Cal State. I was all set to choose a major when . . ." She shrugged. They'd been over this; no sense beating a dead horse. "I guess it wasn't meant to be."

"It's not too late."

"What, and go from a spring chicken to the oldest student on campus?" She laughed, but he'd struck a nerve. Hadn't she toyed with the idea on more than one occasion? "The sad truth is, I'm too young for retirement and too old for college."

"How about something in between?" They'd reached the entrance to the lodge, built of pine logs as big around as casks. Cabins serving as guest accommodations were scattered along the paths that wound through the woods nearby.

"Like what?"

"You could do an internship while working toward your degree."

I might as well wish for the moon. Anna smiled, knowing it would never happen. "Someday, maybe." Meanwhile she had to support herself and possibly her mother, if Monica didn't keep her promise.

Marc looked as though he wanted to say more, but to Anna's relief he let it drop. They stepped into a paneled lobby lined with rustic tables and leather chairs, its walls hung with vintage photos of Carson Springs. There was one of miners panning for gold and another of Old Mission in the days before it was paved, looking pretty much as it did now except that cars had taken the place of horses and parking meters stood where hitching posts once had. Just past the reception desk was a short flight of steps leading down into a spacious cathedral-beamed dining room. A stone fireplace lent a faint smoky smell to the air. Her gaze was drawn to the floor-to-ceiling windows that looked out on the lake, where a molten trail led to the sun sinking below the trees.

Minutes later, seated at a table by the window across from Marc, Anna allowed herself to imagine that they were on a real date. But apparently Marc didn't share that feeling; he appeared lost in thought as he gazed out at the lake. Was he thinking of how much he'd rather be here with his wife?

They ordered drinks, club soda for Marc, a glass of Chardonnay for her. It wasn't until after their waitress had gone that she thought to ask, "Do you mind? Because I don't have to. I mean, I'm not . . ." She bit her lip to keep from blurting, *like Monica.*

"If it was a problem, I'd be in trouble." He cast a wry glance at the lively bar scene. "It gets easier with time. If it didn't, no one would ever get sober."

She thought of the stories she'd heard at family week. "Was it as hard as they say?"

"Harder."

"I don't suppose your . . . the situation at home made it any easier."

"No." He grew very still, his gaze drifting to a point just past her shoulder. Then with a visible effort he shook himself free of whatever memory he'd been in the grip of, saying, "I went out a couple of times that first year—what you normies call falling off the wagon." He flashed her a rueful grin. "One thing about us drunks, we'll grab hold of any excuse. And I was feeling plenty sorry for myself in those days."

"With good reason."

He shook his head. "That's the wrong way to look at it. One time I asked my sponsor, 'Why me?' You know what his answer was? He looked me straight in the eye and said, 'Why not?' After that I stopped asking why and started dealing with what was."

"I know it's not quite the same, but I can relate." Their drinks had come and she sipped her wine. "I've been on every diet known to mankind."

"I wouldn't know it looking at you."

Anna grew flustered. Was he being facetious? No, he wouldn't be that cruel. "You must like the pleasantly plump type," she said with a laugh.

He frowned. "Why do you say that?"

She shrugged. "I've been the butt of fat jokes all my life. I learned early on that it's easier if you laugh first."

He was smiling now, but not in the way

she was used to being smiled at when the topic of her weight came up. "I don't see it. Not even close."

"I've lost a few pounds recently." She felt self-conscious all of a sudden and wished she'd kept her mouth shut. Would he think she was fishing for compliments?

"More than a few, if what you're saying is true." His gaze traveled over her, frankly assessing but in no way patronizing. "Though, personally, I think women make too big a deal of their weight. It's one of the few areas in which men can legitimately claim superiority. We're not afraid to let it all hang out."

They shared a laugh, and she felt some of the heat go out of her cheeks.

Talk turned to other things. While Anna went on marveling that there was at least one man on the planet who didn't see her as pathetic, Marc told her more about his work and about his recent trip to Oregon, where he'd visited his wife's family. Anna, in turn, told him about her come-to-Jesus with Monica.

"She wouldn't even hear me out at first, but I gave her an ultimatum: If she didn't do the right thing, she'd be losing an assistant *and* a sister. Eventually she saw the light."

She waited for the pat on the head she was sure was coming, but Marc merely nodded as though he'd expected nothing less of her. That he saw her as capable as well as normal-sized was almost more than she could take in all at once.

They dined on smoked trout and baby greens, roast duck breast glazed in port, and homemade huckleberry pie topped with ice cream. It was more than she'd eaten all in one sitting in weeks, but oddly enough she didn't regret a single bite.

"Why don't we take our coffee out on the deck?" he suggested. "There's a full moon."

Anna felt as if she were floating as she rose and followed him across the room, stepping through the sliding glass door onto the deck. Luckily, it was deserted—too chilly this time of year even for die-hard romantics, though she hardly noticed. She might have been burning with a fever.

Deep redwood chairs were scattered about. When Marc bent to brush the leaves from one so she could sit down, Anna knew for the first time in her life what it was like to be fussed over by a man.

The moon sailed serenely overhead,

casting its silver net over the water, so beautiful it made her ache. How often had she dreamed of a night like this with a man like Marc? That he was beyond reach seemed grossly unfair.

They sipped their coffee and nibbled on *biscotti.* The only sounds were the soft chirring of crickets and nightjars, and the breeze murmuring secrets to the pines. She heard a faint plop out on the lake. "Do you like to fish?" she asked, desperate for something to talk about that would keep him from guessing what was in her heart.

"My uncle used to take me. Got to be pretty good at it—I once landed a twenty-two-inch bass. They're still talking about it down at the bait shop in Susanville."

"I'll take your word for it." She smiled.

"You don't believe me?"

"Let's just say I've known men to exaggerate."

"We only do it to impress you ladies."

Anna tried to imagine herself as someone worth impressing, and caught a glimpse of the woman he saw, the woman she could be. The words slipped out: "Don't worry. I'm sold." Noting the odd look that crossed his face, she rushed to add, "Not that I'm . . ." She bit her lip. "What I meant was . . ."

"I won't get the wrong idea, I promise." He flashed her a smile, his teeth white in the darkness.

"I wouldn't mind if you did," she blurted, then immediately brought a hand to her mouth. "Oh, God. I knew I shouldn't have had that second glass of wine." She smiled ruefully. "Let's just say it's been awhile since I've enjoyed myself this much. As you can see, it's gone to my head."

"That makes two of us." He wasn't kidding, she could see.

Blood rushed to her head, which buzzed pleasantly. She felt as though she'd drunk a whole bottle of wine. "It . . . it must be lonely without your wife," she stammered.

He sat looking out over the lake, where lights twinkled like submerged flames along the opposite shore. "Let's just say it's given me a new appreciation for funerals."

"How so?" She cast him a startled look.

"They're not for the dead, are they? They're for us. How can you move on otherwise?" He sat very still, the light from inside sending his shadow spilling over the edge of the deck into the deeper shadows below.

"The answer is, you don't. You just go on . . . waiting. For something—anything."

Anna felt something catch in her chest and instinctively reached for his hand. "Thank you."

"For what?" He turned to look at her in surprise.

"For reminding me that I don't have the market cornered on misery."

"I guess it takes one to know one," he said with a mirthless laugh.

"If I told you how I felt right now, you'd laugh."

"Try me."

She drew in a breath. "I was thinking that if this were the last day of my life, I could die happy."

There was a long pause. "Want to know what *I'm* thinking?" he said at last.

"What?" She shivered, hugging herself.

"I was wondering if any of those cabins were vacant." He gestured toward the trees, where here and there a lighted window glowed invitingly. Before she could reply, he said derisively, "You see? I'm no better than the next guy."

Anna was speechless. If she could have found her voice, she'd have told him that far from being offended, she was deeply grateful. Yet all she could manage was, "Did you mean what you just said?"

"To my discredit, yes."

Her heart soared, then she remembered: *He's married.* "It's my fault. If I've led you on—"

He didn't let her finish. "It wasn't anything you did, Anna." He leaned close, the light falling over his face, in which she saw every line etched as if on a coin. "I enjoy your company—it's as simple as that. More than I have any right to." He took hold of her hand and this time drew her to her feet. "Tell me I haven't scared you off for good."

He wanted her. It wasn't just her imagination. The realization was so startling she didn't quite know what to make of it. She thought of Gary Kingman, her first and only boyfriend. They'd dated most of the fall semester of her freshman year before she'd finally relinquished her virginity. And though the experience had been less than magical, he'd made up for it by telling her over and over that he loved her. It wasn't until the following weekend that she found out the truth when Gary's roommate, after one too many beers, informed her that Gary had hung the bloodied sheet out the window of their dorm room the following day—the victor brandishing his spoils. She'd felt so violated she'd broken off with him at once, and for the rest of the semester had crept around campus with her eyes lowered, certain that everyone knew. Even after all these years she couldn't think of it without cringing inside.

But Marc wasn't like Gary.

"I'm not going anywhere," she answered in a surprisingly firm voice.

"In that case, would it be all right if I kissed you?"

Anna nodded dreamily. In the chilly air she could see his breath, and as he drew close, its warmth against her lips was a kiss in itself. The deeper warmth of his mouth, tasting faintly of anise, came as a delicious shock. She grew lightheaded, her insides seeming to funnel down like sand in an hourglass. When she wound her arms about his neck, it was as much to anchor herself as to urge him on.

"Should we see about that cabin?" she murmured against his ear.

Marc drew back, his eyes searching her

face. "I don't want you to do anything you'll be sorry for."

She knew what he was saying, that it would only be this one night. But for Anna even one night would be a gift beyond imagining. "Aren't you the one who's always telling me I can take care of myself?" she asked lightly even as her heart roared in her ears.

There was no reason to rush home—Betty was staying the night with Liz (Monica wasn't the only one Anna had come down hard on)—and as luck would have it, one of the cabins was vacant. The chatty middle-aged man at the front desk gave them a spiel about its being haunted, but Anna only smiled. That legend had been making the rounds since she was a kid—about the newlyweds who'd been struck by lightning in bed on their wedding night. She told it to Marc as they were making their way along the dimly lit path.

"I don't get it," he said. "They were in bed?"

"Supposedly a bolt came down the chimney while they were . . . um . . . you know." She giggled, still feeling the effects of the wine.

"Well, at least they died happy."

They found their cabin and unlocked the door. Anna was relieved to see that it wasn't creepy in any way. There was a bed covered in a patchwork quilt, a pine dresser, and an easy chair. A jug of daisies adorned the antique washstand by the fireplace.

"Maybe we should tune in for the weather forecast." He glanced at the radio on the nightstand. "On the other hand, we could always decide to live dangerously." He grinned, tossing the key onto the dresser. Anna felt the strength leave her limbs as he took her in his arms.

It was like in dreams, only better. The way he was kissing her she wouldn't have noticed or cared if the heavens had opened. When he drew back at last, it was to unbutton her blouse, her best one, cream silk with tiny covered buttons. As it slipped to the floor she instinctively crossed her arms over her chest. He gently pried them away. "No . . . I want to look at you." His gaze was frankly admiring. "You have a beautiful body, Anna."

She shivered, scarcely able to breathe. When he cupped a hand over her breast, her knees wobbled and for a moment she was sure they were going to give out. She murmured, "I think I'd better lie down."

She slid between sheets, cool and crisp as blank paper on which anything at all might be written. They kissed some more, Anna shyly running her hands down his chest and belly . . . and below. He was less tentative with her, though no less gentle. He took his time, almost as if asking permission, before kissing her there . . . and there . . . and there. Anna trembled, nearly overcome by the flood of sensations. She thought once more of Gary and all the nights since—years of loneliness and despair, of lying in an empty bed longing to be touched. Tears came to her eyes now, tears of gratitude that she hadn't gone to her grave without experiencing this.

He drew back at one point, and she tensed, thinking she'd disappointed him in some way. But all he said was, "You're shivering. Should I close the window?"

She shook her head. "I'm fine." They'd left it open a crack to air out the room, and though she knew that to most people it would be chilly, the December breeze was balm against her heated skin. "Just a little nervous, I guess."

He kissed her neck, whispering, "We'll take it slow."

When he entered her at last, she had to bite down on her lower lip to keep from crying out. Not because it hurt, but because it felt so good . . . so *right.* The strangest feeling came over her as she clung to him, arching to meet each thrust: a desire to make it last, to hold on to this forever, even as she rushed toward the climax.

When they came together, seconds later, it was like being released in midair—a moment of exquisite suspension before plummeting to earth.

Afterward they lay tangled together, struggling to catch their breath. She couldn't tell where she ended and he began. "Now I know how those honeymooners felt," she said.

He brushed the hair from her eyes, smiling. "I'm glad we didn't have to die finding out."

"Hold me." She tightened her arms about him, feeling as if he were slipping away even though he hadn't moved. She tried not to think about his wife or the fact that she wasn't the first woman with whom he'd been unfaithful—the condom conveniently tucked in his wallet had testified to that. She didn't want to spoil the moment. And anyway, what did it matter? He didn't owe her an explanation.

"Don't tell me you're afraid of ghosts?"

She shook her head. "That's for people who've run out of real life things to worry about."

"Poor Anna." He stroked her hair. "You've had a tough go of it, haven't you?"

"But look where I ended up." She smiled into his shoulder, peering up at the moon caught in a windowpane. "If it hadn't been for Monica, we wouldn't have met."

"A compelling point."

"And we still have the whole rest of the night. I don't want to waste it feeling sorry for myself."

A little while later they made love again, with less urgency this time, before she drifted to sleep spooned up against Marc, lulled by the sound of water lapping against a dock. Her last waking thought was, *Those honeymooners were lucky in a way. They never had to be parted.*

Anna woke early the next morning to the raucous calling of blue jays. Seeing Marc's head on the pillow next to hers, she wondered for an instant if she were still dreaming. Then he sat up and yawned, scrubbing his face with an open hand and croaking, "Morning."

"Good morning to you, too." How she'd longed to say those words to a man lying next to her in bed.

"You're not in any hurry, I hope."

His eyes traveled down her naked body. She'd thrown off the covers and her legs were stretched out languidly on the mattress in a wedge of sunlight. Normally she'd have tried to hide them, but now she examined them as dispassionately as if they belonged to someone else—a woman lying next to her on a beach perhaps. She observed that they were nicely rounded and curved in all the right spots. How was it that she hadn't noticed until now?

"It depends," she said, injecting a sultry note into her voice, "on what you have in mind."

It was another hour before they climbed out of bed, mindful of the time. They showered and dressed, meandering into the lodge to find the breakfast buffet laid out. Anna helped herself to coffee and a bowl of fruit. Food was the last thing on her mind; all she could think about was Marc. Would she see him again? From time to time, perhaps. But would that be enough? She felt torn between wanting him at any cost and hoping she wouldn't have to find out.

As they were getting up to leave, she forced herself to meet his gaze. *Don't fall in love with me,* his eyes warned, but all he said was, "Don't forget your purse." She'd been so caught up in her thoughts, she'd nearly walked off without it.

In silence they climbed the path to the parking lot. Morning sunlight winked in and out of the branches overhead, falling in bright patches over the ground cushioned with pine needles that crunched agreeably beneath their feet. When they reached his car, Marc turned to face her, taking her hand and saying gently, "I want to see you again, Anna . . . but I'm not sure it'd be such a good idea."

She held very still, like a deer at the edge of a clearing.

"It's not just that I'm married," he went on. "I'm sure you must have realized by now that I'm no saint. But those other women . . ." His eyes searched her face, pleading with her to understand, "You're not like them. I'm afraid you'd get hurt."

Anna longed to cry, *I don't care! I'll take whatever I can get!* It wasn't so much dignity that caused her to hold back as a selfish desire to hoard what little she had: If the memory of last night was all she took away from this, let it stand unblemished.

She took a deep breath of the clean air smelling of pine needles and sun-warmed timber. She could see the lake glinting through the trees below. Leaves from the white oak under which they stood drifted down like spent currency. Her heart breaking, for she was more than a little in love with him already, she said with forced lightness, "Don't worry. You won't hear from me again unless it's life or death."

She'd been thinking of Monica as she spoke. It never occurred to her that it might be her own life at stake.

CHAPTER EIGHT

If I don't look at the bars I won't scream.

Instead, Anna kept her eyes fixed on the cinderblock wall across from her. It was institutional green, its painted-over graffiti faintly visible, like ghosts communicating from beyond the grave. She drew a small amount of comfort from the knowledge that there'd been others before her, if only the likes of Waldo Squires coming off a Saturday night bender; it made her feel the tiniest bit less isolated. At the same time, a voice in her head cried over and over, *This can't be happening. It's a bad dream.*

Except in this particular nightmare, when she closed her eyes, it was only to open them again to the same green walls bathed in the stark light of overhead fluorescents.

She sat on the edge of her hard cot with her knees pulled up to her chest, but she couldn't escape the heat from the vent below that rose in dry eddies, making her skin itch and her lips crack. From behind the steel door at the end of the corridor drifted voices punctuated by an occasional raucous laugh or an order being barked, with the usual backdrop of ringing phones and clanging file cabinets. The very ordinariness of those sounds was an assault, a harsh reminder that though life as she'd known it had ended, to those outside it was just another day.

Please, Laura. Hurry up and get here.

Anna didn't know what, if anything, Laura could do, but she knew she'd feel better once she'd arrived. Which was why she hadn't wasted her one call on Liz. Her sister would have made a fuss and demanded that she be released while Laura would quietly go about accomplishing that.

For a wild moment Anna let herself imagine it was Marc coming to rescue her. But she hadn't seen him in months, not since that night at the lake (the memory of which she'd replayed so often every detail was etched in her mind). He certainly wouldn't want to hear from her now. If anything, he'd move to distance himself. An illicit affair was one thing, being linked to an accused murderess quite another. On the other hand, he'd know soon enough. It was probably all over the news by now.

Remembering the press that had been swarming outside her house, clamoring for blood, she shuddered. Most of her adult life had been spent in Monica's shadow: fans showing up unannounced at her door, as if in touching her they'd be that much closer to Monica. Reporters wanting statements. People she barely knew stopping her on the street, wanting the inside scoop. Were Monica and Nicholas Cage *really* having an affair? Was it true she'd caught her housekeeper in bed with her husband?

After the accident it only got worse. As her assistant, Anna had been thrust into the very heart of it, fielding the hundreds of interview requests that had poured in, weeding through the mountain of letters from well-wishers who said they'd pray for Monica and crackpots who thought she'd gotten what she deserved. Anna became accustomed to seeing reporters and paparazzi camped outside the gates at Lorei-

Linda, and hearing the alarm sound when one of the more intrepid ones managed to sneak onto the grounds. Even as Monica grew more reclusive, her mystique had grown. Nowadays it was mostly would-be biographers and freelancers in search of Hollywood's elusive white whale, and manufacturers and merchandisers eager to cash in on her name. It seemed the cruelest of ironies that even in death, Monica's shadow had eclipsed Anna, cutting her off from the light she'd been struggling toward.

Her thoughts were interrupted by the clanging of the door at the end of the corridor and the *shuffle-clump-shuffle-clump* of someone limping toward her. She looked up to see that it was Benny Dickerson. He stopped in front of her cell, peering in through the bars, his bassett hound eyes seeming to beg her forgiveness in some way.

"Your lawyer's here," he announced.

She blinked at him in surprise. "I didn't know I had one."

"Looks like you do now."

Laura had said something about a lawyer, but Anna hadn't expected her to come through so quickly. How long since they'd spoken—minutes, hours? She'd lost all track of time. Or maybe it had lost track of her.

She rose on legs that felt oddly elasticized, stretching up, up until she felt as if she were floating several inches off the floor. The door to her cell slid open with a clang. As she stepped out into the corridor, he took her elbow, not to keep her from bolting but in a courtly gesture that unexpectedly moved her to tears. He guided her past the empty cell next to hers, ushering her into the visitors' room just beyond. She found a middle-aged woman with blunt graying hair seated at the table that took up most of the bare, windowless space. She rose, gripping Anna's hand.

"Rhonda Talltree. Laura said you might need a lawyer."

Anna's first impression was of great height, but Rhonda was more physically imposing than tall: broad shoulders and generous bosom tapering to narrow hips with muscular arms that looked quite capable of wrestling poor Benny to the floor—an impression her jeans and cowboy boots did nothing to dispel. Anna recalled that

Rhonda was the one who'd handled Laura's divorce.

"Thanks for coming," Anna said. It was all she could manage at the moment.

"Sorry it took so long," Rhonda said. "I was in the middle of something when she called." Up close, Anna saw that her hair had as much black in it as gray. A pair of silver and turquoise earrings swung like pendulums from her ears. "By the way, she sends her love."

"She's not coming?" Anna felt crushed, like a child who'd been expecting her mother to pick her up from school only to have a stranger show up instead.

"Relax—she's just down the hall. I thought it'd be best if we spoke in private first." Rhonda dismissed Benny with a crisp nod before sitting down. "But first I should tell you I don't specialize in criminal defense. If you'd like, I could give you some names."

Anna shook her head. "Laura picked you for a reason," she said, sinking into the chair opposite Rhonda's.

Rhonda smiled, showing beautiful white teeth. "I was a deputy D.A. in Ventura for fif-

teen years—with a pretty impressive conviction rate, I might add—so I know the territory. Except I'm used to locking people up,
not the other way around."

"But I'm innocent. As soon as we clear
this up—"

"Whoa." Rhonda held out a work-rough-
ened hand adorned by a silver and
turquoise ring the size of a walnut. "The
good news is there's no smoking gun. The
bad news is you aren't going anywhere so
fast. Not until after the arraignment."

Anna's heart sank. This wasn't going to
be over anytime soon. "What happens
then?"

"You'll enter a plea and if all goes well be
released on bail."

"You mean there's a chance I might not
be?" Panic closed about her like a sweaty
fist.

Rhonda reached across the table to lay a
reassuring hand on her arm. "I promise I'll
do my best."

Anna thought of something that pushed
her panic up another notch. "I can't afford
to pay you."

"We'll worry about that later on." Rhonda
bent to retrieve a yellow legal pad from the

well-worn briefcase at her feet. "First, let's get one thing straight. If I'm to represent you, I'll need *all* the facts, no holding back." She eyed her sternly, and Anna realized Rhonda wasn't taking anything for granted.

"I have nothing to hide," she said.

"Okay. Let's start with the night in question."

"I was home."

"Any witnesses to that effect?"

She shook her head. "I live alone."

Rhonda scribbled something on her pad. "When did you last see your sister alive?"

"Around four-thirty that afternoon."

"I understand you worked for her." Laura must have given her the lowdown.

"Actually, it was my last day." Struck by the irony, Anna gave in to a small smile.

Rhonda raised a brow. "Was she upset that you were leaving?"

"She wasn't happy about it, no." Anna sighed, pushing a hand through her hair as she struggled to summon the memory she'd spent the past few days trying to block out. "We'd had words earlier in the day. It got a little heated at one point."

"Did you threaten her?"

"No, of course not."

"So as far as you know she had no reason to tell her agent that you were out to get her?"

Anna reeled as though slapped. "Where did you hear *that*?"

"I have a cousin on the force." Rhonda lowered her voice, mindful of Benny on the other side of the door. "Carlos Vasquez. You know him?"

The name was familiar. "He was out at the house once or twice." When Rhonda looked at her blankly, she added, "My mother had a tendency to wander off." And she'd thought Betty was her biggest worry. "So they really think I killed her?"

"It looks that way."

"I don't understand. How—?"

"In addition to an e-mail sent to her agent in which she claims to have felt threatened by you, there's also physical evidence linking you to the crime."

Anna's fevered mind spun. "That's impossible. I told you, I was nowhere near—"

"What can you tell me about Gardener Stevens?" Rhonda cut her off.

"He's Monica's lawyer. Why?"

"It seems that on the day she died, your

sister made an appointment to see him about her will. According to Mr. Stevens, she was planning to disinherit you. As it stands, you and your sister Elizabeth will each inherit a quarter of the estate."

"It's Liz," Anna corrected, too numb to absorb what Rhonda was saying.

"Did you know anything about this?"

"That I was in her will? Monica mentioned something awhile back." Though with her you could never be sure—she'd used money like a carrot on a stick. Anna's only concern had been that Betty would be taken care of. "But even if I'd known she was going to cut me out, I wouldn't have tried to stop her."

"Even so, this leaves you a wealthy woman."

A hot, choking anger momentarily eclipsed Anna's panic. "Are you suggesting I killed her for the money?"

"Relax. I'm on your side."

Anna eyed her warily. "You could've fooled me."

Rhonda leaned forward. "This is only a small taste of what you'll be getting from the D.A." Her dark eyes fixed on Anna with an intensity that made her flinch. "If you can't take the heat, you won't last a minute on the witness stand—if it comes to that."

Anna drew a trembling hand over her face. "I'm sorry. I'm just . . . it's been a long day."

"Understandable. Now, where were we . . . yes, the will. The prosecution is going to paint you as a desperate woman. Your mother's in a nursing home and you're struggling to make ends meet. To top it off, you just lost your job and your rich sister's planning to cut you out of her will." Rhonda paused to let it sink in.

Beneath her forbidding gaze, Anna sensed a compassion that was kept under wraps for reasons that had been lost on her a minute ago but which she now understood—it was of little value in these circumstances.

The enormity of it swept over her in a chilling wave. "So I'm guilty until proven innocent; is that what you're saying?"

"Not quite. The burden of proof is still on the prosecution, and as far as I can see, what they have is mainly circumstantial." Her gaze dropped to Anna's arm. "Want to tell me about those scratches?"

Anna self-consciously lowered her arm into her lap. "They're from my cat."

"I know that's what you told the police."

Looking into Rhonda's flat, disbelieving gaze, Anna felt stupid. What had she expected to gain from lying? In a voice barely above a whisper, she admitted, "Okay, it was Monica. But it was an accident—she was drunk and fell out of her chair. I was helping her up and—" She lifted her arm to show the barely healed scratches extending from the inside of her elbow to her wrist.

"Why didn't you tell that to the police?"

"I didn't want them to think . . ." She drew in a ragged breath. "It was my job to protect her."

"That's not how it'd look to a jury."

Anna felt the bottom drop out of her stomach. "You . . . you really think it'll come to that?"

"Unless we cut a deal, which would mean you pleading to a lesser charge." Rhonda's black eyes bored into her. "But before we go any further, there's something I need to know. Did you harm Monica in any way . . . even unintentionally?"

"No!" Anna realized she'd spoken too sharply and lowered her voice. "I mean, we'd had our differences. And I'll admit things got a little hairy at the end. But I *never* . . ." She broke off, bringing a loose, trembling fist to her mouth.

"Can you think of anyone else who might have wanted her dead—ex-husbands, former lovers, disgruntled employees?"

"It's a long list." Anna gave in to a small, bleak smile. "My sister . . ." She hesitated, not wanting to speak ill of the dead. "Let's just say she wasn't very well liked." Glenn didn't count; he'd been spared the brunt of her wrath. "But no one hated her enough to kill her, not that I know of, anyway."

"Okay. Let's back up a little." Rhonda leaned forward on her elbows, hands clasped in front of her as in prayer. "You said you left your sister's around four-thirty that afternoon. Did you drive straight home?"

"Yes."

"No stopping for gas or groceries?"

Anna shook her head. If only she'd known, she'd have filled her tank, run all her errands, and stuffed her face at Wendy's where everyone could see.

"I asked Laura if she could vouch for you," Rhonda went on, her mouth stretching in a humorless smile. She didn't have to say it: Laura would have done anything for her except lie in court. "Not that it would prove anything even if she had seen you. You could have driven back to your sister's later on."

Anna slumped back in her chair. "I was tired. I went to bed early."

"Other than that, how were you feeling?"

"I'm not sure what you're getting at."

"You weren't angry at Monica?"

"Not really, no."

"Even though you'd had words?"

"I was used to it," Anna said. "She had a temper, but it usually blew over pretty quickly."

She saw something flicker in Rhonda's eyes. Disbelief? Disgust? She glanced once more at her notes. "According to the coroner's report, her blood alcohol level at the time of death was point one three five. That's more than twice the legal limit. You weren't worried about leaving her alone in that state?"

Anna waited for the usual guilt to kick in, but all she felt was shame for having put up with Monica for as long as she had. "It wasn't the first time."

"Laura mentioned that she'd been in rehab."

Anna nodded. "It was only in the past few weeks that I noticed she was drinking again." A deep sorrow welled up in her. It was one thing for Monica to have died so horribly, but for her to have been drunk at the time seemed the ultimate indignity. "I guess the pull was too strong."

"Tell me about it. I work with FAS kids—I teach them to ride. That's where I was when Laura called."

FAS—fetal alcohol syndrome. Anna supposed she ought to be grateful they'd been spared that at least; Monica had never wanted children.

"I've gotten to know some of the mothers," Rhonda went on. "Even the ones who eventually get sober are reminded constantly of how they fucked up." She smiled grimly. "Your sister must've been pissed that you'd stopped picking up the pieces."

"You don't know the half of it," Anna said with a sigh.

"Was that why you quit?"

"Among other things." Anna hesitated, not sure it was worth mentioning. "I used to be fat. I think Monica liked me better that way."

"Let me guess; she wasn't the center of attention anymore?"

"Something like that." The incident with Glenn in the pool house reared its ugly head, but she quickly pushed it away; she didn't want to think about that right now.

"That might explain why she felt threatened. Things can get twisted in people's minds, especially when large quantities of alcohol are involved."

Anna shook her head. "I wish now I'd handled it differently. If I'd stayed the night, she might still be alive."

"Or it might be your funeral instead."

Anna felt a chill travel up her spine. It hadn't occurred to her that she might have been targeted as well. "Do the police have any other leads?"

"They found signs of a trespasser—some footprints in the dirt by the outer wall. But there's no way of determining how long they'd been there." This wasn't news to Anna; she'd been over it all with the police. They hadn't pursued it for precisely that reason—it rained so infrequently in Carson

Springs, the prints could've been weeks old.

Still, she asked, "Do you think there's anything to it?"

"Hard to say. There wasn't a trace of anything tracked onto the patio or into the house. No sign of forced entry either."

"Which puts us back at square one."

"Was she expecting any visitors that night?"

"Not that I know of." Glenn occasionally dropped by on short notice, but with anyone else it would've been on the calendar.

"All right, I'll nose around a bit and see what I can find out." Rhonda tucked the pad back into her briefcase. "In the meantime, I'd like you to put together a list of names. Anyone you can think of who might know something . . . or be involved."

Anna closed her eyes, trying to shut out the image that filled her head: Monica floating facedown in the pool, her limbs pale as water lilies against the dark fabric that billowed about her lifeless form. She shuddered. No, she couldn't think of anyone who'd hated her sister that much.

She jerked at the sound of Rhonda's chair scraping back. "I'll let you know as soon as the hearing is scheduled. We'll talk more then," her lawyer said.

Anna's mind leaped ahead. "Oh, God. The funeral. It's the day after tomorrow."

"We should have you out on bail by then." Rhonda put a hand on her arm, steadying her the way Anna imagined she would a fearful child on horseback. "Try not to worry too much. And get some sleep. We have a long day ahead of us."

Sleep? Anna had forgotten what that was. Every time she started to drift off, the nightmare images would loom. But all she said was, "I'll do my best."

Laura was allowed in for a few minutes after that. In her jeans and sweatshirt, she looked as if she'd been out riding, too. Anna noticed a piece of straw stuck to her flyaway brown hair as they embraced.

"Are you okay? Never mind, that was dumb. How *could* you be?" Laura's brown eyes were bright with unshed tears.

"Thanks for sending Rhonda." Anna struggled to hold her own tears in check. It was as though she'd been lost in the woods, wandering aimlessly for hours, and Laura's dear face had materialized like a lighted window out of the darkness.

"You're in good hands. She's the best."

"She seems to know what she's doing."

Laura mustered a smile. "You'll be out in no time."

"I'll be lucky to get out on bail."

"But you're innocent!"

"That's not how they see it."

"Oh, Anna." A tear slipped down Laura's cheek. "I can't believe it. *You,* of all people."

Anna felt an urge to console her friend, but she knew they'd both end up sobbing. She swallowed hard. "Have you told Finch?"

Laura nodded. "She's in shock, like the rest of us. She said to tell you not to worry about Boots. She'll make sure he gets fed."

"The key's—"

"—under the mat. I know." Laura brushed away her tears. "Is there anything else we can do, anything at all?"

"Call Liz. Tell her everything's set for the funeral; all she just has to do is confirm with the florist. His number's on the pad by my kitchen phone. She'll need to get in touch with Glenn, too. He's coordinating things at his end."

The irony didn't strike her until Laura gave a tearful laugh, saying, "If you wrote it in a book, no one would believe it." Who but Anna would be orchestrating the funeral of the very person she was supposed to have murdered?

She smiled. "I don't suppose they would."

Their time was up. She hugged Laura at the door.

"Is there anyone else I should call?" Laura held on to her, reluctant to let go.

Anna thought once more of Marc. She wanted desperately to see him, but knew how devastated she'd be if he didn't come. She couldn't take that risk. Not now, when she felt so vulnerable. She shook her head, answering, "No one I can think of."

Anna slept fitfully. When she woke, it was to the merciless high noon of the fluorescents. How long had she slept? It couldn't have been more than a few hours for she still felt drugged with exhaustion, her eyes grainy and her head stuffed full of cotton. She sat up, listening for the familiar cacophony of the bullpen, but the only sounds now were the ticking of a heater vent and faint buzzing from the fixture overhead. It was almost a relief when the door at the end of the corridor clanged open and Benny once more shuffled into view, balancing her dinner tray in one hand and holding his bad hip braced with the other.

He pushed the tray through the slot in her cell door—meatloaf and mashed potatoes glistening with gravy. The smell brought a wave of nausea. "I came before but you were out like a light. I warmed it up in the microwave," he said. She was touched by his consideration; it made her feel a little less alone. "Eat up now, you hear. Ain't nothing bad that was ever made good by an empty belly." His voice was low, almost conspiratorial, as if they'd been hatching a plan of escape.

Anna forced a smile. "Thanks, Benny."

"If there's anything I can do . . ." His drooping eyes regarded her dolefully.

"Just keep the faith." She patted the large freckled hand curled about the bars.

Benny started back down the corridor, his shadow lurching along the wall. He was almost to the end when he paused and turned around. "Oh, I almost forgot. There was a fellow here to see you a bit ago."

She felt a surge of hope. Marc? But it

could have been anyone—Hector or Father Reardon. "Did you get his name?" She struggled to keep her voice even.

"Can't say that I did."

"What did he look like?"

"Young fellow. Tall, dark hair." Her heart sank, then she remembered that to an old guy like Benny anyone under fifty would seem young. As if picking up on her thoughts, he asked slyly, "Wouldn't be your boyfriend, would it?"

She didn't bother to deny it. "Did he say when he'd be back?"

Benny dropped his gaze. "Sorry, Anna, but the chief left orders—no more visitors tonight. He says this ain't no hotel."

Anna felt the walls closing in on her. "Benny, please." She was gripping the bars so hard she'd lost sensation in her fingertips. "It's important. Maybe life or death." She didn't know if that was true, but right now it seemed that way. "You've got to help me."

"Well now, Anna, you know I can't do that." He stumped back toward her to whisper sotto voce, "I could get suspended. And with me coming up on retirement." He leaned heavily onto his good leg, his hip thrust out in a pose that might have been comical if not for the anguished look on his face. "But I'll tell you what . . ." He licked his lips, casting a furtive glance over his shoulder. "If your fella shows up while the chief's still on his break, I'll give you a few minutes." He shook his head, as if puzzling over his own foolhardiness. "Guess it's the least I can do . . . after the way you looked after the missus."

Anna recalled that his wife, Myrna, had recently passed away. But what had she done other than drop by the hospital a few times to comfort a dying woman? Anyone would've done the same. "I won't forget it, Benny," she said hoarsely, her eyes filling with tears.

When he was gone she sank down on the cot, drawing her knees up to her chest. The hysteria she'd been staving off crept up on her and she began to laugh soundlessly, tears streaming down her cheeks. She'd longed for Marc, but never in a million years could she have imagined the circumstances that would bring him.

It seemed an eternity before Benny reappeared with a taller man walking a few feet behind him. Her heart leaped.

"Marc," she breathed.

He drew to a halt in front of her cell. His eyes burned in the cold white light, and she had the sense of being embraced though he hadn't so much as touched her. Then the door slid back and he stepped inside.

"Five minutes," Benny muttered with a glance at his watch before discreetly moving up the corridor.

Marc drew her into his arms, roughly almost. "I jumped in the car as soon as I heard. I couldn't fucking believe it."

It was all she could do to keep from dissolving. "Me neither."

He drew back, his eyes searching her face. "Are you all right?"

She managed a small smile. "I've had better days."

"I wanted to call when I heard about Monica, but . . ." His eyes cut away.

She felt a spark of anger. *Why didn't you then?* But she knew it would only have made things more difficult, for both of them. "You're here now; that's all that counts."

"Do you have a lawyer?" he asked.

She nodded. "As of today."

"Is he any good? Because I could make a few calls."

"It's a she, and I'll know more tomorrow." She didn't feel like discussing Rhonda. "Just hold me, Marc. That's all I need from you right now." She burrowed into his arms, conscious of Benny standing just a few feet away.

"Poor Anna." He stroked her hair, and she caught his scent—the same scent that had lingered on her clothing after that night at the lake. Nestled in his arms, she felt safe for the first time all day.

"It all seems so unreal." Her voice was muffled by his shirt. "Even Monica's being dead."

"I'm sorry about your sister."

"You don't think I killed her, do you?" She drew back, eyeing him with something close to panic. If Marc had suspicions . . .

"Of course not." It was obvious there wasn't a doubt in his mind. A wave of relief washed through her. "Do you have any idea who might have?"

She shook her head. "Not a clue."

"We'll deal with that later. Right now, we have to get you out of here."

"My lawyer's on it."

"How can I help?"

"I guess," she said slowly, "that's up to you."

He regarded her in silence. They both knew what it would mean for him to get in any deeper: It could end up doing more harm than good. But all he said was, "I'm staying at the inn. Let me know as soon as you hear anything. I'll be there as long as you need me."

It all came rushing back: the moon caught in a windowpane, the sound of water lapping against a dock, Marc's breath warm against her cheek. The memory was almost more than she could bear. She fixed her gaze on a button on his shirt that was loose—something a wife would have noticed. "I should know more by tomorrow."

"You'll call me?"

She nodded. "There *is* something you could do in the meantime," she told him.

"Name it." He looked relieved to be of some use.

"Liz. Would you talk to her? I'm sure she's worried."

"I'll drop by on my way to the inn."

Anna scribbled her sister's number on the back of one of his business cards. "Tell her . . ." She shrugged. "Nothing. Just that I'm okay."

An awkward silence fell. Then Marc asked, "Does she know about us?"

She smiled and shook her head. "No." She'd seen no reason to tell Liz.

She saw the regret in his eyes. "If it counts for anything, I'm sorry about the way it was left."

"You didn't lie to me, at least." A trace of bitterness crept into her voice nonetheless.

"I thought about you. A lot."

She looked at him long and hard. "I missed you every minute of every day." Before today, she'd have died rather than admit it, but such concerns seemed silly now, like worrying about your clothes getting wet while you were drowning.

He smiled crookedly. "Be careful what you wish for, right?" He brushed his knuckles lightly along her cheek, leaving a faint trail of fire.

"I'm glad you came."

"Me, too."

Benny cleared his throat to let them know their time was up. Marc hugged her tightly. She could feel his heart beating and for a fleeting second mistook it for her own. She tilted her head back and brought her mouth up to meet Marc's. His kiss was balm to her frayed nerves.

Reluctantly they drew apart.

"Tomorrow," he said.

"If I make it through the night."

"Just remember—you're not alone."

She felt some of the tension go out of her. *I love you.* The words were on the tip of her tongue. But all she could do was mouth them to his retreating back.

Marc drove carefully, negotiating the steep, twisting road as if around any bend might lie the answer to the questions gnawing at him. He'd gotten only the sketchiest of details from CNN, but he knew they wouldn't have arrested Anna without sufficient evidence. Had she been framed? And if so, by whom? Only one thing was certain: He wouldn't be getting much sleep tonight. In fact, he hadn't had a good night's sleep since . . .

He gave his head a little shake to clear it. He'd spent the past four months trying to rationalize it out of existence, but the truth was he felt something for her. It had caught him off guard, especially after knowing her for so short a time. He hadn't been hit this hard since that day he'd first laid eyes on Faith, chatting with a friend on the Stanford quad, a breeze flirting with the hem of her skirt—a *skirt,* in the days when you couldn't tell the girls and boys apart from behind. Anna was nothing at all like Faith . . . but the feeling, like a bone in his throat, that was the same.

He couldn't turn his back on her any more than he could on Faith. And maybe he needed something from Anna as well, if only to know that he was making a difference in some way. He couldn't save his wife, but maybe he could save Anna.

He squinted, straining to make out street signs in the glare of his headlights. Liz had told him to look for the one to the hot springs, and finally he spotted it, just ahead on his right.

Moments later he was turning onto a narrow graveled lane. His headlights panned over dense trees and shrubs before an A-frame cabin sided in cedar shingles came into view. Farther up the hill he could see the spa illuminated by floodlights, rustic contemporary with Asian overtones—Frank Lloyd Wright meets I. M. Pei.

A Jeep Cherokee was parked in the driveway next to Liz's red Miata. She hadn't mentioned company. Was he intruding? No, she would have said so. Though surprised to hear from him, she'd seemed eager for any information he could give her.

He knocked, then stood cooling his heels for a good minute or so before the door opened a crack and she peered out at him over the chain. "Marc, hi. I didn't expect you to get here so quickly." She fumbled with the chain and stepped aside to let him in, looking nervous for some reason. "Sorry about the mess," she apologized. "I haven't had a chance to clean up."

He entered a small living room with an open-beamed ceiling and fireplace. On the sofa was a basket of laundry waiting to be folded, but otherwise the room looked neat enough. Liz was a mess, though. In her leggings and rumpled T-shirt, her hair mussed as though she'd just climbed out of bed, she looked nothing like the stylish woman he remembered from family week.

He heard a cough in the next room, and asked, "Is this a bad time?"

Liz darted a glance over her shoulder. "No, not really. My friend, um, he was just leaving. Can I get you something to drink? There's wine in the fridge." Before he could remind her that he didn't drink, she said, "Sorry. I wasn't thinking. How about a soda?"

"A glass of water would be fine."

She made no move toward the kitchen; she just stood there looking up at him, her brow creased with consternation. "Tell me about Anna. I've been worried sick."

"Under the circumstances, she's about as well as can be expected."

"I couldn't believe it when I heard." He saw the hurt in her eyes that she hadn't been the first person Anna called.

"I couldn't, either," he said. "That's why I'm here."

Liz shook her head. "It's like some kind of nightmare. First Monica . . . and now this."

He lowered himself onto the sofa, the smell of clean laundry drifting toward him. "Do you have any idea who might have wanted her dead?"

"You're asking the wrong person. Monica and I . . . well, we weren't exactly close."

She shrugged. "I guess blood isn't always thicker than water."

"You were there for her when she needed you." Though at family week Liz had seemed dragged there against her will. It was only toward the end that she'd opened up.

Liz's mouth stretched in a mirthless smile. "I did it for Anna. As far as I'm concerned she's the only sister I ever had."

He eyed a framed photo on the mantel of a smiling, gap-toothed boy. "Your son?"

Her expression softened. "Dylan. He's eight."

"Good-looking kid."

"He's at his dad's. Brett has him two nights a week."

"Sounds like a good arrangement."

Her cheeks colored as if she'd read more into his offhanded remark. Just then a man's voice speaking low into a phone drifted from down the hall.

Liz hurried out of the room, returning moments later with a tumbler of ice water in one hand and a glass of wine in the other. As she handed him the water, he caught her eyeing him with her old wariness: She had a jaundiced view of shrinks. "Don't take it the wrong way, Doc, but isn't this outside your jurisdiction?" She spoke lightly, but he caught the edge in her voice.

He smiled. "I'm not here in a professional capacity."

She cocked her head, regarding him with a puzzled look. Then her eyes widened in comprehension. "I see." The surprised hurt on her face said it all: Why hadn't Anna trusted her enough to tell her? "I guess I don't know my sister as well as I thought."

He could see that she was curious to know more, but all he said was, "The only thing that matters now is getting her out of jail. I'm here to help however I can."

With a deep sigh Liz dropped into the chair opposite him. "So what happens now? Laura said something about an arraignment."

"We should know more tomorrow."

"But you *do* believe she's innocent?" Marc let his silence speak for itself, prompting Liz to speculate darkly, "I'll bet Glenn had something to do with it. I never trusted that guy."

"Glenn?" He leaned forward with interest.

"Monica's agent. I'm surprised Anna didn't mention him."

"What makes you think he's involved?"

She shrugged. "Who knows? Maybe they were lovers and he caught her in bed with another man. Or maybe he thought he could make more money off her dead. All I know is, he puts the sleaze in sleazy agent."

A man stepped out of the hallway into the living room just then. He was tall and tanned, with the kind of all-American good looks you'd expect to see on a box of Wheaties. "Hi, I'm David." He smiled genially, extending his hand. In his tan slacks and blue Izod shirt, a lock of sun-streaked brown hair dipping over his forehead, he might have been a first-pick NFL draft, though he had to be closer to Marc's age.

Marc stood to shake his hand. "Marc Raboy. Sorry for busting in on you like this. Liz didn't tell me she had company."

"No problem. I was just on my way out." His smile faded, replaced by a look of concern. "How's Anna? I came over as soon as I heard. I thought . . ." He and Liz exchanged a coded glance. "Anything I can do to help?"

"We'll let you know."

David turned once more to Liz. "You'll call me?"

"Of course." She spoke lightly.

"Stop by the café if you get a chance," he told Marc. "It's the Tree House. Ask anyone, they'll point you in the right direction." Marc noted his wedding band. So that's why Liz had seemed so nervous—not that Marc was in any position to judge.

He smiled. "Thanks. I just may do that."

David reached for the blazer folded over the chair by the door. "Well, it was nice meeting you. When you see Anna, tell her that her friends are behind her a hundred and ten percent. If she needs anything, all she has to do is ask."

"I'll walk you to your car." Liz leaped to her feet, looking flushed. Marc didn't think it was from the wine.

When she returned several minutes later, he stood up. "I should be going, too."

She followed him to the door. "I know what you're thinking," she blurted as he was stepping outside. He paused. Clearly she needed to get it off her chest. "He's married, okay, but there's more to it than that." She leaned into the doorway, one bare foot atop the other, an expression on her face like that of a guilty child wanting desperately to be forgiven.

"You don't owe me an explanation," he said gently.

She let out a ragged breath. "You won't say anything to Anna, will you?"

"Like I said, it's none of my business." He didn't add that Anna had far more pressing concerns at the moment.

"David's a friend of the family," she went on regardless. "We all used to hang out together at the café back when David's father ran it. He and I even dated for a while in high school." She gazed sightlessly out at the wooded darkness. "We both got married around the same time. It's only since my divorce that we . . ." She brought her gaze back to him with a rueful little grimace. "And here you thought this was all about Anna." Her eyes searched his face. "What's going to happen to her, Marc?"

"I wish I could tell you . . . but there are times when even shrinks don't have all the answers," he said with a touch of irony.

The phone rang just then, and Liz dashed back inside to answer it. After a moment he heard her say breathlessly, "Okay . . . yeah . . . I'll be there . . . thanks." She hung up and looked back at Marc, standing on the stoop, his heart beating in time with the moth pummeling itself to death against the porch light. "That was Laura," she told him. "The hearing's tomorrow at eleven."

CHAPTER NINE

Anna glanced about the courtroom. The last time she'd been there had been years ago on jury duty—a malpractice suit that was settled out of court. The high ceiling and dark oak wainscoting, the gilded state seal over the judge's bench, had seemed grand then, not frightening. She looked over at Rhonda, seated beside her, cool and poised in her gray suit and pearls, while Anna felt heavy with exhaustion, every muscle aching from her night in jail. A pulse throbbed in one eyelid, and there was a taste like old pennies in her mouth. Glancing over her shoulder, she was relieved to see Laura seated up front, with Hector, Maude, and Finch. Marc and Liz rounded out the row—the six of them forming a bulwark against the reporters and thrill seekers packing the gallery.

The formalities had been dispensed with. Now the judge leaned forward, his gaze directed at Rhonda. "Ms. Talltree, does your client wish to enter a plea at this time?"

Rhonda stood up. "Yes, Your Honor—not guilty. At this time I'd like to move that the charges be dismissed. They're entirely unfounded, and the so-called evidence linking my client to this crime is flimsy at best."

"That remains to be seen, Counsel." His gaze was flat, unreadable. "Motion denied."

Anna found herself staring at the clumps of hair sprouting from the nostrils of the Honorable Emory Cartwright, an otherwise perfectly presentable middle-aged man with pale blue eyes and thinning brown hair. She remembered seeing him in church. An Episcopalian married to a Catholic, he compromised by occasionally attending mass with his wife. She recalled, too, that Leonore Cartwright's contribution to their last bake sale had been a sour cherry pie—her husband's favorite, she'd said.

Rhonda didn't look fazed. "In the matter of bail," she went on smoothly, "I move that

Ms. Vincenzi be released on her own recognizance."

He glanced at the file. "No prior record, I see."

"She also has deep ties to the community and is active in her church." Rhonda rested a hand on Anna's shoulder. "Her mother and surviving sister live here as well. In fact, I've asked Liz Vincenzi to testify today on her sister's behalf."

The judge directed his gaze at the D.A., a heavyset man in a double-breasted suit with a ruddy face and blond combover. "Mr. Showalter?"

Showalter whispered something to one of his cronies and rose. Anna was reminded of a fifth-grade bully looking for someone to pick on. "Your Honor, I'm sure Ms. Vincenzi is kind to animals, too, and that she gives to the March of Dimes." She cringed at his snide tone. "But we've all known wolves in sheeps' clothing. We're talking about a woman who pushed her sister, a paraplegic, into the pool and watched her drown, ignoring her cries for help." He turned slightly as though addressing the thronged gallery, pausing for dramatic effect. "A woman like that would stop at nothing."

Anna felt the blood drain from her face, but Rhonda remained calm. "Your Honor, even if she *wanted* to, my client is in no position to go anywhere." She submitted Anna's expired passport and bank records, before calling Liz to the stand.

"Ms. Vincenzi, what is your relationship to the defendant?" Rhonda asked after she'd been sworn in.

Liz, elegantly feminine in a navy suit and shirred pink blouse, leaned into the microphone. "I'm her sister."

"What was your reaction when you heard she'd been arrested?"

Liz sat up straighter, her eyes flashing. "It's beyond outrageous. Anna wouldn't hurt a fly! Whatever you're up to here—" She shot a fierce look at Showalter.

The judge warned her to refrain from such comments.

Anna felt as if she were observing it all from a distance, hearing them talk about someone she didn't know. Even sounds were distorted, the rustles and coughs and shuffling of feet seeming to echo as if in a cavern.

She felt some of the tension go out of her when the judge pronounced, "Given the defendant's ties to the community, I don't think she poses a significant flight risk." But before she could breathe a sigh of relief, he went on to say, "Nonetheless, due to the seriousness of the charges, bail is set at five hundred thousand." His gavel banged down. "I want to caution you both," he warned, with baleful looks at the lawyers, "that any attempts to try this case in the court of public opinion will *not* be viewed favorably." He pointedly eyed the reporters scribbling in their notepads.

Anna sat there, stunned. Half a million dollars? How could she raise even the 10 percent she'd need to post bond? She was only dimly aware of Rhonda's squeezing her shoulder. She felt numb all over, as if anesthetized.

"Anna?" Her lawyer's voice seemed to come from far away.

She tried to stand up, but her knees buckled and she sagged back into her chair. In a calm voice that bore no relation to the thundering in her head, she said, "I'm fine, really. I just need to . . . to . . ." Suddenly she was having trouble catching her breath.

Rhonda took hold of her elbow, assisting her to her feet. As Anna stood there, swaying unsteadily and gripping the back of her chair, it occurred to her that she was now in the same boat as her mother—dependent on others for every little thing. She turned to her lawyer, saying in a hoarse whisper, "I don't have that kind of money."

"We'll work something out," Rhonda murmured, casting a hopeful glance at Liz. But Anna knew her sister didn't have that kind of money either. Ironically, the only one who could have afforded to bail her out was Monica.

Laura rushed up to throw her arms about Anna. "Thank God! I thought I'd die if I had to sit there another minute." She glared at Showalter and his cronies as they disappeared through a side door. Her eyes were red-rimmed and her nose pink from crying. Pills of Kleenex dotted the front of her dark green turtleneck. "We'll get the money somehow; don't worry." She cast a wild look at Hector. Anna didn't doubt they'd have taken out a loan on their ranch if it wasn't already mortgaged to the hilt.

Hector put a brotherly arm around Anna's shoulders. He smelled of Old Spice and, more faintly, of the barn where he spent most of his waking hours. "I've got a little bit set aside." It wouldn't be nearly enough, Anna knew, but the gesture moved her deeply.

"If only we could use the money from the calendar." Maude's soft little face crinkled with concern. In her ruffled yellow dress, she might have been a canary that had flown in through the window.

Anna recalled that the calendar, featuring tasteful seminude photos of the ladies in Maude's sewing circle, most of them grandmothers, had created quite a stir when it had gone on sale last Christmas. Thanks to an article in the *Clarion,* its modest first printing had sold out in days and it had since gone back to press several times, making minor celebrities of Maude and her friends. But even if it had been offered to her, Anna wouldn't have dreamed of taking money slated for charity.

"This sucks." Finch's dark eyes glittered and slashes of color stood out on her cheekbones. She knew all too well what it was like to be caught in the slowly grinding gears of the system.

"I'll be okay," Anna said softly, touching the girl's rigid arm. "What counts is that you're here. I don't know what I'd do without you guys." She swallowed against the lump in her throat, glancing from one to the other. Her gaze lingered on Marc, standing slightly apart from the others, and he nodded slowly in return.

Liz slipped a folded piece of paper into her hand. "Dylan made it for you." Anna unfolded it to find a crude crayon drawing of her house with Boots in front and a fat yellow sun overhead. Printed in uneven block letters across the bottom were the words DON'T BE SAD.

She felt a hot pressure behind her eyes and willed herself not to cry, knowing that once she started, she wouldn't be able to stop. "Tell him I'll try. And that . . ." She started to choke up. "His aunt Anna sends him a big kiss."

Liz looked close to tears herself. "Everything's all set for tomorrow. I spoke with Glenn. According to him, everyone who's anyone will be there." Her distaste for Monica's agent was written all over her face even as she gave a small ironic smile. "It's too bad Monica isn't here to see it. She'd be loving every minute of it."

Anna felt some of her numbness fade, replaced by panic. In all the excitement over today's hearing, the funeral had slipped her mind. What if she didn't get out in time? Not to be at her sister's funeral . . . it was unimaginable.

The bailiff was approaching and Finch stepped in front of Anna as if to shield her, saying in a fierce low voice, "Remember—they can't get to you if you don't let them." Anna's last image of the outside world as she was led away in handcuffs was of a slender dark-eyed girl in a skirt and peasant blouse, scowling at no one in particular.

"We could go door-to-door. It's always harder for people to say no to your face." Finch glanced from Andie to Simon, then across the table at Lucien, who sat thoughtfully sipping his Coke.

"We could also lose a couple of fingers that way," Simon reasoned.

Andie shot him a dirty look. "I think most people will want to help."

Simon poked at the glasses sliding down his nose. "All I'm saying is that the law of averages—"

Andie gave him a good-natured punch in the arm. "You may be smart, but you don't know everything." At times they acted more like brother and sister, Finch observed, though Simon could be romantic, like the time he'd surprised Andie with tickets to an Enrique Iglesias concert—the last thing he'd've gone to on his own.

"Who's with me on this?" After this morning's hearing, Finch had convened an emergency meeting at the Tree House Café. Now she glanced about the table, well aware that spending their spring break canvassing neighborhoods wasn't anyone's idea of a fun time.

"I'm in," Lucien said. "What do you say we pair up?" He glanced at Finch. "That way if there's any trouble, we'll have backup."

"Good point. I'll be there to protect Simon if anyone gives him a hard time." Andie grinned at her boyfriend, who, it was true, looked more likely to beat someone at chess than with his fists.

"Okay, you go with Simon, and I'll go with

Lucien." Finch kept her gaze averted so Lucien wouldn't read the expression on her face. So far she'd managed to keep him at a comfortable arm's length. They usually hung out with Andie and Simon, and the few times they'd been alone together she'd stuck with neutral topics. After she'd begged off that first weekend, saying she had to work, he hadn't asked her to his house since. Maybe he sensed she wasn't ready.

Andie raised her glass. "To the Anna Vincenzi Defense Fund. I want you guys to know I'm giving up a Little Flowers retreat for this," she said with a laugh. It had gotten to be a joke that because of her mother's association with the church, she was invited to every Catholic Youth event. "What about you?" She turned to Simon.

He shrugged, saying with a straight face, "I was going to jet off to the Middle East to help negotiate a peace treaty, but I guess they'll have to do without me."

Andie and Finch giggled, but Lucien remained silent. Over winter break his dad had taken him skiing in Vail. What exotic locale would it have been this time? She felt a tiny stab of resentment, but realized it wasn't fair. Whatever his plans, he was willing to sacrifice them for Anna.

Get real. He's doing it for you, said a voice inside her head. She pushed the thought away, looking up at a little boy scampering up the ladder of the tree house overhead.

Andie was always teasing her about Lucien's being her boyfriend. In actual fact, they hadn't so much as held hands. Not that she hadn't considered it, but why mess up a good thing? Every guy she'd ever screwed had screwed with her head. As an added bonus, one had given her gonorrhea.

"All for one, and one for all." Simon clinked his glass against Andie's.

"Through thick and thin . . . or should I say sick and sin," Andie seconded.

Finch felt a lump form in her throat—where would she be without her friends? She said briskly, "Okay, let's map out the territories. I think we should start with our own neighborhoods, don't you?"

"Yeah, it's harder to say no when they know you." Andie stirred her soda thoughtfully with her straw. "When I sold Girl Scout cookies, Mrs. Chadwick next door always bought at least ten boxes."

"Hey, I've got an even better idea. We could do a TV pitch." Simon spoke sarcastically, eyeing a table of reporters at the other end of the patio, who, with all their cameras and gear, looked as if they were on safari.

Remembering the scene at the courthouse—the crush of bodies and the barrage of blinding flashes—Finch shuddered at the thought of repeating the experience.

Glancing about the crowded patio, she was reassured by the sight of the portly Reverend Mr. Grigsby with his equally round dachshund Lily, her crippled hind legs strapped to a set of custom wheels. And Doc Henry, who'd been out twice last week to check up on Punch's spavined hoof. Red-haired Myrna McBride from The Last Word bookstore was lunching with Gayle Warrington from Up and Away Travel, and at the table next to them sat Sam's geeky lawyer friend Mr. Kemp with his girlfriend Ms. Hicks from the library. Ms. Hicks caught her eye and waved; she was helping Finch research a paper on honeybees, inspired by Blessed Bee.

She spotted Ms. Elliston, the school nurse, browsing among the shelves of used books in back. She was one of those people you barely knew was there until you had to go to the infirmary—colorless and seemingly humorless, her dishwater hair tucked behind her ears and her eyes faded like something that'd been sitting too long on a shelf. Yet the time Finch had skinned her knee playing soccer, Ms. Elliston had swabbed and bandaged it with the utmost gentleness, speaking in low soothing tones to put her at ease.

The little boy in the tree house called out to his mother below, who sat sipping an iced tea and reading a tattered paperback. Finch wondered what it would've been like to have grown up in Carson Springs, where even people who didn't know you greeted you as if they did and the only real nutcase was old Clem Woolley, who was harmless enough—never mind he never went anywhere without his invisible sidekick Jesus. Then she remembered that though Anna had lived here all her life, it hadn't prevented her from being thrown in jail for something she didn't do, and she shivered a little in the warm sunshine.

The clicking of a shutter—one of the reporters snapping a shot of the centuries-old oak for which the Tree House was named—

caused her to start. Her thoughts returned to the matter at hand. She said, "I know someone who might help."

"Who?" Andie asked.

"Father Reardon. He could make an announcement on Sunday. You know, like for the food drive at Christmas."

Andie perked up. "Great idea. I'll get my mom to ask him." He was one of Gerry's closest friends, thus the natural choice.

"I could also hit my dad up." Lucien spoke lightly, as if not wanting to make a big deal of his father's being rich. "If you get him in the right mood, he's usually pretty generous."

Finch's gaze dropped to the arm draped casually over the back of his chair. Though the day was warm, unseasonably so for April, his long-sleeved shirt remained buttoned at the cuffs. Maybe one day he'd tell her about the scar on his wrist.

Simon excused himself to buy a map from the gift shop in back. When they'd divvied up the territories, Finch pushed her chair back, saying, "Okay, let's get started." The day was half over already, and the Flats, where she and Lucien were headed first, spread out over several miles.

They were making their way across the patio when Simon stopped short. "I almost forgot." He fished a folded piece of notepaper from his pocket and handed it to Finch. "I keep meaning to give you this. Arthur, the guy who wrote the book, turned me on to this other guy who knew Lorraine. Believe it or not, I even got her address."

There was a Pasadena address scribbled on it. In all the excitement over Anna, Finch had forgotten about Lorraine Wells. She thanked Simon, tucking it into her purse. She'd deal with it later—or maybe not at all. Right now, she had more pressing concerns.

Minutes later she and Lucien were heading out to the Flats in his brand-new yellow Aztec, a present from his dad for Lucien's sixteenth birthday. Orange trees slid past in neat rows. In the distance, hills so thick with poppies they looked dusted in gold rose to meet the snow-capped mountains.

"Who's Lorraine?" Lucien asked casually.

"No one." She shrugged, not wanting to get into it.

He didn't press the subject except to shoot her a questioning look. She studied his profile. His features were oddly delicate, almost poetic, like the etching of Byron on the wall in Ms. Miller's class. In the past she'd always gone for the macho type—guys who were older because they'd been held back a grade or two, most of them dark-haired with perpetual five o'clock shadow and attitude to burn. Yet despite his preppie clothes and hands that looked as if they'd done nothing more demanding than scribble in his journal, there was an air about Lucien that she found strangely electrifying. He wasn't afraid, of anyone or anything.

Not even death, she thought, a chill tiptoeing up her spine.

"Tell me it's none of my business, if you like," he said after a minute or so. "Just don't say it's nothing."

"I didn't mean it that way." She looked out at the trees rippling past. "Listen, it's no big deal. Just this lady Simon thought I might want to look up."

"What for?"

"We have the same last name."

"Kiley?"

She hesitated, then said, "No, Wells."

"So that's your real name, huh?" He sounded intrigued. She'd told him she was adopted, but very little beyond that—the less he knew, the better.

"Kiley *is* my real name." Realizing how defensive she'd sounded, Finch softened her tone. "Look, it's nothing against you, but I'd rather not talk about it, okay?"

"Okay." He shrugged.

He was being so cool about it that after a moment she relented. "It wasn't always Finch either. Before that it was . . ." She paused. The only ones besides her family that she'd told were Andie and Simon. "Bethany," she said softly.

"Bethany." He repeated it slowly, enunciating each syllable so that it came out Beth-a-nee. "How'd you end up with Finch?"

"It was one of those spur-of-the-moment things." She didn't elaborate.

"I thought maybe it was a family name."

"I didn't have a family before I came here."

He flashed her a grin. "A woman of mystery. I love it."

"See? I knew I should've kept my mouth shut." She struggled not to smile.

"I didn't mean to bring up a sore subject."

"It's not your fault. It's just that I don't like being reminded of those days." That was another lifetime, and Bethany Wells was just someone she used to know.

Her mind flew back to the day she'd first arrived here. She'd been on a Greyhound bus for days, going nowhere in particular. Carson Springs had seemed as likely a place as any to get off. And by then she'd run out of money, so she'd crashed a wedding reception to get something to eat— one that turned out to be Laura's sister's. If Alice hadn't taken pity on her after she'd been caught, she'd have wound up with a return ticket to New York and a new set of foster parents. She shuddered to think what her life would be like today if not for that simple act of kindness.

"This lady—you really think she might be related?" Lucien's voice broke into her thoughts.

Finch laughed and shook her head, though she couldn't shake loose the tiny kernel of hope chafing inside her like a pebble in a shoe. "It was Andie's idea. She got a bug up her ass, is all. Nothing will come of it."

"Hey, you never know."

"Anyway, it's not like I'm missing out on anything." She kept her voice light, not wanting him to guess the truth: that as much as she loved Laura and Hector and Maude, there was a hole inside her that they couldn't fill.

"Which is more than I can say," he said darkly.

She cast him a sidelong glance. "Don't take this the wrong way, but offhand I know a dozen people who'd trade places with you in a heartbeat." Okay, his parents were divorced, but so were those of half the kids in school, and none as rich as Lucien's. "What, did your parents spank you when you were a kid?"

She waited for him to crack a smile, but his expression remained tight. "Let's just say I'm not exactly a priority."

She felt bad for goading him. It wasn't Lucien's fault that his parents were well off. Gently, she asked, "What's your mom like?" The only thing Finch knew was that she lived in New York.

"You mean other than the fact that she's a drunk?" His jaw tightened. "The only reason I'm here is because she's in rehab."

"Wow," she exclaimed softly. "That sucks."

"Yeah, well, what can I say." His mouth

twisted in a smile that was more of a grimace. "My dad? He's not much better, only he usually holds off until after lunch."

"And I thought poor people had all the problems."

"You think money solves everything?" He smiled, but she could see that he was hurt.

Before she could stop herself, she shot back, "No, but I've noticed that a lot of the people who have it act like their shit doesn't stink."

"I hope that doesn't apply to me," he said stiffly.

"No," she said. "But check back with me in a few years—I might have a different opinion." Lucien laughed, and she felt the tension between them ease. "The next right." She pointed at the intersection ahead, where a large chestnut marked the road to Sam and Ian's.

Sam was on her knees in the flower bed when they pulled in, wearing a floppy straw hat and baggy, grass-stained trousers. She rose and ambled over to meet them. "Finch! Why didn't you let me know you were coming? I'd have put on some decent clothes." She pulled off a dirt-caked glove, extending her hand to Lucien. "Hi, I'm Sam."

"Lucien Jeffers." He shook her hand.

"It's nice to finally meet you."

Finch felt herself grow warm. Would Lucien think she talked about him all the time? "Um, we didn't come to visit," she was quick to say. "We're here because of Anna."

Sam's smile was replaced by a look of concern. "How's she holding up?"

"Okay, considering."

Sam shook her head in dismay. "I would've been at the hearing, but Jack's running a temperature." She glanced toward the house. It was like the ones Finch had dreamed of growing up—white clapboard with blue trim, nasturtiums climbing up over the porch railing. High up on the roof a weathervane shaped like a rooster creaked in the breeze.

"Nothing serious, I hope," Finch said.

"Just a little cold. He'll be fine. In fact, he should be up from his nap any minute." Sam turned to Lucien, smiling as she brushed at the bits of grass and leaves clinging to her shirt. "I don't know if Finch told you, but Jack's quite a bit younger than my girls. I had a baby when my friends were having grandchildren."

"At least you knew what you're getting into," he said.

"You can say that again." She laughed. "At my age, you know every single thing that can go wrong." She started toward the house, motioning for them to join her.

Finch stepped inside to find Jack asleep in his playpen in the living room. As Sam reached to switch off the baby monitor, he stirred and lifted his head, blinking up at them sleepily. His cheeks were flushed and his golden curls mashed on one side of his head. Seeing Finch, he broke into a grin showing four tiny teeth.

"Fah!" he cried, hauling himself upright and holding out his chubby arms.

He knew the way to her heart all right. One look at that face and she was butter. She scooped him up. "Wow. What've you been feeding this kid? He weighs a ton!"

"He takes after his dad." Sam beamed with pride.

"Speaking of the devil, where's Ian?"

"He's doing a civic center in Sausalito. He'll be back next week." Sam didn't seem to mind that he was away a lot—the life of a muralist was a nomadic one—though Ian did his best to limit his trips.

"Down," Jack ordered, wriggling to free himself. Finch lowered him onto the rug, watching him toddle over to Sam, who wrinkled her nose as she lifted him into her arms. "Phew. Somebody needs his diaper changed. Be right back, guys. There's lemonade in the fridge—help yourselves." She waved toward the kitchen, where a large bowl heaped with lemons sat on the counter. "Lupe brings them over by the bushel. I've run out of things to make with them."

"Cool grandma." Lucien voiced his approval when Sam was out of the room.

Finch smiled. "She is, isn't she?" Sam was one of the best things about being adopted into this family. They wandered into the sunny kitchen that looked out over the backyard, where Finch poured them glasses of lemonade. By the time Sam returned with a freshly diapered Jack, they were seated on the sofa leafing through an album of his baby pictures. Finch smiled at one of Jack on his first birthday. Instead of blowing out the candle, he'd gone straight for the cake. His chubby cheeks were smeared with chocolate frosting.

Sam set him down, and he immediately

toddled over to the basket of toys by the fireplace, dumping a cascade of puzzle pieces, alphabet blocks, Playskool trucks, and plastic farm animals onto the rug. She gave an indulgent sigh as she sank into a chair, asking Lucien, "Do you have brothers or sisters?"

"Nope, but I always wondered what it'd be like," he said, smiling at another photo of Jack covered in mud. "It looks like there's a fair amount of cleanup involved."

"You don't know the half of it." Sam laughed, and Finch was once again struck by how easy she made it seem—balancing grown daughters with a toddler. Always the perfect hostess, too.

But they hadn't come to socialize. Finch cleared her throat. "Um, about Anna—"

"It's awful, isn't it?" Sam shook her head. "I just wish there was something I could do."

"Actually, there is." Finch raised her voice to be heard over the sound of Jack happily bashing at his Busy Box with a toy truck. "We're raising money for her legal expenses."

Sam brightened. "What a wonderful idea."

"Whatever you can afford," Finch was quick to throw in, not wanting her to feel pressured.

"Keep an eye on Jack. I'll just be a sec." Sam darted from the room, reappearing moments later with a check in hand.

Finch gasped when she saw the amount—a thousand dollars! "It's . . . uh . . . I don't know what to say," she stammered.

"It's the least we can do," Sam said, though Finch knew it was far more than she and Ian could afford. "In fact, if it weren't for Jack, I'd be out there with you knocking on doors." She paused, looking thoughtful. "Come to think of it, there's no reason I can't make a few calls."

"Um, that'd be great." Finch found her voice at last.

"I knew my old Junior League directory would come in handy one of these days." There was a glint in her eye as she stood to see them out. Under that PTA mom's surface beat the heart of a rebel: She'd love nothing more than to hit up those ladies, many of whom would be horrified at the idea of giving to an alleged murderer. Sam hugged her at the door, and when Lucien put out his hand, she ignored it to hug him, too. "Any time you want to try on a kid brother for size," she told him, "you can borrow Jack."

He grinned. "Thanks, I'll keep it in mind."

They were almost out the door before Finch remembered to ask, "Will you be at the funeral?"

"I wouldn't miss it for the world." Sam sounded more matter of fact than mournful. And why not? Monica hadn't gone out of her way to endear herself. Though the funeral was sure to draw a crowd, if for no other reason than to gawk at all the celebrities, few would shed a tear at her grave.

By the end of the day they'd canvassed a dozen more homes, raising several hundred dollars on top of Sam's contribution. At the Ochoas', she and Lucien had politely nibbled on cookies and at the Sharps', coffee cake. As they were leaving the Ratliffs', where Mrs. Ratliff's elderly mother had insisted they try her homemade strudel, Finch had muttered under her breath, "I'm not sure my stomach can take any more."

In the car, on their way back to town, she said, "Not too bad for our first day."

"Only one person slammed the door in our faces."

"Did you believe that old hag?" Though Mrs. Wormley hadn't exactly slammed the door, she'd said snippily that the police didn't go around arresting people without good reason and she, for one, wasn't in the habit of aiding and abetting criminals. "It's probably because Anna wouldn't join her stupid church committee."

"They're the biggest hypocrites, those religious types."

"They're not all like that." Finch thought of her friend Sister Agnes. That time she'd run away from Laura's, it was Sister Agnes who'd found her and brought her back. "Hey, pull over. I want to show you something."

They were headed south on Old Schoolhouse Road, and Lucien drew to a stop in front of its namesake, a ramshackle building long abandoned, its windows boarded over and the weeds surrounding it waist high. It was where Sam's father had gone to school, and his grandfather before him, but now it was mainly a make-out spot for the kids who went to Portola High across town.

He cast her a dubious look. "*This* is what you want to show me."

"Are you coming, or not?" Finch got out, motioning for him to follow her.

They picked their way through tall weeds and brambles, mindful of the broken glass and rusty beer cans scattered about. When they reached the schoolhouse, she saw that the railing was missing from one side of the steps that creaked ominously as she climbed them. She pulled a strip of peeling red paint from the door to reveal traces of the original blue underneath.

"Do you know the movie *Stranger in Paradise*?" she asked.

"I think I saw it on TV." He eyed her with interest.

"One of the scenes was filmed here. It was a wreck then, too, but they fixed it up. I heard about it from Sam. Her mother spent a day on the set—she knew the director or something."

"I didn't know you were into old movies."

She went on as if he hadn't spoken. "That's how I know about Lorraine Wells. She was listed in the credits." Finch paused, turning to him. "I know it's dumb. I mean, what are the chances we're related?"

"Next to none," he agreed.

"Still, I can't help wondering: Maybe there's a reason I ended up in Carson Springs." She pushed against the door, but it was wedged shut. She delivered a hard kick, and the hinges gave with a rusty squeal. "Don't get the wrong idea—I'm not into all that New Age crap. It's just a thought."

"Creepy," Lucien said as they stepped cautiously inside. She turned to find him looking apprehensively about.

"I wouldn't want to be here alone." She hugged herself amid the gloom.

The room was dark and smelled like a hundred years' worth of neglect and debris, its only light the pale shafts that had found their way through the holes in the roof. As they crunched over drifts of dried animal droppings and leaves, stepping around chunks of decayed flooring and warped boards, Finch and Lucien were greeted by a furious skittering. She nervously eyed the potbelly stove in one corner, rusted through in spots and home, from the sounds of it, to legions of mice.

Lucien turned to her with his slow-breaking smile that took away some of the chill. "It's not much to look at, is it?"

She glanced about, trying to picture the walls hung with colorful maps and diagrams, but all she could see were rotting studs and peeling tar paper. "I guess some things are better left to the imagination."

She began to shiver, drawing the sleeves of her jersey down over her fingers. It seemed only natural, like one heartbeat following another, when Lucien wrapped his arms around her from behind. His breath was warm against her ear.

"We should go," she said, making no move to pull away.

"Yeah." He tightened his arms about her.

With a sigh, she swiveled around to face him. But whatever she'd meant to say, the words died on her lips. His eyes were so black in the half light that when he kissed her, it felt as though she were melting into all that velvety darkness. She parted her lips, letting the tip of his tongue play over hers. *Stop,* a voice cried in her head, *you'll ruin everything.*

After a moment she drew back, breathing slowly and deliberately until her heart stopped pounding. "We really should be going," she repeated in a trembling voice.

He just stood there, looking at her. "What are you afraid of?"

"Who said I was afraid?"

"You didn't have to say it."

She ducked her head, letting her hair slide past her ears so her face was hidden from view. "It's not you."

"Whoever he is, I'm not like him."

Her head jerked up. "Who said it had anything to do with anyone?"

"I can see that you've been hurt."

Her eyes filled with tears, and the smell of rotting leaves and wood given over to termites grew more pungent. "It wasn't just one guy," she said in a strange choked voice. "I . . . I can't even remember all their names." She waited for him to draw back in disgust.

"That was then; this is now." He lowered his head, his lips brushing over hers.

"I don't know if I can—"

"We'll go as slow as you like."

"I can't make any promises."

"I'm not asking you to."

"Either way, we'll still be friends?"

"That's up to you." He smiled, taking her hand and wrapping it around his.

She felt a burden lift from her. The acceptance she saw in Lucien's face was what she'd needed without knowing how to ask.

They retraced their steps. Outside, the sun was setting, bathing the mountains to the east in a reflected rose-colored glow, the pink moment that drew tourists from miles around. The wonder of it wasn't lost on Finch, either. She stood with her head tipped skyward, her long hair catching the breeze and lifting off her shoulders like a bird taking flight. When Lucien slipped an arm around her shoulders, she scarcely noticed.

"I wonder how Andie and Simon made out," she said.

"I've never known either of them to take no for an answer."

"About tomorrow," she said, "how tacky would it be to hit people up at the funeral?"

"On a scale of one to ten, I'd say about eleven or so."

"That's what I was afraid of." She thought of Anna, alone and frightened, and her spirits sank with the sun dipping below the mountaintops.

Lucien drew her in so that her head was tucked under his chin. "You're doing everything you can. That's all anyone could ask."

By morning Anna had lost all hope. As she sat staring sightlessly at her breakfast, long since gone cold on its tray, all she could think of was that an hour from now the mourners would be filing past Monica's casket, the famous rubbing elbows with those whose closest encounters with celebrities thus far had been occasional glimpses of the ones that frequented the spa and La Serenisa. Liz would be in attendance, along with their mother. Anna's friends, too, and people from church. The only one who wouldn't be there was the one person who'd known Monica the best— Anna herself.

I'm sorry, Monica. However bad things had gotten toward the end, she felt no rancor toward her sister, only the most profound pity. No one deserved to die the way she had.

The sound of footsteps brought her head

up so sharply she felt something crack in her neck. Not Benny this time, but a pimple-faced rookie who scarcely looked old enough to drive, much less carry a gun. He stopped chewing his gum long enough to announce, "Bond's been posted."

"What?" Anna wasn't sure she'd heard right.

"You're free to go." The door to her cell clanged open.

Anna's mind spun. Who had that kind of money? None of her friends, that was for sure, unless it was borrowed. She rose shakily to her feet, feeling as she had when she'd been bedridden with pneumonia. As she stepped into the corridor she held out her hands to be cuffed before remembering. She quickly dropped them. The rookie handed her a paper bag with her things, pointing toward the shower room. "You can change in there."

Expecting to find only the clothes she'd been wearing when she arrived, Anna was surprised to find a brand-new dress in a soft shade of gray as well, along with pantyhose and a pair of black pumps from her closet. *Laura,* she thought. She'd guessed there wouldn't be time for her to go home before the funeral. She and Hector must have been the ones who'd posted bond, though God only knew where they'd gotten the money. Anna felt a rush of gratitude mixed with shame for what she'd put them through.

The dress looked as if it would be too small, but when she slipped it over her head it was a perfect fit. Moments later she was being ushered into the visitors' area, where another surprise was in store. It wasn't Laura and Hector who awaited her, but Laura's younger sister, stylishly dressed in a slim-fitting navy coatdress and high heels, her handsome husband at her side. Alice stepped forward, seizing hold of her hands. "I'm sorry it took us so long, but we were out of town when we heard. We didn't get back until late last night."

Anna stood there, gaping at them. "I don't understand. I thought—"

"Laura phoned us in London. We would've been here sooner, but our flight was delayed."

"You mean *you're* the ones who—"

"We were happy to help." Wes spoke as if it were fifty cents, not fifty thousand.

"I . . . I don't know how to thank you," Anna stammered.

"You don't have to." Alice took her arm, smiling. "We'd better hurry or we'll miss the service."

Minutes later Wes was pulling into the only parking space they could find, several blocks from the church. As they made their way down the street, Anna could see the crowd of reporters and paparazzi on the front steps. Parked along both sides of Calle de Navidad were TV vans sprouting satellite dishes, some with cables linking them to live feeds. She could almost picture Monica stepping through the doors into the spotlight with a shimmy of her hips and toss of her auburn mane.

Luckily they managed to slip in through a side door without being seen. Inside the church it was standing room only. Scanning the pews, Anna spotted Sallie Templeton, who'd played Monica's mother in *Victory Tour* three face lifts ago. And golden-haired Wyatt Van Aken, Monica's costar in *The Good Die Young,* whom the press had dubbed Robert Redford Light. Sniffling theatrically into her handkerchief was forever forty-nine Bessie Parker, whom Monica hadn't seen in years and privately couldn't stand, but who was carrying on as if they'd been bosom buddies. Glenn, in a dark gray Armani suit, was escorting another aging star down the aisle, her face hidden behind a veil.

She saw the familiar faces of friends and acquaintances as well: Norma Devane from Shear Delight in a fitted black jacket glittering with jet beads; David Ryback and his blond wife Carol, looking more tired and faded than usual; the elderly Miller twins, Olive and Rose, their gray heads draped in matching black mantillas; and bleached blond Melodie Wycoff from the Tree House Café, with her policeman husband Jimmy, one of the few who'd been nice to Anna while she was in jail.

Liz, accompanied by their mother, had saved her a seat up front. As Anna slid in next to them, her mother, dressed in a suit and pearls, her hair coiffed for the occasion, gave her a smile of such tender sweetness that for a moment Anna was a child again, safe in her arms—until she realized Betty was smiling at everyone that way. Someone tapped her shoulder. She turned to find Laura, squeezed in between Hector and

Finch, mouthing a silent hello. Maude, on the aisle, peeked out from under a wide-brimmed hat to give her a wink.

Sam and Ian, with Aubrey and Gerry and her kids, sat behind them. Claire shot Anna a sympathetic look, as if to say, *I know what you're going through.* A reminder that her adoptive mother had passed away earlier in the year—sadly without having seen the success she'd made of Tea & Sympathy.

There was no sign of Marc. Anna tried not to feel let down—she couldn't expect him to stick around forever—but it gnawed at her nonetheless. Then Father Reardon emerged through a door into the chancel, looking biblical somehow with a shaft of light from the stained glass window over-head highlighting the silver in his hair, and she forgot everything else. He spoke briefly but warmly of the contributions Monica had made, not only to the world, but to the community in which she'd lived—a stretch, given the tiny sums she'd donated to vari-ous local charities through the years. He ended with a verse from Ecclesiastes, read with such heartfelt emotion it brought tears to Anna's eyes.

"Or ever the silver cord be loosed, or the

golden bowl be broken, or the pitcher be broken at the fountain, or the wheel broken at the cistern. Then shall the dust return to the earth as it was: and the spirit shall return to God who gave it."

She gazed in wonder at the still figure stretched out in the coffin. Monica had stipulated an open-casket funeral, but though Anna had dreaded this moment, her fears vanished at the sight of her sister looking as lovely as she had in life. Not a marble effigy, but so radiant she might have been asleep. Her auburn hair glowed like banked fire against the ivory satin pillow over which it was arranged, her slender hands folded about a white calfskin prayer book that Anna recognized with a small shock as the one she'd been given when she was confirmed—never mind that Monica hadn't been to church in years. Even the gown she was dressed in, one that Anna had picked out, layers of chiffon in her favorite shade of green, seemed to float about her. The thing that struck Anna most, though, was the faint smile on her lips—as if she'd gotten the last laugh somehow.

"She looks so beautiful," she whispered to Liz.

"You know Monica; she never left the house without being camera ready." There was no sarcasm in Liz's voice, just sadness.

"What's going on? Who died?" Their mother tugged on Anna's sleeve, looking bewildered.

"It's okay, Mom." Anna tucked a hand as light as a fallen leaf under her arm. "It'll all be over soon."

"Will I be back in time for tea?" Betty asked fretfully. "I don't want to be late. Mr. Harding . . ." she leaned close to confide, "always takes more than his share."

Anna shared a smile with Liz. It seemed the ultimate irony that their mother didn't know it was her own daughter in the casket, but maybe it was for the best.

Her mother subsided with a sigh. The days when she'd attended mass without fail, drawing comfort from the liturgy, were behind her. Nowadays it was the Sunshine Home where she was most content.

Glenn stepped forward to give the eulogy, looking pale and drawn. If anyone had a reason to mourn, it was he. Even with Monica's career in permanent hiatus, there'd been a steady trickle of endorsements, advertising revenue, and percentage payouts

from movies enjoying a second life over-
seas. But Anna knew that wasn't the only
reason he'd miss Monica. The bond they'd
shared was closer in some ways than that
of lovers.

Once again Anna was remembering the
incident in the pool house—weeks that felt
like years ago. And she'd thought being
seen in a swimsuit when she was fat had
been bad; nothing could have prepared her
for what had come later, when she was thin
. . . and seemingly desirable. She shuddered at the memory. Then Glenn cleared
his throat and began to speak. "I'm not here
to talk about what Monica Vincent meant to
me personally. She belonged to the whole
world, a shining star who made everyone's
lives a little brighter, even when the light in
her own had dimmed . . ."

He went on about Monica's courage in
the face of the accident that had left her
wheelchair bound, and how despite her
handicap she'd remained radiant to the
end. When he was finished, a select handful
got up to pay their respects as well. Not the
usual aunts, uncles, and cousins—Monica
hadn't bothered with them in years. The
only people she'd cared about were the

ones coming forward now, one by one, to sing her praises: Melissa Phelps, who'd produced several of her pictures, and balding mogul Len Shapiro, head of Unicorn Pictures, who spoke glowingly of Monica's professionalism—every movie she'd starred in had come in on schedule, he said. Last, but not least, was Giorgio Frangiani, the Italian heart throb with whom Monica was rumored to have had an affair and who spoke of her in such loving terms it would have been easy to imagine him carrying the torch—that is, if Anna hadn't known for a fact he was gay.

No one mentioned the ghastly circumstances of her death, and Anna was grateful for that. It was enough that she'd have to contend with the lion's den outside.

The organ in the choir loft began to swell and a voice known to millions sent goose bumps up the back of Anna's neck—how on earth had Glenn gotten Bette on such short notice?—as it opened throttle on "The Party's Over," Monica's favorite song and one that seemed particularly suited to the occasion. As the last chord soared into the rafters, there wasn't a dry eye in the church.

Even those who'd despised Monica were moved by the spectacle of her death.

What would they think if they knew what really *happened that day?*

The doors were flung open and sunlight flooded in. As Anna was borne down the aisle by the river of people making their way outside, she could see the mob of reporters and paparazzi on the steps jockeying for shots of the celebrities scurrying toward their waiting limos, shielded by the handful of B-list stars who'd paused for photo ops. Anna ducked her head, praying more fervently than she ever had in church, that she might slip through the crush unnoticed. But she'd scarcely set foot outside when a deep voice yelled, "It's her! Hey, Anna!"

Others joined the chorus:

"Anna, how does it feel to be out on bail?"

"Can you comment on the funeral?"

"Give us a shot, Anna, come on, be a good girl . . . just one."

She brought her hands up to cover her face. Blinded by the storm of camera flashes, she stumbled and would have fallen if a strong hand hadn't gripped her elbow. She couldn't see who it was through the black dots swarming like tiny insects across her field of vision, but then a familiar voice boomed, "Move aside! Give her some room!"

Marc. She went weak with relief.

"Don't look back," he muttered, his grip tightening about her arm as he steered her down the steps onto the curb where his Audi was double-parked. Shoving aside a stringy-haired man with a camera who'd stepped into their path, he wrenched open the passenger door and none too gently pushed Anna inside. Before she could say a word they were roaring up Calle de Navidad.

CHAPTER TEN

It was a standard line that Holy Name Cemetery, which boasted one of the best views in Carson Springs, was wasted on its residents. Tucked into a bend of the road that meandered up the hill to Pilgrim's Peak, it was shaded by centuries-old oaks and honey mesquite and remained green year-round due to the stream that could be heard faintly murmuring through the trees. It was where Anna's father and grandparents were buried as well as many of St. Xavier's earliest parishioners, but since the fancy gated cemetery across town had lured away most of its business, the sight of picnickers was more common now than mourners. As she looked about at the modest headstones, many moss-grown and tilting askew, Anna couldn't help being struck by the irony of Monica's being laid to rest in obscurity.

The graveside service was brief, with only the immediate family and close friends in attendance. Jimmy Wycoff had set up a roadblock at the foot of the hill to hold the press at bay, for which Anna was deeply grateful. Her nerves were so raw that a squirrel scampering up a tree nearly caused her to jump out of her skin. Standing by the open grave, trying to hold her balance with her high heels sinking into the turf, she was conscious only of Marc's hand on her elbow. Years before, her mother had signed her up for ballet lessons (which had succeeded only in making her feel even fatter and clumsier), where she'd learned to pirouette, eyes fixed on a single point on the wall to keep from growing dizzy. Right now, Marc was that point.

Father Reardon read a verse from Psalms, and she watched dry-eyed as the casket, gleaming mahogany with brass rails, was lowered into the ground. She felt as though she were seeing it all from a distance: Glenn standing with his hands solemnly clasped in front of him, the sun winking off his Rolex; Liz staring grimly ahead, in the grip of memories she clearly wished no part of; Betty looking anxious and befuddled, as though wondering what any of this had to do with her. As if in a dream, Anna stepped forward to pitch a shovel full of dirt into the grave, thinking as she did of when she and her sisters were little, the prayer they said every night before bed: *If I should die before I wake, I pray the Lord my soul to take.*

Then they were drifting toward the parking lot, where everyone was saying their good-byes. The faces blurred together. There were only traces of perfume, the glimmer of earrings, flashes of sunlight off dark glasses as they pressed in. Only Laura stood out, her sweet smile a reminder that for all that was bad in the world there was an equal measure of good . . . and Finch, her somber gaze giving her the look of someone far older than her years.

She hugged Anna, murmuring, "Don't worry. We won't let anything happen to you."

"If you need anything, just call," Liz told her. She clearly meant it, whereas in the old days she'd only given it lip service.

Then Anna was back in Marc's car, sinking into her seat with a sigh of relief—all she wanted was to be home soaking in a hot bath. "My place isn't far," she reminded him as they started down the hill. "At the bottom take the first right, then—"

He didn't let her finish. "From what I've seen, it looks like the entire Fifth Division is camped out in front of your house. They'd be all over you like ants at a picnic." Anna's vision of her home as a safe haven dissolved. "Tonight you're staying with me." He spoke as if it were all settled.

She protested even so, "Marc, I can't ask you to do this. You've put yourself on the line enough as it is. Besides, I don't have any of my things."

"We'll pick up whatever you need along the way."

"What about you—don't you have to be at work?"

"I'm taking some time off."

She fell silent, unable to wrap her brain around the idea that a man, any man, much less Marc, would go to such lengths for *her.* What did it mean? She gazed out her window at the coyote brush forming a dense berm along the road. It was covered in white blossoms that scattered in their wake, whirling up into the air—not blossoms after all, but butterflies, hundreds of them.

"I have some vacation days coming," he went on in the same matter-of-fact tone. "My boss has been after me to take them, so I figured now was as good a time as any."

"Still, it's . . . I don't know what to say."

"You can't do this alone. You need help."

"I thought that's what my lawyer was for." Besides, Rhonda had warned her to keep a low profile. If the press got wind of her spending the night with a married man, it might only make matters worse.

"She can only do so much, and since the police don't seem to be pursuing any other leads," he went on determinedly, "I thought we should do a little digging of our own."

"I'm not sure that's such a good idea."

"Do you always play by the rules?" He cast her a challenging look.

He had a point. Where had playing it safe gotten her? She couldn't be any worse off, that was for sure. "Any ideas on where to start?" she asked hesitantly.

"You tell me."

She thought for a moment. "Well, there's her ex-husband."

"Which one?"

"Her fourth, and last—Brent Carver."

"The actor?"

"She talked about him?"

"Not much. Just said he was a real shit."

"He's not. Just . . . kind of flaky. They had a weird relationship."

"It must have been hard for him, playing second banana."

"I don't think it bothered him as much as it did Monica. Except for being a hunk, he wasn't much fun to show off. Most of the stuff he does is pretty low rent—bit parts on TV, a few commercials here and there. He's big on the auto show circuit."

"I take it the divorce was less than amicable."

"Yes and no. Monica was angry at him, but Brent didn't put up much of a fight. He knew he had it coming. She'd caught him cheating on her—seems he'd charged the hotel rooms to her card."

Marc let out a low whistle. "The guy has balls, I'll give him that."

"He spent like a drunken sailor, too, though she would've forgiven that. The funny thing is that once they split up, they got along better than when they'd been married."

"Can you think of any reason he'd have wanted her dead?"

"No. Except . . ." She frowned. It came rushing back, the fight she'd overheard that day—the last time he'd been over at the house. "She'd threatened to cut off his alimony." Anna hadn't thought too much of it at the time. Brent, perpetually in debt, was always hitting her up for more, but he usually backed down like a little boy with his hand slapped. "She knew he couldn't afford to take her to court."

"Does he stand to inherit anything?"

"I doubt it," she said. She would know more after she'd spoken with Gardener Stevens.

"Have the police talked to him?"

She nodded. "Apparently, he has an alibi."

"That doesn't rule out a contract hit."

She smiled; it was all so . . . theatrical. Contract killing . . . hit men . . . like something out of *The Godfather.* "Knowing Brent, he'd have charged it to Monica's Visa."

Marc's expression remained thoughtful. "Do you have his address?"

"It's in my Rolodex." In her mind, she saw her office sealed off with crime-scene tape, and sighed. They were approaching the turnoff to Route 33 when she thought of something else. "His agent would know—a guy named Marty Milnik."

"The name rings a bell."

"He used to be on CTN."

"I'm sure he's listed. We'll give him a call when we get to the house."

He drove in silence, as if pondering various angles. They were nearing the top of the hill with its sweeping view of the valley when he asked, "What can you tell me about this Glenn character?"

Anna tensed. "What do you want to know?"

"Liz told me she didn't trust him."

"She's never liked him."

He flicked her a glance. "What's your take on him?"

The memory surfaced once more. With everything else that had been going on, she hadn't wanted to relive it, but there was no getting around it this time. Besides, if there was even a remote possibility it was in any way connected to Monica's death . . .

She smiled grimly. "If you'd asked me a few weeks ago, I'd have told you he was a nice enough guy."

"Something happen to change your mind?"

Anna felt herself grow warm. She understood now why women who'd been victimized felt it was their fault somehow, though rationally she knew that if anyone should be ashamed it was Glenn. "He came on to me," she said tersely.

"I'm not surprised."

"It wasn't like that. He . . . well, he was pretty insistent." She didn't go into the details; she could tell from the sudden tightening of his expression that he got the picture. "Monica wasn't too happy about it, believe me."

"Funny, I wouldn't have pegged her as the protective type."

"She wasn't. It was *me* she was mad at, not Glenn. I'm sure she thought I was encouraging him."

"She was probably jealous. Were they lovers?"

"Not that I know of."

"Still, it's worth looking into."

"I suppose." She didn't relish the idea of confronting Glenn, not after the way he'd looked right through her at the funeral; clearly, he blamed *her* for Monica's death.

Besides, she had a more imminent concern. "Marc, why are you doing this?" She eyed him intently. "I mean, it was only one night. It's not like you owe me anything." It pained her to admit it—to her it seemed like so much more—but that was the plain fact of it.

His eyes remained fixed on the road. After a moment he said softly, "Maybe I need to."

"Superman to the rescue?" she said lightly, wondering if it had less to do with her than with his wife.

"Just don't ask me to leap any tall buildings in a single bound." He flashed her a grin. "My days of being a caped crusader ended in the fourth grade when I did a swan dive off the roof of our garage."

She laughed for the first time in days. It felt good, like the sunshine warming her. "I wanted to be Nancy Drew."

"It looks as if you got your wish," he said.

Anna gave a small ironic laugh. "The trouble is that except for Brent and Glenn, I don't have a clue who to start with. Most of those people at the funeral she hadn't seen in years."

"Do you think any of them had it in for her?"

Anna had wondered the same thing herself. The past forty-eight hours she'd had little else to do. But she shook her head. "I can think of a few who would've stabbed her in the back the first chance they got, but only in the figurative sense."

"Sometimes there's a fine line."

She yawned, feeling profoundly sleepy all of a sudden. "Can we talk about this later? I need to close my eyes." As her eyelids drifted shut, she felt as though she were plunging down in an elevator. A moment later she was sound asleep.

She woke to find that darkness had fallen and jerked upright. "Where are we?"

"Almost there," he told her.

"What time is it?"

"Time to eat." He'd pulled off Highway 1 and they were bumping slowly along a pier lined with tourist shops, bait shacks, and saltwater taffy concessions. "I hope you like seafood."

"Anything's fine . . . as long as it doesn't come on a tray." Funny. Her life used to be measured in meals and now food was the furthest thing from her mind.

Minutes later they were seated in a booth at the Rusty Anchor, tucking into seafood platters the size of small skiffs, everything freshly caught and batter-fried to a crisp. Anna, whose appetite had returned with a vengeance, thought she'd never tasted anything so delicious.

"I eat here at least once a week," Marc told her.

"I can see why."

"It's not just the food."

"I know. Eating alone gets old after a while." No one knew that better than she.

"That's the part that never seems to get easier." His gaze drifted toward the window, where his ghostly reflection shimmered in the darkened glass.

"Does your wife like to cook?" *In for a penny, in for a pound,* she thought.

He brought his gaze back to her, smiling faintly. "See, that's what I like about you. Anyone else would've put it in the past tense."

"She's not dead."

"To most people she is."

"Well, I guess I'm not most people."

He put his fork down, pushing his plate away. "You know my favorite? When they try to relate by comparing it to some crazy relative in their own family—like they have a fucking clue what *real* crazy is." He gave a bitter laugh.

"I'm sure they're only trying to make you feel better."

"Or themselves." He signaled for the check. "To answer your question, yes, my wife likes to cook—when she's not burning the house down."

"And I thought it was just my mother." She caught herself, and grimaced. "Sorry."

"It's okay. I don't have the market cornered on crazy relatives." He laughed, and some of the tension went out of his face. "Speaking of your mother, how is she?"

"Better . . . or maybe that's just what I want to believe. She seems happy, at least. Tea time at the Sunshine Home is a major deal."

"I have one of the local beauticians come in once a week to wash Faith's hair. She looks forward to it."

Anna knew the feeling. Any contact with the outside world, however small, had meant the world to her when she was in jail. "How often do you visit her?"

"I used to go every day. Then it was once a week. Now . . ." He shrugged. "I go when I can."

Anna nodded in understanding. Her visits to the Sunshine Home had tapered off, too, though her mother didn't seem to notice. "It's the sameness, isn't it? The fact that it never gets any better."

He reached for her hand. "You asked me before why I was doing this. Maybe it's because I *can*." When Anna didn't reply, his fingers tightened about hers. "We'll find a way out of this," he said. "Do you believe that?"

"I want to." She managed a small smile.

Marc reached up to brush her cheek. "You look tired. We should get you to bed."

"It's been a long day."

Anna fell asleep again in the car, waking up when he pulled to a stop in front of his house. She was surprised to see that it wasn't on the ocean, but surrounded by trees and scrub.

She yawned, and said sleepily, "I thought you lived in Malibu."

He smiled. "It's not all beachfront mansions and movie stars."

Inside, the house was snug with a pitched roof and skylights. Sliding glass doors opened onto a deck that looked out over a floodlit slope carpeted in ice plant.

"Water tends to be a luxury in these parts," he told her. "We planted stuff that'd grow in the desert."

He led the way through a cozy living room lined with books, down a hallway to the master bedroom in back. She sank onto the bed, covered with a colorful woven spread. Everywhere were touches of a female hand—the handblown perfume bottles on the oak dresser, the collection of antique fans on one wall, the cedar chest at the foot of the bed—yet none of it was fussy or overdone.

Marc pulled a blanket from the chest. "Lie down," he said sternly. "Doctor's orders."

Anna kicked off her shoes and stretched out, deliciously aware of the down pillow into which her head sank—it seemed ages since she'd enjoyed even this simplest of pleasures. Marc covered her with the blanket and kissed her lightly on the cheek. An instant later she was once more sound asleep.

When she awoke, there was only the glow from the floodlight out on the deck by which to grope her way to the bathroom, where she found a toothbrush in an unopened box on the sink. Tears filled her eyes. It was the little things, she thought—the small kindnesses that under ordinary circumstances might not have meant so much. She brushed her teeth and splashed water on her face, returning to find Marc seated on the bed.

"How long was I asleep?" she asked.

"A few hours."

"Why didn't you wake me?" She felt guilty, knowing she'd kept him up. After all that driving, he had to be exhausted.

"You needed to rest." He drew her onto the bed, putting his arms around her. "Feeling better?"

"Much." She wriggled down so that her head was resting against his chest.

"I spoke with Marty Milnik."

"What did he say?"

"It seems he and Brent had a parting of the ways. Marty didn't go into it, but he gave me the address of a studio in Covina where Brent's supposedly got a gig. I thought we'd drive out there in the morning."

Anna wondered what kind of studio it could be. Covina was the boondocks as far as Hollywood was concerned. But she only nodded and said, "Sounds like a plan."

Marc kissed the top of her head. "Want to sleep some more?"

"I feel like I could sleep for a week."

"In that case, how about some company?" Anna responded by wrapping her arms around his neck and kissing him with an intensity that surprised them both. He drew back to smile at her. "I didn't necessarily mean that kind."

She arched a brow. "Are you withdrawing the offer?"

"Well, no . . ."

In less than a minute they were under the covers with their clothes off. Snuggled beside him, she tried not to dwell on the fact that this was the same bed he'd shared with his wife. They kissed a little while longer before he pushed aside the covers, his fingers trailing over her skin. She closed her eyes, reveling in the sensations. Most of what she knew about sex came from *Cosmopolitan*; every other article, it seemed, was about ways to make the most of the experience with men who were clueless otherwise. But Marc's touch was expert, each brush of his lips and fingertips awakening parts of her she'd scarcely known existed. Anna thought, *If I've died and gone to heaven, I don't ever want to go back to earth.*

Now his mouth was grazing her belly . . . and . . . oh, God . . . below. She began to tremble uncontrollably. She'd read about *this,* too. But no words could convey how it felt.

"Please," she begged, not knowing if she wanted him to stop . . . or go on.

He drew his head up, gently kissing her on the mouth, her taste like some strange fruit on his lips, before whispering in her ear, "I want to make you come this way."

She blushed, feeling self-conscious. But she soon forgot her shyness and there was only his tongue, featherlight. The sensations mounted to a white-hot pitch. Dear God. How could she have gone the rest of her life without knowing this? Without *him*?

When she came it was a feeling like none she'd ever experienced, not even the first time with Marc. She arched back with a cry, the pleasure so exquisite it was almost unbearable, spilling through her like warm liquid. Afterward she collapsed, breathless.

Bit by bit her heart stopped racing. The world crept back in: the sound of a car laboring up the road, its headlights wheeling across the ceiling; moths thumping against the sliding glass door—she could see them in the floodlight's yellow glare, spiraling away stunned, only to return with renewed vigor to the task of beating themselves to death. Anna wondered if the reason she felt so alive, so conscious of everything around her, was because she was on the verge of losing it all.

Marc stretched out beside her, and she snuggled against him. She could feel that he was aroused, but he gently pushed her hand away when she reached to touch him down there, murmuring, "No."

"But—" She felt selfish.

He placed a finger over her lips. "Tonight was for you."

Her throat tightened. Marc had wanted her to have something that was hers alone. He was showing that he cared, that she wasn't just a stand-in for his wife. It was all Anna could do to keep from letting go of the tears pressing hotly behind her eyes.

She drifted to sleep in his arms thinking of Monica—not the nightmare images that had haunted her these past few nights, but her sister as she'd looked on her wedding day, standing at the altar beside Brent, a vision in antique ivory lace, a look on her face as if to say, this was it, the brass ring she'd been reaching for. Only it hadn't been. For all her wealth and fame, Monica had died empty-handed.

The studio in Covina turned out to be an industrial warehouse a stone's throw from the railroad tracks, with a discreet sign on the corrugated siding that identified it as the home of Blue Knight Productions. Marc told the crackling voice over the intercom they were there to see Brent. A moment later they were buzzed in.

A punk-haired twentysomething sporting a tattoo on one shoulder and holding a steaming Styrofoam cup in each hand, greeted them as they walked in. "So, you guys are, like, legit, right?" she said. "The feds were out here last week—a hot tip that we were using minors. Yeah, as if." She rolled her kohl-lined eyes. A gold stud over one eyebrow flashed in the overhead fluorescents.

"As far as I know, we're legit." Marc gave her his most disarming smile.

The girl tilted her head to one side, appraising him frankly—never mind she looked young enough to be his daughter. In a throaty voice, steam from the cups she was holding curling up around her face, she said, "Come with me. They're still setting up, so you have a few minutes."

They followed her down a narrow corridor fashioned out of Sheetrock. At the end, Anna could see cameras and floodlights, cables duct-taped to the floor, and a head-set-wearing technician flitting in and out of view. They turned a corner, stopping at a door with Brent's name printed on an eras-able board. The girl gave it a kick, yelling, "You got company!" Coffee sloshed over onto one hand and she winced, cursing un-der her breath as she continued on.

The door swung open, and Anna stifled a gasp. The only thing covering Brent was the towel he was holding over his privates. He grinned as if unaware that he was naked. "Hey, Anna Banana." She cringed at the nickname. "What brings you all the way out here? Don't tell me you missed me." He winked.

Several possible responses flitted through her mind before she settled on the most innocuous. "Brent, this is Marc. We, uh, were wondering if we could have a word with you." She was careful to keep her eyes from straying south.

Brent high-fived Marc. "Any friend of Anna's is a friend of mine."

Brent was so boyishly exuberant, he was impossible to dislike. He was also impossible not to look at, naked or clothed. Well over six feet, with a muscular build bronzed from regular visits to the tanning salon, a Colgate smile, and perennially tousled blond locks, he was the kind of guy you'd expect to see tossing a Frisbee on the beach. Unsurprisingly, the highlight of his career had been a bit part on *Baywatch.*

The problem wasn't apparent until you were up close: Brent was old—not *old* old, but in terms of Hollywood, where most actors were washed up at forty.

"Have a seat." Brent gestured toward the ratty sofa, reaching casually for the robe on a hook on the door. The unmistakable sounds of a couple having sex drifted toward them.

Anna had guessed, of course—Blue Knight Productions, and that girl's talk of the feds. She wondered how Brett could have sunk so low, but it didn't really surprise her. In a way, hadn't he been working toward this his whole career?

"I didn't see you at the funeral," she said.

His smile faded as he sank into the chair opposite the cluttered dressing table. "Look, I'm sorry. I just couldn't face it." He spread his hands in a helpless gesture.

She wondered briefly if there was another reason. "I'm not here because of that," she said. "I guess you heard what happened."

"Oh, Jesus, yeah. Guess they had to pin it on someone, the bastards." His brow wrinkled in sympathy, but just as quickly smoothed. "But, hey, you'll beat it. I mean, they might as well arrest the fucking Pope."

She wasn't sure if she appreciated the comparison. "I was hoping you could clear up a few things," she said.

"Sure. Anything I can do to help." He sat back, spreading his arms.

Marc leaned forward. "Where were you that night?"

"What the fuck. You think *I* offed her?" Brent's benign expression turned angry.

"We're not saying that." Anna was quick to soothe him. "We just thought that if you *were* there, you might have noticed some-thing suspicious." She averted her eyes from the gap where his robe didn't quite meet.

"Afraid I can't help you there." He frowned, reaching for the pack of cigarettes on the dressing table. "I was at a bar with some friends. The police checked it out. The last time I saw her was that day at the house." He shot Anna a meaningful look, and she blushed.

"I heard she was getting ready to cut you off without a cent." Marc eyed him dispassionately.

Brent lit his cigarette and took a long drag, sending a stream of smoke jetting toward the ceiling. "Yeah? Well, you heard wrong. She blew off steam from time to time, but it didn't mean shit. You know how she was." He looked at Anna, then back at Marc, his eyes narrowing. "Not that it's any of your business."

"We're not accusing you of anything," Anna reiterated.

After a moment Brent relented and said, "Yeah, okay. She heard I was pulling in some bucks doing this." He shrugged. "I know what you're thinking. But, hey, it's a business just like any other. Guy who owns it is married with three kids, goes to church on Sunday. You know who our best customer is? Bristol Hotels." He snorted. "Adult pay-per-view is big with traveling salesmen."

"Look, I don't care what you do for a living," Anna told him. In light of her own situation it didn't seem so shocking. "I'm just trying to get to the bottom of all this."

"Man, if I knew who did it, he'd be one sorry fuck after I got through with him." Brent shook his head, looking more sad than angry. It hadn't occurred to her that he'd miss anything other than his monthly check.

"Any idea who it might've been?" Marc zeroed in.

Brent took a languid drag off his cigarette. "Why don't you talk to Lefevour?"

"You think Glenn had something to do with it?" The uneasiness she'd felt seeing him at the funeral crept back in.

"You tell me." In the mirror over the dressing table she could see that Brent's sun-bleached hair was starting to thin in back. The moans on the other side of the door grew louder. Anna heard a female voice urge breathlessly, "Oh yeah, baby, yeah. Give it to me. Oooooohhh . . . harder . . . *harder* . . ."

Suddenly the memory came rushing in, and this time she couldn't stave it off. Was it only three weeks ago? It seemed like a year. She closed her eyes, reliving that day . . .

Anna sat staring at the computer screen, frowning and nibbling on a thumbnail.

From: kssnkrys@aol.com
To: monica@monicavincent.com
Subject: Life sucks

Dear Monica,
Sorry i haven't written in a while. The thing is, i got fired. The Bitch didn't like me from the get go and was always on my case ragging me about every little thing, even stuff i didn't do. And that was while Brianna had the mumps and was keeping me up all night. So I guess i sort of lost it. I let her (The Bitch) have it. Even told her what a skank she is and i don't know how her old man can stand to look at her. I know. I should've kept my mouth shut, but i was sick and tired of her acting like I was something she stepped in.

Like she was doing me this big fat favor or something. Don't i deserve some respect? Is that too much to ask?

Well, anyway, now my parole officer is on my case. It won't be easy finding another job but I won't give up. Sometimes I think the only thing that keeps me going is knowing you care.

Your friend,
Krystal

Anna's frown deepened as she typed her reply:

From: monica@monicavincent.com
To: kssnkrys@aol.com
Subject: Re: Life sucks

Krystal,
I DO care . . . very much. And I understand about your boss being on your case . . . believe me. But there are better ways of handling those kinds of situations. And if all else fails, you can quit without burning bridges. I'm not

saying this to kick you when you're down. I know what you've been through. But look at it this way—if you can make it this far, you can go the rest of the way. Who cares what someone else thinks? It's what you think of yourself that counts.

As ever,
Monica

Anna felt bad about deceiving Krystal, her more than anyone, but would she take her advice if she knew it was Monica's no-body of a sister giving it? Also, if the tabloids ever got wind of it . . .

She sighed. She had enough problems without that. Like the fact that Monica had started drinking again. And the way she'd been acting lately, like a tire on a speeding car about to blow. At the moment she was lighting into Brent, who'd dropped by a little bit ago, no doubt to ask for money. Angry voices drifted up the backstairs.

"You've taken me for my last dime, you sorry son of a bitch," Monica shrieked at the top of her lungs. "In fact, you can kiss your alimony good-bye!"

"Yeah? Well, in that case *you* can talk to my lawyer." Brent was all bluster and no bite.

She gave a harsh laugh. "What are you going to pay him with, a postdated check? God, you're pathetic."

"Okay, okay, I'm sorry I didn't tell you about the gig. But like I said, it's only short term." His voice turned wheedling. "The thing is, I'm a little low on cash right now. If you could slide me some, I'll pay you back as soon as I get caught up."

"When would that be, in twenty years or so?"

"Please, babe."

"Don't 'babe' me. In case you haven't noticed, we're divorced."

"Okay, okay. Calm down."

"That's what you said when I found out you were fucking that bimbo. I swear it ought to be coming out of *your* hide, not the other way around."

"Look, it's not much. You pay your friggin' gardener more." Anna could hear the fear in his voice even as he attempted to stand up for himself.

"And how, exactly, have you earned it?"

"Christ, Monica, I was *there* for you. I worshiped the ground you walked on."

"Oh, really? And just how does charging whores to my American Express figure into all this worship?" Monica was really getting into it now. Anna could tell she was enjoying herself.

"You cut off a guy's balls, what's he supposed to do? *You* were the one I wanted."

"And that's supposed to make me feel better?"

Anna got up and closed the door. She could still hear them, but the voices were muffled now. There was a time when she'd have felt compelled to rush downstairs in case things got ugly, but no more. The only reason she was still there was because she had yet to line up another job. It wasn't easy when she had to make calls in secrecy and sneak off for interviews feeling like an FBI operative.

The muffled bleating on the other side of the door grew louder, and Anna felt a twinge of alarm. Suppose things *did* get out of hand? Like the time Monica threw a vase at Brent, missing his head by inches.

Anna sighed. Now that she'd made the decision to leave, each day was unbearable, a Sisyphean boulder to be pushed up-hill, the task made even more difficult by Monica's being so keyed up—almost as if she sensed a shift in the wind.

Then she thought of Krystal, struggling to make a go of it against nearly impossible odds. *Why should I feel sorry for myself?* Things were better now that her mother was at the Sunshine Home. She'd joined a gym and was spending more time with Liz and Dylan. She'd even spoken to Marge Fowler at the museum about becoming a docent. Marge, in turn, had steered her toward the Women's League, which was looking for volunteers to conduct tours of historic homes. In preparation, Anna was reading everything she could get her hands on to refresh her memory of the town's history. As a result, she'd become friendly with Vivienne Hicks at the library. They'd gotten together for coffee a few times, and the other day Vivienne had complimented her on her weight loss.

Others had begun to comment as well. Anna no longer shopped in the plus size department at Rusk's. She'd even started wearing makeup—not much, just enough to give her a little color and bring out her eyes.

(If she'd learned anything from all the beauty tips she'd been doling out through the years, it was that less is more.) Norma Devane had even persuaded her to add a few subtle highlights to her hair.

Her thoughts turned to Marc, the memory of their night together like a precious gem tucked away for safekeeping. If he hadn't called, it wasn't because he didn't want to see her, she knew, but because he was afraid of hurting her. Her friends might tell her she was naive, but the look on his face when he'd said good-bye—no one was that good an actor. She'd seen how torn he was, wanting what she was offering and at the same time knowing it wouldn't be enough for either of them.

She could almost hear Liz's derision. Welcome to the real world, she'd say. But the last thing Anna wanted was to be lumped in with Liz. The mere fact that Marc had kept his distance proved he was better than her sister's married lover, whoever he was.

With an effort, Anna brought her attention back to her screen: One message was from a fan who'd seen every one of Monica's movies numerous times and suggested a remake of *Dark Victory* in which Monica could do the

Bette Davis role, crippled instead of blind. Another from Susieq555@earthlink.com wanting to know what Monica thought of interracial dating, on account of she had the "hots" for this black guy at work. And one from a retired nurse named Dottie, who after years in an abusive marriage had found the courage to leave her husband. She thanked "Monica" for her encouragement, saying it was the extra push she'd needed.

Thank goodness she hadn't heard from Hairy Cary in a while. Maybe he'd been scared off by her last e-mail telling him not to worry about security at LoreiLinda, that in addition to a state of the art alarm system, it was patrolled by security guards with attack dogs. A bit of a stretch maybe, but how was he to know otherwise?

She was logging out when she realized she could no longer hear Monica and Brent. Had they made up, or merely taken it to another part of the house? She got up and cautiously cracked open the door. It was past lunch and she was starving. She weighed the risk of a trip to the kitchen, which might result in her being dragged into the fight.

In the end hunger decided for her. She

tiptoed downstairs to find the kitchen empty except for Arcela, washing up after lunch. She opened the fridge to find it stocked with the low-fat cheese and sliced turkey breast Arcela bought just for her. "What's the latest from Cherry?" she asked as she was spreading mustard on a slice of whole wheat bread.

Arcela brightened. "She coming soon. Lawyer say everything okay." She hesitated, then said softly, her eyes filling with tears, "Thank you, Miss Anna."

"It was nothing, really." All she'd done was get Maude's friend, Dorothy Steinberg, to write a letter saying that Cherry would have work at the hospital when she arrived in the States. "I'm just glad it worked out. I can't wait to meet her."

Anna was about to bite into her sandwich when she heard a peal of laughter out on the patio. She looked out the window, catching sight of Monica and Brent, who seemed to have forgotten their tiff. Not only that, they'd been joined by Glenn. She hadn't heard him buzz—Arcela must have let him in. These days she was so preoccupied, she could hardly concentrate on her job.

Monica summoned her with a wave. Oh, God. There was no way she could ignore it. Monica wouldn't buy the excuse that she was on her lunch break, and these days Anna had been going out of her way not to ruffle any feathers. When the time came, she wanted to part on good terms, for their mother's sake if nothing else.

Leaving her sandwich, she slid open the door and stepped out onto the patio. She hadn't seen either Brent or Glenn in a while. Prepared for the standard greetings—a meaningless wink from Brent and hearty hello from Glenn (like a teacher urging a shy child in a sing-along)—she was surprised to find them staring at her as if they'd never before laid eyes on her.

Brent let out a long low whistle. "Well, what do you know?" He eyed her up and down before turning to Monica. "Your sister's a stone fox."

"Not that you haven't always been gorgeous," Glenn was quick to interject. "But this . . ." He stepped back to get a better look. In his black silk T-shirt and gray Armani jacket, beads of sweat nestled like jewels in his gelled hair, he looked almost . . . vulpine. "I'd sign you in an instant." He caught himself, adding, "Though you'd have a tough time competing with my star client."

"Yes, isn't it amazing?" Anna detected a cold undercurrent in Monica's voice. "I've been after her to let me buy her a whole new wardrobe, but she insists on taking in her old clothes. She's always been too practical for her own good."

Even Anna, who knew better than anyone what her sister was capable of, was struck by the deftness with which Monica had transferred the focus from Anna's slender new figure to the baggy slacks and top she had on—clothes that had fit just weeks ago—at the same time reminding Brent and Glenn of how generous she was.

Anna's cheeks warmed, and she dropped her gaze. "I don't have much time to shop," she said lightly, thinking of all the times she'd pushed her sister up and down Rodeo Drive without Monica's once offering to buy her so much as a pair of pantyhose.

"Not to worry, babe. With a bod like that, you don't need to get all dolled up." Brent's eyes roamed up and down.

Glenn said heartily, "What do you say we all go for a swim?"

Anna's heart sank. But before she could mutter some excuse, Monica smiled her little cat smile, saying, "Just what I feel like."

Anna cast a desperate glance at Brent, to no avail. He was in no position to call the shots. Whatever Monica wanted, she got. The only reason she railed at him from time to time was because she liked reminding him of who the boss was.

Anna gave it her best shot nonetheless. "I'd love to, but I promised Thierry I'd get back to him about those changes—you know how he hates to be kept waiting."

Monica acted as if she hadn't heard. "There should be enough towels, though with Arcela you never know." She sighed— the long-suffering employer, too softhearted for her own good. "Why don't you run and check?" she told Anna.

Blood rushed up into Anna's cheeks. She wanted to slap her sister, but to Brent and Glenn it would look as if it were coming out of left field. Plus, there was no limit to what Monica would do to get back at her—like cutting off payments to the Sunshine Home, which on more than one occasion she'd threatened to do. She took a deep breath and set off toward the pool house.

Minutes later, she was reaching into the drawer where the swimsuits were kept when it occurred to her that her old one would hang on her like an elephant's skin. She dug through the tangle of bikinis her sister had favored before the accident, choosing the least skimpy. Keeping her eyes averted from the mirror, she wriggled into it. When she finally risked a peek, a shock wave rippled through her. Not only was the bikini a perfect fit, she looked . . .

Sexy. Anna wasn't just flattering herself: There was no denying what she saw in the mirror—breasts that swelled pleasingly from her halter top and a butt that didn't jiggle when she moved this way and that. It wasn't just that she'd lost weight; her workouts at the gym were paying off. How was it she hadn't noticed until now?

She stepped outside just as Brent and Glenn were emerging from the changing room on the other side. Brent let out another wolf whistle while Glenn just stared.

Monica, who'd been wearing her swimsuit when Brent arrived, was clearly none too pleased that she'd been upstaged, if only for the moment. She eyed Anna from across the pool, the stony look on her face saying it all. Then she called with forced cheer, "When you guys are done checking out my sister, I could use a hand over here!" She turned to Anna as she drew near. "I'd forgotten I still had that old thing. Well, you're welcome to it. God knows *I* couldn't get away with it these days."

"What are you talking about?" Glenn delivered his line without a hitch. "You're still the most gorgeous woman on the planet."

"Who isn't getting laid." Monica spoke lightly, as if it were the most marvelous joke.

Only Anna knew that it was the truth—that Monica hadn't been to bed with anyone since the accident. Not that there wouldn't have been a line forming to the left should she so much as crook a finger, but her pride wouldn't allow it. She preferred instead to foster the illusion of being a femme fatale, flirting outrageously with everyone from Glenn to the gardener's sons, occasionally even overstepping the line, like with Andie's boyfriend. She did nothing, either, to discourage the rumors that flew fast and thick, such as the one about the piano tuner with whom she'd supposedly had an affair—a rumor that had surely enhanced his reputation as much as hers. But underneath it all, Anna felt certain, lay the desperate re-alization that she'd lost everything that had once defined her as a woman.

It was enough to make Anna feel sorry for her. Almost.

She slipped into the pool, and after swim-ming a short distance found it wasn't so ter-rible now that she didn't feel like a hump-back whale. She paddled about while the two men kept Monica company in the shal-low end, and as soon as she could do so without drawing attention to herself, climbed out.

Arcela, knowing she must be starved, had brought out a tray of fruit and cheese. Anna helped herself to some grapes, stretching out on a chaise longue. She was surprised to find she wasn't having such a bad time. It was better than being in her stuffy office upstairs, though six months ago if anyone had told her there'd be a day when she wouldn't hate the sight of herself in a swimsuit, she'd have laughed.

It wasn't long before Glenn announced regretfully that it was time for him to go—he was having dinner with Harvey, he said, dropping the name of one of the most im-portant producers in Hollywood the way wealthy women did their fur coats. Anna seized the chance to make her own excuses as well.

She was in the changing room struggling with the clasp on her top when the door eased open. She swung about in surprise to find Glenn poised just inside the doorway, the light slanting through the louvers making him look sinister somehow, like Claude Rains in *Notorious.* "Need some help with that?" he asked.

"Glenn. What are you doing in here?" Anna's arms dropped to her sides, and she eyed him uncertainly.

"I'm not making you uncomfortable, I hope." He smiled disarmingly.

"No, of course not." She wanted to kick herself. Why had she said that? He had to know how awkward this was.

"I didn't want to embarrass you out there, but the way you look in that," his gaze traveled downward, "should be illegal."

Anna cringed inwardly. She'd heard better pickup lines in B movies. "Thanks." She spoke offhandedly, ever so casually reaching for the towel she'd discarded.

"But, then, I've always thought you were beautiful."

Liar, she thought. But he sounded so sincere she was momentarily thrown off guard. When he walked over and pulled her into his arms, she was too stunned to protest.

Then his mouth was on hers. Oh, God.

There was a time she might have welcomed his kiss, but now all she was aware of were his clammy trunks sticking to her skin and his tongue thrusting hotly into her mouth. She tried to squirm away, but he only held her tighter, as if she were doing it to excite him. She let out a little cry, pushing against him. "Glenn . . . no. Please."

He drew back with a mock injured look. "You're kidding, right?"

"No, I'm not." She put as much force into the words as she could without shouting. She didn't want the others to hear. "I like you. Let's keep it that way, okay?"

It was the exact wrong thing to have said. "I like you, too." His voice grew husky and his eyelids drooped. He traced the line of her collarbone with his fingertip. She'd never noticed before how hairy he was, even the backs of his hands—like an ape's.

"I didn't mean it that way," she protested weakly.

"I know, but can't friends have fun, too?" He tugged playfully at one of her straps.

"Come on, Glenn. I'm serious." She injected a lighthearted note into her voice, hoping against hope that she could keep this from escalating.

"Me, too." He grinned, his wet trunks leaving nothing to the imagination.

"Look, if I gave you the wrong idea, I—"

He covered her mouth with his, thrusting his hips forward and grinding into her. A finger worked its way under the elastic of her bikini bottom. As she struggled to escape, it only seemed to inflame him further.

"Stop it!" she hissed. "Stop right now, or I'll—"

"Scream?" His voice was low and intimate, almost amused, as if they shared a secret, which in a way they did: They both knew who Monica would blame.

Again, Anna hesitated—just long enough for him to take it as compliance. Now he was forcing her legs apart with his knee. She could feel him hard and hot under his damp trunks, and was swamped with panic. She thought of Marc, how gentle he'd been. It gave her the strength she needed.

Anna threw her head back and screamed at the top of her lungs.

Glenn jerked back, scowling. He clearly hadn't expected this, not from mousy Anna. Before he could gather his wits and re-arrange his trunks, the door flew open. Over Glenn's hairy shoulder Brent stood silhou-etted in the doorway.

"What the—hey, get your hands off her!" He lunged forward, shoving Glenn, who staggered backward.

He caught hold of a chair, righting him-self. And in the split second before he charged, Glenn's true self was revealed: the kid from Compton who'd traded Echevarria for his mother's maiden name and spent as much time studying the habits of the studio executives he'd chauffeured around as he had his college textbooks.

He launched himself at Brent, not like a boxer but like a street fighter, aiming low. Though Brent was taller and outweighed him by at least twenty pounds, his muscles were mostly for show. The blow caught him in the belly and sent him reeling back against the wall with a grunt of expelled breath. Like a stunt man in a western, he slid slowly to the floor, landing with a muffled thud.

Anna stood frozen. Even Glenn didn't move as he stared at Brent huddled on the floor, gasping for breath. She had an image of the three of them caught like this forever, a Pompeian tableau, then a shadow fell over the doorway. She looked up to see Monica, her eyes glittering with a hatred so intense Anna felt an icy chill trickle down her spine.

Leaving her sister wasn't going to be as easy as she'd hoped. But staying might be even harder.

The memory receded, leaving Anna chilled as she sat hugging herself in Brent's seedy dressing room. "Glenn? I don't see him as a murderer, if that's what you mean." He might be a lot of other things, but not that.

"That's not what he's saying about *you.*" Brent took another drag off his cigarette. "He told the cops you'd threatened Monica. They asked me if I ever noticed anything along those lines."

Anna burned at the indignity of it. "What did you tell them?"

"That from what I could see it was the other way around. The way she treated you, I wouldn't've blamed you if you *had* offed her."

Anna felt the blood drain from her face. Brent might have meant well in his own way, but he'd only succeeded in making her look worse.

Marc took hold of her hand, squeezing it. "How do we know he isn't blowing smoke to cover his own ass?"

Anna shook her head. "You don't slaughter your cash cow."

"Maybe we're looking too hard for a motive."

"A crime of passion?" It had occurred to her, but as far as she knew they hadn't been romantically involved, which ruled out the jealous lover scenario.

Before they could speculate further the door cracked open and the punk-haired girl stuck her head in. "They're ready for you," she told Brent. "Need to warm up?"

He winked to let her know it wouldn't be necessary. While Anna did her best not to think too hard about what sort of warm-up she'd had in mind, he rose to his feet. "Listen, I'm sorry—you got a bum rap," he told

Anna. "Anything I can do, you know where to reach me."

"Thanks," she said, thinking he'd done more than enough already.

He kissed her on the cheek and was out the door, leaving a trail of Brut.

"So much for Brent," she observed dryly to Marc as they were pulling out of the parking lot. "We're no further ahead than when we started."

"Except that we now know exactly where things stand with Glenn."

"Yeah, I know that he's a liar and a snake in the grass."

This time she didn't hold back, giving him a *full* account of that day—how Glenn had pawed her, and how if Brent hadn't stopped him, he'd have forced himself on her. Marc didn't say a word. It wasn't until she was finished that he abruptly veered off onto the shoulder.

"You know it wasn't your fault, don't you?" he said sternly, twisting around to face her.

"Rationally, yes."

"What would happen if you put the blame where it belonged?"

"I'm not sure what you're getting at," she said.

"Maybe you're afraid you'd have to do something about it."

She gave in to a small smile. "You sound like a shrink."

"Just promise me that the next time you're pissed off at someone, you'll let them have it."

"Even if it's you?"

"Especially me."

Anna hadn't realized she was trembling until he pulled her into his arms and she felt a deep calm settle over her. "I still don't see him as a murderer." Much as she might like to.

"Would you have pegged him for a rapist?"

"He didn't—" She stopped herself. "No."

Marc drew back. "Okay, then, let's see what he has to say for himself." His expression was dark as he shifted into gear and edged back out onto the road.

"Assuming he'll even talk to us."

"With any luck, we'll catch him off guard."

She wondered what good it would do. If by some stretch of the imagination Glenn *had* killed Monica, how on earth could they prove it? Even so . . .

She gave Marc directions to Glenn's office, adding, "If we hurry, we might catch him before he goes to lunch."

CHAPTER ELEVEN

As Anna and Marc were making their way south on the Santa Monica freeway, Finch was eyeing the envelope propped on her dresser. She'd been out since breakfast exercising Cheyenne in the ring, and had dashed inside to shower and throw on some clean clothes before meeting Andie. They were hosting a birthday tea at Tea & Sympathy for a bunch of preteen girls, the first one having been such a huge success they were now booked months in advance.

But thoughts of squealing thirteen-year-olds vanished as she picked up the letter, no doubt left by Maude, who usually fetched the mail. It was pale blue and crinkly and smelled faintly of lavender.

When she noted the return address, her heart began to pound.

Miss Lorraine Wells
1345 Bellvue Manor
Pasadena, CA 91105

She sank down on the bed, tearing open the envelope. When she'd written to Lorraine, she hadn't expected to hear back so soon. In fact, she hadn't expected to hear from her at all. Now she withdrew the single sheet of stationery with a trembling hand.

Dear Miss Kiley,
Thank you for your letter. I would like to meet with you, if possible, but unfortunately I don't get out much these days. I'm eighty-seven and have had two hip replacements. If you could come to me, I would greatly appreciate it. I'm sure we would have lots to talk about.

I can be reached at (626)555-8976. I look forward to hearing from you.

Yours truly,
Lorraine Wells

Finch read it again, frowning. What did it mean, exactly?

She's probably just a lonely old lady looking for company. All she'd get would be an earful of stories she had no part in. That is, if Lorraine still had her marbles.

But from her letter, she seemed sane enough. And suppose, just suppose, they were related. She slid the letter back into its envelope, tucking it away in a drawer. *Wait'll I tell Lucien.*

The thought took her by surprise. Why him, and not Andie? One kiss didn't make them a couple. Neither did the fact that tomorrow she was going to a barbecue at his house. Never mind that Lucien had joked that his dad was so laid back he could have a girl spend the night and the old man wouldn't bat an eye.

He's not like other guys, she told herself. Most of whom were forever trying to get into your pants. Unless he was just playing it smart, like the last guy she'd been with, who'd pretended to love her but who was only using her to get back at his ex-girlfriend, it turned out.

Pushing aside the memory of those days, she glanced about as if to get her bearings.

Her room off the barn was pretty much as it had been when it was Hector's, with the exception of the quilt on the bed, a present from Maude's sewing circle when her adoption had become final, and the posters she'd hung—one showing a herd of mustangs galloping across a plain, and another of an Appaloosa mare and her colt. Stuck in the frame of the mirror over the dresser was a snapshot of Andie and her mugging for the camera at Ian's most recent gallery opening, and one of Laura and Hector surrounded by the entire Kiley-Delarosa clan on their wedding day.

Finch showered and threw on a dress. Normally she lived in jeans, but all the girls at the party would be dressed up. She didn't want to look shabby in comparison.

"My, don't you look nice," Maude said as she breezed into the kitchen, the screen door banging shut behind her. "I don't believe you've met my friend Dr. Steinberg." She gestured toward the woman seated beside her at the table, not as old as Maude; her hair was more brown than gray.

She looked familiar. "Aren't you . . . ?"

"Miss November," she said with a laugh, thrusting out her nearly flat bosom.

"Though I'd prefer if you called me Dorothy."

Finch recalled that Dorothy, while not an official member of the sewing circle, had been asked to pose for the calendar since it had been inspired partly by her—the profits would go toward a research program she'd spearheaded. It had all started the year before when Maude sent flowers to thank her for saving Jack's life—Dorothy was head neonatologist at Dominican—which had led to Dorothy's asking her to help out at the hospital's annual book drive. They'd been fast friends ever since.

"Are you guys planning an encore?" Finch teased, glancing at the photos strewn over the table, outtakes from the shoot. She eyed a sepia-toned nude of Mavis Fitzgerald at the piano, a fringed shawl draped artfully over one shoulder.

"Heavens, no. Once was enough." Maude hastened to explain, "We're trying to decide which of these would work best for the label. It's for the Easter bake sale. You know how the club always put up a batch of jam? Well, Dorothy thought up the perfect name—Well Preserved. How's that for catchy?"

Finch shook her head, smiling. She knew she ought to be used to Maude's antics by now, but this one took the cake. "Aren't you guys famous enough as it is?"

"More like *infamous.*" Maude's blue eyes twinkled.

"How about this one?" Finch pointed at a group photo of the ladies holding potted plants over their strategic areas, with Maude in the center, peering out from under a large straw hat. It was so . . . well, *Maude.*

"You don't think I look too—" Maude broke off with a giggle.

"Sexy?" Finch teased. "Yeah, you'll give old Waldo ideas." It was well known that the caretaker at the country club had a crush on her, though Maude went out of her way to discourage it. She'd had enough of watching a man drink himself to death, she'd say crisply, referring to her late husband. Finch dropped a kiss on her cheek, which smelled of lilies of the valley. "Gotta run. I'll be back in time for supper." She waved to Dorothy on her way out. "Bye. Nice meeting you."

Rattling down Old Sorrento Road in Hector's pickup, her thoughts turned to Anna.

Reporters were still camped out in front of her house—only a handful now, but evidently enough to keep her at bay. Finch was eager to share her news—they'd raised almost three thousand dollars so far!—but last night when she'd gone over to tell her, no one was home. She consoled herself with the thought that there'd be even more money by the time Anna returned. Today she and Andie planned on hitting up some of the mothers at the party.

She arrived at Tea & Sympathy to find Claire bustling about in her apron, putting the finishing touches on the table settings. "I'm not late, am I?" she asked. Claire was always so together, you felt as if you'd come up short somehow.

"Right on time." She stuck a sprig of clematis into a bud vase and straightened to smile at Finch. "Andie's in the kitchen. I'm sure she could use a hand."

Claire's hair, the color of maple syrup, was twisted into a top-knot from which curly tendrils escaped to trail down her slender neck. The gold heart locket her husband Matt had given her when they got engaged—a photo of him and his two children

tucked inside—peeked from under her ruffled silk blouse.

Their wedding last Christmas was the
most romantic one Finch had ever seen: a
candlelight ceremony at St. Xavier's, with
Miss Hicks from the library, who had a surprisingly good voice, singing "Ave Marie,"
followed by an elegant indoor reception at
Isla Verde.

From out back came the banging of ham-
mers and buzz of saws—Matt and his crew
converting the garage he and Claire would
eventually move into. The work was almost
done. All that was left was choosing paint
and wallpaper and tiles—something that
bored Andie to tears, but which Finch,
who'd grown up never knowing a real
home, found endlessly fascinating.

In the kitchen she found Andie arranging
miniature strawberry tarts on doily-covered
plates. She reached for one, and Andie
slapped her hand. "Uh-uh. Remember last
time."

How could she forget? A group of twelve-
year-olds, who collectively couldn't have
weighed more than Matt, had scarfed up
every crumb and clamored for more. Luckily, the freezer was stocked for just such

emergencies. A minute or so in the microwave and the girls were gobbling up warm brownies and lemon squares.

"Let's hope today's crew is a little less ravenous," she said.

Andie handed her a knife, pointing her toward the pan of brownies on the stove. "Make sure to cut them small so it looks like more."

Minutes before the guests were due to arrive, each table had been set with a tiered silver étagère on which plates of finger sandwiches, the strawberry tarts, miniature cream puffs and éclairs, and bite-size cookies and brownies were displayed. Claire had bought the étagères from Delilah Sims, a Tree House regular, who'd discovered them in the china closet at her grandmother's last year when she was getting ready to auction off the estate. (Finch hadn't even known what they were called until Claire told her, and now she was always careful to use the correct French pronunciation—it made her feel sophisticated.)

Claire stepped back to admire the effect. "It almost makes me wish I were thirteen again."

"What were you like?" Andie licked a

smudge of chocolate frosting from her finger. It was odd seeing the two of them together—so alike in some ways, so different in others. Andie hadn't even known Claire existed until a little more than a year ago, but now they were as close as sisters who'd grown up together. Andie had been the maid of honor at Claire's wedding, and when Claire's adoptive mother died last year, Andie had flown with her to Miramonte for the funeral.

Claire smiled. "I thought I was a freak, but I'm sure it was mostly in my head. Of course, it didn't help that I was a foot taller than the tallest boy in the class."

"You should hear Justin." Andie made a face. Her little brother had shot up this past year and sounded like Kermit the Frog. "Last year girls were radioactive. Now all he and his friends can talk about is which ones are wearing bras."

Claire poured milk into a creamer. "I was the last girl in my class to get one. I used to pray in church that I'd grow breasts."

"Luckily, that's something I've never had to worry about." Andie glanced down wryly at her chest, the envy of every girl at Portola

High. "With me, it was acne. I looked like a pizza with all the extras."

"Pizza? I thought this was a tea party."

All heads turned to Andie's mother as she breezed in through the door wearing form-fitting jeans and a leather jacket over a stretchy pink top. You didn't have to look further than Gerry to see where Andie had gotten her boobs.

Andie rolled her eyes. "We were talking about—" She broke off. "Never mind."

Gerry shrugged—she was used to Andie's treating her like she was from an-other planet—plunking the paper bag in her arms on the table by the door. Every week she brought over grocery sacks of lemons from the trees at Isla Verde, which Claire put to good use—everything from lemonade to her famous lemon tarts. "Who's the birth-day girl?" she asked, eyeing the hand-painted banner over the door.

"Reverend Griggs's daughter," Claire told her.

Gerry eyed the spread longingly. "Lucky for you I'm on a diet, or I'd be all over that like ants at a picnic." She claimed to have gained weight while in Europe, but Finch couldn't see it.

"Mom." Andie groaned good-naturedly when Gerry sampled a stray crumb. There were times when she acted more like the parent. It had gotten worse since her mom had remarried. In addition to acquiring a new step-dad, Andie had had to leave the house she'd lived in since she was born. Though having a bedroom twice the size as her old one went a long way toward making up for it, as far as Finch was concerned.

Gerry turned to Finch. "Any word yet?"

Finch felt a moment of panic, thinking Andie must have told her about Lorraine, before realizing she meant the baby. "They're still waiting," she said. The agency said it might take awhile."

"Tell them I'm keeping my fingers crossed," Gerry said.

The oven timer pinged. "My pie." Claire hurried to get it, Gerry clopping after her in chunky-heeled espadrilles, carrying the sack of lemons.

Finch heard a car pull into the driveway, and looked out the window to see a gaggle of thirteen-year-old girls in their Sunday best spilling from a black Subaru Outback, a harried-looking mom shepherding them up the path.

"Girls! Mind your manners!" she cried as they surged in through the door, squealing in delight. Finch recognized her as Mrs. Leahy, who owned the craft shop next door to Delarosa's, a small aerobicized woman with short, fluffy blond hair and Sally Jessy Raphael glasses. She turned to Finch with a weary sigh. "They slept over at our house last night. They were up until all hours, so they're a little wired."

"I think we can handle it," Finch said with a smile.

"In that case, they're all yours." She shot a warning look at a chubby redhead picking at one of the tarts as Andie rounded up the others, showing them where to put the presents. "I'll be back at three to pick them up."

She was almost out the door before Finch got up the courage to say, "Um, Mrs. Leahy? We're collecting money for the Anna Vincenzi Defense Fund. I was wondering if you'd, uh, like to make a donation. Anything you can spare. Every dollar helps."

Mrs. Leahy's smile faded, and Finch thought, *Uh-oh.* She'd had pretty good luck so far, but there were those who'd written Anna off as guilty until proven innocent.

Finch knew she was one even before she replied coolly, "I'd like to, but it might look as though I were taking sides."

"But she's innocent!" Finch blurted.

Mrs. Leahy shot her a sharply reproving look. Clearly she considered it an inappropriate topic to be discussing around the girls. "I think that's up to a jury to decide," she said in a pointedly hushed tone, taking a step back as if to distance herself. "Now, if you'll excuse me."

Finch felt blood rush up into her cheeks. How could anyone be so cold? She nearly gave the bitch a piece of her mind, but due to the occasion held her tongue. "I'm sure if you knew her . . ." Her voice trailed off. The look on Mrs. Leahy's face would've stopped traffic.

"I'll admit she doesn't seem the type, but you know what they say—it's the quiet ones you have to watch out for."

Finch swallowed the angry retort she longed to hurl at the woman's retreating back. She was almost glad for the distraction of the party; it kept her from her own murderous thoughts. She and Andie spent the next couple of hours pouring lemonade and hot chocolate and tea and replenishing the sandwiches and sweets that were gobbled up as fast as they could fill the plates. They smiled and cracked jokes and organized games, but all the while Finch felt a growing sense of dread. What chance would Anna have if the majority felt as Mrs. Leahy did?

Before long Claire was carrying out the cake, swirled with white chocolate frosting and decorated with sugar roses. The birthday girl's eyes widened as it was placed before her. The other girls clapped and cheered, and it took Natalie two attempts to blow out all the candles. The poor girl was asthmatic, though you wouldn't know it from her rosy cheeks and shining eyes.

Mrs. Griggs arrived promptly at three to pick up Natalie. After the brush off she'd gotten from Mrs. Leahy, Finch felt reluctant to approach her. But Mrs. Griggs had always been friendly, and Finch couldn't afford to wimp out, not with so much at stake.

She waited until Natalie was racing off to the car, a shopping bag of opened presents in each hand, but before she could open her mouth the pastor's wife gushed, "I can't thank you girls enough. I don't know when I've seen Nat so happy. I only wish I could've been here." She looked wistful. Gone were the days of playing den mother; Natalie had made it clear she wasn't to show her face.

"We took lots of pictures," Andie assured her.

"I can't wait to see them." From the expression on her face, it seemed thirteen would be as hard on Mrs. Griggs as on her daughter.

Finch cleared her throat. "Um, by the way, we were wondering if . . ."

Picking up on her hesitation, Andie rushed in. "We're collecting money for Anna Vincenzi's defense fund."

Finch waited dry-mouthed. The Reverend Mr. and Mrs. Griggs had a lot of influence in the community. If they had their doubts about Anna . . .

But Mrs. Griggs, round and plump like her husband, with a heart-shaped face accentuated by a widow's peak, put her out of her misery. "All I have on me at the moment is forty. Will that do?" She pulled out her wallet, taking out two twenties and pressing them into Finch's hand. "Please tell Anna she's in our prayers. As a matter of fact, my husband will be mentioning her in this Sunday's sermon." She confided in a hushed tone, "There are those who have a tendency to rush to judgment. They need reminding that it's that very thinking Jesus preached against." She tucked her wallet back into her purse with the smile of a woman hoping to make a difference in the world, however small. Finch could have kissed her.

There was a time she hadn't believed in God. But right now, watching Mrs. Griggs bob down the path, it seemed anything was possible—even miracles.

"Almost there." Lucien beeped his horn and a dog unfolded from the saffron cloud of dust hovering over the road.

Finch hadn't realized he lived this far out in the boonies. Noting the row of mailboxes tilting at angles amid a tangle of weeds, she wondered if his father was as well off as she'd thought. Casually, she said, "You never told me what your dad does."

"He's retired." Lucien wore the tight look he always did when the subject of his father came up.

"From what?"

"Life."

"I didn't know you could retire from that."

"You can if you're rich." From his cynical tone it was obvious that it wasn't something he was proud of. "My grandfather made a shitload of money in real estate," he explained. "Dad's been living off it ever since. He's sort of the black sheep of the family."

Black sheep or no, he might still be a snob. "I wonder what he'll think of me," she said nervously.

"He's in no position to judge, believe me." He must have realized how it sounded, for he was quick to add, "But I'm sure he'll like you. Why wouldn't he?"

Finch could think of a few reasons, but kept her thoughts to herself.

At the end of a bumpy dirt lane that made the road to her house seem like a freeway, they turned down a graveled drive and Lucien's house rose into view, a rambling split-level shaded by majestic live oaks. Higher up on the hill was a stable and corral. "I didn't know you had horses," she said.

"We used to—not anymore. They were all sold off." He pulled to a stop behind a string of cars. The yard was nicely landscaped—

there was even a koi pond with a miniature waterfall, but it looked unkempt.

"Too bad." She thought of how devastated she'd be to lose Cheyenne.

Lucien shrugged. "They were mostly for show, anyway."

Finch found it hard to imagine anyone owning a horse the way they would a sculpture, but refrained from saying anything as she followed Lucien into the house. The drapes were pulled, but even in the dim light she could see that it hadn't been cleaned in a while. Everywhere she looked were overflowing ashtrays, empty beer cans, and coffee mugs. Bits of what felt like pretzels and potato chips crunched under her soles as she made her way across the carpeted living room.

Voices punctuated by hearty male laughter drifted from out back. Finch stepped through a sliding glass door onto a cabana-shaded patio, where a group of middle-aged men sat around a table drinking beer. One lifted a hand in greeting without taking his eyes from a bald guy in a Hawaiian shirt who was telling a joke. When the punch line came, all five men roared with laughter. Only then did the one she assumed was Lucien's dad hoist himself out of his chair, cigarette in one hand, beer in the other, and amble over to greet them.

"Dad, this is Finch." Lucien looked nervous as he introduced them.

"Hey there. Glad you could make it." A fleshy hand engulfed hers, and she found herself looking up into a florid face vaguely resembling Lucien's.

"Thanks for having me, Mr.—"

"Guy. We're not sticklers for formality here." He winked. "What can I get you to drink?"

"A Sprite, if you have one." She had a feeling he'd have mixed her a martini if she'd asked.

"I'll get it." Lucien disappeared inside, leaving her alone with his father.

"I understand you're a fellow New Yorker." Guy dropped into a chair, gesturing toward the one beside it. "We had a duplex on Seventy-second and Madison. View of the park, the whole nine yards. Hell, I'm still paying for it," he said, a reference to the alimony he paid his ex-wife, no doubt.

"I lived in Flatbush." Finch felt a twinge of perverse pleasure seeing the look on his face. For people like Lucien's dad, that part of Brooklyn might've been the moon.

He quickly recovered and said a touch too heartily, "Well, it's not where you're from, it's where you end up that counts." He peered blearily up at Lucien, who'd reappeared, drinks in hand. "In' that right, son?"

"Right, Dad." Lucien wore a small tight smile.

"Take me, for instance. I got sick of the old rat race and threw in the towel. Decided it was time to enjoy life."

It looked to Finch as if he'd been enjoying it a bit too much, but all she said was, "You have a nice place."

"Fifteen acres of heaven. Is this living, or what?" He threw his arm out in an expansive gesture that toppled the beer can on the table at his elbow. It bounced off the tiles at his feet with a hollow, tinny sound before rolling off into the shrubs. "Just look at that view." He gazed out at the tawny hills rolling off into the distance. When he looked back to Finch, there was a beat in which he seemed to be wondering who she was and what she was doing there. Then he smiled and said, "But, hey, don't let me keep you. Why don't you two kids go for a swim?"

"I thought I'd show her around first." Lucien looked as if he couldn't wait to escape.

"Sure, take your time. I'll give you a shout when the steaks are on." He heaved himself from his chair with a creak of plastic webbing and headed back to his friends.

Lucien set their drinks down and steered her through a side gate onto a path that led up the grassy slope to the stable. After a moment Finch ventured cautiously, "Your dad seems nice."

"Yeah, he's a real barrel of laughs." Lucien cast a dark look back at the house.

"Everyone always thinks their own parents are the worst." She thought of Andie's dad, who acted as if she and Justin were relics from his first marriage that he no longer had use for but didn't have the heart to throw away. "Anyway, it can't be too bad, or you wouldn't be here."

"Let's just say it's the lesser of two evils."

"Well, at least you *have* parents."

"When they know I'm around." He kicked at a rock, which spun off into the tall grass. Then with a crooked smile he said, "But you're right, it could be worse. Besides, one more year and I'm outta here."

She felt a little pang, thinking of college. Lucien would be applying to Harvard and Yale; she'd be lucky to get into a state college.

They continued on in silence, the grass swishing at their legs. Insects swirled in the shafts of sunlight slanting through the trees and fat clouds scudded overhead, brindling the surrounding hills with their shadows.

When they reached the stable, Lucien poked his head in to make sure no wild creatures had taken up residence. Finch could see that it'd been awhile since anyone had been up there, yet it had the feel of something abruptly abandoned, as if the horses had been taken out for a ride one day and just never returned. The stalls were strewn with moldering straw, and dusty tack hung from pegs on the wall. Several pairs of mud-caked boots were lined up by the door.

"Do you ride?" she asked, fingering a bridle thick with dust.

Lucien nodded. "My mom used to take me. There's a stable in Central Park." He looked wistful, as if remembering happier times. "We stopped going after a while. It got so she could hardly stay in the saddle, she was so drunk."

She touched his arm, saying gently, "It won't be like this forever. You know that, don't you?"

He shrugged, looking unconvinced. "Yeah, I know. It just feels that way." He held her gaze and she knew he was going to kiss her.

This time she gave into it, letting his tongue play over hers. She didn't start to tense up until he drew back, asking, "You trust me, don't you?"

"Depends." This was where he'd suggest that they take their clothes off, that it wouldn't have to go any further than that, she could keep her bra and panties on if she liked.

He cocked his head, eyeing her with bemusement. "You still don't get it, do you?"

"What?"

"I feel like the luckiest guy on the planet just being with you."

Finch didn't know what to say. The idea that a guy would want her for herself, not just for what she could give him, was almost more than she could take in. "You do?" she croaked at last.

He nodded, his eyes searching her face. "Do you want to go back?"

She hesitated, then said softly, "No."

They unearthed a pile of saddle blankets from a trunk in the tack room. Lucien spread them over what was left of the hay in the loft and they stretched out. In the warm, still air under the rafters, they kissed some more. After a while she sat up and peeled off her T-shirt. She wasn't wearing a bra. Lucien lazily traced the tan line from her bikini.

"You're sure?" If she hadn't loved him before, she did then. It was obvious he wanted her, but he wanted even more for it to be *her* decision.

She remembered when she used to hand over her body like a coat at the door. "It's been awhile since—" she broke off.

He regarded her solemnly. "Did someone hurt you—is that it?"

She pulled her knees up to her chest, shivering in the warm air. "You know Suzy Wentworth?" He smiled, as if to say, *Who doesn't? She's the school slut.* "Well, that was me. They didn't even have to get me drunk." She felt a need to punish herself, to paint a picture so ugly Lucien would turn away in disgust.

"I don't care if you took on the entire football team," he said.

She felt something tightly wound inside her loosen just a bit. "It wasn't like I even wanted them. It was like . . ." she struggled to put it into words, "like the rest of the time I was invisible, and when I was with someone, I knew I was there."

Lucien nodded slowly. "I know the feeling."

She pushed his sleeve back, lightly running her fingertips over the angry purple scar on his wrist. This time he didn't pull away. "Your turn," she said.

"There's nothing much to tell." His voice was matter-of-fact. "It wasn't like I decided to off myself because my parents got divorced. Honestly? It was better without them going at each other all the time." He fell silent for a moment, staring up at the rafters, where motes of dust floated lazily in a shaft of sunlight. "Then, I don't know, a year or so ago it all just sort of fell apart. You know the saying, that's the way the cookie crumbles? That's how it felt, like little pieces of me breaking off."

Her fingertips moved up to his palm. "All the king's horses and all the king's men—"

"—couldn't put Humpty Dumpty together again." He gave a hoarse laugh.

"I saw someone die once."

"Really?" He turned to look at her.

After all this time it seemed less a memory than a half-remembered nightmare. "My foster mom's boyfriend. I watched him bleed to death and didn't lift a finger to help."

"I'm sure you had your reasons."

"Yeah, I hated him."

"Then he deserved to die."

"Nobody deserves to die." She was taken aback by the vehemence with which she spoke.

After a moment she stretched out beside him, listening to the measured beat of his heart and picturing the blood pumping in and out.

This should have been my first time, she thought when they made love at last. Instead, it only felt like the first.

She knew it wasn't the first time for him either, not just because of the condom in his wallet; she could tell from the careful way he moved inside her, as if not wanting to come too soon. After a few minutes she urged softly, "It's okay."

He drew back to look at her. "What about you?"

"I don't think I can." She hadn't with any of the others.

He smiled. "We'll see about that."

He rocked against her. With her previous lovers it had been quick, but with Lucien it was more like a slow dance with their clothes off. The sensations mounted—not the surging tide of romance novels, more like warm water lapping against her in little waves. Then all at once she arched back with a gasp. "Oh!"

Lucien cried out too, and after a moment rolled onto his back. Lying beside him, drenched with sweat, her heart racing, she recalled the halfhearted murmurs of affection that would be followed by the groping for clothes and gotta-run-I'll-call-you-in-the-morning dash out the door. But when Lucien stirred it was only to prop his head on one elbow and look down at her. "Just think, we could've gone swimming instead."

"Very funny."

His expression grew serious, and he gently brushed a strand of hair from her cheek. "You're beautiful, you know that?"

"You're just saying that."

"Why would I lie?"

"I don't know."

"You're going to have to trust someone sometime," he said. "It might as well be me."

She thought about what he'd said as they were heading back down the hill. Did she trust him enough to share her hopes and dreams? "I heard from that lady," she said cautiously.

"What lady?"

"The one I told you about—Lorraine Wells."

"What did she say?"

"She wants to meet me."

"When?"

"I was thinking of driving down next weekend."

"We could take my car."

She hadn't anticipated that he'd want to come along, and was quick to reply, "It wouldn't be much fun."

"Beats hanging around here."

She looked down, more grateful than she wanted him to know. At the same time a voice in her head cried that it wasn't too late; she could still back off without getting hurt. She paused, looking up at him. "You meant what you said before? This won't change anything?"

Lucien pulled her close, wrapping his arms around her and saying softly, "Why does change have to be bad?"

She arrived home that evening to find Laura and Hector seated on the sofa, holding hands and looking dazed. It was so rare to see either of them sitting still that Finch froze in her tracks, glancing apprehensively from one to the other, dire thoughts about Anna flitting through her head.

"What's wrong?" she asked.

Laura looked at her uncomprehendingly. Then a dreamy smile spread across her face. "Nothing," she said.

"The agency called." Hector stirred as if from a deep sleep, his broad brown face tilting slowly upward.

"On Sunday?" Finch stepped forward,

her foot coming down on a rubber dog bone that let out a strangled squeak.

"Susan couldn't wait to tell us." Laura's voice trembled with emotion. "They have a baby for us."

Finch felt a burst of relief—Anna was okay!—before it hit her: She was going to have a sister. "Omigod. Are you serious?"

"See for yourself." Laura levitated off the sofa, wafting over to the battered rolltop on which the computer sat, colored cubes floating across its screen.

She clicked the mouse and the floating cubes were replaced by a photo of a smiling, fat-cheeked baby with a thatch of black hair that stuck straight up. Finch felt her heart swell.

"Her name is Esperanza." Laura drew a finger across one of the baby's fat cheeks as tenderly as if it were flesh and blood. "Isn't she beautiful?"

"When do we get her?" Finch asked breathlessly.

"Susan says it'll be at least six weeks."

"It helps that I speak Spanish." Hector grinned like a proud papa, propping his dusty cowboy boots on the coffee table made from an old wooden shutter during what Laura referred to as her Martha Stewart meets Little House on the Prairie phase.

Finch stared at the photo. "She's so cute." *Esperanza.* Spanish for hope.

"I hope you're as happy about it as we are." Laura slipped an arm about her waist.

Laura didn't want her to feel any less important, she knew. "Are you kidding? Now I'll earn twice as much baby-sitting." Finch didn't trust herself to say what was in her heart. The last thing Hector needed was a pair of bawling women on his hands.

Laura laughed. "Lucky Jack. Now he'll have *two* nieces."

"Have you told Maude?" Finch felt a wet nose pressing against her leg and bent to stroke Pearl's head. Though half blind and just as deaf, she seemed to sense the excitement in the air.

"We will as soon as she gets back." Finch remembered that the sewing circle met at Mavis's on Sundays. "Don't you think she looks a little like Hector?" Laura had gone back to gazing rapturously at the screen.

"Who, Maude?" Finch teased.

Hector got up off the sofa and wandered over. "You know what they say—all us Mexicans look alike," he said with a wink.

As if it were just now sinking in, Laura threw her arms around Hector with a whoop of glee. He lifted her off her feet, twirling her around and around until they were both breathless.

The thought of Anna crept in. How could they celebrate? Because life went on. You couldn't separate the bad from the good anymore than you could the past from the future. Hadn't she learned that today with Lucien?

Before she knew it, she was joining hands with Laura and Hector, the three of them dancing about the room while poor old Pearl stood there with her tail wagging, looking on in confusion.

CHAPTER TWELVE

"Did I mention the D.A. is up for reelection this year?" Rhonda frowned as she looked up from the papers strewn across the table, absently reaching for a cookie.

The reporters camped outside her office around the clock had forced them to find other places to meet, and when Anna suggested Tea & Sympathy, her lawyer had leaped at the idea. But Rhonda looked so out of place amid the flowered curtains and tablecloths, her teacup balanced in a hand more accustomed to hoisting saddles and tightening girths, Anna couldn't help but smile.

"So?" She didn't see the significance.

Rhonda set her cup down in its saucer with a decisive clink. "He'll want to make his bones. A high-profile case like this? Made to order. He'll milk it for all it's worth."

"Are you always this optimistic?" Anna was too weary to get worked up.

"Only when I know they're out for blood. Speaking of which, let's have another look at that autopsy report." She shuffled through the files and papers spread in front of her.

Anna sighed. "We've been *over* it a hundred times."

Rhonda's head snapped up. "I have news for you, kiddo. Real life isn't *L.A. Law*—no last-minute evidence that somehow got overlooked, no surprise witnesses popping up at the zero hour."

"I'm sorry, I didn't mean—"

"It's about all the boring fine print and combing over every detail. *That's* how cases are won," Rhonda went on as if she hadn't spoken.

"What are the chances of its getting thrown out?"

"I'll give it my best shot, but don't get your hopes up." At the preliminary hearing in three weeks, evidence would be presented to determine whether or not a trial was warranted, though Rhonda had warned that it was only in rare instances, usually involving a procedural screwup, that cases were dismissed. "It doesn't help that our friend Mr. Lefevour has a restraining order against you."

Anna winced at the reminder. What had seemed a stroke of luck at the time had bitten her in the ass big time. She and Marc had caught Glenn just as he was stepping out through the revolving door to his building. Taken off guard, he'd been civil at first, but quickly grew hostile when he realized why they'd come.

"You want to talk? Okay, let's talk." He'd whipped out his cell phone. "I'm sure Detective Burch would like to be in on this, too."

"For God's sake, Glenn, you *know* me! You can't honestly think . . ." She was stopped cold by the seismic shift taking place in his face. He fought to control it, his jaw clenching and unclenching and a muscle twitching over one eye. It was then that she'd fully understood his love for Monica. Not romantic, but the love of the strong for someone in need of protecting—a pull she understood all too well.

His eyes burned like suns in a distant

galaxy behind the graduated lenses of his Vaurnets. "All I know is you're the reason she's dead. Now if you'll excuse me . . ." He'd pushed past them, striding toward his BMW idling at the curb, attended by a red-jacketed valet.

Since then Anna had refrained from further sleuthing, which wasn't as easy as it had seemed in all those Nancy Drew books she'd devoured as a child. She was leaving it to the private investigator Rhonda had hired.

The autopsy report surfaced, and Anna sipped her tea as Rhonda studied it. "Here's the thing I don't get," she said after a moment. "Toxicology results show a blood alcohol level of point one three five, which is more than twice the legal limit. Yet she put up a damn good fight." She withdrew a batch of eight-by-tens from a manila envelope, selecting one and passing it to Anna. "Look at the bruising on her arms. It's pretty extensive."

Anna forced herself to look at it the way she might have subjected herself to a minor but uncomfortable medical procedure. However many times she'd seen these photos, the horror never wore off. This one showed only Monica's neck, shoulders, and upper arms, the bruises standing out like ink smudges on pale blue stationery. A crumb from the cookie she was nibbling on caught in her throat and she coughed, reaching for her tea.

"I'm sorry." She dabbed at her watering eyes. "This might sound strange, but I still have a hard time believing she's dead. Every time the phone rings, I think it's Monica."

"It's hard losing a sister." From her tone, Anna didn't doubt she spoke from experience. Yet Rhonda didn't pat her back or offer words of comfort, which was a relief. What this ordeal had taught Anna was that there was only so much sympathy you could take.

"It's not that I miss her—that's what's so awful. Most of the time I wanted to wring her neck." She caught herself and winced, glancing about to make sure no one had overheard.

"Apparently you weren't alone." Rhonda gave a grim smile.

Anna was thankful for their table in a corner away from the window. It was just after eleven, with only a few holdovers from breakfast and the lunch crowd not due for another hour. The only ones close enough to overhear were Tom Kemp and Vivienne Hicks, but they were too absorbed in each other. Anna had heard that they'd become engaged and wanted to congratulate them, but the conversation would naturally turn to her predicament. She didn't want to rain on their parade.

"It's ironic," she said. "People hated her, but at the same time they wanted her approval." Like Lenny Duckworth, the contractor who'd done some work at Lorei-Linda last year and had sued after being stiffed on the bill. The other day he'd come up to Anna on the street and shocked her by bursting into tears. It seemed that for all his tough talk, he felt terrible that Monica had died thinking ill of him.

"Fame," Rhonda observed archly, "is a double-edged sword."

"It was like that even when she was a kid." Anna recalled how Monica had sweet-talked her teachers into giving her special treatment. And who was the only one who could tame their dad when he was on one of his tears? "It was as if she always knew she was special."

"Even dead, she's in the spotlight."

"Wherever she is, I'm sure she's enjoying every minute of it." Anna gave in to a small bleak smile.

They spent the next hour or so going over every detail of the report. Rhonda was even flying in an expert witness, a former county medical examiner, to testify at the preliminary hearing. They were winding up when Rhonda's cell phone trilled its digitalized rendition of the *William Tell Overture.*

"Yeah? Oh, hi." She listened, jotting something on an envelope. "Thanks." She hung up, informing Anna, "The results just came back on those prints—boys' size eight Nikes." Anna assumed she meant those belonging to the mystery trespasser.

"A kid?" Probably on a dare. She felt her whole body sag. She hadn't realized how much she'd been pinning her hopes on this wild card until now.

Rhonda didn't seem too perturbed. "It rules out one theory, at least."

"Which is?"

"That they were yours."

Anna gaped at her. "Why would I risk my neck climbing the wall when I could let myself in through the gate?"

"To make it look like an intruder."

Anna hadn't thought of that.

By the time they finished, it was close to noon. The tea in the pot had long since gone cold and a few scattered crumbs were all that remained of the cookies. From where she sat, Anna had a view of the sunny kitchen where Claire was bustling about—measuring, mixing, kneading, and occasionally bending to slide something in or out one of the ovens. Matt was at the table eating lunch; all she could see were the broad slabs of his shoulders and the back of his shaggy reddish-blond head.

Seeing them together reminded her of Marc and how close they'd grown these past weeks. He'd taken refuge at Laura's when the reporters had tracked him down at the inn, pestering him to comment on their relationship. Recalling the blurry photo in the most recent issue of the *Enquirer,* which showed them ducking into a car like a pair of fugitives, she winced inwardly. How long before he got tired of it and threw in the towel?

The bell over the door tinkled and Finch and Andie sailed in. Spotting her, they made a beeline for her table. "I *thought* that was your car out front." Finch's dark eyes danced—something was up. "We couldn't wait to show you." She dug into her canvas tote, pulling out a folded check. "You'll never guess who it's from."

"Marguerite Moore?" Anna joked.

Finch rolled her eyes at the idea of that mean-spirited busybody donating so much as a nickel to the fund. "I'll give you a hint. Think lottery ticket."

Anna recalled an item in the *Clarion* some weeks back, but she'd been too preoccupied to give it much notice. Now it came to her. "Clem Woolley?"

Finch tripped over her words in her eagerness to tell the story. It seemed the town eccentric and author of the self-published tome *My Life With Jesus* had purchased a pair of lottery tickets—he always bought two of everything, from sandwiches to seats for whatever was showing at the Park Rio—one of which had left him five thousand dollars richer. "He said that Jesus wanted you to have it."

"I don't know what to say." Anna shook her head in disbelief, smiling at the idea of Jesus' bailing her out with a winning lottery ticket—it gave new meaning to being saved.

"Guess the old coot's not as crazy as everyone thinks."

Anna looked up to find Mavis wiping her hands on her apron. Andie's grandmother had been keeping a respectful distance, but with all the commotion couldn't resist putting in her two cents.

"Grandma should know. He used to have a crush on her." Grinning, Andie slipped an arm about her waist. Where Andie was petite with curly dark hair, Mavis was tall and angular, her once-red hair the color of rusted iron.

Mavis snorted. "Don't be listening to her lies! And me a married woman." Even now that she was widowed and in her eighties, there were vestiges of the Irish war bride who must have turned more than a few heads. She leaned close to confide, "Though truth to tell, he was a little peculiar even back then."

"Maybe Clem only sees what the rest of us can't," Finch said thoughtfully.

"Don't tell me you've gone religious on us?" Mavis teased. "Better watch out, or before you know it Father Reardon'll be pouring water over your head."

Finch handed the check to Anna, who in turn passed it to Rhonda. She'd have to think of some way of repaying Clem, not to mention Finch and Andie. "You guys . . ." Looking at them, she felt remarkably blessed for someone facing the prospect of a life behind bars. "I don't know what to say."

"What goes around comes around." Mavis cleared away their cups and plates, stacking them on a tray. "After Glenda Greggins fell and broke her hip, who looked in on her nearly every day? And who volunteered when we needed someone to organize the church picnic last summer?"

Anna blushed, dropping her gaze. "It wasn't that big a deal." What she remembered most about old Mrs. Greggins was feeling bad that she couldn't do more.

"When it's for the right reasons, it never is." Mavis gave her a motherly pat. "How about another cookie, dear? We can't have you wasting away."

Anna smiled at the idea. "As if."

Finch eyed her in disbelief. "Have you looked at yourself in the mirror lately?"

Anna couldn't recall the last time she had. The very thing that had once consumed her was now the least of her worries. All she'd noticed was how loose her clothes had gotten.

"You're skinny as a rail," Andie said.

Anna looked down at her baggy slacks, saying dryly, "I guess there's a silver lining to every cloud."

A line was forming at the display case, and Mavis hurried off, tightening her apron strings the way a ship captain might secure the rigging on a sail. Rhonda stuffed the papers into her briefcase, saying she had to run. When she was gone, Anna scooted over to make room for the girls.

"When do you go back to school?" she asked.

"Thanks for reminding us." Andie groaned.

"Tomorrow." Finch slipped into Rhonda's empty chair.

Anna felt a twinge of guilt. "It wasn't much of a break for you, was it?"

"So much for getting a tan." Andie looked down at her pale arms, heaving an exaggerated sigh.

"Why bask in the sun when you can go door to door?" Finch teased.

"We couldn't have done it without Simon and Lucien," Andie put in loyally.

"I'll have to thank them, too." Anna found herself leaning toward the girls the way she would toward a campfire on a cold night. Their high spirits and enthusiasm were just what she needed. "What else have you guys been up to?"

"Oh, this and that." Finch dropped her gaze.

Anna cast her a stern look. "You know the best thing you could do for me? Talk about anything—I don't care if it's the weather— as long as it's not about this damn trial."

"Okay, what about you and Marc?" Finch shot her a mischievous look. "He hasn't ex- actly been sleeping alone every night."

Anna had fallen into the habit of slipping out after dark to visit Marc, who was stay- ing in Finch's room off the barn, but appar- ently it was the worst kept secret in the Kiley-Navarro household. "I don't know what you mean," she deadpanned.

The girls exchanged knowing looks.

"Where is he, anyway?" Finch asked. "I haven't seen him since yesterday."

"He had some things to take care of." Anna suspected it had something to do with his wife. "He should be back in a day or two. You sure you don't mind giving up your room?"

Finch shrugged. "Are you kidding? Marc's great. In fact, I think Maude's secretly in love with him." She pressed her lips together to keep from giggling. "But don't worry—she's not his type."

"I told her she could stay with us," Andie said. "God knows we have enough room." She pretended to hate living at Isla Verde, but there was no getting around the fact that it was palatial compared to her old house.

"If Maude's snoring gets any worse, I just might take you up on it," Finch said.

Andie nudged her with an elbow. "Finch has some news. Go on, tell her."

Anna smiled. "I'm all ears." It couldn't be the baby; she'd heard all about it from Laura.

"Remember that lady I wrote to a while back?" Color bloomed in Finch's cheeks. "Well, she wants to meet me."

Anna felt a twinge of apprehension,

knowing Finch was almost sure to be dis-appointed. "Really? That's great."

"She lives in Pasadena." Andie seemed even more excited than Finch. "We're driv-ing down on Saturday, me and Finch and the guys."

"We were going to go last weekend, but Lorraine wasn't feeling well," Finch said. "Not that anything will come of it," she was quick to add.

Claire swept into the room just then with a tray of turnovers fresh from the oven. Anna watched her arrange them inside the case while Maude manned the register. She wondered if Claire, too, had had qualms be-fore going off in search of her roots. From what she'd heard, her adoptive parents had kicked up quite a fuss, although with her mother dead, she'd recently patched things up with her father.

That reminded Anna: She was meeting Liz at the Sunshine Home in less than an hour. Just the thought made her feel weary. The most she could hope for was that it would take her mind off her other troubles.

"I hope you find what you're looking for," she told Finch. Though in some ways the biggest mystery of all, she thought, is the family you know.

Felicia Campbell ushered them into the parlor. "Your mother's just finishing her bath. Why don't you make yourselves comfortable?" Anna sank down on the plush sofa, and after a moment Liz joined her. "Can I get you something to drink?" In her flowered silk dress and pearls, Felicia looked more like the proprietress of an elegant bed and breakfast.

"Nothing for me," Anna said.

"I'm fine."

Liz looked about apprehensively, as if remembering their last visit when old Mr. Henshaw had wandered in naked from the waist down. But the residents were having their afternoon "lie-down," as Felicia liked to call it. The only sign of life was the gardener out back, drifting in and out of view between the swagged velvet drapes.

Felicia sat down across from them, eyeing Anna with concern. "How are you holding up, dear?"

"I'm still standing. That's something, at least." Anna mustered a small smile. It was nice to know that for every Marguerite Moore there were a dozen like Felicia. "My mother hasn't said anything, has she?" With her face all over the news, Betty, even at her most confused, might have picked up on it. She was relieved when Felicia shook her head.

"How is she?" Liz asked tentatively.

"Physically, she's fine. Mentally, well, I don't have to tell you—she has her good days and her bad days. Today she's in fine fettle." Felicia brightened as she rose from her chair. "But why don't you see for yourselves?"

Anna was pleasantly surprised when they walked in to find Betty seated in a chair by the window, dressed in slacks and a top, her hair fluffed into a silvery froth.

Her eyes lit up. "Girls!"

Liz took a cautious step forward. "Mom?"

"Yes, Elizabeth?"

Liz eyed her in disbelief. "You know me?"

"And why wouldn't I know my own daughter?" Betty beckoned to them, patting the arm of her chair. Her face, which had grown less wrinkled with each passing year as the hardships that had left it furrowed melted into oblivion, was as smooth and pink as the inside of a shell. "Come over here where I can see you. Anna, you cut your hair." She fingered the ends as Anna bent to kiss her on the cheek. "It suits you."

Her mother hadn't been this lucid in months. Anna was seized with a kind of desperation, knowing it couldn't last. There was so much she wanted to say; how could she fit it all into one visit? "I'm glad you like it." She ran a hand through her hair.

"And just look at you—skinny as a rail." Betty pursed her lips in disapproval. She'd always encouraged her to eat, which was one reason Anna had been so fat. She opened her mouth to respond, but Betty was already peering past her, asking fretfully, "Where's Monica?"

Anna felt a great heaviness descend over her. *I can't handle this right now. Not on top of everything else.* Liz must've sensed it because for once she stepped up to the plate. Lowering onto her haunches so that she and Betty were eye to eye, she said gently, "Mom, don't you remember? You were at the funeral."

"Funeral, what funeral?" Betty spoke

sharply. "What in heaven's name are you talking about?"

"Mom . . ." Liz looked close to panic. "Monica's dead."

"What an awful thing to say! I won't listen to another word!" Betty clapped her hands over her ears.

"Mom, you know I wouldn't make up a thing like that."

"You girls were always jealous of her. Both of you." Betty glared at them.

"Fine. Think what you like." Liz rocked back on her heels with a disgusted look.

"It's true, Mom." Anna stroked her mother's hair. "Monica's . . . with Jesus now." It was what Betty used to tell them whenever someone died.

But already the light of sanity was receding from her mother's eyes. "You're lying!" She cast about wildly, calling in a shrill voice, "Precious? You can come out now. It's okay, nobody's going to hurt you." *Precious.* Anna cringed at the pet name she'd had for Monica as a child.

"Mom, please." Tears pressed hotly behind her eyes.

All at once it seemed to sink in, and Betty began to rock back and forth, her arms folded tightly over her stomach. "My little girl. My Precious," she keened softly, the sound she was making almost inhuman.

Liz cast Anna a stricken look.

She remembered the pride their mother had always taken in Monica, keeping a scrapbook and bragging about her famous daughter to anyone who would listen. She never seemed to notice Monica's disregard that bordered on contempt. "All my fault." Her voice was a thin whisper. "I should've stopped it."

Anna forced her mother to meet her gaze, but Betty's eyes were fixed on some distant plane, one that was visible to her alone. "Stopped what?"

"I told him . . . I said if he ever laid another hand on her . . ."

The small hairs on the back of Anna's neck stood up. "Did Dad do something to Monica?"

"I'll go to the police, Joey. I mean it this time." Betty was lost to them now. "What kind of a father would do that to his own child?" Her hands flew up to cover her face. "No, Joey . . . please . . . not the face . . . noooooo . . ." Pale eyes peered out between her spread fingers like those of a caged animal.

Liz grabbed her by the shoulders, shaking her, roughly almost. "What happened? *What did he do to her?*"

"Don't . . . please . . ." Betty whimpered. "The children . . . think of the children . . ."

Anna was too shocked to speak or even move. Everything was falling into place. Daddy's little girl. And why Monica had hated their parents so. Even she and Liz— how she must have resented them! And having to hide the shame all those years, act as though nothing had happened.

The blood had drained from Liz's face. She muttered, "I think I'm going to be sick."

Anna took her aside. "Did he—?"

"God, no." Liz looked aghast. "You?"

Anna shook her head.

Their mother continued to rock back and forth, making that awful moaning sound. Anna felt her stomach clench and thought she, too, might be sick. Slowly, ever so slowly, she lowered herself onto the bed. "Poor Monica. If only we'd known."

Liz shook her head. "She wouldn't have wanted our sympathy."

"She must have been so ashamed. All those years . . ."

"No wonder she hated them."

Anna nodded. How could she not? Their mother had been too weak to put an end to it, and by the time Monica left home, the damage was done.

"She showed him, didn't she?" Betty's head jerked up, eyes glittering with triumph. "His famous daughter who'd as soon spit on him as look at him." A horrid smile momentarily animated her face, and her shoulders shook with soundless laughter.

Anna thought of her mother's scrapbook, every article and photo lovingly pasted onto its black vellum pages. And all the while the real Monica had been lost to her. The degree to which Betty had been deluded even then was staggering.

Felicia chose that moment to pop her head in. "Everything okay in here?"

Anna started as if at a thunderclap. It seemed as if a hundred years had passed since they'd set foot in this room. "My mom's a little upset, as you can see," she heard herself reply in a remarkably calm voice. "I think it'd be better if we came back another time."

"What could we have done?" Liz said.

"Nothing." There was a lump in Anna's throat like a dry swallowed aspirin.

They were sitting on the front porch, collecting themselves before the drive home, which at the moment neither was in any condition to do.

"I feel sick just thinking of it." Liz was pale.

The old-fashioned glider creaked rhythmically beneath them. "I remember this one night when Dad came into my room," Anna recalled. "I must've been eight or nine. He was kissing me goodnight when Monica walked in, hogging all the attention as usual. She wouldn't leave until he did. Now I wonder if she was trying to protect me."

Liz shook her head. "Mom knew. I can't believe she *knew*. Why didn't she *do* something?"

"It wasn't that simple."

"There you go, defending her again."

"All I'm saying is . . . never mind." Anna sighed. What was the point? She and her sisters had grown up under the same roof, but it might have been different universes.

"Look, whatever her reasons, it was inexcusable. She should have gone to the police, or at the very least divorced him."

"Shoulda, coulda, woulda . . . it's too late now."

Anna couldn't argue with that. "You know something? I don't think Monica was ever happy, even when she got famous. It was always like she was acting the part."

"The greatest role of her career." Liz's mouth twisted in a wry smile.

"What about you?" Anna asked softly, lulled by the creaking glider and rustle of leaves overhead. Somewhere down the street a power mower droned.

"Am I happy?" Liz gave a harsh laugh. "It depends on which day of the week you ask. Monday through Friday, I'm usually too busy to notice. It's the weekends that pretty much suck."

She didn't need to spell it out: With married lovers, weekends were generally reserved for wives and kids. "How often do you two, uh, see each other?" She was careful to remove any trace of judgment from her voice. Who was she to talk?

The glider squealed to a halt. "Not as often as I'd like, if that's what you're getting at." Liz looked miserable. "He keeps saying he's going to leave her, but I'm beginning to wonder if it's worth all the agony even if he does. Besides, there's his kid. I can't stop thinking about what it'd do to him." She swallowed hard, darting a sheepish look at Anna. "Listen to me. Here you're on trial for murder and I'm crying over a stupid affair." A tear rolled down her cheek. "Why can't I be noble like you?"

"Being noble isn't much fun," Anna said. "Anyway, I'm not as noble as you think."

Liz gazed at her bleakly. "I know I don't always show it, but I worry about you, Anna."

"I'll be okay." Anna was amazed to find she believed it, for the moment at least.

Liz rose heavily. "I should be going. I have to pick up Dylan at school."

Anna pulled herself to her feet with an effort. "Will you be home later on?"

"Where else would I be? I don't dare step outside for a breath of air in case he calls." Liz gave another harsh laugh.

"Good. We can talk then."

Anna's thoughts turned once more to Marc. Was she chasing rainbows as well?

What would become of them when all this was over? Even these past few nights without him she'd been lonelier than she would've thought possible. She'd grown used to slipping across the field under cover of darkness like a Bronte heroine, and to the sight of Marc poised in the doorway of Hector's old room, the light from inside spilling out around him. She missed their long talks and the hours lost in each other's arms when they didn't speak at all. Tonight she would lie awake again thinking of him. The question was, Would he be thinking of her?

She recalled their last night together, when she'd shown him the latest e-mail from Krystal. After it had been made public that she'd ghost-written for Monica, she'd been bombarded by phone calls and letters. Some were like the one from the Texas grandmother who was crocheting her a shawl for those cold nights in jail, but most were irate. One woman hoped they locked her up and threw away the key; another wrote that burning in hell was too good for her. Only the message from Krystal was an enigma.

From: kssnkrys@aol.com
To: monica@monicavincent.com
Subject: ????

Monica,
I know you aren't who i thought you were but you were still right about everything you said. You don't deserve this. I know your innocent. I wish i could tell them.

Please don't hate me. I have to think of my kids. It'd kill them (and me) to be taken away again.

Krystal

"What do you make of it?" she'd asked Marc.

"I don't know, but it strikes me as odd." They'd been lying in bed, the window open to let in the night air.

"She obviously feels guilty about something, but the question is *what*?"

"She might know something."

"How could she?" Unless she was there that night, which Anna rejected as too far-fetched.

He frowned in thought. Outside, the dogs had begun to bark, probably at a raccoon that had gotten into one of the garbage cans. "Still, it's worth looking into."

"I wouldn't even know how to reach her. All I have is an e-mail address."

"I have a friend—hacker for the rich and famous. He makes a living tracking down cyberstalkers."

"I suppose anything's worth a try at this point." Though her hands were tied, there was no reason he couldn't do a little digging on his own.

Now, of course, she knew it was a dead end. Even if Krystal wasn't who she claimed to be, how could a boy of twelve or thirteen, judging from his shoe size, have fooled her into believing he was a thirty-four-year-old single mom? More to the point, why go to all that trouble? It didn't make sense.

Anna walked Liz to her car, feeling oddly protective of her. To the world, her sister might appear poised and polished, but Liz was more fragile than she let on. Anna hugged her tightly, ignoring the sharp corner of Liz's purse digging into her ribs. "I'm glad you were here. Thank God I didn't have to go through it alone."

Liz drew back with a loud sniff, her eyes glistening. "We'll get through this, won't we?"

Anna didn't know whether she meant the shock of their mother's revelation or their own predicaments, but she smiled and said with far more conviction than she felt, "Don't we always?"

CHAPTER THIRTEEN

He stopped at the second set of reinforced steel doors, leaning into the intercom. "Dr. Raboy to see Dr. Fine." It was a line that always seemed to carry a hint of the burlesque each of the hundreds of times he'd spoken it. *Hello, Doctor. Nice to see you again, Doctor. How's our patient? Fine, you say? Glad to hear it, Doctor.* Whenever he visited Faith, he always stopped for a word with her doctor before continuing on down the hall—exchanges that had begun to feel less and less like the relaying of important information and more and more like a ritual.

The door buzzed, and he stepped through it.

"Hey, Shirley."

His favorite nurse broke into a wide grin

that turned her cheeks into shiny dark plums. She wore a light blue smock that snapped up the front (standard issue on this ward, where buttons had a habit of getting torn off and occasionally swallowed) and a bright pink scrunchie about one wrist—Shirley always braided Faith's hair before every visit, a small kindness that touched him more than he could say.

"Hey there, Doc. How y'all doin'?" It'd been more than twenty years since Shirley had lived in Alabama, but each word still came out dipped in molasses.

"Hanging in there." His standard response. With any luck she hadn't caught his fifteen seconds of fame—the shot of him scurrying down the courthouse steps with an arm about Anna.

"You lookin' a little scrawny. They feedin' you at that rich folk's resort?"

Marc smiled. Shirley considered his work at Pathways a Sunday stroll in the park compared to her frontline combat in the trenches of Thousand Oaks, and she never failed to rib him about it. He ignored it this time to ask, "How's everything?"

"Same old same old." Her massive shoulders rolled in a shrug.

"How's Faith?" He spoke casually, too casually perhaps. Shirley had been on to him since day one: She wasn't fooled by his laid back friendliness and somewhat detached air.

She leaned across the desk. "She been askin' after you, Doc. That skinny white dude with the attitude? I say. And she give me that look—you know the one, all innocent like. Then she say, 'Why, Shirley, don't you talk that way 'bout my husband. He not a bit skinny.' " She let loose a laugh that rolled up in waves from her generous bosom, one he'd often longed to lay his head against the way he once had his mother's. "I swear, sometimes I think she just foolin' on us."

He smiled knowingly. One of the more reassuring, and at the same time maddening, aspects of the disease was that one's personality remained basically intact. Faith hadn't lost her droll sense of humor. "I wouldn't put it past her," he said lightly, handing Shirley the box of See's chocolates he always brought.

She slipped it out of sight with a conspiratorial wink. "Don't want folks thinkin' you gone sweet on me." She waved a plump hand toward the corridor, where the speckled green linoleum shimmered with a fresh coat of wax. "Go on now."

Bernie Fine was hanging up the phone when he walked in. He rose and stepped out from behind his desk, a large man running to fat with an untidy shock of gray hair and thick glasses that magnified his eyes, giving him the look of a sweet and somewhat goofy cartoon bear—never mind his was one of the sharpest minds in the field.

"Marc, good to see you. You're looking well."

Marc smiled. "Not according to Shirley. She thinks I'm underfed."

Bernie chuckled. "She'd feed the whole world if she could."

"I don't doubt it."

"What's up with you these days?"

Marc considered telling him, just to see the look on his face, but Anna's woes were bad enough without being mined for shock value. "This and that. You?"

"Can't complain." Bernie, perched on the edge of his desk, looked like a pile of clothes that'd been dumped there. "My youngest graduates in June—magna cum laude." He glowed with pride. "Did I tell you he got into Harvard Med?"

"That's something. I mean, well . . . Harvard."

"We're treating him to that trip he's always wanted."

Marc reached into his memory banks. "I've heard New Zealand is beautiful."

"Best surfing in the world, according to Zach. Go figure, my son the future doctor. But, hell, he's earned the right to play beach bum for a couple of weeks."

Marc had never met Bernie's wife or three sons. He knew them only from the framed photos on Bernie's desk. He waited for the little beat signaling that this portion of the program was over, then cleared his throat. "How is she?"

Bernie's expression sobered. "Nothing much to report. We took her off the Paxil— she was having a bad reaction to it. We're waiting to see how she does with the Wellbutrin." He didn't have to explain: With schizophrenics, the ever-shifting regimen of antipsychotics and antidepressants was like mixing a Molotov cocktail.

"Has she—?"

"No." Bernie pulled a crumpled handkerchief from the pocket of his corduroys and began polishing his glasses. "We're keeping a close watch, though."

Three months before, Faith had stabbed herself with a letter opener swiped from the front desk. Fortunately, the wounds had been superficial, but it had given them all a scare. Yet Bernie Fine, to his credit, hadn't suggested that perhaps another facility would be more suited to her "particular needs"—maybe out of kindness or professional respect, but more likely because she was that rarest of all patients, the kind whose monthly bill was paid in cash. She'd come into a little money when her grandfather died, enough so that Marc was able to avoid the inevitable quibbling and delays that came with insurance, or worse, governmental red tape.

"Does she seem depressed?" *Stupid question,* he thought. Who wouldn't be in this place, even if they hadn't been depressed to begin with? On the other hand, with the meds she was on, most of the time she was too doped up to feel much of anything.

"Not unusually so. In fact, I've seen some improvement." Bernie spoke cautiously.

"Can you be a little more specific?" Marc asked.

"She's been sharing more in group. In our private sessions as well." He returned his glasses to his nose, his eyes swimming back into large focus. "She's expressed a fair bit of anxiety about your visits."

"I know I don't come as often as I used to." He felt a stab of guilt, but didn't reach into the usual grab bag of excuses. He didn't owe an explanation to this man, with his healthy wife and three healthy sons, however kind and helpful he was.

Bernie regarded him curiously. "I've never heard her complain. If anything, she blames herself. She's concerned about how this is affecting you. Part of her, I think, would like to set you free."

Marc gave a bitter laugh. "Free? That's a relative term." Sure, he could divorce Faith. But what good would it do? Every morning when he woke up she'd still be the first thing on his mind. He could no more abandon her than he could Anna. And therein lay the rub.

"I'm not telling you what to do, Marc."

Bernie sighed. "Frankly, I don't know what *I'd* do in your shoes."

He smiled. "You just keep putting one foot in front of the other and hope the shoes don't wear out."

"How've you been—really?" Bernie leaned forward, his cartoon bear's eyes fixed so intently on Marc it was unnerving.

Marc shrugged. "I'm taking some time off work."

"So I gather." Bernie fished a newspaper clipping from the clutter on his desk—an article from last week's edition of the *Star,* complete with requisite blurry photo: Marc and Anna ducking into his car. He handed it to Marc. "One of the nurses brought it in."

Marc glanced at it, and handed it back. "Thanks, I've seen it."

"They spelled your name right at least."

"Personally, I like the part that reads 'boyfriend of accused killer.'"

"Anything to it?"

"Since when do you believe what's in the tabloids?"

"Look, Marc, if you're seeing someone . . ." Bernie shrugged as if to let him know it wasn't his place to judge. In his kind face Marc saw acceptance—not just of him per se, but of the accommodations that must often be made in situations like his.

"Does Faith know?" Marc felt a dull throb of apprehension. She could've seen it on TV or heard it from the same helpful nurse who'd brought the clipping in.

"If she does, she hasn't mentioned it."

"That's something, at least." Marc had one foot out the door when he turned and said, "Just for the record, I'm in love with her."

Bernie didn't have to ask whom he meant. He only smiled and said, *"Mazel tov."*

If Marc had been dreading this visit, his reservations melted the moment he laid eyes on Faith. She sat cross-legged on the window seat in the library, reading aloud to one of the other patients under the watchful eye of Rolly, the Jamaican orderly (whose dreadlocks were an endless source of fascination on the ward). Bent over her book, elbows propped on her knees and her braid trailing down one shoulder, she looked all of eighteen—the age she'd been when they met. He paused in the doorway, captivated by the words rolling off her tongue like music.

"The bride kiss'd the goblet, the knight took it up,
He quaff'd off the wine, and he threw down the cup.
She look'd down to blush, and she look'd up to sigh,
With a smile on her lips and a tear in her eye."

Lochinvar. A tale of star-crossed love. He smiled at the irony, his gaze shifting to the woman on the floor at Faith's feet. She had to be twice Faith's age and at least double her weight, but she sat like a docile child, eyes half closed and mouth parted.

"Faith," he called softly.

She looked up. "Marc." As quickly as her face had lit up, it clouded over. "I wasn't expecting you until after lunch," she said with a tentativeness that was heartbreaking.

The library was the coziest of the common rooms at Thousand Oaks, with its carpet and comfortable chairs, its rows of freestanding shelves filled with books on every subject, yet as he crossed it he felt a chill travel through him.

He'd nearly reached her when a hand

closed over his ankle. He looked down to find a sly moon face grinning up at him.

"Would you like Faith to finish reading to you?" he asked, extracting his ankle from the woman's grip.

She nodded vigorously, her lank gray hair flopping about the doughy mounds of her shoulders. Looking up at Faith, she demanded, in a child-like voice, "Go back to the beginning."

Faith bent forward to ruffle her hair with an affectionate laugh, and for a fleeting instant she was his wife again: patron saint of the helpless. "Not now, Iris. I'll read to you some more after group, I promise. Right now, I need to be alone with Marc." She seldom referred to him anymore as her husband and although it hurt, he preferred to think it was out of sensitivity for those with no husbands of their own or visitors of any kind, for that matter.

Iris heaved herself to her feet, muttering to herself as she shuffled from the room, tugging at her shapeless smock. Faith and Rolly exchanged a look—like parents of a difficult child—that pierced Marc's heart like a tiny poisoned dart. Then Rolly ambled over to clap a hand on his shoulder, saying in a low voice, "I'll be outside in the hall. You need me, just give a shout." With his Jamaican accent it came out "shot."

Not until they were alone did Faith gracefully unfold from the window seat, offering her cheek to be kissed. She was wearing a gray Nike tracksuit that made it look as though she'd been out jogging, an illusion furthered by the light sheen of perspiration polishing her cheeks and forehead. Tiny wisps of hair had sprung loose from her flaxen braid; in the sunlight they sparkled like spun gold.

"Nice save," he said.

Faith smiled. "Iris can get possessive at times."

They settled on the sofa facing the shelves marked R-T, Marc at one end and Faith at the other, her bare feet tucked under her. He noticed the dark circles under her eyes. Had they been as pronounced before? She looked thinner, too. Was she eating enough?

"Your parents send their love," he told her. "They've been trying to reach you all week." He was careful not to make it sound like an accusation. Besides, they were used to her mood swings. Sometimes whole weeks would go by when she'd refuse to take any calls.

"I've been busy," she said with a shrug.

"They wanted you to be the first to know." He hesitated, then said, "Cindy's pregnant."

"No kidding? That's great!" She sounded genuinely delighted. Even so, he eyed her closely.

"The baby's due in November."

"Wow. I'll finally be an aunt."

He waited for the cracks to appear, but when none did, he relaxed a little. "They're pretty excited. Your mother's already maxed out her Visa buying baby things."

"I'll bet." She laughed knowingly.

There. That shadow in her eyes just then—like something flitting below the calm, clear surface of a lake. He drew in a breath, bracing himself for the plunge. "They weren't sure how you'd take it."

The dark thing rose to the surface, slowly spreading over her face. Marc waited, his heart thudding. "Does it always have to come back to *that*? God, I'm so sick of it all!" She pulled her knees up against her chest, wrapping her arms around them.

"Would it have been better if I hadn't told you?"

"Does it matter what *I* want?"

"I didn't mean to upset you."

"Don't worry. I'm sure there's a little colored pill that will fix it." She gave a hollow laugh. In her temples, tiny blue veins stood out like cracks in an eggshell.

Marc's mind reeled back to that awful day. He'd hurried home from work, concerned because she'd sounded so strange over the phone. Something to do with the hormones she was taking, he'd thought. They'd been trying for years to have a baby, and she'd taken some time off work to give it one last shot. That morning she'd been feeling nauseated and, though cautiously hopeful, he'd begun to suspect it was something other than an early sign of pregnancy. More and more often he'd call home in the middle of the day to find her still in bed, depressed and lethargic, classic signs of mental illness. Yet he'd ignored them—he, of all people, who should've known. But the fear that had been growing in the back of his mind didn't burst into full bloom until he'd walked in that day to find Faith unconscious on the bathroom floor in a pool of blood.

His first thought was that she'd miscarried—until he saw the bloody ice pick in her hand. As he dropped to his knees, feeling for a pulse, he'd felt as though he were plummeting down through the floor.

In the ambulance she'd grabbed his shirt, pulling him down to whisper hoarsely in his ear, "Is it *out*?" Her face was the color of the sheet pulled up under her chin.

"The baby?" His horror ratcheted up another notch at the thought that she might have aborted their child.

She shook her head weakly. *"It."*

Days later the story came out: the voices clamoring in her head that sometimes communicated over the radio, whispering of the devil growing in her womb that would eventually kill her if she didn't get rid of it first. She could *feel* it she said, never mind the X rays and tests that showed nothing was wrong. So she'd taken matters into her own hands. Listening to her calmly recount the events leading up to the terrible scene he'd witnessed, Marc had wept with both horror and a profound sense of helplessness. It was like watching her drown while he stood on shore, unable to jump in to save her.

Yet incredible as it now seemed, he'd been optimistic. And for a time, with therapy and meds, she *had* seemed to improve. But it was always one step forward, two steps back, with the ensuing years bringing a succession of hospitalizations. Twice she'd attempted suicide. Once, when he'd caught her holding a knife to her wrist, she'd gone after him instead. That was the final straw: The following day she'd checked into Thousand Oaks. She'd been there ever since—eighteen months—not counting brief supervised forays into the outside world.

But hadn't he been locked away, too, from the kind of love he'd once taken for granted? Until Anna. The question was, where did he go from here?

"Are you angry because I couldn't come last week?" he asked gently.

"*Should* I be?" she shot back.

"You tell me."

She sighed, as if the answer should have been obvious. "What I *want* is for it not to be an obligation. If you're sick of me, just say so. I won't hold it against you. I'm sick of me, too."

He reached for her hand. "I don't want to stop seeing you."

"Then where have you been?"

"I told you—I took some time off work. I've been staying at a little place up the coast."

Faith cocked her head, eyeing him intently, and for a tense moment he was certain she knew. "Well, that explains it," she said.

He felt himself go cold. "What?"

"Why you're so tanned."

He relaxed. Whatever she suspected, she wouldn't probe; she had to know she'd only end up being hurt worse. "I'm going for the George Hamilton look."

"I don't see that it's hurt him any with the ladies." That was as close as she'd get to the truth.

Marc was quick to change the subject. "How's the painting going?" Bernie Fine had suggested she take up art as a form of therapy, and Faith seemed to enjoy it.

"Okay."

"Anything you want to show me?"

"Not yet."

"Well, when you're ready—"

"Don't patronize me." She eyed him coldly.

"I didn't realize that's what I was doing."

"Well, you are. You know as well as I do it's only to keep me from going off the deep end. Like the meds, only it comes in more colors."

"Well, at least you haven't cut off your ear." He'd found that it helped sometimes to joke; tiptoeing only made it worse. But this time she didn't laugh.

"Not funny," she said.

"You're still angry with me, I see."

"Damn you." She glared at him, her eyes filling with tears.

"Faith—" He put out a conciliatory hand, but she shrank from it.

"I *hate* it."

"I know." At least she hadn't said she hated *him.*

"No, you *don't* know," she cried. "Most of the time I can bear it. But when I see you, I'm reminded all over again of everything I'm missing. *That's* what's so hard." Her voice broke. "It's not your fault. And I'm not

saying I'm ready to go home. The truth is, I
. . . I feel safe here."

As always, he felt tugged in opposite directions: wanting his wife back and wishing
he could walk away for good. And now
there was Anna.

"Would you rather I not visit for a while?"
he asked gently.

Faith stared at him so long and so hard
he could feel it in his chest: a dull ache. He
remembered what Sundays used to be like:
lounging half the morning in bed, waffles
drenched in maple syrup, long walks hand
in hand. Would he ever know those things
again, or was it purely wishful thinking?

Her face crumpled and she began to
weep.

He gathered her in his arms. "Shh . . . it's
okay."

She wept softly into his shirt. "I d-don't
want you to s-stop coming."

"In that case, you're stuck with me." At
times like these he almost wished he still
drank—anything to numb the ache.

She burrowed into him like a small child.
He thought once more of her sister. When
the time came, Cindy and her husband
planned to fly down with the baby. Marc

had discussed it in depth with Cindy, as he did everything involving Faith—like a military maneuver. Cindy worried what it would do to her sister, but she was more worried about the baby.

"What if she wants to hold it?" she'd asked, her voice low and ashamed. He'd understood how she felt: What kind of person would deny her sister such a thing?

Just as Marc's heart had broken for his sister-in-law, it was now breaking for his wife. He stroked her hair, murmuring reassurances. In a little while he was going off in search of a woman named Krystal about whom he knew nothing except the address in Encino that his friend Keith had given him. But all he could think of right now was that maybe the real insanity in this world was love itself—a dumb beast that would sooner beat its head against a brick wall than leap over it.

Las Casitas was like a dozen other apartment buildings he'd passed along the way: several stories of drab cinderblock wrapped around a central patio and pool, its rows of doors accessed by outdoor ramps. As he climbed the metal stairs the smell of chlorine rose about him like vapors from a chemical dump, along with the sounds of children splashing in the pool.

When he reached the door to 3-F, he could hear a child was crying inside and the muffled voice of a mother at wit's end, her tone alternately threatening and cajoling. He knocked, and after what seemed an eternity the door eased open a crack.

"Yeah? What do you want?" Peering out at him was a thin, tired face framed by scribbles of permed yellow hair.

"I'm a friend of Anna's," he said. "I was wondering if I could have a word with you."

"I don't know anyone named Anna."

"You knew her as Monica."

Recognition momentarily animated her tired blue eyes. "Oh, *her.* Yeah, I read about it in the paper. Tough break."

"That's why I'm here. Mind if I come in?" he asked.

She hesitated, then the door opened a little wider, revealing a wiry woman in shorts and a halter top. Her muscles looked to be from hard physical labor rather than workouts at the gym. "Look, this isn't a good time," she said. "My kid's sick and I have to be at work."

"It won't take long."

Her eyes narrowed as she looked him up and down. "How'd you know where to find me?"

"It wasn't hard." Keith had gotten the name off her AOL account. It turned out Krystal Longmire had quite a history, though she'd moved around some since her last known address—Lompoc State Penitentiary. "By the way, I'm Marc." He put out his hand, which she shook reluctantly, still eyeing him suspiciously.

The child inside began to whine. "Brianna, honey!" Krystal yelled over her shoulder, "Drink your juice like a good girl!" She turned back to Marc. "I'd better go."

"Please. It's important."

Krystal heaved a long suffering sigh. "All right, but only a minute."

She'd stepped out onto the ramp and was easing the door shut behind her when the little girl wailed piteously, "Leave it open so I can see you!" He caught a glimpse of a small, pale face amid the murky depths of the shade-drawn living room.

Krystal folded her arms over her chest.

"Look, mister, I don't want no trouble. I'm having a tough enough time as it is."

Not as tough as Anna, he thought.

"I'm not here to make trouble."

Her mouth kinked in a hard little smile. "Yeah? That's what they all say. I got two kids and three years of hard time from the last guy who sold me that bill of goods."

"Anna told me about you. She seems to think very highly of you."

Some of the hardness went out of her face, and she nibbled on a thumbnail before self-consciously lowering her hand. "Look, I feel bad about what happened to her. I mean, she was nice and all. But it's not like there's anything I can do. Now if you'll excuse me—"

She was turning to go when he took a last wild shot. "You were there that night, weren't you?"

It had the desired effect. Krystal froze, and an arm riddled with old tracks shot out to yank the door shut, unleashing a wail from inside. "Listen, I don't know what you're up to," she hissed, "but if you're not outta here in thirty seconds or less, I'm calling the cops."

"I think," he said in the same mild tone,

"that if you were going to call the cops, you'd have done it weeks ago."

She sagged against the cinderblock wall. "What do you want?"

"Answers."

"I only know what's in the papers."

"Where were you that night?"

"Home with my kids."

"Can you prove it?"

She glared at him. "I don't have to."

"Not to me. But I'm sure the police would like to know." He reached into his jacket, pulling out his cell phone.

She put out a hand to stop him from punching in a number, flags of red standing out in her cheeks as if she'd been slapped. He didn't know if it was guilt or just the fear of someone who'd spent time behind bars. "Don't. They'll think I had something to do with it."

"*Did* you?" He held her gaze.

"No." Her voice was faint. Inside the whines were quickly escalating into howls. "I'm coming!" Krystal called over her shoulder, the expression on her face that of a battle-fatigued soldier gearing up for yet another assault. She turned back to Marc. "My little girl? She's been in foster homes half her life. She cries all the time and can't sleep unless there's a light on. My parole officer gets wind of this, I'll be back in jail so fast I won't know what hit me. I can't do that to my kids."

"You seem pretty worried for someone with nothing to hide."

"They get you on something. They always do." For a fleeting moment he almost felt sorry for her. "You don't know what it's like. *She's* the only one who gave a shit. And look where she ended up."

A howl ending in a hacking cough worthy of Mimi in *La Bohème* arrived as if on cue. "Here's how I figure it," he said. "You wanted to see with your own eyes if Monica, or should I say the person you *thought* was Monica, was as great as she'd seemed. Just a peek, then you'd be on your way with no one the wiser. How am I doing so far?"

"Not bad. You oughta get a job working for one of those tabloids." Her flat gaze gave nothing away.

"Look," he said, "you don't owe me a thing. But you *do* owe Anna."

"Even if I knew something, which I don't,

my kids come first. Anyway, how do I know you're not a cop?"

"You'd be on your way downtown for questioning if I were."

"And you'd have a couple of screaming kids on your hands," she lobbed right back.

"I could still have you taken in."

"Maybe, but you won't."

"What makes you so sure?"

"You're decent, that's why." She made it sound like an insult.

Marc looked at her long and hard, as if to disprove her assessment of him. But she'd clearly endured worse than anything he could dish out. She would bend, but she wouldn't break. The only hope was for Anna to appeal to her in person.

The wailing from inside grew louder.

Krystal was pushing open the door when she paused to look over her shoulder. He was surprised to see her washed-out blue eyes glittering with unshed tears. "Tell Anna . . ." her voice broke a little, "tell her I'm sorry."

The following night, back in his room at Laura and Hector's, he filled Anna in. "I think she knows something," he said. They were in bed, Anna nestled in the crook of his arm. "Either that, or she's just plain scared."

"Of what?"

"Getting thrown back in jail."

"Why would she feel guilty if she hadn't done anything wrong?"

"She's an addict. We think everything bad that happens is our fault because most of the time it is." He smiled ruefully.

He told her about his brief conversation with the detective in charge, a tough former marine who, from the looks of it, was no stranger to the bottle himself. Burch had brushed him off, informing Marc that he wasn't interested in pursuing any new leads. His exact words were, "If her lawyer wants to blow smoke out her ass trying to pin it on someone else, I don't have to play along." But Marc omitted that part.

"So we're back at square one," she said gloomily. He could see every minute of the past four weeks in her face: the dark circles under her eyes, the faint lines like parentheses on either side of her mouth.

"I had my friend do a search on that other guy, too." The man known only as Hairy

Cary, whose fascination with Monica had bordered on obsessive had turned out to be a married man with five kids—a Baptist minister, no less. "I pity his poor wife, not to mention his congregation."

"Do you think he had something to do with this?"

"Anything's possible. There's only one problem: He lives in Kentucky."

"Last I heard, they have flights out of Kentucky."

"I'm not ruling it out," he said. "In fact, I've put in a call. In the meantime I think it'd be worth paying another visit to Krystal." He smiled. "You might have better luck."

Anna pulled the covers up around her, shivering despite the space heater that glowed like a coal in the darkness. "It's funny. I wouldn't have pegged her as a stalker."

"They come in all shapes and sizes," he said, thinking of Hairy Cary.

"Do you think she's a murderer?"

Marc shook his head. "Call it a hunch, but no I don't."

"It could have been an accident."

"All I know is, the sooner we find out what, if anything, she's hiding, the better."

He looked out the window. The barnyard was a barren moonscape, the elongated shadow of the dog ambling across it like some alien creature.

"If she won't talk, we could have Rhonda subpoena her."

"She'd be a hostile witness. It could backfire."

"You think she'd lie on the witness stand?"

"Without an eyewitness, who could prove she was lying? Besides, we don't know for certain that she is."

Anna sighed. "I guess we'll know tomorrow." They planned to drive down first thing in the morning.

"Speaking of which, we should get some sleep. It's going to be a long day," he said.

Anna rolled onto her side, winding her arms around his neck. "I'm not sleepy."

He kissed her on the lips. "Miss me?"

"Would you think less of me if I said yes?"

"I didn't know it was a bad thing to miss someone."

"It is if the person you're missing doesn't miss you, too."

Marc tilted his head, smiling. "You know

what I wish? That you could see yourself the way I do."

"Tell me what you see." She regarded him gravely.

"A beautiful, brave, sexy woman."

"Do I sense an ulterior motive?" Smiling, she slid a hand under the covers.

He seized hold of her wrist, pulling it to his mouth and kissing her open palm. She smelled of freshly cut flowers, lavender or hyacinth. "Krystal wasn't the only one I saw yesterday."

Her smile faded. "I take it you mean Faith."

He nodded. "I've never kept anything from you and I'm not going to start now."

She tensed, drawing away. "Is there a point to this?" A steely edge had crept into her voice.

"I just thought you should know."

"That you're married? I'm well aware of that fact. I also know that you have no intention of divorcing your wife."

"I don't have a choice." Would he have married Faith if he'd known what lay ahead? He honestly didn't know, but it was pointless to wonder. The plain fact was he loved two women, and one of them, for better or for worse, was his wife.

"There's always a choice. Weren't you the one who told me that?" Anna was sitting up now, eyeing him with the same wariness Faith had. With her hair tousled and her shoulders gleaming in the moonlight, she'd never looked more beautiful.

"Some choices you can live with; others you can't."

"So what you're saying is that when all this is over, assuming I'm a free woman, we'll go back to the way it was before? Or maybe you see us as weekend lovers—no strings attached, no questions asked." She shook her head. "I'm sorry, Marc, you don't get to call the shots this time. If nothing else allow me to make my own decisions."

Marc wanted to applaud her even as he drew back in surprise. Clearly, the fire she'd walked through had galvanized her in more ways than one. "Fair enough," he said. "I have just one request. Can we table it until then?"

She stared out the window. He'd begun to worry that she was lost to him already when she brought her gaze back to him. She reached for his hand, running her thumb along his wedding band. "Does your wife know?"

"I think she suspects."

"I'm sure she doesn't expect you to be celibate."

"If that's the case, she hasn't said anything."

Anna burrowed into his arms, kissing him deeply as she pressed up against him. He felt an answering tug in his groin, and pushed a hand between her legs. She was wet. Jesus.

"Yes, damn it, I missed you," she whispered in his ear.

He rolled her onto her back, straddling her. They were both breathing hard. Normally he took his time, stroking and kissing until passion took over where her shyness left off, but he could see it wasn't going to be that way tonight. She drew him into her, wrapping her legs about him, meeting each thrust with an intensity that matched his own. Moments later he felt her shudder as she threw her head back in a soundless cry.

Then he was coming too—a rush so intense he nearly blacked out. When Anna's face swam back into focus, he saw that her cheeks were flushed and her mouth curved in a little smile.

"Remind me to go away more often," he said. He'd meant it as a joke, but her face fell. He wanted to kick himself.

But she quickly recovered, saying with a lightness that tore at his heart, "If anyone's going anywhere, it's me."

Marc led the way up the stairs, the metal risers ringing faintly beneath his feet. The sun hadn't fully risen and already it was hot, the bedraggled plants around the pool drooping. The sounds of people up and about drifted through the closed doors he passed: muffled voices, the whirr of a coffee grinder, a TV weatherman announcing today's forecast: "Sunny and clear, folks, with temperatures headed on up to the high eighties. Time to crack out those coolers and crank up that air conditioner . . ."

They reached Krystal's apartment and Marc knocked. When no one answered, he tried the knob. The door swung open. No one was home. They walked wordlessly from room to room, the empty drawers and closets, the crusty rings on the medicine cabinet shelves bearing silent witness to what he'd known the moment he walked in: Krystal had bolted. All that was left besides the furniture were the dirty dishes in the sink and a bowl of cat food on the floor.

Mentally he kicked himself. *My fault. I let her get away.* On the other hand, what could he have done to stop her?

He turned to Anna. "The super might know something." She nodded, but he saw his hopelessness reflected in her face. He very much doubted Krystal had left a forwarding address.

The super turned out to be the landlord as well, a paunchy middle-aged man with beige hair sticking up in tufts around his bald pate. When they told him about Krystal, asking if he had any idea where she might've gone, he cursed under his breath. "Like to know myself. Bitch owed two months' back rent." He fished a pack of Camels from the sagging pocket of his terry robe and lit one, squinting at Anna through the smoke curling up around his head. "You look familiar. Have I seen you before?"

She blanched, but kept her cool. "I don't think we've met."

The man obviously hadn't made the connection, but he eyed her dubiously even so, as if wondering what she could possibly want with the likes of Krystal. Then he shrugged—it was no skin off him either way. "You find her, give her a message from Louie. Tell her next time I see her, it'll be in court."

"Do you think anyone here might know where she went?" Marc asked when Anna fell silent at the mention of court.

The landlord took a deep considering drag off his cigarette. "You could try her neighbors, but I doubt they'll know anything. She kept to herself. All she cared about was them kids."

It seemed he was right. After an hour or so of knocking on doors and getting nowhere, their worst fears had hardened into certainty: Krystal and her children had vanished without a trace.

"Now what?" Anna sank onto the stairs, defeated.

He sat down beside her. "I wish to hell I knew."

The only sure thing was that they'd come up against a dead end.

CHAPTER FOURTEEN

As Anna and Marc were leaving Las Casitas, Finch and her friends were pulling up in front of Bellevue Gardens not more than twenty miles away. The extended care facility where Lorraine Wells lived was a flat-roofed stucco building bordered by oleander, with a large tree shedding something sticky onto the sidewalk out front. A pink-smocked older woman greeted them pleasantly as they walked in.

"Lulu's very excited to meet you," she told them as they signed in. "She doesn't get many visitors."

Finch and Andie exchanged a glance that said, *I'll bet.* The place was enough to give anyone the creeps. While Simon looked about with interest, as if mentally taking notes for an exposé on nursing homes, Lucien said smoothly, "We're looking forward to meeting her, too."

They'd been on the road for hours due to a traffic jam. Several stops—one for gas, another to pee, followed by breakfast at Burger King—had put them in Pasadena shortly before eleven. Now, eyeing the fake wood paneling and the rubber tree collecting dust in one corner, Finch wondered if it had been a wasted trip. What could possibly come of it?

At the same time, a voice in her head whispered, *Maybe it's not a wild goose chase after all.* She'd heard of coincidences too bizarre to be anything but fate. Like the woman in *People* who'd spied a baby photo of herself while leafing through a friend's family album—it turned out she'd been adopted and that she and her friend were actually cousins. And what about that funny feeling she'd had getting off the bus in Carson Springs that first day? Like she'd been there before.

They walked down a hall smelling of disinfectant and lined with mummified old people slumped in wheelchairs. It had been several weeks since she'd arranged this meeting. In the meantime, she'd been so busy with school and fund-raising (not to mention Lucien) that she'd scarcely given it a second thought. Now she paused outside the door to Lorraine's room, her stomach executing a slow underwater roll.

Lucien reached for her hand. "It'll be okay."

"Is it too late to turn back?" she muttered.

"Think of the story it'll make," Simon said.

Andie shot him a dirty look. "You wouldn't dare."

They entered the room to find an ancient woman sunk deep in an easy chair, her head bent over a book. "Ms. Wells?" Finch called softly.

The woman looked up, breaking into a wide smile. "Lulu, please." She set the book aside, and with some effort hoisted herself to her feet. Tall and gaunt with a mop of curls so improbably red it had to be a wig, she looked like an aged Orphan Annie. "My Lord, I didn't expect so many of you." She glanced about in delight.

"Lucien drove." Finch jerked a thumb in his direction.

"And we tagged along," Andie said, introducing herself and Simon.

"Well! Let's hope I can keep all your names straight." Lorraine looked from one to the other as if at gifts, trying to decide which one to unwrap first. "Sit down, make yourselves comfortable. My roommate won't mind." She gestured toward the twin beds, one of which was stripped bare. "Gertie passed on last week."

"I'm sorry," Finch said.

"Don't be." Lorraine settled back in her chair. "All she did was bitch and moan. About drove me crazy, the old cow." They must have looked startled, for she added with a twinkle in her eye, "You know the one good thing about getting old? You can say whatever you damn well please. Anyway, you get used to people dying in this joint— kind of goes with the territory."

"Have you been here long?" Simon asked.

"Long enough to wish it was me that'd kicked the bucket. But I suppose my time will come soon enough."

Finch's gaze strayed to the framed photos on the wall: eight-by-ten glossies of movie stars, some of whom she recognized and each one personally autographed to Lorraine. "You *know* all these people?"

"Sure. That one over there, that's Derek Lord." Lorraine pointed out a handsome man with a pencil mustache and dark wavy hair. "Weren't no bigger star in his day. Spent like a drunken sailor, though. He died without a cent."

"Were you an actress?" Finch got up to examine a photo of a much younger Lorraine standing next to a dark-haired beauty she recognized with a jolt as Vivien Leigh.

"Me? Lord, no." She helped herself to a cookie from the tin on the table at her elbow before passing the tin to Finch. "I order 'em special. Food here's for the birds. Now, where were we? Oh yeah, my glamorous career. No, I was never an actress. Sure, I had dreams like every other starry-eyed girl just off the hay truck, but the trouble was I stunk at it. I wound up behind the scenes instead." She pointed at a color photo of a young Lorraine pinning the hem of a spangled red gown worn by none other than Lana Turner.

Simon whistled. "Wow. I'll bet you have stories to tell."

Lorraine leaned forward, saying in a confidential voice, "All those perfect figures? I knew every flaw—the boobs that were mostly foam rubber, the butts that needed a little lift. Leading lady put on few pounds? It was up to me to make her costumes fit. One—I'm not saying who—had me sew a secret pocket inside his trousers for his flask. Second day on the set he passed out cold right in the middle of his big scene." She cackled, a sound like pebbles rattling in a jar.

"Isn't that Selma Lamb?" Andie peered at a photo of Lorraine arm in arm with the buxom blond star of *Stranger in Paradise.*

Lorraine broke into a grin, showing a mouthful of crooked teeth. "None other. Oh, she was a pistol! From day one, we got on like a house on fire. When she found out I was from Deaf Smith, Texas, same as her, *well.*" She expelled a breath.

Finch studied the photo, recognizing the backdrop of snow-capped mountains and the red schoolhouse closer by. Remembering the day she'd gone there with Lucien, she felt something loosen in her belly.

Lorraine heaved herself to her feet once more and shuffled over to point out the rugged-looking man standing off to one side in the photo. "That there's the director, Hank Montgomery. He and Selma had a—what do you kids call it nowadays?—a thing."

"My great-grandmother knew him," Finch told her. Sam never tired of telling the story of the day her mother visited him on the set, the very one depicted in the photo.

"Her and a few hundred other gals." Lorraine gave a knowing wink. "Wasn't a woman within miles could resist his charms."

It occurred to Finch that Lorraine herself wouldn't have been immune. Suppose she'd gotten pregnant? Which would mean it was entirely possible that . . .

Goose bumps swarmed up the back of her neck. She stammered, "Did you and he—?"

Lorraine laughed, and Finch saw that her bright red lipstick had crept into the pleats around her mouth. "Lord, no. I was too smart for that. Which is more than I can say for some."

"But I thought—" Finch broke off, embarrassed. It seemed silly now. How could she have imagined that they were related?

Lorraine cast her a faintly apologetic look.

It was obvious Finch and her friends had been lured here under a false pretext. Finch swallowed her disappointment. She wanted to be angry but couldn't find it in her heart. Lorraine had only acted out of loneliness, something she understood all too well.

"I would've told you over the phone," Lorraine said. "But some things are best said in person. There *is* a story, only you're not part of it. See, there was this one gal— sweet young thing, no bigger than a minute. Hank, he had her weak in the knees and seeing cross-eyed. I'd have bet the ranch she was a virgin, but that didn't stop neither of 'em. When Selma got wind of it, well, you wouldn't have wanted to be within shootin' distance of her that day."

"This is better than *Dawson's Creek,*" Andie muttered.

"Grace Elliston was her name," Lorraine went on. "I remember 'cause Selma couldn't stop talking about it. When Grace wound up pregnant, Hank paid her to keep it quiet and they went their separate ways, but Selma wouldn't let that be the end of it. After the baby came, she was always saying things like, 'How's it feel to be a daddy?' or 'You planning on visiting your baby girl anytime soon?' About drove him round the bend. I think he felt bad—not so much about Selma, but about not being there for his kid. Far as I know, it was the only one he ever had."

Elliston? The name was familiar. "I know a Martha Elliston," Finch said. "She's our school nurse."

"Well, let's see, she'd have to be . . ." Lorraine did the arithmetic. "Forty-five, forty-six."

Finch didn't know Ms. Elliston's age, but that sounded about right.

"Doesn't she live with her mother?" Andie put in. "I see them in church sometimes. I assumed she was a widow—the old lady, I mean—but come to think of it, I've never heard her mention a husband."

"I always wondered what happened to Grace," Lorraine said. "It couldn't have been easy for her."

Or Martha, either—growing up without a father under a cloud of scandal. No wonder she always looked so beaten down.

They stayed awhile longer, Lorraine telling them more about the old days, but the whole time, beating in Finch like a second heart, was the knowledge that she would very likely never know her real family. She was doomed to a life of wishful thinking and dreams of what might have been. All at once she felt like crying. She was grateful when Lucien, as if picking up on her thoughts, squeezed her hand.

At last she dragged herself to her feet. "We should be going," she said. "It's a long drive." Lorraine looked sad to see them go. After a moment of hesitation Finch walked over and planted a kiss on her forehead, as leathery as an old wallet.

Lorraine clutched her hand, peering up at her with watery eyes. "I hope you find what you're looking for, dear."

Finch forced a smile. "Me, too." But she knew she had no more hope of her finding her family than of flying to the moon.

Laura and Hector were assembling the crib when she walked in. "No, you've got it backward, this thingamajig goes *there.*" Laura glanced up from the sheet of directions she was peering at to jab a finger at the bracket Hector was bolting in place. He nodded and calmly kept on with what he was doing. Other parts were scattered over the braided rug in front of the fireplace along with sections of the crib.

"I'm back," Finch announced when they failed to notice her standing there.

Laura cast her a distracted look, blowing at a wisp of hair that had fallen over one eye. "Whoever wrote these," she said, waving the flimsy sheet in her hand, "is either an idiot or playing a practical joke." She tossed it aside with a snort of contempt.

"How do we know it's not a she?" Even with his head bent low Finch could see that Hector was smiling.

"No woman would risk having this thing collapse with a baby in it."

He rocked back onto his heels, holding out the screwdriver. "In that case, be my guest. Wouldn't want to be accused of getting off on the wrong foot with our kid."

Laura tried to look angry, but she was giggling too hard. The giggles soon turned to hiccups, and she collapsed onto her back, gasping for breath. Pearl and Rocky ambled over to investigate, nudging at her with their noses. This Laura was a stranger to them, a woman who walked around humming incessantly all day, occasionally laughing out loud for no reason. She misplaced things around the house, and at the grocery store forgot half the items she'd meant to buy. The only thing on her mind, it seemed, was the baby arriving in just a few weeks.

Finch was beginning to feel just the tiniest bit left out.

"Need a hand?" she gestured toward the half assembled crib.

"Oh, I think Hector can manage on his own." Laura sat up, looking like a large pink-cheeked child, her hair crackling with static. "I know when I'm not wanted." She shot him a mock injured look as she struggled to her feet amid wet noses and wagging tails. Almost as an afterthought, she asked, "How'd it go today?"

Finch shrugged. "I'll tell you about it over dinner."

She followed Laura into the kitchen, where Maude was rolling out dough while a frying pan sizzled on the stove. "Your favorite, chicken pot pie," she said, offering a floury cheek to be kissed.

The familiar sight of Maude making supper brought a lump to her throat. "I'll set the table."

"Hector's almost done with the crib,"

Laura announced as she grabbed a handful of napkins from a drawer.

Maude snorted. "Hardly enough room in there for a cradle much less a crib." She was talking about the alcove off Laura and Hector's room, which they'd converted into a nursery.

"Babies don't need much room," Laura said with a shrug.

"They grow."

"Well, it'll do just fine for now." Laura drifted about, setting out the milk carton then a moment later returning it to the fridge. "When she's older we'll add on. And don't forget, it won't be long before Finch is away at college."

Finch had been looking forward to it, but now the thought brought a pang.

Maude pursed her lips. "Even so . . ."

Laura gave an airy laugh. "Admit it, you want her in with *you.*"

It was a moment before Finch realized she meant the baby, not her.

Maude gave another snort, thumping at the dough with her rolling pin. She could deny it all she liked, but there was nothing she'd love more than a baby to fuss over night and day.

Finch felt suddenly out in the cold. She recalled her years in foster care, where the best stuff and biggest helpings always went to the littlest and cutest kids. How could she compete with a baby? And from the way Laura was mooning, it would only get worse once Esperanza was there.

"Well, at least she'll have plenty to wear." Maude was sewing a whole wardrobe of little dresses, an opportunity she'd been deprived of when Sam's baby turned out to be a boy.

"Just no ruffles, please." Laura was filling a pitcher at the sink.

"Knowing you, she'll be on horseback before she's even learned to walk. Another tomboy—just what we need," Maude grumbled good-naturedly.

"By the way," Laura said, "Alice wants to throw me a shower. I told her—"

"Is that all anyone thinks about around here!" Finch slammed a plate down on the table. "What about Anna? She could go to prison, and all you care about is that stupid baby!"

Laura looked stunned. "I haven't forgotten Anna," she said. "As a matter of fact, I told Alice that if she wants to throw a party, we should make it a fund-raiser." She set the pitcher down. "Finch, what's going on? Are you upset because—"

Finch didn't hear the rest; she was already bolting out the door. Outside, the air was cool against her burning cheeks amid the gathering dusk as she pelted across the yard.

In the barn she was greeted by the horses nickering in their stalls. She heard a rustling noise and her mare's sleek chestnut head appeared over the door to her stall. Finch pressed a cheek to her silky neck, breathing in her horsey scent. Weren't they both rejects in a way? Like Punch and Judy before her, Cheyenne had come to them through Lost Paws, where Laura was on the board—a track horse that had outlived her usefulness.

She heard the barn door slide open and turned to find Laura eyeing her with concern. "Finch, what is it?"

"Nothing."

"I was afraid of this." Laura sighed, sinking down on the bench. "It didn't turn out the way you'd hoped, did it?"

Finch walked over and sank down beside her, oblivious to the delicious smells wafting across the yard. "She's just a nice old lady. I feel stupid for ever thinking . . ." She struggled to keep from crying. "I guess that kind of stuff only happens in movies."

There was a long silence, broken only by the horses nickering for the sugar cubes Laura usually had tucked in her pocket. At last she said, "I'm sorry. I wish there was something I could say that would make it better."

"It's okay." Nothing was going to make her feel better right now.

"You don't need to hear you have a family with us; you already know that."

Finch nodded dispiritedly. "I feel like such an idiot."

Laura put an arm around her shoulders. "When I was your age, I dreamed of a big family, at least six kids. It wasn't meant to be, but you know what? I wouldn't have it any other way. You and Hector and Maude, you're everything to me."

"With the baby, that's five. You'll need one more to make it six." A corner of Finch's mouth hooked up.

Laura laughed. "We'll see how it goes with this one first, though with all the trouble we've gone to putting together that crib it'd be a shame not to put it to more use."

Finch told her then about Hank Montgomery and Grace Elliston. Laura didn't seem surprised; she only nodded and said, "Nana said he was the most magnetic man she'd ever met. I got the feeling he was a real heartbreaker."

"I wonder if Martha knows he's her father."

"She's certainly never said anything. If she had, it'd be the talk of the town." Hank Montgomery might have slipped into obscurity elsewhere, but in Carson Springs he was legendary. "Come to think of it, though, I *do* remember some old gossip about Grace. In those days a baby out of wedlock would have caused quite a scandal. Poor woman." She shook her head.

Finch studied her face, dear and familiar. Who was to say Martha wouldn't have been better off had her mother given her up for adoption?

"Do you think I should say something to her?" she asked.

"I'm not sure it's your place."

"I'd want to know if I were her."

Laura frowned in thought. "Maybe if we went to Grace instead—"

"We?"

"You think I'd let you go alone?"

Finch felt something loosen in her chest. "We could invite her over after mass this Sunday. You know, for lunch or something."

"We'd have to invite Martha, too. No, I think our best bet is to drop by during the week when Martha's at work. Of course, I'd have to write you a note for school." Her eyes sparkled the way Andie's did when the two of them were plotting some intrigue.

"As long as she doesn't ask what's wrong with me. I'd hate to have to lie to her face when she's the reason I'm absent."

"Good point. I'll say it's a checkup."

They lapsed into companionable silence. Finch had forgotten all about dinner until Laura said, "What do you say we head back inside?"

Finch realized she was starving. "I'm so hungry I could eat a—" She looked up to find her mare eyeing her reproachfully, or so it seemed. "Never mind."

Minutes later she was sitting down to a steaming plate of chicken pot pie and biscuits, green beans, and Maude's famous pickled beets. They bowed their heads while Laura said grace. When they got to *Amen,* Finch said it louder than the others.

Laura smiled at her across the table and for a frightening moment Finch thought might make a corny speech—about how blessed they were to have each other and how they all had to stick together—but all she said was, "Butter, anyone?"

CHAPTER FIFTEEN

The day of the preliminary hearing the courthouse was packed, the steps outside a sea of reporters and bobbing Minicams. Local TV jockeyed with print and radio while the network heavies seized control of prime space. There were stringers from *Le Monde* and the Brits' favorite sleazemonger, the *Mirror.* And a reporter from the *Globe,* a particularly disreputable character by the name of Lenny Buckholtz, with "more balls than a bowling alley," as Maude sniffed, had been placed under arrest for attempting to bribe a clerk in the coroner's office into slipping him postmortem photos.

Each new development in the ongoing soap opera of *State of California* v. *Anna Vincenzi* was like a scrap of wood tossed onto an already roaring blaze. An editorial in the *New York Post* postulated that Anna had killed Monica for the money. The *National Star* ran an exclusive interview with a former housekeeper who described her years of mistreatment at Monica's hands, suggesting that Anna's motivation had been one of revenge. In the midst of it all, Anna, the *real* Anna, had become lost somehow, replaced by a figment of the public's imagination. The truth was irrelevant. People wouldn't welcome it any more than they would the truth about themselves.

Now, as she scanned the packed gallery, she knew what it was to be a Christian in the lion's den. Her underarms were soggy despite the antiperspirant she'd lathered on, and if her stomach didn't settle down, the coffee she'd gulped on the run would soon have her regretting that she'd worn pantyhose.

She glanced at Rhonda beside her, scribbling something on her legal pad. She looked poised and confident. Too confident? Would she rub the judge the wrong way as she had the last time? Well, at least no one could say she wasn't prepared. After weeks of plotting and planning, her lawyer was in full battle mode.

But what if that wasn't enough?

Krystal, their ace in the hole, had vanished along with any chance of the real killer's being found. The investigator Rhonda had hired, a retired LAPD detective named Barney Merlin, had reported, not surprisingly, that Krystal's children weren't in school and that her boss at Merry Maids hadn't heard from her; she hadn't even bothered to pick up her check. Wherever she'd gone, it was obvious she didn't want to be found.

"All rise for the Honorable Judge Emory Cartwright. Court is now in session."

Anna was jerked to her feet as if by an invisible leash. These days her body was like an obedient dog, operating according to whatever command it was given: Sit, stay, lie down, play dead.

Rhonda remained on her feet after everyone else had retaken their seats.

"Your presence is duly noted, Ms. Talltree," the judge said dryly. "I just hope, in your enthusiasm for this morning's proceedings, you're mindful of my ulcer."

"I'll do my best, Your Honor." A wave of

chuckles rippled through the courtroom as Rhonda, erect as a military attaché in her navy suit and crisp white blouse, lowered herself into her chair.

The judge, looking more dyspeptic than ever, stilled the rustling in the gallery with a sharp rap of his gavel. "In the matter of *State of California* v. *Anna Vincenzi* . . ." He rattled off the charges for the benefit of the court reporter, a tall, rail-thin man hunched like a question mark over his machine, before nodding to the district attorney, who was flanked by a pair of his deputies, a young man and woman who looked fresh out of law school. "Mr. Showalter, you may proceed."

The D.A. rose to his feet, smoothing his tie. In his double-breasted, pin-striped suit, he looked like a pork barrel politician stumping the campaign trail. "Your Honor," he began, "the people will show that the defendant, on the night of April 17, 2001, did intentionally cause the death of Monica Vincent. Ms. Anna Vincenzi," he swung around to level an accusing finger at Anna, "was not only her sister but her trusted assistant. And on the night in question, the defendant drove to the victim's home, also her place of employment, with one thing in mind: murder." He paused for dramatic effect, fingers steepled under his chin.

"We may never know Ms. Vincenzi's motive," he went on. "Was she jealous of her older sister's fame and fortune, or was it simply greed? In any case, we intend to show that somewhere between eleven and midnight, following what appears to have been a struggle, she pushed the victim into the pool. This wasn't a prank gone awry, Your Honor. Monica was in a wheelchair, paralyzed from the waist down and helpless to defend herself. Though it appears she put up a good fight, as evidenced by the bruises she sustained as well the scratches on the defendant's arm at the time of her arrest, she was unable to swim to safety. Nor was there anyone to hear her cries—except the defendant, who coldly stood by and watched her drown." Another pregnant pause. "Your Honor, if there was ever a case of first-degree murder, this is it."

Anna felt the blood drain from her face. Who was this woman he was describing, this cold-blooded killer? How could anyone possibly think that of *her*?

When it was her turn, Rhonda rose to her

feet. "Your Honor, there's nothing to suggest that Ms. Vincenzi was anywhere near her sister's house that night; there are no eyewitnesses and only the flimsiest of circumstantial evidence. It's easy to point the finger at a woman whose only crime was that she had easy access to her sister. Let's face it; she's a sitting duck—or should I say a bird in hand." She cast a pointed look at Showalter. "Monica Vincent is dead, yes. But my client didn't kill her. Don't make her a victim of this terrible tragedy, too."

Judge Cartwright's face registered nothing other than general distaste for the proceedings. But however much he might have liked this to be someone else's ulcer, circumstances had dictated otherwise. "Ms. Talltree, Mr. Showalter, let me remind you that this is a preliminary hearing, not a trial, so please spare me the theatrics," he cautioned before instructing them on which evidence and testimony he would allow.

There *would* be a trial; Anna was almost sure of it now. And what then? Her mind swam with visions of lockdowns, tattooed inmates, high walls topped with razor wire. In panic she glanced over her shoulder, catching sight of Marc, seated next to

Laura in the first row. He didn't smile or mouth words of encouragement; he just held her gaze, his blue eyes focused on hers with the steadiness of a lighthouse beacon. *I'm here,* they seemed to say. *And I'll be here tomorrow and the next day and the day after that.*

She felt some of the tension drain out of her. Whatever happened, she'd been blessed. Instead of a life half lived, she'd known what it was to fall asleep in the arms of a man who adored her, who shielded her the way a windbreak prevents topsoil from being scattered every which way.

Detective Burch, looking like a bull with blood in its eye, was the first witness for the prosecution. He presented postmortem photos, a log of latent prints, and impressions lifted from the house and immediate vicinity, as well as e-mails recovered from both Monica's and Anna's computers. But most damning of all were the DNA test results.

The state's expert, a gaunt, white-haired man with a goatee, Colonel Sanders on a starvation diet, was called up next to interpret those results. From the sprightliness with which he strode toward the stand and the collegial nod with which he greeted Showalter and his deputies, he was clearly no stranger to the courtroom.

"Doctor, would you please state your full name," Showalter said when he'd been sworn in.

The man leaned into the microphone, and in a deep voice that was at odds with his appearance boomed, "Orin Webb."

"What is your occupation?"

"I'm a forensic scientist."

"How long have you been practicing in this field?"

"A little over thirty years."

Showalter turned to address the bench. "Your Honor, I'd like to offer Dr. Webb as an expert witness in the field of DNA analysis."

The judge leaned onto his elbows. "Any objection, Ms. Talltree?"

"None whatsoever—he seems qualified enough." She sounded almost cheerful. Anna might have wondered if Rhonda hadn't explained that the advantage to this hearing was the chance to scope out the prosecution's strategy.

Cartwright nodded. "You may proceed."

Dr. Webb rattled off a number of scientific terms about pattern searching and gene coding and nucleic acid patterns before producing a detailed graph of what he called repeats.

"Could you explain what this means in laymen's terms?" Showalter pointed at the graph propped on an easel, its rows of densely packed lines as unreadable as bar codes.

"Well, it's like a blueprint. We try to match tandem patterns of a specific size; in this case, a user specialized size from one to three nucleotides—" He caught himself and cleared his throat and gave a little smile. "Basically, what it means is that there's a ninety-eight-point-nine percent probability that the DNA from under the victim's fingernails matches the defendant's."

A low hum went through the packed gallery like a power surge, accompanied by the furious scratching of pencils on paper as courtroom artists hastened to captured the scene.

Anna bit down on the inside of her cheek to keep from crying out.

There was more discussion of techniques and probability before Showalter produced his trump card: a blowup of a police photo taken the day of Anna's arrest. "Doctor," he asked, "in your opinion could the DNA you refer to have come from *these*?" He jabbed a finger at the barely healed scratches running up the enlarged photo of Anna's arm.

Rhonda shot to her feet. "Objection, Your Honor. Pure speculation."

"Sustained." Cartwright directed a stern gaze at Showalter, who only smiled smugly. His point had been made.

When it was Rhonda's turn to cross-examine, she strode confidently to the stand, heels clicking on the scuffed oak floor. "Doctor, is there any way of determining whether this DNA you refer to dates from the time of death or, say, several hours beforehand?"

He hesitated, his gaze shifting to Showalter. "Not with any degree of accuracy, no."

"So it could have been the result of a separate incident earlier in the day?"

He frowned, stroking his goatee. "Well, given the circumstances, it's reasonable to assume . . ."

She didn't let him finish. "Doctor, this isn't a game of Clue," she said with a smile that had all the warmth of an air conditioner turned up full blast. "All I'm asking is whether or not you can definitively state that this DNA is concurrent with the time of death."

"Well . . . no," he conceded grudgingly.

"Thank you, Doctor, that will be all."

Anna scarcely noticed when he stepped down. The world seemed to be receding in a gray, grainy tide as memory rushed in to engulf her.

"I'm throwing a little party this Friday," Monica had announced one day out of the blue. "It's for Rhys, to celebrate his nomination."

Anna looked up in surprise from the mail she was sorting through. Rhys Folkes, who'd directed several of Monica's pictures, was up for an Oscar that year, but if the party was this weekend, why was she only just now hearing of it? She studied her sister closely, but saw nothing to arouse suspicion. It had been two weeks since the episode with Glenn, which neither of them had referred to and which Anna had almost, but not quite, succeeded in putting behind her. In fact, surprisingly, Monica had been on her best behavior. Maybe she'd had a change of heart, or maybe it was because Anna was no longer putting up with her bad behavior.

"I'll call Dean," she said, thinking it'd be a miracle if she could book the caterer on such short notice.

"All taken care of." Monica gestured airily. Stretched out on the sofa in her dressing gown, she might have been Cleopatra on her pallet. "It'll be cocktails and a light buffet supper, informal but elegant."

This was even more extraordinary, Monica making her own arrangements. "Is there a list of people you'd like me to call?" It was too late for printed invitations.

"I've taken care of that, too." Monica began leafing through the magazine she'd pulled from the stack on the coffee table. "I'd like it if you could come—as a guest, of course." She flashed her most disarming smile. "Are you free that night?"

In the old days she would have taken it for granted. It was on the tip of Anna's tongue to accept—Monica was making an effort; shouldn't she meet her halfway?— but something stopped her, the Charlie Brown who'd had the football snatched from under her one too many times. "I'll have to check my calendar," she said.

Monica shrugged. "Fine. You can let me know tomorrow." Anna braced herself for the usual sarcastic dig, something along the lines of, "If you can possibly spare an evening out of your *busy* schedule . . ." But it didn't come. Monica only lifted her head to say nonchalantly, "If you don't have anything to wear, I could loan you something of mine."

"I thought you said it was informal."

"Well, yes . . . I meant something that *fits*." She smiled to let Anna know she'd meant it as a compliment. "Besides, it's a special occasion. You know that crowd."

Anna's suspicion deepened. Though Monica was occasionally given to bursts of generosity, it was unimaginable that she'd risk being upstaged, not after what had happened with Glenn. "It's nice of you to offer, but I don't think—"

Monica didn't let her finish. "Why don't we have a look upstairs?"

"Now?" She eyed the mail she'd separated into two stacks: the letters marked personal, which she'd leave for Monica, and the ones from fans, a few bulky with some personal item the sender wished to have autographed.

"Come on, don't be such a party pooper. Leave that." She dismissed the letters with a wave. Clearly, she was warming to the prospect of playing fairy godmother.

Upstairs in her sister's room, Anna felt a ripple of apprehension as she eyed the evening gowns Monica hadn't worn in years, glimmering in their plastic shrouds—not one larger than a size six. Was this another exercise in humiliation, having her try on dresses that wouldn't fit?

She sucked in her breath . . . and her stomach . . . as she pulled one of the less fitted over her head. Magically, it cascaded down past her hips, bringing a rush of heady delight. It was tea length, the color of an evening sky with tiny beads that twinkled and changed in hue as she twirled in front of the full-length mirror. Now she knew how Cinderella must have felt.

"It fits you like a glove." Monica smiled at her from the doorway.

"You don't think it's too . . . much?" Anna recalled the last time her sister had worn it: Swifty's post-Oscar bash the year Monica had been nominated for *Miami, Oklahoma.* Her last official outing before the accident.

"It looks like it was made for you. Besides, it's not as if I'll be wearing it again anytime soon," Monica added in the tone Anna had mentally labeled The Heroine Bravely Holding Up. Not that she didn't receive dozens of invitations to gala events, but would any of them be as much fun as the pity party she threw every night at home?

"I don't know . . ." She frowned, chewing on her lip. "I'm afraid I might spill something on it."

"Never mind. It's yours."

"You mean—"

"Don't look so surprised. I would've given it to you sooner if . . ." *You'd been thin,* Anna could almost hear her say. "Well, it suits you perfectly, that's all that matters."

Anna was too stunned and delighted to protest. "I . . . I don't know what to say. It's beautiful."

"You deserve it. Look at you—you're a shadow of your former self."

"I wouldn't go that far," Anna said with a laugh. She'd have needed a shoehorn to get into most of these gowns. "I just wish . . ." Her mouth clamped shut. She'd been about to say that she wished Marc could see her, but there was no sense giving Monica ammunition she could use later on in a less munificent mood.

She had a harder time keeping him out of her thoughts. She pictured Marc as she'd last seen him that morning at the lake, the wind ruffling his hair, his eyes the deep blue of the sky overhead, and felt an almost visceral longing. So far she'd resisted the urge to call, and for the most part had refrained from wallowing in self-pity. All it took to toughen her resolve was seeing how miserable Liz's affair had made her.

Monica eyed her curiously. "You wish what?"

"Nothing."

Another time she'd have tried to worm it out of Anna, but now she only shrugged and said, "Wear it in good health."

By the time Friday rolled around, Anna found she was actually looking forward to the party. She'd even splurged on a pair of silver sandal heels and made an appointment at Shear Delight. Arriving at Lorei-Linda that evening, she felt like Cinderella stepping from her carriage.

Arcela, taking coats at the door, stepped back to admire her, exclaiming in a hushed tone, "Miss Anna, you look like princess!" At the same time she appeared vaguely troubled. It wasn't until Anna stepped out onto the patio, twinkling with the fairy lights she and Arcela had spent hours stringing earlier in the day, that she understood: The guests, several dozen in all, stood chatting about the pool, drinks in hand, no one dressed in anything more formal than the flowing silk caftan Sallie Henshaw had on.

Anna stopped cold, feeling suddenly conspicuous. But it was too late to turn back. People were eyeing her, some drifting closer to get a better look.

"Monica, you naughty girl, you told us casual chic. I feel positively underdressed." Rayne Billings, in a midi blouse and capris, cast Anna a coolly ironic smile.

And now Sallie was wafting over, the hem of her caftan fluttering about her ankles. They'd spoken a few times over the phone, but had never met in person until now. "You must be Anna. I'm Sallie." As if everyone in America didn't know who she was; Sallie's career as an actress might be on the wane, but she'd kept busy in her twilight years hawking everything from paper towels to denture cream. She put out a plump hand on which flashed an emerald ring the size of the olive in her martini. "I must say, you look stunning in that dress. You're putting us all to shame." She sounded sincere enough, but Anna could only mumble something inane before escaping to the bar, her face on fire.

What made it so awful was that she'd been set up. And hadn't she walked right into the trap? She, of all people who should have known. For a brief moment she'd allowed herself to believe there was a real person underneath her sister's wiles, but now she couldn't escape the truth: Monica was just a monster in a human suit.

Somehow she made it through the rest of the evening. Several glasses of champagne downed in quick succession helped, as well as the attention she got from some of the men, notably Rick Rasche, the blond hunk from the hit series *Malibu.* But the whole time she felt like a sore thumb. All she wanted was to be home in bed, Boots curled at her side. Tomorrow she would kill Monica. Right then, she was too miserable.

The following morning she arrived at work hung over in addition to being fed up. This time there would be no rehearsed speech, nor was she going to wait until she'd lined up another job. She was giving notice, effective immediately.

She found her sister in the sunroom, her feet propped on an ottoman, her hair ablaze in the sunlight that poured in through the bank of French windows overlooking the rose garden, as she sat with the morning paper sipping espresso. In her silk kimono that matched her scarlet nails, she was no longer a fairy godmother, more like Cruella DeVil.

"Did you have fun last night?" She barely glanced up, which only enraged Anna further. When she didn't answer, Monica went on blithely, "I should think so—you were the belle of the ball. Rick Rasche couldn't keep his eyes off you."

"No wonder. I stuck out like a sore thumb." Anna's voice was frosty.

"Funny, I always thought he was gay." She lowered the paper, smiling innocently.

Anna glared at her. "It's no use, Monica. I'm on to you."

"Well, look who got out of the wrong side of the bed this morning," she scolded with an airy laugh, setting her doll-sized cup in its saucer with a musical clink. "Just because you had too much to drink last night, don't take it out on me."

"You know perfectly well why I'm upset."

"Do I? Well, let me guess. It must be because I gave you a knockout dress to wear to my party, where men most women can only dream about were all over you like white on rice." Her voice dripped with honeyed sarcasm. "I'm very sorry if I offended you. Next time I'm feeling generous I'll give to the Salvation Army."

"You can drop the act; I'm not buying it." If her sister thought she could bully or cajole her way out of it this time, it was only because all she saw were the outward changes in Anna. "You set me up on purpose. You wanted me to look like a dumb little hick. I couldn't have felt more ridiculous if I'd been naked."

"Don't be so melodramatic," Monica scoffed. "No one thought anything of the kind. As a matter of fact, a number of people complimented you, as I recall."

"This is payback, isn't it? You can't stand that I'm finally getting some attention, that you're not the sole focus of every man within a mile radius. No one looked twice at me before, and that suited you just fine. If anything, I made you shine all the brighter." Anna trembled with twenty years of suppressed fury. "Well, guess what? I quit, this time for good. Get yourself another whipping girl, though I think the kind you want went out with indentured servitude."

"You're quitting? Because of some stupid little misunderstanding?" Monica laughed, but Anna caught a glint of fear in her eyes. She'd gone too far this time, and she knew it.

"The only misunderstanding," Anna said in a barely controlled voice, "is my thinking there was a real person underneath all your bullshit." She leaned in close and caught a whiff of Monica's breath. She'd been drinking something other than espresso.

"You can't leave. What will I do?" Monica's eyes filled with tears. She looked small and lost. But Anna had been down this road before; she knew enough not to be sucked in.

"Try the Yellow Pages," she snapped.

"You're giving me a headache." Monica brought a hand to her forehead in a gesture so theatrical Anna almost laughed. When it failed to elicit the desired sympathy, her eyes narrowed. "You're not going anywhere. You wouldn't dare."

"Oh, really? And just how do you plan on stopping me?" If Monica threatened to cut off payments to the Sunshine Home, she'd threaten in return to go to the press. Monica wouldn't want it spread all over kingdom come that her mother was being tossed out onto the street because she was too cheap to pay for a nursing home.

She remained unmoved even when Monica hissed, "I'll make your life a living hell."

Now Anna *did* laugh. "You've already done that."

A hectic flush bloomed in Monica's cheeks. "You think I don't know what this is really about?" She strained toward Anna, gripping the arms of her chair. "Now that Mom's out of the way, you want to be rid of me, too. Well, it doesn't work that way. You need me as much as I need you!"

"Maybe I did once, but not anymore." The anger had gone out of Anna, and now she eyed her sister with something close to pity. She knew her better in some ways than Monica knew herself: how comforting it was to be the victim, which meant you were never to blame, and how self-pity warmed like a blanket on a cold night.

"Don't expect me to go on paying Mom's bills."

Anna shrugged. "Do what you like."

Her indifference only enraged Monica further. "I don't owe her a cent! What did she ever do for me? Name one goddamn thing!"

Anna was taken aback by the depth of Monica's enmity. She'd always assumed her contempt had more to do with wanting to distance herself from her humble roots. Softly she said, "She worships the ground you walk on, you know," though it was unlikely Betty would even recognize her at this point.

"Oh sure, *now* she does. But where was she when I was growing up? She was as much to blame as he was! You don't know. You don't know what I—" She broke off with a choking sound, her mouth twisting into a grimace as she snatched up her cup and hurled it at the wall, where it shattered into tiny eggshell shards. "God, you're so blind. You and Liz, stupid little nobodies with your heads in the sand!"

Anna stared at her, knowing she should feel something but too weary to summon more than mild disgust. Her sister was right about one thing. Her head *had* been in the sand. All this time she'd thought Monica was using their mother to manipulate *her,* but there was obviously more to it than that.

The thing was, she no longer cared. Whatever her sister's demons, let her wrestle with them on her own.

But Monica's tantrum had passed. Now she sat there, staring sightlessly ahead, the fury of the moment before gone like the beige foam soaking into the rug. When she finally looked up, she seemed almost surprised to see Anna still standing there. "Would you help me into my chair?" she asked in a slurred voice, gesturing with a limp hand in the direction of her wheelchair.

Some speck of compassion must have survived in Anna after all for she found herself walking toward her sister. Not that her resolve was weakening, but there was one thing Monica hadn't been able to rob her of: simple human kindness.

She was lifting her into her wheelchair when Monica's weight abruptly shifted, throwing her off balance. Monica cried out, clutching at her. Anna tried to right herself, but they both went down, collapsing in a heap onto the rug. It was a moment before she managed to wriggle out from under Monica, pulling herself upright. Feeling a stinging sensation, she looked down at her arm to see bloody scratches extending from the inside of her elbow to her wrist. Monica lay puddled beside her, weeping.

"Are you all right?" Anna gasped.

Monica didn't appear to be hurt. But she was clearly more than a little drunk—at nine-thirty in the morning, no less. "I'm sorry. Please don't hate me." Her cheeks were wet, not crocodile tears this time. "I didn't mean any of those things I said."

Anna struggled to her feet, careful to avoid the shards of china that had landed nearby. She stood there looking down at her sister. "I don't hate you," she said. She had once, but now all she felt was . . .

What *did* she feel? Nothing.

"I know I've been awful to you. I know." Monica sat up, her mouth twisted in a smile that was awful to behold. With her hair tangled about her shoulders and makeup running ghoulishly down her cheeks, she was a parody of the woman adored by millions— more *Picture of Dorian Grey* than picture perfect. "But please . . . don't leave me. I'm begging you. I'll make it up to you. I swear."

Anna felt goose bumps swarm up her arms. Monica sounded exactly like their father after one of his drunken tirades, when he'd plead for Betty's forgiveness. "It's too late for that," she said, shaking her head.

"Just until I find someone else?" Monica eyed her piteously.

Every instinct cried out for her to run, but she found herself saying, "I'll give you until the end of the day." What was a few more hours after all she'd endured?

With Arcela's help she managed to lift Monica off the floor and into her wheelchair, but it was like hoisting a sack of grain. Never mind. If she was three sheets to the wind, it was no longer Anna's concern. She had bigger worries, like how she was going to support herself until she found another job.

She spent the rest of the day clearing off her desk and packing up her things. There wasn't much to show for the four years she'd worked there: a few family photos, a souvenir mug from Monica's last trip to Cannes, a teddy bear she hadn't had the heart to toss into the box she donated each month to Goodwill—love offerings from fans. Tomorrow she'd deal with the reality of being out of work. For now it was enough that she was finally, blessedly free.

Then it was time to go. She descended

the stairs to find Arcela in the kitchen but-toning up her coat—it was her night off. Anna hugged her good-bye. *Poor Arcela. She'll bear the brunt of it now.* But Arcela only whispered, "I happy for you." Anna drew back to find her dark eyes shiny with tears, those of a small brown animal not fleet-footed enough to escape.

Anna felt a twinge of guilt, yet nothing could take away from her giddy sense of re-lease. She longed to share the good news with Marc; he'd be happy for her, too. But it would only open a door better left shut. "We'll still see each other," she told Arcela, who smelled faintly of cinnamon and Lemon Pledge. "And you know you can al-ways call if you need me."

Now all that was left was to say her good-byes to Monica. Anna took a deep breath before heading down the hall. She knocked on the door to her sister's study, and in a surprisingly chipper voice Monica called, "Come in."

Expecting to find her a wreck, Anna was unprepared for the sight of Monica's tap-ping away at her computer. She glanced about the room, done up in French provin-cial and pickled pine, but nothing was out of place, and all she smelled was the potpourri in a shallow dish on the antique trestle. Nor was there anything in Monica's demeanor to suggest that this morning's horror show had taken place.

She cleared her throat, saying, "I'm on my way out. I just wanted to say good-bye."

Monica looked up at her with a faint, ironic smile. "Don't be so dramatic. You act as though we'll never see each other again." As she wheeled out from behind her desk, Anna could see something hard and implacable in her eyes. "We're still family, aren't we?" She spoke lightly, but Anna caught a queer undercurrent that sent a shiver up her spine.

She shrugged. However hard Monica tried to bait her, she wasn't going to bite. "This is for you." Anna handed her the folder with everything her replacement would need. "I included a list of employment agencies. I'm sure you'll have no trouble finding someone."

Monica tossed it onto her desk without a glance. "You're not leaving me much choice, are you?"

Anna smiled thinly. "Now who's being dramatic?" She could sense it like a low pressure front: Any minute now the storm would break. "Come on, Monica, we both know this is for the best."

"For *you,* maybe."

"Look, I'd like it if we could part on good terms. So why don't I go before this gets ugly?"

She'd made it halfway to the door before Monica wheeled around sharply, blocking her path. "You think you're better than me, don't you?" she spat. "Miss Goody Two-shoes whose shit doesn't stink. No wonder you and Liz were Mom's favorites—you're both a pair of spineless wimps. At least *I* had the guts to get out." She glared up at Anna. "You know something? I'm *glad* you're leaving."

"That makes two of us." Anna stepped around her as if she were no more than a bump in the road to freedom. The relief she felt was so powerful she seemed to float out the door and down the hall.

But her freedom was short-lived.

She was awakened early the next morning by the ringing of the phone. Groggy, her first thought had been of her mother, but when she snatched up the receiver, it was Arcela's voice at the other end. Something about an accident was all she could determine from the housekeeper's hysterical babbling. The police were on their way . . .

Now, weeks later, as she sat in the courtroom where a new drama was being played out, she nearly laughed out loud at her naïveté. How could she have believed she was free? Even with her sister dead, Anna was more firmly caught in her web than when she'd been alive.

When it was her turn, Rhonda summoned her own forensics expert, a man as portly as his predecessor was lean, wearing horn-rims and a tweed jacket with elbow patches—a professor straight from central casting.

"Dr. Dennison," she asked, "would it be accurate to say that skin cells contain little or no DNA?"

He was perspiring in his heavy jacket but otherwise looked composed as he leaned into the microphone. "Technically, that's true," he said. "Nucleated cells are typically transferred to the skin surface through sweat."

"Would it be fair to say that under certain

conditions—say, if the body has spent some time underwater—those secretions might wear off?"

"To some extent, yes."

"So it's entirely possible the DNA from under the victim's fingernails could conceivably have come from someone *other* than Ms. Vincenzi?"

"Technically, yes."

"Thank you, Doctor. You may step down."

Anna understood where Rhonda was going with this: She was throwing a monkey wrench into the works by suggesting that the test results linking Anna to the crime could have been false, that it might have been someone else's DNA—the *real* murderer's. But would the judge buy it? From the impassive expression he wore, it was impossible to tell. And for the purposes of this hearing, did it even matter? All the prosecution had to show was probable cause for him to order a trial, which would be a sentence in itself, entailing months of preparation while she struggled to make ends meet.

Cruel fingers closed about her heart. It was all she could do not to let her panic show.

When they recessed for lunch, she and her supporters convened at the Tree House Café, where David Ryback was keeping reporters at bay by informing them that all the tables were reserved.

"Where's Finch?" Anna glanced about, wondering if she'd decided against skipping a day of school.

Laura glanced at Hector, then at Maude. "She, uh . . . had some stuff to do."

Anna sensed something afoot. "Is there something you're keeping from me?"

"You might as well tell her," Sam said to Laura. "She'll know soon enough."

"She wanted it to be a surprise." Laura dropped her voice so Althea Wormley, seated at the next table with several other members of the altar guild, wouldn't hear. "She organized a rally. She didn't tell you because she was afraid you'd try to talk her out of it."

"Oh, God." Anna was aghast. Hadn't she generated enough publicity as it was? Only CTN had been restrained in its coverage, and that was due to Wes.

"Well, I think it's a nice show of support," Maude piped.

"I'm grateful for *all* your support, but . . ."

Anna cast a nervous glance at Rhonda, who was calmly buttering a slice of bread.

But Rhonda surprised her by saying, "Actually, it might work in your favor. At least we'll be getting some positive press for a change."

"Look at OJ," Liz said, then blushed. "Sorry. Bad example."

"You've got to hand it to her. The girl is nothing if not enterprising," Marc said with a chuckle.

Laura darted an anxious look at Hector. "I just hope she doesn't get in over her head." She was probably remembering the time Finch had joined the rally to save the oak tree at Los Reyes Plaza that was slated to be cut down. There'd been over a hundred supporters, but only Finch and a handful of others had been arrested for disturbing the peace, complete with a photo on the front page of the following morning's *Clarion.*

Melodie Wycoff took their orders. Normally chatty, she'd kept a fairly low profile these past weeks, her husband being a cop. The rumors swirling around Melodie were enough—she'd supposedly had an affair with one of his buddies—without her making matters worse. But now she leaned down to whisper sotto voce, "We're all rooting for you, hon. Hang in there." Warmed by her support, Anna nodded in response, too choked up to speak.

"It looked as if you scored some points with the judge," Marc said to Rhonda when Melodie had bustled off.

"Maybe," she said, frowning. "But if it goes to trial, we'll have to do some fancy footwork for the jury to buy that it was someone other than Anna."

"My money's on Krystal," Liz said darkly. If anything she was even more outraged than Anna was that the police weren't looking for her.

"Don't forget Hairy Cary," Marc said.

"Hairy Cary?" Maude looked confused.

"One of Monica's e-mail pals," he explained. "We thought he might have something to do with it, even though he doesn't exactly fit the profile."

"He's a minister," Anna put in.

"So was Jim Bakker," Sam noted wryly.

"I finally got through to him," Marc went on. "He claimed to have been out of town at some Baptist conference, but he seemed pretty nervous. I couldn't tell if it was because he didn't want his wife to find out he'd been sending those creepy messages or if it was something more."

"Creepy in what way?" Hector asked.

"He'd want to know stuff like her shoe size, and what kind of perfume she wore," Anna told him. "Once he sent her a gift—a nightgown."

"Did she keep it?" Liz wanted to know. Anna shot her a dirty look, not bothering to respond.

"I ran a check to see if he had a record," Rhonda said. "There *was* something, but it was pretty far back—an incident involving lewd behavior. I couldn't get the details. He was given a suspended sentence, then presumably found God. He's been clean ever since."

"So that's it, you just drop it?" Laura said.

"Not on your life." Rhonda wore her steeliest look. "I'm having Barney fly out there next week."

"Every time you look in the paper there's a story about some celebrity stalker," Liz said. "Look what happened to John Lennon. And remember that guy Monica got a restraining order against awhile back?"

"I think it was one of her ex-husbands," Anna said.

"Whatever." Liz was clearly warming to the subject. Anna remembered that she hadn't been the only one who'd devoured *Nancy Drew* books when they were kids. "And another thing, has anyone considered the possibility that it might have been someone on staff? The gardener, or even Arcela."

"Arcela? You can't be serious." It was all Anna could do not to roll her eyes. Her sister meant well, she knew; she'd even been hitting up some of the spa's wealthier clients for donations. But she was out on a limb here—the affair must have blown a fuse in her brain. Half the time she didn't even appear to be listening. Anna watched her sister track David with her gaze as he led a party of four to their table. She seemed on edge.

Liz brought her gaze back to Anna. "I know she doesn't seem like the type, but maybe she'd finally had enough and just snapped."

"You're talking about a woman who survived the Marcos regime," Anna reminded her.

"Speaking of which, have you seen all those shoes in Monica's closet? There must be over a hundred pairs." Liz's feeble attempt at humor brought only a few pained smiles.

Anna shook her head. "I'd stake my life on Arcela."

"You may be doing just that," Rhonda said.

Anna looked at her. "What do you mean?"

"She's the only one besides you who saw what went on in that house."

Rhonda would be calling the housekeeper to the stand when they returned, but Anna couldn't think of any reason why she should be worried. "She wouldn't say anything to make me look bad."

Rhonda eyed her across the table, a large woman who made no apology for her size and who in fact seemed empowered by it. "She might not mean to." She didn't have to exlpain; Anna knew all too well how the D.A. would twist her words.

It was all Anna could do to choke down her food when it came. As they were getting up to leave she spotted an old man eating alone at one of the tables in back. Well, not quite alone—there was a plate beside his with an untouched sandwich on it. Recalling Old Clem's generosity in donating his lottery winnings, she signaled to Melodie.

"Would you send over two pieces of olallie berry pie on me?" She pressed a ten-dollar bill into Melodie's hand and pointed to Clem, serenely oblivious to all but his invisible companion as he munched on his sandwich.

Back in the courtroom, Rhonda called her next witness. Arcela approached the stand wearing her Sunday best and clutching something Anna recognized as her rosary beads. Their eyes met, and Arcela's slid away. Anna's heart began to pound.

Arcela stated her name and occupation in a voice that was barely audible even though amplified by the mike. "Mrs. Aguinaldo," Rhonda asked, smiling to put her at ease, "could you tell the court how long you'd worked for Ms. Vincent at the time of her death?"

"Four year," Arcela squeaked.

"Did you live in?"

She nodded, a birdlike jerk of her head. "Yes."

"So you had occasion to observe what went on in the house?"

Anna had noticed on other occasions

that Arcela's English, serviceable at best, deteriorated when she was under stress. Now she stared at Rhonda with wide, uncomprehending eyes until the question was repeated before answering, "Yes."

"How would you describe the relationship between Ms. Vincenzi and Ms. Vincent?"

Arcela's eyes darted to Anna, her hands twisting in her lap. "Miss Anna, she work very hard."

"Aside from that, how did they get along?" Rhonda prodded gently.

"Miss Monica, many time she angry."

"Why was she angry?"

After a moment of hesitation Arcela replied, "She mad because she no can walk."

"So it wasn't anything Ms. Vincenzi did or said?"

Arcela shook her head. "Miss Anna try hard. But Miss Monica . . ." Her expression hardened. "She bad person."

"In what way?"

"All the time, she yell and scream."

"Mrs. Aguinaldo," Rhonda turned to look out over the gallery, "did you ever see Ms. Vincent drunk?"

Showalter surged to his feet. "Objection, Your Honor. Irrelevant."

"I'll allow it." Cartwright gave a desultory wave.

Rhonda repeated the question, and this time Arcela didn't hesitate. "Many time, yes."

"Do you recall a time when she was so drunk she fell out of her wheelchair and was knocked unconscious?"

Arcela nodded, clutching her rosary beads. "She go to hospital. Long time she no come back."

"Were you aware that Ms. Vincent was in rehab?"

Arcela looked confused until Rhonda explained what rehab was, then she replied, "Miss Anna say it good thing; she get better." She sat up straighter, her lips pressing into a tight line. "But she no better. She same mean."

Rhonda nodded, seemingly unaware of the murmurings in the gallery. "So she continued drinking after she got out of rehab?"

Some of the fear left Arcela's eyes. "She say to me, no tell Miss Anna. But I think Miss Anna know. I think that why she go."

"Did you observe her drunk on the day she died?"

"Yes." Arcela flicked another glance at

Anna. Hadn't it taken the two of them to scoop Monica up off the floor?

"It was your night off. Is that correct?"

"Yes."

"So it's possible that she'd gone *on* drinking after you left that evening?"

Showalter jumped to his feet. "Objection, Your Honor. This is pure speculation."

The judge lowered his gaze at Rhonda. "If there's a point to this, Ms. Talltree, I wish you'd get to it."

"Your Honor, it's well established that Ms. Vincent was accident prone." Rhonda spoke calmly. "I have hospital records going back a dozen years, the most recent from April of this year. I'm suggesting that it's entirely possible her death as well was the result of an accident. How do we know she didn't *fall* into the pool?"

A ripple went through the courtroom. Anna knew it was out of left field, but hoped that Rhonda had succeeded in planting a seed of doubt. She watched her turn back to Arcela, saying with a small satisfied smile, "Thank you, Mrs. Aguinaldo. That will be all."

Showalter approached the stand, and Anna's heart began to race. "Mrs. Aguinaldo, how would you describe the work the defendant did for Ms. Vincent?" He was careful to maintain a slight distance, as if not wanting to appear overbearing.

"She do everything."

Anna had to smile. It was closer to the truth than anyone realized.

"Did Ms. Vincent receive much fan mail?"

"Oh yes." Arcela brightened. "Everybody know Miss Monica."

"And these fans . . . did Ms. Vincent ever write them back?"

"Yes."

"Personally?"

Arcela frowned, not understanding.

"Did Ms. Vincent answer those letters herself . . . or was that one of Ms. Vincenzi's jobs?" Showalter rephrased it.

"Miss Anna, she write."

"Under her own name or Ms. Vincent's?"

Arcela looked confused. He tried again. "Did the people getting those letters know that it was Ms. Vincenzi who'd written them?"

After a moment she answered, "I don't think . . . no."

Anna had taught her the rudiments of the computer so she could e-mail her family in

Manila. She'd been like a kid with a new toy. Anna would often arrive at work to find Arcela at her desk. She must have seen some of the correspondence.

Rhonda shot to her feet. "Objection. Anything my client might have done was with the full knowledge and consent of her employer."

"Overruled," Cartwright said.

The D.A. deftly switched gears, asking, "Mrs. Aguinaldo, you've stated that Ms. Vincent and Ms. Vincenzi didn't always get along. Can you recall any specific incident?"

Something flared in Arcela's eyes, and she momentarily forgot her shyness. "She give Miss Anna dress for party. But it wrong dress. Miss Anna, she very, very mad."

Showalter wore the look of a shark scenting blood. "Are you referring to the party that took place the night of April sixteenth, the day before Ms. Vincent was murdered?"

"Yes."

Anna wanted to cry out for her to stop. She was only making matters worse.

But Showalter was just getting warmed up. He cocked his head, smiling. "You told the police that you'd overheard them arguing. Is that true?"

"Yes," she said with a small sigh of resignation, as if realizing too late that she was being led down the garden path.

"Can you tell us what was said?"

"Miss Anna, she say she quit."

"How would you describe Ms. Vincent's reaction to that?"

"She cry. She say Miss Anna be sorry."

"Sorry in what way?"

Arcela darted Anna a stricken glance. "The mother, she sick. Miss Monica say she no more pay for doctor."

Anna's heart sank even further as Showalter swung around to face the bench. "Your Honor, may I remind you that Mrs. Vincenzi suffers from Alzheimer's and is currently in extended care." He turned back to Arcela. "So to the best of your knowledge, if Ms. Vincent had made good on her threat, the full burden of caring for their mother would have fallen on the defendant?"

Arcela gripped her rosary beads. "I . . ." She shook her head. But it was too late; the damage had been done.

Showalter turned to face the gallery, linking his hands behind his back and rocking forward on the balls of his feet. All eyes were on him as he closed in for the kill. "Mrs. Aguinaldo, where were you the night of April seventeenth?"

"With my friend Rosa." She looked relieved. "We see movie. Jackie Chan." She wrinkled her nose in distaste. "Rosa like Jackie Chan." There was a ripple of appreciative chuckles, and even Showalter smiled.

"When did you return home?"

"I stay with Rosa, come back early in the morning."

"So you didn't go back to the house at any time that night?"

"No."

"In other words, if the defendant had returned to her sister's, say to pick up some things she'd forgotten, you wouldn't have known?"

She glanced again at Anna. "I . . . no."

Now it was Showalter's turn to look smug. "Thank you, Mrs. Aguinaldo. That will be all."

Rhonda introduced police records going back several years, showing half a dozen incidents involving stalkers, one of which had resulted in an arrest. She argued that just as it couldn't be ruled out that Monica's death had been an accident, it was also possible that it was the work of a deranged fan. To which Showalter coolly responded that there was absolutely no evidence to support that theory: no prints, hairs, fibers, body fluids, or signs of forced entry. Whatever the judge was thinking, he kept it to himself.

It was a warm day made even warmer by a faulty air conditioner that did little more than stir the tepid air, and by midafternoon Anna's blouse was clinging to her like a second skin. Even so, she used her handkerchief sparingly, almost stealthily, only dabbing at her forehead from time to time. She didn't want to appear nervous.

She could feel the stares like knives in her back. Occasionally she sneaked a glance over her shoulder. The crowd was mostly made up of reporters, with the locals divided into two camps, those who'd been outspoken in their support and those who'd just as openly aired their suspicions.

A woman in back caught her eye, a washed-out blonde in a sleeveless denim top. She seemed to be eyeing Anna with unusual intensity . . . but it was probably just her imagination. Lately it had been playing tricks on her. The other day, walking down the street, she'd caught the tail end of a remark that sounded like ". . . she ought to be hung." But it had turned out to be Miranda McBride instructing an employee on where she wanted a sign hung.

When the judge banged his gavel, declaring a ten-minute recess, it was like a thunderclap breaking a long heat spell. Spectators surged to their feet en masse, pushing their way toward the double doors in back. Had it not been for Marc guiding her through the lightning storm of strobe flashes and TV lights, Anna might have been swallowed up. Out of the corner of her eye she saw Hector roughly shove aside a microphone-wielding reporter while Maude delivered a swift kick to the shin of a skinny dark-haired man who'd leaped into her path.

"This way . . ." Laura grabbed her elbow, steering her through the teeming crush. Dead ahead was the ladies' room. "Go on. I'll guard the door," she muttered, propelling her inside with a small push. The door swung shut behind Anna, and she found herself staring at a row of blessedly empty cubicles.

She slipped into the nearest one, bolting the door. The babble in the hall faded to a muffled roar. Faintly she heard Laura shout, "Tough luck. Hold it in, for all I care!" She sank down on the toilet with a sigh. She was beyond tears, beyond praying even. What good had it done, all those hours on her knees? If God was looking out for her, He was doing a lousy job of it.

The roar momentarily grew louder, and she heard the door click shut. Someone had slipped past Laura. Anna tensed as a pair of muscular calves ending in grubby sneakers small enough to be a child's appeared below the metal divider separating her cubicle from the one next to it.

A woman's voice whispered, "Anna?"

A reporter? She wouldn't put it past those buzzards. But even for them this was a new low. "What do you want?" she hissed back.

"Relax. I'm on your side."

And I have a bridge in Brooklyn you might like to buy. "Then why don't you show your face?"

"It's not important."

Tiny hairs prickled on the back of Anna's neck. "Who *are* you?"

"A friend."

"Prove it."

"Listen." The voice grew more urgent. "They've got it all wrong." Anna rose as quietly as she could. She had one foot on the toilet seat, preparing to climb up and peek over the top of the stall, when the woman cried sharply, "Don't! I swear, I'll be outta here so fast you won't even see my back."

Anna sank back down. "Okay. I'm listening."

It was like in Confession, just a thin wall between her and salvation. She stared at a square of toilet paper stuck to the dirty tiles at her feet, her heart pounding. Was it possible her fate hinged on a faceless stranger in a bathroom stall? Or was this some kind of cruel joke?

"I was there. I saw what happened."

Realization went through Anna like an electric shock. "Krystal? Is that you?"

There was a long silence, then she said grudgingly, "Yeah, it's me. But I'm only here to give you the four-one-one. That's as far as it goes."

"Can't we talk about this face-to-face?"

"It's better this way."

"All right." Anna let out a shaky breath.

"Look, I shouldn't even be here. I could get in a lot of trouble."

"What kind of trouble?" The longer she could keep her talking, the better her chances of convincing Krystal to come forward with whatever she knew.

Krystal sighed. "You know how it is. Every time you get a leg up, they drag you back down. I guess that's why I'm here. You made me feel like I was somebody, like I had a chance. I mean, yeah, I was pissed off at first when I found out it wasn't Monica giving me all that advice. But, hell, I wouldn't have gotten my kids back if it hadn't been for you. If only I'd quit while I was ahead." She gave a harsh smoker's laugh. "But, no, I had to fuck it all up. I had to see for myself if she was the real deal. All I wanted was a peek, I swear. I'm not one of those friggin' crazies you see on TV."

"Why didn't you just ask to meet me—I mean her?"

Another harsh laugh. "That woulda been too easy. Us junkies, we do everything the hard way. Now I wish to God I'd stayed away. Then I wouldna seen—" She broke off.

"What?" Anna thought her heart would knock a hole through her chest.

"Your sister wasn't murdered." Anna went very still. "It wasn't an accident, either."

"Are you saying—?" Anna's head spun, unable to grasp what Krystal was saying.

"I saw her by the pool. Looked like she was crying. She was talking to herself, too." In the deserted restroom Krystal's voice echoed as if in a cavern. "The next thing I know there's a splash and she's gone. I swear I couldn't move. It was like in the Bible, that lady who turns into a pillar of salt."

"Lot's wife," Anna said woodenly.

"By the time I got to her, it was too late. She . . . she was floating facedown. So I ran. Maybe I coulda saved her, I don't know. But you see, don't you? Why I couldn't go to the cops? They woulda pinned it on *me*."

Anna was too stunned to speak. If Krystal was making this up, she was a damn good liar. But if what she was saying was true, that it was suicide, wouldn't Monica have left a note? And what about all the evidence pointing to *her*? Was it just a coincidence? Or . . .

She set you up one last time, a small, still

voice rang out amid the whirling maelstrom in her head. *She wanted it to look as if you'd done it—the ultimate payback.*

The graffiti scratched into the beige metal walls of her cubicle seemed to jump out at her: MARCY SUX COX. STELLA LUVS RICO, and in bold crooked letters that sent a chill up her spine, YOU CAN'T FIGHT THE MAN. She brought a fist to her mouth to muffle the cry that rose. What had she done to deserve such hatred? The only explanation that made sense was the one their mother had provided: In some strange, twisted way Monica had blamed her and Liz, and most of all Betty, for what she'd suffered at their father's hands. A long simmering resentment that had come to a full boil when Anna shed her fat, thus disturbing the status quo.

A more immediate fear took shape. This information would be useless unless Krystal agreed to cooperate. "You have to tell them," she pleaded. "Once you explain—"

"You don't get it!" A fist thumped against the side of the stall, rattling the toilet paper holder and causing Anna to jump. "I could lose my kids, this time for good."

"My lawyer will help. She—"

Krystal didn't let her finish. "No fucking

way. I know that game, and I always end up losing. Like I said, I shouldn't have come at all."

"Then why did you?"

"I don't know. It was dumb, I guess. See, you were wrong about me. Some people are born with the deck stacked against them, and I'm one. Anyway, for what it's worth, good luck. I hope you get off." There was a rustle of movement on the other side, and Anna heard the click of the cubicle's latch. If she didn't act quickly it would be too late.

"I know why you came," she said in a rush, "because you couldn't live with yourself otherwise. Because I don't deserve to go to prison for something I didn't do. You know what prison is like, Krystal. Could you really do that to me, knowing I'm innocent?"

"I'm sorry." The creak of a door opening. "Really, I am." Krystal sounded close to tears.

"Wait—" Anna lurched to her feet, scrabbling with the bolt. Her clammy fingers slipped, found purchase, then slipped again. Anna hammered at it with the heel of her hand, then it slid open and she was

stumbling out into the open. "Krystal!" she yelled, but there was only her own pale, stark reflection in the mirror over the sink by which she stood. She caught a flash of movement from the corner of her eye, and spun about in time to see someone disappear through the door.

Anna stumbled out into the corridor, spotting a skinny blonde in a too-short skirt and a denim blouse pushing her way through the crowd. As she started after her, Laura fell in behind her. They hadn't gone more than a few yards when the reporters surged in around them. A microphone was shoved in Anna's face, and she was momentarily blinded by a barrage of camera flashes. A woman's voice, crisp and modulated, cut through the din, "Anna, can you comment on the hearing so far?"

Anna pushed past her, shrieking, "Out of my way!"

Voices roared in her ears. Bodies pressed in. Cameras and microphones were launched at her like heat-seeking missiles.

"Anna, have you ruled out a plea bargain?"

"Do you think it'll go to trial?"

"This way, Anna! Over here!"

Over the sea of bobbing heads and Mini-cams, she caught sight of Krystal plowing her way toward the exit. "Stop her!" Anna screamed at the top of her lungs.

She set off in pursuit, Laura at her heels. They'd nearly reached the exit when they were joined by Hector and Marc, looking like nothing so much as a pair of Wild West gunslingers as they muscled reporters and cameramen aside. Someone cried out. A Minicam crashed to the floor, unleashing a stream of curses. A dark-haired man wearing headphones leaped into their path, but Marc batted him aside as if he'd been a mosquito.

Then, like the parting of the Red Sea, a narrow channel appeared and they dashed through it. Marc held the reporters at bay while Hector shepherded the women through the door onto the steps outside. Anna glanced frantically about, but Krystal was nowhere to be seen. *Please, God,* she prayed. *Don't let her get away.*

She scanned the crowd spilling down the steps onto the lawn below—not reporters, she saw, but protesters shouting and waving placards. She spotted Finch, bullhorn in hand, bellowing, "INNOCENT PEOPLE DON'T BE-

LONG BEHIND BARS! THE SOONER YOU LET HER GO, THE SOONER YOU'LL FIND THE REAL KILLER!" Police had formed a loose cordon, but the crowd seemed orderly for the most part. Yet Anna could have wept. How would she ever find Krystal in this crush?

Then God took pity on her at last, and Anna spotted her. She charged down the steps to snatch the bullhorn from a startled-looking Finch. "Stop that woman!" she cried, pointing toward Krystal, who was jogging in the direction of the parking lot.

Her amplified voice had the effect of a gunshot. For an instant everyone froze, even Krystal. Then she was once more on the run, this time with more than a dozen people in pursuit.

It had taken countless phone calls and flyers, but with the help of her friends, Finch had managed to round up enough people for the rally. There were kids from school, Claire and Matt and some of the regulars from Tea & Sympathy, Gerry and Aubrey, Sam and Ian, parishioners from St. Xavier's and congregants from First Presbyterian, along with those who simply felt Anna was getting a bum rap. Even Sister Agnes had shown up, a round little figure in a black habit and veil waving a placard that read THE TRUTH SHALL MAKE YOU FREE, JOHN 8:32. Ian had painted a huge banner that was held up at either end by Alice and Wes. And Bud McVittie, a retired army officer and president of the local VFW, had provided the bullhorn, though Finch had politely declined his offer of gas masks.

No sooner had they assembled outside the courthouse when an anchor from Channel 7, a buttery-tressed Career Barbie in a caramel-colored suit and hot pink blouse, had broken away from the pack to come scurrying down the steps, trailed by her crew.

"So you believe Anna's innocent?" She shoved a microphone into Finch's face.

Finch, squinting in the bright light directed at her by the cameraman, was all at once tongue-tied.

Andie nudged her, hissing, "Say something."

Finch cast about wildly before her gaze settled on Lucien, who flashed her an encouraging grin. She found her voice, saying indignantly, "The only crime here is Anna being arrested for something she didn't do!"

Career Barbie's lips curved in a fake smile. "How can you be sure she didn't do it?

"Because she . . . she . . ." Finch faltered before blurting, "She wouldn't hurt a fly!"

"Yeah, she's no more a murderer than I am!" Andie chimed in. Her cheeks flushed a deep crimson, as if she'd realized how it might sound to those seeing her on TV.

"The D.A. was looking for a scapegoat; that's the only reason she was charged." Simon stepped to the fore, looking a good deal older than his age in a dark gray blazer and open-collared shirt. "Are you aware that he's up for reelection this fall? A conviction in such a high-profile case would of course . . ." He was off to the races.

More reporters had migrated toward the ever-widening circle of protesters on the lawn, where a table was set up and Claire was doling out Dixie cups of lemonade and freshly baked Toll House cookies.

Nearby, Olive Miller brandished a placard with a drawing of the Liberty Bell and the words LET FREEDOM RING! She and her identical twin Rose, wearing matching blue shirtwaists, certainly looked old enough to have witnessed the birth of the nation firsthand. A man in a toupee that screamed Carpeteria shoved a microphone at them.

"What're a couple of nice ladies like you doing in a place like this?" he asked with a wink.

"We were on our way to rob a bank—" Rose began sweetly.

"—but we decided this would be more fun," Olive finished for her.

The man's mouth dropped open, and it was a moment before he recovered his wits.

A short distance away, waving banners and shouting at the top of their lungs, were Rose's towheaded granddaughters, Dawn and Eve. They were accompanied by their parents, who looked every inch the aging, potgrowing radicals they were with bandannas tied around their graying heads, wearing tie-dyed T-shirts and Birkenstocks. They hadn't been this worked up since they'd marched against the war in Vietnam.

"*Screw the system!*" yelled the twins' bearded dad.

"*Hands off me, pig!*" his wife screamed at a startled-looking cop who'd accidentally bumped into her.

Burly, tattooed Herman Tyzzer had closed up shop for the afternoon. Anyone wishing to rent a video at Den of Cin would have to wait until the following day. At his side was his wife, Consuela, wearing a black *abuelita* dress with a large gold crucifix around her neck. She looked more like an ex-nun than Andie's mom, who was anything but demure in tight slacks and a stretchy red top that showed off her cleavage. Gerry had caught the attention of at least one cameraman: On the late news on Channel 11 there would be a cutaway shot of her boobs bouncing past. But right now she was all over the map, shouting and waving a sign that read WE LOVE YOU, ANNA! Beside her Aubrey brandished his own placard as enthusiastically as if he were conducting Beethoven's Ninth.

Sam and Ian brought up the rear. Ian looked like a sixties protester, with his ponytail and earring; Sam as if she'd stepped out of the Lands' End catalogue. They'd left Jack with Mavis, who'd been prevented from attending the rally by a flare-up of her arthritis.

Nearby, Tom Kemp and his fiancée chanted at the top of their lungs. Finch had never seen Ms. Hicks so fired up, her cheeks flushed and eyes sparkling. She'd never be beautiful, but at least she no longer looked as if she'd been on the shelf too long.

Finch was glad to see that Edna Simmons had come, too. She hadn't seen Edna since Betty had gone to the Sunshine Home. Now, watching her clump past in her work boots, her horsey braid swinging at her back, Finch felt that maybe it would all work out for Anna, just as it had for her mother.

She spotted Fran O'Brien, owner of Francoise's Creperie. An Energizer Bunny with flaming red hair, she was flanked by her hulking teenage sons, whom Finch knew from school. She wondered if Fran had any idea that Tommy, the elder of the two and star of the varsity wrestling team, was gay. He'd confided it to Finch one day after school, maybe because he'd sensed she had secrets of her own.

A short distance away, David Ryback was pouring lemonade at the refreshment table. He and Claire were just friends, but from the way Claire's husband acted, always finding some fix-it job around the house whenever

David stopped by, you'd think he had reason to worry. Finch doubted that was the case, though she couldn't say the same for David and his wife. From what she'd seen of them in church and around town, their marriage wasn't in such great shape.

But right now the only one she could concentrate on was Anna. In those first frantic days, Finch had had fantasies of storming the jail, like in old westerns, but she'd since realized that if Anna was to get off, it would only be through sheer persistence. Little by little, others had joined the effort, like Monica's former publicist, who'd given an interview on CTN revealing what Monica was *really* like. And the reporter who'd had the guts to say that for someone dubbed by one tabloid as the "Sister from Hell," Anna seemed to have an amazing number of supporters.

Finch was raising the bullhorn to her lips when a sudden commotion drew her attention to the courthouse steps, down which Anna was now barreling. Before she could wonder what it was all about, Anna had snatched the bullhorn from her hand. "Stop that woman!" she bellowed into it, her voice booming out over the sea of bobbing heads and placards.

Finch spun around to see a frizzy-haired blond woman bolting across the lawn. Scarcely aware of what she was doing, or why, she dashed off in pursuit, her friends falling in behind her. Tommy O'Brien joined the chase as did grizzled Doc Henry, loping like an old horse with a stone in one shoe. Out of the corner of her eye she caught sight of Father Reardon, in civilian duds, running full tilt with the petite church organist, Lily Ann Beasley, clinging to his arm as if for dear life.

The blonde was closing in on the parking lot when Finch, in a burst of speed, broke ahead of the pack. She was close enough to see the dark half moons of sweat under her arms and her shoulder blades thrusting beneath her creased denim blouse. The gap closed and Finch caught hold of her elbow. She heard a grunt, then they were both tumbling onto the grass.

"What the f— *Get off me!*" the woman shrieked as she struggled to free herself.

Finch straddled her, holding her pinned in a wrestling move Tommy O'Brien had taught her. When she looked, it was into a circle of gaping mouths and astonished eyes and Minicams aimed at her like guns in a firing squad. She spotted Career Barbie and her Ken counterpart. Then Anna, red-faced and panting, pushed through the crowd. Krystal stopped bucking and collapsed in defeat.

Cops hauled them both to their feet, and while Minicams whirred, capturing the sound bite that in the days to come would be aired nearly as often as that of Clinton denying any involvement with Monica Lewinsky, the blonde lifted a contorted face flecked with bits of grass to wail, "I didn't do it! I swear it wasn't me!"

CHAPTER SIXTEEN

Soon after Krystal was taken in for questioning the story came out. She told of scaling the wall at LoreiLinda in the dark of night, and her shock at seeing Monica go into the pool. She hadn't gone to the police, she said, because they'd have found a way to pin it on her, or at the very least busted her for violating her parole. And what would happen to her kids?

Rhonda stepped in, finding her a lawyer, an old friend and former deputy D.A. from the district attorney's office in Ventura who went to work hammering out a plea bargain. In the meantime, Krystal was free on bail.

It seemed Anna had dodged a bullet as well. When the preliminary hearing reconvened, Rhonda moved that the case be dismissed. And after hearing Krystal's testimony, made all the more compelling by her reluctance to come forward, Judge Cartwright ruled that there was "substantial doubt as to whether a crime had indeed been committed."

Showalter went ballistic, refusing to drop the charges and vowing in a press conference on the courthouse steps to do everything in his power to see that Anna went to trial—a threat Rhonda dismissed, saying he wouldn't risk egg on his face a second time, not this close to reelection.

Anna knew she ought to be overjoyed, but she was too numb to feel much of anything. In the days that followed, she drifted about in a haze, scarcely aware of the reporters snapping at her heels, begging for a comment. Then, just as quickly as it had descended, the swarm of locusts moved on: The clock had run out on her fifteen minutes of fame. The only ones who would miss them, it seemed, were the shopkeepers whose tills had been ringing steadily for weeks. Myrna McBride reported her highest spring sales ever, and her ex-husband's rival bookstore across the street had enjoyed a similar bonanza. The Blue Moon Café catty-corner to Delarosa's installed a new awning and outdoor zinc bar with its earnings, and Higher Ground took over the defunct notions store next door—to the delight of java junkies who'd been crammed into their narrow space—while Ingersoll's had been inundated with mail orders from those who'd become addicted to their old-world crullers and strudels.

Anna consented to a single interview, with Emily Frey at CTN; it was the least she could do to repay Wes for all he'd done. She was flown to the studio in Wes's private helicopter, Marc at her side. As a child, she'd been deathly afraid of heights, but looking down at the sprawl of buildings below, the freeways like long necklaces strung with cars, her only thought was that she'd survived far worse than anything she could have imagined. And wasn't the better part of fear the uncertainty of not knowing how you would handle a catastrophe? Her ordeal had shown her what she was capable of, and there was comfort in that, at least.

She returned home that evening thoroughly wiped out. Marc was subdued, too, as they drove back to her house. They dined on Chinese takeout in near silence, both reluctant to broach the subject they'd been avoiding. It wasn't until they were getting ready for bed that Anna forced herself to look it square in the eye: Going on with her life would mean going on without Marc.

Even so a voice whispered in her head, *Maybe there's a way.* They'd grown so close these past weeks she couldn't imagine being without him. She was a different person, too, from the woman who'd once expected so little out of life, grateful for crumbs off the table. She knew now what she hadn't that day at the lake: that if you want something badly enough you have to go out and get it, or die trying.

Seated on the bed in her nightgown—not the negligee Monica had given her last Christmas, which was tucked in a drawer in anticipation of the honeymoon she'd probably never go on, but her oldest cotton nightie worn sheer by numerous washings, its daisy pattern faded to near invisibility—she waited for Marc to come out of the shower. Her hair was caught up with a butterfly clip, stray wisps trailing down around her neck, her face scrubbed of the heavy makeup she'd worn for the interview. Had she looked in the mirror just then she might have been fooled for an instant into imagining it was her younger self, a teenage girl full of hopes and dreams that hadn't yet been put on hold.

Where had all those years gone? In some ways it felt as though she'd merely picked up where she'd left off that long ago day, returning home for her father's funeral. For one thing, she'd moved out of her childhood room into the master bedroom left vacant by her mother. Gone now were the clunky Grand Rapids suite and peeling nosegay wallpaper. In their place were clean white walls and a simple bed covered in an old quilt from the attic. All that was left to remind her of the past were family photos and a pen-and-ink of the old schoolhouse drawn by her grandmother.

She stared at the blank canvas of the freshly painted walls and wondered what the rest of her life would look like. Would she go on to a job as fulfilling as her last one was stifling? Were marriage and motherhood in the cards?

Marc emerged at last, a towel around his waist, his hair standing up in wet spikes. He looked so irresistible she was tempted to postpone any talk of the future. But tomorrow he was going back home, and she couldn't let him walk away a second time without knowing exactly where they stood.

He caught her looking at him and paused to smile at her, a trail of footprints glistening on the newly refinished floorboards. Mistaking her preoccupied look, he said, "Don't worry, you did great. You'll see when it airs."

The interview was the furthest thing from her mind, but she replied, "I just hope I made sense. I can't remember half of what I said."

"You said everything you needed to."

She drew her legs up, hugging them to her chest. "I suppose it doesn't really matter in the end. They'll think what they like." Let them believe it was despair that had driven Monica to drink, and ultimately to suicide. That was something they could wrap their brains around, a Lifetime movie played out in real life.

"And by this time next week no one will even care." He sat down next to her, putting his arms around her. "The only one who matters is *you*."

"I'll be all right," she said, then smiled. "I guess the shock still hasn't worn off."

"It takes time." He drew her close so that

her head was tucked under his chin. He smelled of Ivory soap and the essence that was his alone, the scent that he would take with him when he left.

"I can't help thinking if I'd done it differently—stood up to her sooner . . ."

"You can't second guess these things."

"How could she hate me that much? Her own sister."

"It wasn't about you." With her head against his chest, his voice was a comforting rumble. "You held up a mirror, that's all, and she didn't like what she saw."

"She wasn't always that way." Once they'd lain in bed at night whispering secrets to each other. Monica had looked out for her then, when kids in school teased her about being fat . . . with their dad, too. It wasn't until her sister got older that everything changed. She became closed off and haughty, leaving Anna to wonder if it was something *she'd* done—imagined crimes she'd gone to great pains to make up for, setting in motion a pattern she would carry with her into adulthood.

"I could see that," he said, though she suspected he was only being kind.

"Once she became famous . . . well, it was like a car without brakes."

He nodded in understanding. "It's like the worst thing that can happen to a drunk is winning the lottery."

"There was that, too. Her drinking."

"Drink enough, and you go crazy."

"Is that what happened to you?"

He drew back to smile at her, and she saw the lines around his eyes that hadn't been there before. "I drank to *keep* from going crazy—or at least that's what I told myself."

"Because of Faith?"

"I thought so at the time, but that was only an excuse. I had demons of my own."

Gathering up her courage, she asked softly, "Marc, what's going to happen to us?"

For the longest time he didn't respond, and she felt a pocket of cold form around her heart. She wanted to snatch her words back. Couldn't she have waited until morning? Did she have to spoil what little time they had left?

"I wish I could tell you what you want to hear." He released her and pulled away, his arms dropping heavily to his sides. "But it's not that simple." He meant Faith, of course.

"I know." She thought of all she'd been through these past months; it hadn't killed her and this wouldn't, either. "I was just thinking aloud."

"Anna . . ."

"You should throw something on. You'll catch cold," she told him in a queer dead voice that didn't seem her own.

He held her gaze, not moving. She watched a bead of moisture dribble down his neck. After a long moment he went to retrieve his robe. For some reason, that's what got to her most: the sight of his blue terry bathrobe reflected in the mirror on the bathroom door as it swung open. It looked so . . . connubial somehow slung on the hook next to hers. She realized she'd come to depend on such things to reaffirm his existence in her life—his toothbrush and razor in her medicine cabinet, his battered Dockers on the closet floor. But she'd only been fooling herself.

When Marc reappeared, hair combed into wet tracks, she rose slowly from the bed, feeling more sure of herself than she had in years, even with her heart in free fall. "I know you have to go," she said firmly. "But I don't want to stop seeing you."

"Are you sure?" From the pained look he wore, she knew it had been weighing on him as well.

She knew what it would mean: weekends here and there, the occasional romantic getaway, enormous phone bills the only thing she'd have to show for it. And if his wife found out? Anna could only hope she'd want Marc to have the happiness she couldn't give him. She thought selfishly, *Why should I be the one making all the sacrifices?* "I don't want to lose you," she said. "I know I won't see you every day or even every week, but I can live with that."

Marc shook his head slowly. "I'm not sure I can."

"So that's it? It's over?"

"Maybe it'd be best if we gave it some time."

Anger flared in her. "I expected more from you than that tired old line."

"I'd give anything if it didn't have to be this way."

She turned away so she wouldn't be moved by the heartbroken look he wore, saying coldly, "I see it now. What you get off on is rescuing people. Now that I'm out of the woods, you can move on to the next damsel in distress." Anna knew it was true in only the most superficial sense, but she wasn't going to let him off the hook. "I guess that's what your wife has over me. She'll always need you more than I do."

"Anna, please."

She spun around. "It's true, isn't it? I'm being punished because I'm stronger."

"Don't." His voice cracked.

Don't be this way. Don't ruin it. Don't say what you're feeling. The mantras she'd adhered to all her life, but they were no longer working. She *had* changed, and in some ways not necessarily for the better. This new side of her—well, it was faintly and disturbingly reminiscent of Monica. But if her sister had been too caught up in herself, Anna realized she hadn't been self-centered enough. Maybe it was time she stopped depending on others to stick up for her and started sticking up for herself.

"I waited all my life for this." Her eyes filled with tears. "I don't want to let go."

"Me neither." The few feet that separated them might have been an ocean.

"I won't necessarily be waiting if and when you're free."

A corner of his mouth crooked up, but the smile didn't reach his eyes. "There isn't a good way to do this, is there? I could tell you I love you, but you already know that. I could say I'm sorry, but you know that, too."

"I guess all that's left to say is good-bye." She eyed his suitcase in the corner, asking in a remarkably steady voice that carried only a faint cool hint of irony, "Need a hand packing?"

He shook his head, looking more bereft than he had a right to be when, after all, he was the one leaving. "It can wait. Unless you'd like me to go now."

She sighed wearily, climbing under the covers. She had no more strength left. "Do what you like. I'm going to bed," she told him, burrowing into the sheets that smelled faintly of their lovemaking. She was sick of being noble. Sick of being brave, too. Right now, the only thing she wanted was to fall into a deep, dreamless sleep.

"Anna." She felt the mattress sink down, then his hand stroking the back of her head.

In a small, choked voice, she asked,

"Was it always going to be this way, Marc? Was there ever a time when you thought it would turn out differently?"

"I didn't let myself think that far ahead." He spoke softly.

She rolled onto her back, looking up at him. "I'm not going to make this easy on you," she said fiercely. "I love you too much."

His jaw clenched, and she saw the battle being waged behind his carefully constructed facade. "The last thing I want to do is pack that damn bag." He flashed a resentful look at the suitcase as if it were the enemy, the cause of all this grief.

Then don't, she wanted to cry. But she only turned over onto her stomach, pressing her face into the pillow so he wouldn't see her tears. It would only make him want to rescue her all over again, and she didn't want that. All she wanted was to stand on her own two feet with the man she loved at her side.

She was nearly asleep when she felt him slip in under the covers. She held very still so he wouldn't know she was awake; it was only when he began stroking her hair that she could feel her body giving in, traitor that it was. His hand moved lower, his thumb tracing the outline of her shoulder beneath the flimsy cotton of her nightgown. When he kissed her neck, the last of her resistance melted. She rolled to face him, offering her mouth to be kissed, and feeling how aroused he was. She marveled anew that she could stir such desire, that he never seemed to tire of her.

She sat up and peeled off her nightgown. His eyes, glinting amid the shadows, seemed to ask, Are you sure, or will this only make it worse? In response, Anna stretched out before him naked, her body no longer a source of shame but something precious to be offered. Marc didn't need a second invitation.

There was a sweet, almost elegiac unhurriedness in the way he stroked and kissed her, exploring the yielding wetness between her thighs. When he finally entered her, it was with exquisite care. They took their time making love as well, reveling in each other as if there were no reason it couldn't go on this way forever, night after night into the twilight of their years.

It wasn't until they drew apart, sated, that

the real world crept back in. Anna lay awake with her eyes closed, cradled in his arms, knowing he couldn't protect her from the one thing she dreaded most: finding a way to live without him.

It started to rain, the first real downpour in weeks, and she listened to it drum against the roof and gurgle in the gutters. Tomorrow when the sun came out, the fields would be covered in a soft green fuzz, and the poppies that had been nodding their furled heads would be drifts of gold, but for the moment the world was contained in the ticking of the clock on the nightstand, measuring out the precious last minutes in Marc's arms.

In the days that followed, she threw herself into the seemingly Quixotic quest for a job, which kept her from wallowing in misery and at the same time reminded her hourly of the price of being infamous. It seemed no one wanted to hire her, most of the places she inquired at turning her away before she could get so much as a foot in the door— like Phil Scroggins at the pharmacy, who'd told her the job had been filled when it was only that morning that the ad had appeared in the *Clarion*.

Liz told her not to worry, reminding her that once the will was probated, they'd both be rich. But that could take months, Anna knew, and meanwhile there were bills to pay, a car in need of a new transmission, and a cat that had developed mysterious oozing sores requiring repeated trips to the vet. It occurred to her that her life hadn't really been on hold all this time, as she'd imagined. While she'd been off fighting to prove her innocence, it had been quietly accruing in her absence, like the stack of unread mail on the table in the foyer and the thick coating of dust everywhere she looked.

On the plus side, there were friends willing to stick their necks out. Like Myrna McBride, who'd offered her a job at The Last Word, and Laura, who'd insisted she'd have her hands full when the baby came and could use another clerk at the shop. Anna had turned them both down. She'd made up her mind about one thing: She wasn't going to be hired out of pity, nor would she work for a friend or, God forbid, a relative.

It was Andie's boyfriend who'd suggested she try the newspaper. They were looking to replace the person at the front desk, and no one was more qualified, Simon teased, than she, who'd been headline news in the *Clarion* for weeks. Bob Heidiger, the editor in chief, a tough no-nonsense veteran of the *Los Angeles Times,* must have seen the cosmic irony in it, too, for he agreed to hire her on a trial basis.

By the end of her first day the piles of paperwork on her desk had been cleared away, the files organized, and the contents of the drawers placed in order. The following week everyone else on staff, it seemed, was throwing her the little jobs they didn't have time for: from emptying wastebaskets and tracking down Fed Ex packages to blue-pencilling a column on acorn woodpeckers for an editor out sick with the flu. Bob was impressed, and on Friday made it official, saying gruffly, "Hell, I just hope you decide to keep *us.*"

What he didn't know was that she welcomed even the most menial tasks. The busier she kept, the less time she had to dwell on her thoughts. Nights were when she gave in to loneliness. But like the food with which she'd once salved her misery, the tears she shed into her pillow brought only fleeting relief.

Laura urged her to see someone, and Anna agreed to it only because she wouldn't have left her alone otherwise. She made an appointment with a therapist, a seventies throwback with long graying hair parted down the middle and an office scattered with cushy pillows and plants and New Age crystals. Joan Vinecour had listened with furrowed brow, occasionally murmuring something in response, and after two sessions informed Anna that she was suffering from PTSD—post-traumatic stress disorder. Anna thanked her, wadding up the prescription for Prozac she'd been given and tossing it into a trashcan on her way out. If she was depressed, it was because she had every reason to be. Nothing would be gained from numbing herself against the pain.

But the picture wasn't all bleak. There was pleasure in small things—time spent with friends and her new closeness with Liz. After her first week on the job, when her sister offered to treat her to an afternoon at the spa, she didn't hesitate to accept. The following Saturday, a day that normally would have been given over to chores, found her winding up Agua Caliente Road, eagerly anticipating the pampering that awaited her.

The atmosphere at the spa was one of orchestrated calm, heightened by the Carlos Nakai flute music drifting from hidden speakers in the walls. A Native American bark painting hung over the polished oak reception desk, where a smiling young woman in drawstring trousers and a gauzy white top greeted her when she walked in.

Then Liz appeared to usher her into the locker room, where she was issued a pair of rubber sandals and a waffle-weave robe that her sister informed her was made of organically grown cotton. Women strolled about half dressed, some naked, while others sat blow-drying their hair and putting on makeup in front of mirrors so flatteringly lit that the Bride of Frankenstein would've looked good. A table along the wall held pitchers of herbal iced tea and chilled spring water in which slices of lemon floated.

"I've booked you with Eduardo. He's the best," Liz informed her. Anna had declined the Peruvian hot rocks massage; the no-frills kind would do.

Soon she was lying facedown on a padded table in a room softly lit with aromatic candles. "Don't fight it," soothed a heavily accented voice as sure, strong fingers dug into the knotted muscles in her shoulders. "Let it go." But every time she started to relax, she felt as if she were falling and tensed up again.

An hour later, her muscles pummeled and kneaded into submission, she staggered outside. A flight of stone steps meandered down a slope so lush with ferns and foliage it looked almost primeval. She passed under a pergola laced with vines, then over a wooden bridge spanning a creek. It was the forty-niners, she knew, who'd made the discovery that over time had proven more valuable than gold: water bubbling from the earth, warmed by underground thermals to a constant eighty-four degrees.

These days the water was fed through pipes into man-made pools so cleverly designed she could almost believe they were natural. She sank into the nearest one, which, blessedly, she had all to herself, only dimly aware of voices wafting through the tall bamboo along with the faint strains of Native American flute music.

She was dozing off when Liz materialized unexpectedly out of the mist. She'd changed out of her work clothes into a robe, which she dropped as she slipped in beside Anna with a contented sigh. "The pay sucks, but, ah, the perks . . ."

"I should've taken you up on your offer," Anna said with a dreamy smile, referring to the job Liz had offered her.

"It's not too late."

Anna shook her head. "No way. I've learned my lesson: Family and work don't mix."

"I sincerely hope you're not comparing me to Monica," Liz replied in a faintly injured tone.

"Don't start." She nudged Liz playfully with her toes the way she once had in the bathtub when they were kids. "Besides, in a few months we can both retire if we want."

"Somehow I don't see it." Liz looked tense even as she stretched out. "Don't get me wrong, I *live* for Dylan, but the truth is I'm just not cut out to be a full-time mom."

Anna felt a stab of envy. "It's nice that you have a choice, at least."

"You'll have kids of your own someday."

"I'm not so sure."

Liz eyed her knowingly. In the secret language of sisters things didn't always have to be spelled out. "You miss him, don't you?"

Anna nodded. There was no use denying it.

"I guess we both knew what we were getting into." Liz sighed. "And look where it ended up."

"You, too?" Anna cast her a quizzical look.

Liz's face constricted in a spasm of grief, then smoothed over as if through sheer force of will. "Last night was the last straw," she said in a matter-of-fact voice. "He asked if he could come over, said he had something to tell me that he couldn't say over the phone." She gave a bitter laugh. "I thought it would be that he was divorcing his wife. It's been over between them for years. Ever since Davey got sick—" She broke off, darting Anna a look that was half sheepish, half defiant. "Okay, so now you know. But spare me the lecture. It's a little late for that."

David Ryback? Anna wouldn't have

guessed it. She'd heard that his marriage was in trouble, sure, but had chalked it up to the strain of their son's illness. "Does Carol know?"

"Deep down, don't most wives?"

"I wouldn't know," Anna said dryly.

Not one to pass up an opportunity to inject her jaded view on the subject, Liz said bitterly, "Believe me, you're not missing out on much. Marriage is vastly overrated, in my opinion."

Easy for Liz to say—she'd had her shot. And as far as their being in the same boat, Anna would never have crossed that line if Marc and his wife had had anything close to a real marriage. On the other hand, who was she to judge? If she'd been disapproving once, now all she felt was pity for all involved. There were no villains in this story, just good people who'd lost their way.

"Just because it didn't work out with Perry—" she started to say.

But Liz wasn't interested in hearing about her ex-husband; she was too preoccupied with David. "Are you shocked?" she asked with a look that both dared Anna to say something and begged for her to understand.

Anna recalled seeing David and Carol in church; they'd looked less at odds with each other than defeated somehow, their son, small and pale, wedged between them like a buffer. "After what I've been through, nothing could shock me. Besides," she added, "people in glass houses shouldn't throw stones."

"It was different with you and Marc."

"I thought so, too." Anna felt the knots that had been pummeled into submission start to tighten once more.

Liz shook her head in sympathy. "You were so perfect together. I really thought—" She broke off, her face crumpling.

Anna put her arms around her sister. In the warm water Liz was shaking all over, as if chilled. "Don't cry. It'll get better. It has to." Carlos Nakai had given way to Enya, and through the dense bamboo floated the sounds of laughter and the slap-slap of rubber sandals making their way down the steps.

Liz choked back a sob. "I'm sorry. You're the last person I should be dumping on."

"It's all right," Anna said. She was used to it.

Liz drew back to eye her with a mixture of

awe and resentment. "I wish I knew what your secret was. How the hell do you do it?"

Anna smiled. "I guess it's like climbing a mountain—you only look at what's in front of you."

Liz gave a teary laugh. "Fuck it. Just throw me the goddamn rope."

When they emerged at last, flushed and glowing, Anna said casually, "I thought I'd stop in to see Mom on the way home. Want to come along?"

She waited for Liz to say that she couldn't take the time off work, or she had to pick up Dylan, or she was meeting a friend. But she only shrugged and said, "Sure. Why not?"

They both knew it was little more than a ritual to be observed. These days Betty just sat all day staring into space, lost in a world that existed only in her mind, filled with people and events long gone. But Anna continued to visit, with Liz occasionally tagging along. How was she supposed to face the future if she couldn't reconcile the past?

"Great. We can stop for a bite to eat afterward," she said.

"As long as it's not the Tree House." Liz mustered a small smile.

"I was thinking more along the lines of Burger King. I'm a little short on cash at the moment."

"I'd loan you some, but . . ." Liz didn't have to say it. Being a single mom meant always coming up short one way or another. They were halfway up the slope when she asked guardedly, "Have you thought about what you'll spend it on?" For the most part, they'd avoided any discussion of the inheritance. It seemed macabre almost, the idea of profiting from a tragedy of such Shakespearean proportions.

"My lawyer's bill," Anna said without missing a beat.

"I have my eye on a brand-new BMW convertible."

"I'd settle for a new transmission."

Liz smiled, as if at the hopelessness of Anna's ever being anything but thrifty. "You've got to think *big.* How about a new house, or a trip to Europe? You've always wanted to see Paris. You've been talking about it since we were kids."

Anna thought for a moment, then shook her head. The one thing she wanted more than anything in the world no amount of money could buy. "Thanks," she said, "but I've had enough excitement to last me for at least the next hundred years."

CHAPTER SEVENTEEN

Now that she no longer had Anna to worry about, Finch became caught up in the excitement at home: In less than a week, Laura and Hector would be on their way to Mexico to complete the final phase of the adoption. Meanwhile, the house was in an uproar and Laura a human roller coaster—belting out "La Vida Loca" in the shower at the top her lungs one minute, and the next fretting over whether or not it would all fall through at the last minute.

Hector went about his business as usual—seeing to the horses, repairing things around the ranch, attending classes at night—but Finch could see that he was preoccupied, too. He'd be reading a book, and minute after minute would pass before

he'd turn a page; or he'd become so absorbed in his thoughts while currying one of
the horses, you could practically see your
reflection in its coat when he was through.
Where Laura had become almost as forgetful as Maude, turning the house upside
down in search of misplaced keys or a pair
of reading glasses, Hector, normally reserved, had become positively chatty, regaling them over dinner with tales of growing up in a family of sixteen. Needless to
say, he was an old hand at changing diapers.

The party had been Maude's idea. She'd
wanted to throw one for Anna, who'd politely declined, saying all she wanted right
now was some peace and quiet. Not to be
denied, Maude had turned her efforts toward welcoming Esperanza into her new
home with fanfare. Everyone had been invited, including Sister Agnes. Sam was in
charge of flowers and Alice of party favors
(she was keeping it a secret as to what they
were). Claire would supply the desserts.
And Ian was painting banners—one in English, the other in Spanish. Maude had even
jokingly suggested that her sewing circle do

a striptease, which brought horrified groans all around.

There was only one thing casting a shadow over the occasion: Lucien would be going back to New York as soon as school let out. His mother, just out of rehab, had lined up a summer internship for him at his uncle's firm. Finch didn't even know if he'd be back in the fall. Lucien had been evasive whenever the subject came up.

The thought nagged at her so that when Laura announced one day out of the blue that the time had come to pay a visit to Martha Elliston's mother, Finch was glad for the distraction. The perfect opportunity had presented itself: Laura had heard the old lady was laid up with a case of shingles. Wasn't it their Christian duty to look in on her? she said with a wink.

The following day they were barreling along Old Sorrento Road in Laura's Explorer, a loaf of banana bread wrapped in tin foil and still warm from the oven cradled on Finch's lap. Martha and her mother lived out near Mavis, it turned out, in a clapboard house painted canary yellow with blue trim, which came as a pleasant surprise, since Martha herself was so drab. They rang the bell. When no one answered, Laura tried the door, and found it unlocked. She poked her head in, calling, "Hello? Anyone home?"

A feeble voice from somewhere in the back of the house demanded querulously, "Who is it?"

"Laura and Finch Kiley from church!" Laura stepped inside, not waiting for an invitation.

They found the old woman in her bedroom down the hall, a small mound under the down quilt that covered her. An untouched breakfast tray sat on the nightstand at her elbow along with various vials of medicine. A tiny apple doll's face peered up at them dubiously from a pile of pillows.

"We heard you were sick," Laura said brightly. "We thought you could use some company."

Finch had expected the old woman to be surprised—after all, they barely knew one another—but instead she wore the look of someone for whom surprises were a thing of the past. "I'm not much for company these days," she said, pulling herself upright and patting a wisp of white hair into place. "But since you came all this way, you might as well sit down."

Laura settled into the easy chair by the bed, but Finch remained standing. There was a faint unpleasant smell in the air, not just of sickness but of despair, as if the old lady had given up on more than the cross-word puzzle that had slid, or been tossed, onto the floor. "My aunt had shingles once." Laura launched into the awkward silence that had fallen. "She said it was almost as bad as when she'd had her babies." A Freudian slip that brought a flush spreading across her collarbone and up her neck. "But she's fine now."

"It's always something," the old lady muttered darkly. "When you get to be my age, nothing works. Every bone in my body aches and I haven't had a decent bowel movement in years."

It was all Finch could do to keep from wrinkling her nose. Ugh. No wonder Martha always seemed so beaten down. Who wouldn't, having to listen to this all day?

"Have you tried sauerkraut?" Laura was undeterred. "Maude says it works wonders."

"Nothing works for me." The old woman seemed almost proud of the fact. "I could drink a gallon of prune juice and eat bran till it was coming out my ears, and it wouldn't make a dent."

"Well, in that case . . ." Laura glanced at Finch with something close to panic.

Finch stepped forward. "We brought you some banana bread." She held out the tin-foil-wrapped loaf, which the old woman eyed suspiciously.

"Does it have nuts in it?" she asked. "Because I'm allergic to nuts. One bite and I'd swell up like a balloon."

"Maybe your daughter would enjoy it then," Laura said in a last-ditch effort.

"She's not here."

"Well, when she gets back . . ."

"Don't know when that'll be."

Finch eyed her in amazement. Mrs. Elliston spoke as though she didn't know perfectly well that Martha was at school, where she always was this time of day. The thought of her trudging home to someone who didn't even appreciate her hard work was almost more than Finch could bear. Anna's mother couldn't help it, but this old bag clearly enjoyed being a pain in the ass.

"It must be nice that your daughter's a nurse," she said, "you so sick all the time."

The old lady shot her a narrow look, as if

suspecting that Finch was being sarcastic. "We're meant to suffer," she said with a martyred sigh. "It says so in the Bible."

"I don't agree at all." Laura spoke lightly, but Finch could see that the old lady had struck a nerve. "If God had wanted us to be miserable, He wouldn't have given us so much to enjoy. Doesn't the Bible tell us to lift up our hearts and rejoice?"

" 'Eternal glory in Christ after ye have suffered awhile.' First Peter, Chapter Five, Verse Ten," she quoted triumphantly. She'd perked up and seemed to be enjoying herself now. "There's coffee on the stove; help yourselves if you like. Can't drink it myself. Gives me heartburn," she said.

"We should be going." Laura cast another desperate glance at Finch.

"We only stopped in to see how you were doing," Finch was quick to add.

"Martha put you up to this?" The old lady eyed them suspiciously.

"She doesn't even know we're here," Laura told her. That much was the truth, at least.

But Mrs. Elliston didn't look convinced. "Last week it was a woman from the agency—as if I'd want some stranger hanging around all day. You can't trust them, you know. They all steal. With my friend Pearl it was every last piece of her family silver. I won't have it. I told Martha as much. But she's afraid something will happen to me, being here all alone." At the same time, Finch doubted she missed an opportunity to rub it in that she was alone, and thought with disgust: *She'll probably outlive Martha.* Wasn't Maude always saying that it was the ones pickled in brine who often lived the longest?

"She's a good nurse," Finch blurted. "I mean, well, you should be proud of her."

The old lady cocked her head, peering up at her like a wily old parrot. "Who says I'm not?"

"All I meant was . . ."

Laura stood up. "We really should be going." She spoke more forcefully this time. "I'm sure you need your rest."

"I'll leave this in the kitchen." Finch held up the banana bread.

"Be sure to lock the door behind you," the old lady called after them. God forbid some other well-meaning soul should drop by to wish her well.

It wasn't until they were outside that they

dared look at each other. Laura let out a breath. "Whew! I wasn't sure we'd make it out of there alive." She rolled her eyes. "Next time I have a bright idea, remind me to drink prune juice instead." She started to giggle, and before long they were both doubled over, hands cupped over their mouths to stifle their laughter as they made their way up the walk.

"I notice you didn't mention Hank," Finch said when they were in the car.

"Are you kidding? I was afraid she'd levitate right off the bed." Laura turned the key in the ignition. She must have accidentally pressed down hard on the gas pedal for they went lurching out of the driveway with a squeal. "If she keeps it up, Father Reardon will have to perform an exorcism."

This unleashed a fresh onslaught of giggles. "I'm glad we didn't say anything," Finch said when she could catch her breath. "I wasn't sure it was such a good idea."

It hadn't really been about Martha and her mother, she realized. She'd thought she'd feel better knowing that her search for her family hadn't been a complete bust. Instead, it had been brought home to her that sometimes, even when things look grim, the grass isn't always greener on the other side of the fence. Suppose her real mother had been like Martha's?

"I wonder what he saw in her—Hank, I mean," Laura said. "It's hard to imagine Grace Elliston as the kind of woman who'd be seduced."

"Lorraine said she was pretty once." Finch had a hard time imagining it, too.

"I suppose she blames Martha for ruining her life." Laura shook her head. "I wonder if she's ever stopped to think what a blessing it was."

"I never thought I'd feel sorry for someone who *wasn't* given up for adoption," Finch said with a laugh.

"It was different in those days. It must have been hard for Grace."

"Not as hard as for Martha. Um, aren't you going a little fast?" Finch eyed the speedometer, which showed they were doing fifty in a thirty-five-mile-an-hour zone.

Laura shot her a sheepish look and eased her foot off the gas. "Guess I'm in a hurry to get home."

"Me, too." The plan had been for Laura to

drop her off at school, but she knew there would be no school today.

Soon they were bumping along Old Sorrento Road. "Well, if you can play hooky, I guess I can, too," Laura said. "What do you say we saddle up the horses and go for a ride? It'd be a shame to stay indoors on a day like this."

Finch grinned. "Just what I feel like."

The night before Laura and Hector were due to leave, Finch sat cross-legged on the bed in their room, watching Laura pack. Usually she tossed things into suitcases willy-nilly, but now she was taking her time, half a dozen outfits spread out over the bed while she agonized over which ones to take. She wanted to make the right impression, she said, not come across as some gringo snob.

"No one would ever take you for a snob," Finch assured her.

"I hope you're right." Laura chewed on her lip as she studied two nearly identical outfits laid out side by side.

"Even if you were wearing the crown jewels," she threw in for good measure.

"I'm not sure that's a compliment, but thanks anyway," Laura said with a laugh.

"You're sure you packed enough for the baby?" Finch teased, eyeing the bulging duffel bag crammed with diapers, formula, receiving blankets, little overalls and footie pajamas, and a bonnet to guard against the Mexican sun.

"You're right. I probably won't need all that stuff." Laura sank down beside her on the bed. It was unclear whether she was referring to the fact that she'd packed enough for triplets, or that the adoption could still fall through, even at this late date.

"It's going to be okay." Finch patted her arm.

"I know. I'm just nervous, is all. I still can't believe it—a baby." Laura pushed a hand through her hair, making it stand up in a staticky halo. "Just when I thought I'd be lonely with you going off to college next year."

"Like you could ever be lonely in this house."

"Still . . ." Laura was getting that look again, as if at any minute she was going to cry. "I'll miss you."

College, which had seemed so far away,

was all at once a reality. Her throat tightened. "I'm not going anywhere for a while."

"You'll be so sick of changing diapers by then, you'll be out of here like a shot." A corner of Laura's mouth turned up in a lopsided smile.

Finch flopped onto her back, looking up at a stain on the ceiling in the shape of a rooster's comb. "I wonder what it'll be like having a sister."

"I remember when my parents brought Alice home from the hospital. I thought she was all mine." Laura's voice grew soft. "I used to dress her in my doll clothes until she got too big. And the way she'd look at me with those big blue eyes of hers, like I was the sun, the moon, and the stars—well, I'd never felt so important." She smiled down at Finch. "There's nothing like a sister. You'll see."

Right now all Finch wanted was for time to stand still. She scooted over, laying her head in Laura's lap. When she was younger, she'd watched in envy as mothers cuddled their kids, but she'd learned it was better not to want what you couldn't have. Now the warm weight of Laura's hand on her brow was reminding her all over again of everything she'd missed out on that her little sister would take for granted.

"Oh, hell," Laura swore under her breath. Finch lifted her head to find her holding a crumpled tissue to her nose, looking sheepish. "I promised myself I wouldn't cry. If I don't watch out, I'll be a sobbing wreck by the time we land."

Finch sat up. "You'll be fine. Come on, I'll help you finish packing."

She went through the suitcase, double-checking to make sure it had everything Laura would need while weeding out what she wouldn't wear. Hector popped his head in at one point, then with a roll of his eyes disappeared. Maude brought a travel sewing kit for last-minute emergencies. Even the dogs ambled in, Pearl tucking her tail under her legs at the sight of the suitcase.

When there was nothing left to do, Finch wandered into the living room to watch TV, where she dozed off half an hour into a *National Geographic* special on Alaskan wildlife. She woke much later to the sound of murmuring voices. Light spilled from under the door to Laura and Hector's room.

They wouldn't be getting much sleep tonight, she knew.

She envied them. Whatever else happened, they had each other. While all she'd have of Lucien were memories and an e-mail address. Would she ever see him again? Suddenly she couldn't bear not knowing. How had she gone from wondering what to do with him to wondering what she'd do without him?

"What are you thinking?" she asked as they strolled hand in hand across the quad, no different from the couples she'd once secretly made fun of.

Lucien shrugged. "I was just wondering if it's possible to get a decent grade for a paper you wrote in your sleep."

Finals were upon them and from the tense looks around campus, he wasn't the only one preoccupied with grades. Finch knew she ought to be worried, too, but with everything else that was going on, she couldn't seem to get too worked up about whether she got a B or a B minus on some stupid paper.

"If it's for Ms. Goodbee," she said, "you

could turn in recopied Cliffs Notes, and she'd give you an A."

"So now I'm a teacher's pet?"

"You said it, not me."

"Must be my irresistible charm." He let his eyelids droop in an attempt to look mysterious.

"To a woman who hasn't been laid since the sinking of the *Titanic,* anyone would look good."

He laughed, saying, "I take it you mean the actual *Titanic,* not the movie. Anyway, how would you know?"

"Have you noticed how she walks? Like there's a two-by-four up her rear."

"You're in a good mood this morning."

"I didn't get much sleep last night." She ignored Courtney Russo, standing with her posse by the cafeteria, eyeing her and Lucien like she knew something they didn't.

"Join the club."

Finch felt irritated all of a sudden. Was that all he could think of, acing his finals? "I wasn't up all night studying," she snapped. "I just had trouble sleeping, that's all."

Lucien eyed her warily. "Something on your mind?"

"Well, let's see. It could have something

to do with the fact that my parents are bringing home a baby any day."

"When do they get back?"

"In a week."

"You'll know then."

"Know what?" Was he suggesting the adoption might fall through?

"What it's like having a baby in the house." He frowned. "What's eating you anyway?"

"Nothing." She shrugged, letting go of his hand.

But Lucien knew her too well. These past weeks they'd grown close, falling into a rhythm so perfectly tuned that even now she looked down to note with dismay that her stride matched his. She slowed at once, letting him pull ahead of her, but they hadn't gone far when he caught hold of her wrist, drawing her into an empty classroom.

"I'm not letting you off the hook until you tell me what's wrong," he said.

"We'll be late for class."

"Fuck class."

"Yeah, right. Who cares? Next year you won't even be around." The words slipped out.

"So that's it." He nodded slowly in understanding, then with a sigh slumped onto the nearest desk.

"So it's true," she said softly. "You're not coming back."

He stared down at the floor. "It looks that way."

"Was it your idea, or your mom's?" She had to know.

He looked up at her, the picture of misery. "She's not forcing me or anything. It's just . . . she's having a tough time right now, but she's trying, you know? I don't want to make it any harder on her." There were tears in his eyes.

"Will we still see each other?" She swallowed against the lump in her throat.

"I'll be back Christmas week. My dad's taking me skiing." He didn't have to say it: His vacation plans didn't include her.

"Whatever. I'm not sure I'll be around either," she said coolly. "My aunt and uncle have a place in Cabo." She liked the way it sounded. *Cabo.* As if she were the kind of person used to jetting off to places like Cabo San Lucas at a moment's notice. And it wasn't a lie, exactly; Alice and Wes *did* have a condo in Cabo, which they were always offering to let them use, even if Laura and Hector would sooner fly to the moon. What would they do in Cabo with a baby? Laura had said.

He looked crestfallen. "Really? Because I was kind of hoping . . ." He shrugged. "Never mind. It's no big deal."

"What?"

"I was going to ask my dad if you could come with us."

"Really?" Her heart soared, then just as quickly plummeted. She couldn't ask Laura and Hector to finance such a trip; every cent of their savings had gone toward the baby. "I'd love to," she said as casually as she could, "but my parents are kind of expecting me to spend Christmas with them. I don't want to disappoint them."

"We wouldn't leave until the day after."

"Look, for your information I don't even *know* how to ski," she told him, angrily almost.

"I'd teach you."

"What about skis?"

"You can rent those."

"Not everyone can afford it, you know." She glared at him as if he were somehow to blame for the fact that she was poor.

He cocked his head, giving her that slow-breaking smile that got to her every time. "Look, I wouldn't have offered if I'd expected you to pay your way. It'd be my dad's treat. He'd be thrilled, believe me. Anything that keeps me out of his hair."

She was flooded with relief. Even so, she held back, saying, "How do I know you won't have another girlfriend by then?"

"You could just as easily have another boyfriend," he lobbed right back.

"As if."

"Don't tell me you haven't noticed the way Alan Dorfmeyer looks at you."

"You're making this up."

He grinned. It wasn't until they were walking to their next class that he asked, "So how about it, do you want to come or not?"

She took a deep breath. "I'd have to ask my parents, but I'm pretty sure they'll say okay."

Lucien pulled her to him and kissed her deeply, oblivious to the students strolling past. "Preview of coming attractions," he whispered in her ear.

"I guess this means Alan's out of the running," she said.

"He lays a finger on you, I'll beat the living crap out of him."

The bell rang. Lockers banged. Out in the hallway, voices called raucously to one another. The vice principal announced over the PA system that there'd be a special assembly after lunch. "We better hurry," she said.

"Mrs. G. can live without me for once." He didn't move except to tighten his arms about her.

"I'm not sure I can." She was horrified to realize she was on the verge of tears.

Christmas seemed a long way away. She thought that if she could survive this, skiing would be a cinch. Even if she got hurt, what was breaking an arm or a leg compared to falling in love?

Two days before Laura and Hector were due back, Finch and Andie took on the task of cleaning the house, top to bottom. They sorted through the odds and ends that had collected on the back porch—mud-caked boots, dog-chewed Frisbees, half-empty bags of potting soil—filling several large garbage bags. They bathed the dogs, clipping a bow atop Rocky's curly head that five minutes later ended up trampled in the yard. They even whitewashed the fence along the driveway. When there was nothing left to clean or polish, Finch looked about at the gleaming woodwork, the cat-scratched sofa covered in a freshly laundered bedspread, and the spray of pussy-willows in the milk can by the fireplace, feeling an enormous sense of accomplishment. The place hadn't looked this good since Laura and Hector's wedding.

At the last minute, Anna stopped by to see if she could lend a hand. She seemed subdued, and Finch guessed it had to do with missing Marc. At the same time, she seemed determined to get on with her life. Where in the past she'd always seemed to be running on empty, there was an air of quiet strength about her these days.

They were chatting on the porch when the Explorer pulled into the driveway amid a plume of dust. Finch watched with her heart in her throat as Laura and Hector climbed out. Where was the baby? Had something happened? She'd heard horror stories about adoptive parents setting off with high hopes only to return empty-handed because of some last minute glitch or Third World snafu.

Then Laura opened the rear door and bent over to retrieve something from the backseat. All Finch could see from where she stood was a blanket-wrapped bundle from which a pair of plump brown arms emerged, waving like an orchestra conductor's. Laura spotted them and broke into a grin as she headed up the path, treading as carefully as if she were carrying a fragile newborn, not a chubby six-month-old. A wave of relief washed over Finch.

Esperanza was even cuter than her picture, with a round face and dimples, and a thatch of jet-black hair that stuck straight up like a punk rocker's. When Finch put her hand out, the baby grabbed hold of her index finger with surprising strength, cooing and kicking with delight. Finch's heart tipped over inside her chest.

"Would you like to hold her?" Laura handed her over without further ado.

"She weighs a ton," Finch said with a laugh, afraid that any minute she'd start crying.

"Half of it's diaper. I haven't changed her

since the airport." Laura spoke as if even diaper duty were a privilege.

"Look at that face." Anna tickled a fat brown foot, gazing into eyes like Hershey Kisses, with lashes so long they curled back to brush her brows. Jack would have to watch out; he'd have competition.

Maude stepped out onto the porch just then, and seeing what all the commotion was about clapped a hand to her bosom. "Gracious." She scooped the baby from Finch's arms and set about inspecting her from head to toe. Esperanza seemed equally fascinated with Maude as she cooed, "We're going to get along just fine, aren't we, sweet pea?"

"Is she crawling yet?" Anna wanted to know.

"She hasn't quite figured it out yet, but she's trying," Laura told her.

Maude's blue eyes shone. It had been ages since she'd cared for a baby—her son was now middle-aged with a family of his own—but she knew exactly what to do when Esperanza began to whimper, pacing back and forth while patting her back. Immediately, the baby stopped fussing.

When she began to nod off, Laura took

her from Maude, already an old hand as she pushed open the door, Esperanza drooping against her shoulder.

"I take it everything went well," Anna said to Hector.

"Had a little trouble at the embassy, but after that it was smooth sailing. As of yesterday, Uncle Sam has a brand-new citizen." He grinned, showing his chipped front tooth.

"Thank God. I was so worried." Anna had obviously feared the worst. Would she spend the rest of her life imagining that disaster loomed around every bend?

Hector asked, "How's the new job?"

Anna brightened. "Harder than I thought it would be, but I'm learning something new every day."

Anna was being modest, as usual. "Her boss said she should try doing a story," Finch told him. "If it's any good, he'll run it."

"The operative word being *if*. Either way, it sure beats . . ." Her smile fell away. "Sitting at home," she finished weakly.

Finch wondered how she did it. If Monica had been her sister, she'd have been throwing rocks at her grave.

"Glad to hear it." Hector regarded her affectionately, and Finch knew he slept easier these days knowing she was safe from harm. "Heard from Marc?"

"He called just the other day." Anna ducked her head, but not quick enough to hide her pained look.

Hector was careful to maintain an even tone as he said, "Next time you talk to him, tell him we sure do miss him around here."

"I'll do that." She managed a small smile, then a moment later excused herself, saying she had some things to do back at the house.

When they were alone, Hector slung an arm about Finch's shoulders. "Nice job," he said, nodding in the direction of the newly whitewashed fence.

"I figured you'd have your hands full with the baby," she told him.

"Good guess." He cast a wry glance toward the house. "In fact, I have a feeling nothing's gonna be the same from here on out."

"You sure you don't want your old room back?" she teased.

Hector grinned, the deep creases at the corners of his eyes curving to meet his temples, where she noticed for the first time a light dusting of silver hairs. "You're welcome to it," he said.

"Does she cry a lot?"

"No more than most babies."

"Do you mind that she's not—" She caught herself.

"Mine?" he finished for her. "Sure, I always thought I'd have kids of my own, but it worked out the way it was supposed to." He looked at her, his dark eyes alight with equal measures of humor and affection. "It's all your fault, you know. If it hadn't been for you, we wouldn't have known what we were missing."

"Just do me a favor and don't adopt twelve more," she said with an embarrassed laugh. But she was secretly pleased to hear how he felt, this accidental father who'd turned out to be better than one she might have picked.

After a moment of companionable silence, he nodded toward the car, saying, "Want to give me a hand with those suitcases?"

Finch fell in behind him as he started down the steps. Inside the house she could hear the baby crying in a sleepy, halfhearted way while Laura warbled a lullaby in her off-key voice. She looked up to see a hawk wheeling lazily in a sky so blue it seemed to crackle, and for an instant imagined herself soaring alongside it. She was brought back to earth by the smell of lasagna in the oven and the sight of Hector holding up an over-size sombrero nearly as wide as his grin.

CHAPTER EIGHTEEN

Each day on the job brought new challenges. The first two pieces Anna did on spec were summarily tossed out, Bob Heidiger gruffly pronouncing them sophomoric, but one on a local battered wives' shelter caught his interest. He called her into his office and shut the door—not a good sign usually, though this time the news wasn't all bad. He got right to the point. "You're still a long way from being a reporter, but you do have a knack for getting to the meat of the matter. I guess you've heard Suzette's hanging it up the end of the month—" Suzette Piggot of "Suzie Says," the *Clarion*'s sixty-eight-year-old advice columnist. "I was thinking of going with one of the syndicateds, but why don't you take a crack at it?"

Anna had stammered a reply before floating back to her cubicle. An hour later she was sifting through a pile of letters she'd collected from Suzette. The first to catch her eye was from a woman named Tanya, who was torn over whether or not to put her elderly father in a nursing home. Anna wrote in response that it was natural to feel guilty but that it would only muddy the waters and possibly result in her making the wrong decision. She suggested Tanya see a counselor, and listed several organizations she'd come across when she'd been in the same situation herself.

She found that it wasn't much different from when Monica's fans had written for advice. Bob even insisted that she remain anonymous when he finally gave it the green light, saying her notoriety might put people off. Some letters required careful thought and research; others, merely a dose of common sense, like the one from a woman who complained that her next-door neighbor was in the habit of dropping by unannounced, often hanging around for an hour or more. When "Penny for Your Thoughts" debuted, it featured Anna's response to Fed Up:

Dear Fed Up,
A tap on the brakes is certainly in order. Next time your neighbor drops by uninvited, I suggest you greet her with, "Perfect timing! I'm just taking a five-minute coffee break." That way, you'll be letting her know there's a time limit without offending her. And if she doesn't get the hint, give her the boot. If her hide's that thick, she won't even feel it.

Penny

But as much as she loved her job, she still had to go home to an empty house. The difference was that nowadays she wasn't allowing herself to sink into the mire. She'd found another therapist, one she liked, a no-nonsense older woman named Corinne, who reminded her of Rhonda. It was Corinne who'd steered her toward ACA— Adult Children of Alcoholics. Anna attended meetings once a week and had come to a deeper understanding of what had caused Monica to act as she had. More and more, too, she was seeing the part *she'd* unwittingly played in it all. Hoping it would benefit

Liz as well, she'd urged her sister to join her, but Liz had declined, saying she'd used up all her frequent flier miles on *that* particular trip to hell.

Anna didn't blame her. There was a fine line between delving into the past and dwelling in it. Hadn't she obsessed enough about Marc? The only remedy, she'd found, was staying one step ahead of it. She'd joined the music festival committee at Sam's invitation, and as a volunteer for the historical society would be conducting tours of historic homes during Christmas open house week. The weekend before, she'd attended the garden club's annual orchid show and the one before that she'd taken a trip to Big Sur with Liz, where they dined on Dungeness crab and had too much to drink before falling into their respective beds, giggling themselves into hiccups.

Her greatest pleasure was baby-sitting for Esperanza, nicknamed Essie, on the odd occasion when everyone at the ranch was tied up. Essie laughed more than she cried, and nothing short of an earthquake could wake her. Anna didn't doubt that at the party in her honor, set for the week after school let out, she'd be the belle of the ball. The only downside was the deep hunger she stirred in Anna, who wondered about the children she might have had with Marc. She knew she ought to count her blessings, yet couldn't help feeling as though she'd been robbed.

But wasn't that just what had been drummed into her growing up, that no woman was complete without a husband and kids? (Though God knows her parents had been anything but models of domestic bliss.) Why couldn't it be enough that she was finally discovering what she wanted out of life? The trouble was that her solitude had a face: Marc's. At night she couldn't close her eyes without seeing him. A breeze blowing her hair across her cheek brought memories of his caress. Even the coffee mug he'd favored brought a pang each time she opened the cupboard and saw it sitting there.

He called every so often, but their conversations seemed forced and always left her more depressed than ever. It was getting harder and harder to settle for so little when she wanted so much. The irony was that men looked at her twice in the street

now, and not just because she was the local Madame X. A few had even asked her
out, like Howard Newman at the *Clarion,* an
attractive divorced father of three. Over
lunch at the Tree House, they'd talked
about their work and his kids, and what
they enjoyed doing in their time off—
Howard was an avid hiker—but though she
enjoyed his company, she didn't see it going anywhere. The only man she wanted
was taken.

On a Tuesday morning in mid-June, when
the riotous spring blossoms that'd blan-
keted the valley had given way to the deep
green of summer, she got the call she'd
been dreading. "It's your mother," Felicia
Campbell said. "She's taken a turn for the
worse . . ."

Anna's initial reaction was to smile at the
quaint expression, as if Betty had taken a
wrong turn on an unfamiliar road and lost
her way. Then it hit her: Her mother was ill,
possibly dying. She'd known it could happen at any time—old age and the years of
abuse at their father's hand had taken their
toll—but it came as a shock even so. As
soon as she hung up, she phoned Liz and
arranged to meet her at the hospital.

By the time they arrived it was too late. A soft-spoken Pakistani resident took them aside, explaining gently that Betty's heart had given out. Anna stood speechless while Liz demanded answers. Had they done everything they could to resuscitate her? Why not? What the hell kind of hospital was this anyway?

It was left to Anna to inform her that their mother, whose biggest fear had been a slow death hooked up to machines, had left a living will. "It's what Mom wanted. It's better this way, really."

Liz stared at her in disbelief, then after a moment bowed her head and began to weep. Anna had known it would be like this: that her sister's heart, hardened against their mother, would be the first to crack. Her tears weren't just for Betty, but for all that would forever remain unresolved. That she'd missed that boat long ago—their mother had been beyond reach for years— didn't seem to matter. She was gone; that was all Liz knew.

"The arrangements have all been made." Anna spoke quietly. They might have been stranded on a rock amid the ER staff swirling around them like surf: harried-look-

ing nurses and residents tending to the patients, some holding bloody towels to
wounds or cradling injured parts of their
bodies.

"Why didn't you tell me all this before?"
Liz lifted her head, her bloodshot eyes filled
with accusation.

"You never asked."

"When did she . . . ?"

"When dad died."

"I suppose she wanted to be buried next
to him." A bitter note crept into Liz's voice.

"No. She was very definite about that."
Betty had wept at their father's funeral—
tears not unlike the ones Liz was now shedding—but the one thing she'd been firm
about was where she was to be buried
when her time came. "She'll be next to
Grandma." On the other side of the cemetery, as far from Joe Vincenzi as possible.

"Thank God for that, at least."

"I should call the funeral home."

"Do you need me to do anything?"

Liz looked incapable of anything more
than wiping her own nose at that moment.
"It can wait until tomorrow," Anna said gently, making a mental list of the friends and

relatives they'd have to call. "Do you want me to have someone drive you home?"

"Why don't we ask David? He's probably upstairs with his son. And Saint Carol, of course. She'd insist he take me home." Her voice cracked as she leaned against the wall, eyes squeezed shut. Betty's death and the breakup with David had somehow become tangled together in her mind.

"I'll take you," Anna told her. "We'll come back in the morning for your car."

Liz looked as though she were going to protest, but instead surrendered with a sigh, saying, "You're probably right. With my luck, it'd be a double funeral. In fact, the way I feel right now, it might end up being one anyway."

"You'll live." Anna spoke briskly. She knew that what Liz wanted was sympathy, but she was no longer in the business of providing full-time care and comfort.

Her sister's mouth stretched in a bleak smile. "Oh, sure. I'll live. Chin up, isn't that what Mom used to say?"

"You still have Dylan."

"Believe me, he's the only thing keeping me sane."

"You have me, too."

"I don't know why you don't hate me." Slumped against the wall, her arms folded tightly over her stomach, Liz might have been one of the patients. "I wasn't much help, was I? With Mom or Monica."

No, you weren't. "I forgive you," Anna said.

Liz looked at her in surprise. Clearly, she hadn't expected Anna to agree so readily that she was at fault. But her expression quickly turned sheepish. "I'm sorry. Really. I'll try to make it up to you."

Isn't it a little late for that? said the cold voice in Anna's head. But there was no point in beating a dead horse. "I'll make a list of people for us to call. We'll each take half."

"Just be sure to put David and Carol in *your* column," Liz said bitterly. They were on their way out when she asked, "What about Marc—are you going to let him know?"

Anna thought for a moment, then shook her head. He'd insist on coming, and she couldn't cope with *that* on top of everything else. On the other hand, if she told him not to, it would become even more glaringly obvious that theirs wasn't a real friendship, but some strange hybrid. Friends looked after one another at times like these; they held your hand and kneeled with you in prayer. If Marc couldn't be there for her as he'd once been, what was the point in pretending?

Marc sat in a circle of patients and family members in Room C-4, which looked over the lawn, where at that moment one of his colleagues, Dennis Hodstetter, was consoling a distraught young woman seated cross-legged on the grass. He thought of Anna. He'd read somewhere that there were fifty words in the Eskimo language to describe snow. Shouldn't there be at least that many to define all the ways to miss someone?

It had been a particularly intense session so far: One of his patients, a bearded young artist named Gordon, had divulged earlier on that he'd been sexually molested as a child—by the very man seated across from him now, his older brother. Gordon was crying and so was his brother while their parents looked on in anguish.

They went around the circle. A number of people expressed anger and disgust, while

Mohammed B.—a recovering coke addict whose traditional Muslim parents sat mute with shock—commended both Gordon and his brother for having the courage to confront this. Melanie S., an incest survivor herself, broke down in tears. Jim T. said in a strangled whisper that he didn't trust himself to speak; he might say something he'd regret.

Marc reminded them all of their confidentiality pledge before inviting Gordon and his brother to pull their chairs into the center of the room. Gordon went first, speaking in a choked near whisper of the damage that had been done and the many ways he'd suffered through the years. His brother Tom, as clean-cut as Gordon was shaggy-haired, listened with tears streaming down his cheeks, nodding every so often as if to acknowledge what he'd done and the pain it had caused.

This was the hardest part of Marc's job: checking judgment at the door. However disgusted or angered by what he heard, he had to find a way to get past it. Healing didn't come from shaming, he knew; it was a function of open and honest discussion, allowing each person to have their say. The end result wasn't always forgiveness; some things were too deep or painful to forgive. But in this case, Gordon might learn to forgive himself, if not his brother, and be able to move on with his life.

Marc's thoughts turned once more to Anna. He'd known it would be hard, but the ache hadn't lessened with time. He thought about her constantly. He wrote letters that ended up crumpled in the wastebasket, e-mails that were deleted unsent, and for every time he phoned, at least a dozen times he'd hang up before punching in her number.

And where was Faith in all this? Was he clinging to lost hope, a dead love? The husband in him had begun to think it was merely wishful thinking that she would ever be well, but the doctor knew that advances were being made, if not every day, then at a rate that was meteoric in the once-hidebound field of mental health—a field that not so long ago had relied on electroshock and insulin therapies, with lobotomy as a last resort. He'd seen miracles like the woman in group just last week, a self-described recovering schizophrenic who'd spoken frankly and intelligently about her struggle with her disease. And she hadn't even been a patient; she'd been here for her son. So, yes, it was possible that one day in the not-too-distant future he'd look across the dinner table and see the woman he'd married smiling back at him. If he didn't believe that, there'd have been nothing to hold him back. He'd have gone straight to Anna.

In a choked voice Gordon haltingly read aloud his list of confrontations. "The time you accused me of lying when I told Dad what you'd done, I felt anger, shame, and pain. That day at the lake when you made me swear on my life that if I ever . . ."

When his brother finally had a chance to respond, it quickly became clear there was no real villain here—it turned out that Tom, too, had been molested at an early age— only wrongful acts with consequences that had multiplied exponentially over time.

Marc wrapped it up in time for lunch. There was a collective sigh of relief as they all gathered up their things and headed for the door. When the last person had filed out, he looked about the empty room, the carpet littered with crumpled tissues reminding him of a battlefield. Yet if anyone was defeated, it was he. The work that had sustained him in the aftermath of Faith's illness was showing signs of wear and tear; tiny cracks had appeared in his armament, letting in the thoughts and feelings he'd managed for the most part to vanquish by using the tools of his trade.

He drove home at the end of the day amid a breaking thunderstorm. The rain hadn't started in earnest yet, but sodden gray clouds hung low overhead, lightning flickering like a faulty circuit to illuminate the fat droplets gathering on his windshield. He'd been planning to stop for a bite to eat, but thought better of it. He'd be lucky if he made it from his driveway to his front door without getting soaked. The thought depressed him even more than the afternoon's group. He still wasn't used to eating alone. But each time he sat down in front of the TV, a bowl of reheated chili or slice of leftover pizza in hand, he'd picture his mother shaking her head in disapproval. It had been one of Ellie's most firmly held beliefs that such practices were for "those who didn't know any better."

On impulse he decided to pay a visit to Faith. Not that it would necessarily lift his mood, since he never knew what to expect.

Sometimes she'd be in a good frame of mind, even upbeat, other times agitated and depressed. To his everlasting shame he often prayed for the latter, as he did now. For in the absence of all hope, he'd be able to move on.

Shirley wasn't at the nurses' station when he arrived; she was off duty tonight. A dour gray-haired nurse he didn't recognize informed him that visiting hours were over. Perhaps if he'd phoned ahead, special arrangements might have been made, she told him with a pointed glance at the rules posted on the wall.

Too weary to argue, he simply continued on down the hall, not running or even walking particularly fast. His shoulders sagged, the rain that had soaked his hair running in warm rivulets down his neck. When she caught up with him, red-faced and indignant, he ignored her as if she'd been a fly buzzing about his head, not even breaking his stride.

A patient who'd stepped out into the hall, a henna-haired woman with a feather boa around her neck, shrank from him as if he were a potential rapist, clutching the lapels of her pink satin robe, while a gaunt young man who resembled a concentration camp survivor with his hollow eyes and shaven head gave him only a cursory glance as he passed.

He found Faith lying on the bed in her room, listening to Schubert on the CD player he'd given her. She sat up, and he thought he saw a flicker of alarm, then her expression smoothed over. "It's all right, Adele," she said in a clear firm voice. "I spoke to Dr. Fine. He said it was okay."

The old battle-ax went on ranting for another minute or so . . . rules were rules . . . how was she expected to do her job if people didn't . . . they didn't pay her enough to . . . but at last she retreated into the hallway, muttering to herself.

"Whew." Faith let out a breath, breaking into her old impish smile. He noticed when she got up to switch off the CD player that she'd put on a few pounds, and was encouraged by it.

He smiled, walking toward her. "I'm in Dutch, as my mother would've said."

"Don't pay any attention to Adele."

"What's her problem?"

"She's scared, that's all."

"Of what?"

"That one day it'll be us patients running the asylum."

"It might be a welcome change in her case."

Marc felt his apprehension recede. She was having one of her good days. Except for the shadows like old bruises under her eyes, she was almost her old self. He sank down beside her on the bed, fighting the urge to stretch out and close his eyes.

"You look tired," she said, her brow wrinkling with concern.

"It's been a long day."

"Have you been getting enough sleep?"

"In this heat?" The temperature hadn't dropped below ninety degrees all week.

Outside, rain slammed against the window in furious bursts. The storm had broken the heat spell though he doubted he'd get much sleep tonight.

Faith regarded him with an expression he knew all too well: half exasperated, half resigned. She knew something was eating at him, but would wait until he was ready to tell her—or until she lost patience. It had been like that when his mother was dying: She'd endured his brooding silences, waiting until Ellie was in her grave before saying with the same quiet firmness with which she'd just addressed the nurse, "I'm sorry about your mother—I loved her, too—but I'm afraid shutting me out isn't an option anymore. We're in this together whether you like it or not."

"I finished those books," she said now, glancing at the pile of paperbacks he'd brought her last time.

"Any in particular that you liked?"

"The Larry McMurtry—it made me think of Wyoming." She looked wistful all of a sudden.

His chest constricted. They'd talked about buying a house there someday. The first twelve years of her life, before her family had moved to Oregon, they'd lived in Jackson Hole. She and Marc had spent their honeymoon in a log cabin by Jenny Lake, where he, too, had fallen under Wyoming's spell.

"We'll get back there one of these days," he said lightly.

"No, we won't." The sad certainty with which she spoke was like a cold blade through his heart.

"You don't know that."

She shook her head. "It's no use fooling ourselves, Marc."

He put his hands on her shoulders, forcing her to meet his gaze. "I know it doesn't seem that way right now, but one of these days you'll be coming home. You have to believe that." He hoped it sounded more convincing to her than it did to him.

Her mouth twisted. "In some ways that scares me even more than the idea of spending the rest of my life in here."

A memory of their honeymoon surfaced: They'd been out hiking and had come across a dead rabbit caught in a tangle of barbed wire; it had torn itself to shreds trying to escape. Faith was like that rabbit in some ways. "You wouldn't be alone," he reminded her. "You'd have me."

"Don't bullshit me, Marc." She went on regarding him with those sad, knowing eyes, making him wonder who the crazy one was here. Outside, the storm rattled against the window like someone trying to get in—or out—rain sheeting down its reinforced glass to cast a ripply film of shadow over her face. She asked softly, "Who is she?"

The words went through him like the

lightning that flared just then, setting off a low buzzing in his head. He thought about denying it. But she fought so hard for every scrap of reality that to leave her thinking she'd imagined it would be the ultimate cruelty. After a long moment, he answered, "No one you know."

Faith drew in a breath, her bruised eyes seeming to grow larger, more luminous. "Are you in love with her?"

He let his silence speak for itself.

She just sat there staring at him, a range of emotions playing over her face.

With a groan, he pulled her to him, burying his face against her neck. She smelled sweet, but it was the hothouse scent of someone who rarely ventured outdoors. Faith didn't pull away, nor did she return his embrace.

"I'm sorry . . ." he said in a choked whisper.

"Would you have told me if I hadn't asked?" She spoke in a hoarse whisper.

"I don't know."

"It's all right, Marc. I don't blame you."

"I never expected it to happen. I know how that sounds but—"

She drew back to place a finger to his

lips. "It's time we faced this. We should have done it years ago."

"What are you saying?"

"I've filed for divorce."

He let out a startled, disbelieving laugh, remembering when they'd been newlyweds and she used to joke that if they ever got divorced, he'd have to take her as part of the settlement. "You're not getting rid of me that easily," he told her.

"I don't want to be rid of you."

"Then—"

"I want to see you . . . just not for a while." Her eyes pleaded with him to understand. "This isn't about you, Marc. If I'm ever to get well enough to go home, it has to be for *me*. I can't do it for both of us. I've tried. It . . . it's too much."

"Faith—" He reached for her, but she gently pushed him away.

"Please. Just . . . *go*." When he made no move to leave, she lay down on her side with her back to him, knees pulled in toward her chest.

Marc felt as though he were literally being torn in two. A part of him had wanted this, yes. Prayed for it, even. Not just for this Sisyphean struggle to end, but for it to be someone else's decision. Shouldn't he have been relieved?

A good sentry doesn't abandon his post, he thought.

But if what she said was true, then it wasn't his battle.

At last he rose. Faith lay so still she might have been sleeping. Gently, so gently it might have been the wind stealing in through a crack, he leaned down and kissed her forehead, then quietly slipped from the room.

The days that followed were harder than he could have imagined. He went to work each day emptied out and came home filled with the pain of others. Pain that shielded him against his own, muffled the rage and sorrow that pounded at him with thwarted fists. He stopped shaving and when his stubble became a beard, trimmed it only so that he wouldn't appear a raving madman. His eyes were mildly but perpetually bloodshot from lack of sleep. Though the urge to drink was faint, like the clanging of a distant bell, he phoned his sponsor late one night.

"Jim? It's me, Marc. Did I wake you?"

There was a brief silence at the other end, and he pictured Jim squinting with one eye shut at the clock by his bed. "It's after midnight," he growled. "Of course you woke me up, you son of a bitch." A low, sustained chuckle. "What gives? Engine giving you trouble again?"

Jim Pennington, mechanic to the stars—the only one to whom the likes of Steven Spielberg and Tom Cruise would entrust their Jaguars and Bentleys—had done eight years of hard time at Lompoc for running a chop shop before he sobered up, in more ways than one. That had been twenty-five years ago and he'd been on the straight and narrow ever since.

"Car's fine," Marc told him. "I'm not so sure about me."

"Okay, I'm listening." The jollity went out of his voice. Jim, with whom he had less in common than with anyone he knew, was the one person he could confide in.

"Faith filed for divorce." Marc had told him about Anna, and now hastened to add, "It's not what you think. She says I'm holding her back."

"Do you believe that?"

"I don't know what to believe anymore."

"Okay, what do you *want* then?"

"I want her back."

"Which one?"

"I don't know that either." Marc dropped his head against the back of the recliner in which he sat, holding a tumbler of tonic water, sans gin, on one knee. The room was dark, illuminated only by the light in the kitchen that he'd forgotten to switch off. "And here I thought I was supposed to have all the answers."

"Don't flatter yourself, Doc." He heard the rough affection in Jim's voice. "None of us knows shit."

" 'We have come to accept that we know only a little,' " Marc quoted from the big book of AA.

"You know what your problem is, Doc? You think too much." Jim referred to the program he worked as the meat and potatoes variety. "Stop trying to figure it all out and just go with your gut."

"That's what got me into this mess to begin with." If he hadn't followed his instincts, he wouldn't have rushed to Anna's aid. But how could he be sorry for that?

"Dude, did it ever occur to you that this so-called mess might be the best thing that's ever happened to you?"

Marc stared into his glass at the ice

cubes gleaming silver in the light that sloped from the kitchen doorway. "Maybe you should think about switching careers," he said with a smile. "You'd make a good shrink."

"And you'd make a lousy mechanic. You can't talk an engine into running. You got to crawl underneath and get your hands dirty."

Marc sighed. "I thought I wanted this divorce. And now all I want to do is crawl into a hole."

Jim was silent for so long, Marc thought he'd gone back to sleep. Then in his deep rumble of a voice, coarsened by his years of drinking and the two-pack-a-day cigarette habit he had yet to break, he said, "When I was doing my time, the only thing that kept me sane was the thought of going home to my wife. But soon as I got out I saw the truth—we were just two drunks hanging on to each other to keep from falling down." Marc heard a voice murmuring sleepily in the background. Jim had remarried, a woman he'd met in AA. They had two kids, one in college, and were happy, as far as Marc knew. "What might've been right at one time isn't always in the long run. Shit happens; things change. You got to face it, dude. You aren't the one working the levers; you're just the guy that got caught in them."

"Thanks, Jim. I can always count on you to put things into perspective," Marc said with the appropriate dash of irony.

"For five hundred bucks, I'll throw in a new muffler."

"I might take you up on that. I don't like the way mine's been sounding lately."

"Want some free advice, Doc? Get yourself a new set of wheels."

"Is there supposed to be a metaphor in this?"

"No, but I've got a friend who can give you a honey of a deal."

"I'll think about it." Marc gave a dry chuckle. "Now go back to sleep before Irene kills me."

"Sounds like you're doing a pretty good job of it all by yourself."

"Sweet dreams."

"Same to you, Doc. Same to you."

Hours later he still wasn't sleepy. He stared fixedly at the TV, too lost in his thoughts to even know what was on. After the storm a cold front had moved in, and now he felt a chill in the air that lay pooled about his bare feet and ankles. He brought his glass to his mouth to down the rest of the tonic but it was empty, though he had no memory of having drunk from it. He knew he should go to bed but couldn't seem to summon the strength. *You're in mourning, Doc,* said a voice in his head that sounded suspiciously like Jim's. If that was true, then it was long overdue.

A news bulletin on TV caught his attention: Monica Vincent's mother had died. An old photo of her with Monica flashed onto the screen, but all he could think of was Anna. Jesus. To have to cope with this on top of everything else. He was reaching for the phone when he thought better of it. Not because of the lateness of the hour but because just the prospect of hearing her voice had brought a flood of adrenaline. A cheap fix, he thought, was the last thing either of them needed.

He lowered his arm heavily into his lap, where his empty glass lay tilted on its side like something washed ashore. *If only I could get some sleep.* But his eyelids were wired open, a low buzzing in his veins like something alcohol-induced. Right now, what he could use more than anything, he thought, was a drink.

Mavis Fitzgerald was among the last to leave. After she'd helped clear up, she lingered in the kitchen, asking repeatedly if there was anything more she could do. Of all Betty's friends, Mavis had probably been the closest. Anna remembered that she used to drop by at least once a week, though it was miles out of her way. She'd assumed it was because Mavis enjoyed the company—being widowed at such a young age—but in time she'd come to realize that it was more than that: Mavis had been keeping an eye out. She knew what Joe was like and that her mother was powerless to stand up to him. Once, in a foul mood, he'd come thundering into the kitchen to demand that Betty "get up off her ass" and make him some coffee. Wearily, she'd dragged herself to her feet, but Mavis had said firmly, "You sit, Betty. *I'll* make it—nice and *strong.*" Joe had fixed her with a baleful, bloodshot gaze, fists flexing at his sides, but she'd looked straight back at him unflinchingly. Recalling it now, Anna was struck anew by how brave she'd been. More than that, Mavis had opened her eyes, showing Anna that her father wasn't as invincible as he'd seemed.

Those same blue eyes, faded but still alert, studied her now across the table crowded with half-eaten platters of food. "Sure I can't help wash up?"

"I'm sure." Anna spoke firmly.

All she wanted was to be alone. The funeral had been an ordeal. Not in the way that Monica's had been, but because reactions to her mother's death had been mixed. *It's a blessing,* a number of people had murmured, with Olive Miller voicing every old person's fear—being robbed of your mind—in saying, *Your mother would've wanted it this way.* But Anna realized she didn't have the slightest idea what her mother had thought or felt. Look at what she'd put up with all those years. Maybe in some ways it was losing her mind that had been a blessing.

"Well, all right then . . ." Mavis pulled her into a quick fierce hug smelling faintly of cloves. "Call me if you need anything. Promise?"

"I will." Anna saw her to the door, waving to her as she climbed into Olive Miller's blue Pontiac Cutlass, idling in the driveway. In the living room, Laura and Finch were still tidying up.

"Enough." She wrested the Dustbuster from Laura's hand. "Liz and I will do the rest."

"We're almost done," Laura protested— as if Anna didn't know what this was all about: Like Mavis, Laura didn't want her to be alone.

But it wasn't her job to provide full-time moral support. "Go home to your baby." Hector had left nearly an hour before with Essie slung over one shoulder, fast asleep.

Laura ignored her, stooping to pick up a crumpled napkin off the floor. "Hector's per-fectly capable of looking after her himself," she said.

"It's no use, Anna. We're not leaving," Finch said.

"You don't have to baby-sit me. I'll be fine. I promise." She scooped up her cat, winding in and out between her legs, his loud purring more comforting than the con-dolences she'd been fielding all day. From the bathroom down the hall came the muted clink of bottles and vials as Liz cleared the medicine cabinet of their mother's things—something Anna had been putting off doing.

Laura and Finch exchanged a look. Anna knew what they were thinking: that it wasn't just her mother. And they weren't wrong. Thoughts of Marc had lapped at her all day in cold little waves. But if being alone was hard, there was something even worse, she knew, and that was *fear* of loneliness, which could drive you to cling like a barnacle to familiar habits, however bad.

No, she'd get through this somehow.

"Any of that coffee left?" Laura retreated into the kitchen, returning moments later with a steaming mug and a chocolate chip cookie. She sank down on the sofa next to Finch, who sat perched on one of its arms.

Anna had no choice but to pull up a chair. "You guys." She smiled. "You know the biggest favor you could do me? Take home the rest of those cookies."

"Oh, I don't know. You'll have to twist my arm," Laura said, biting into her cookie.

"Did Claire make these?" Finch reached over to break a piece off Laura's.

"Actually, I think it was David." The Rybacks had stopped by briefly. Naturally Liz had managed to stay busy in the kitchen until they left.

Anna looked out the window at a yellow Lab that had wandered into the yard, not Pearl—she seldom ventured past the front porch these days. It must be her neighbor's from down the road; Herb Dunlop had dropped in earlier to pay his respects.

"I remember when my grandmother died," Laura said. "She'd been sick for a long time, but I still wasn't prepared for how hard it hit me." She eyed Anna with concern over the rim of her mug, the one Marc favored, blue ceramic with a director's chair and the words RELAX. GOD'S IN CHARGE. "Are you sure you don't want one of us to stay the night?"

Anna mustered a smile. "I'm sure."

"I wish I'd known your mother before she, uh, . . ." Finch faltered, not wanting to say it: *before she went crazy.* "What was she like?"

"Sweet. Funny." The corners of Anna's mouth crept higher. "She loved to read, too. If she'd had to rescue one thing from a burning house, it would have been her library card. I can't help thinking what her life would've been like if . . ." Her voice trailed off.

"I don't think there was a mean bone in her body," Laura put in.

"That's because they'd all been broken at one time or another."

They all turned toward Liz, who stood at the entrance to the hallway, a cardboard box in her arms. Anna sighed. "Please, Liz." She didn't have the strength for this. "Can't you give it a rest?"

"Sorry." Liz lowered the box onto the breakfront, looking chastened—an improvement over the old days, when she'd have countered with some caustic remark.

An awkward silence fell. Then Finch said, "And I thought I'd had it bad."

"Nobody's family is perfect," Anna said.

"There's no such thing," Laura said. "Perfect family is an oxymoron."

"The secret is to pick your own." Finch cast a wry look at Laura.

"We didn't have that luxury." Liz wandered over to where Anna sat, dropping onto an arm of her chair. "But it wasn't a complete wash. I got one halfway decent sister out of it, though frankly I don't know why she puts up with me."

"Beggars can't be choosers," Anna teased. "You're the only one left."

Talk turned to other things. Laura told them that Hector was teaching Maude how to use the computer, and Anna voiced her suspicion that the litter of kittens down the road at the Fosters' had been fathered by Boots. Liz regaled them with the latest misdeeds of celebrities who'd visited the spa.

When it was time for them to go, Anna hugged Laura and Finch at the door while Liz hung back, wearing a wistful look. She'd confided earlier that her own best friend, who was close to the Rybacks as well, had cooled toward her since the affair. Anna was glad her friends weren't so quick to judge.

"Thanks for taking care of that," Anna said when she and her sister were alone. She nodded toward the cardboard box on the breakfront.

"It was the least I could do." Liz carried it through the kitchen, and a moment later Anna heard the clang of the lid going down on the garbage can out back. When her sister reappeared, she was holding her purse and jacket. "I should be going. I told Dylan I'd be back in time for dinner."

Liz had wanted to spare her son the funeral, saying he was too young and that it would only upset him, but the truth was he'd scarcely known his grandmother. Somehow Anna found that to be the saddest thing of all.

She was walking Liz to her car when a familiar sight caused her to stop short: Marc's silver Audi turning into the driveway. He must have heard about her mother on the news.

All else faded from view as she watched him climb from his car and start toward her, tall and lean and better looking than any man had a right to be. He paused halfway up the drive, lifting a hand as if to ask, *Okay? You won't shoot me?* Anna stood rooted to the spot, unable to move or even speak, a line from *Jerry Maguire* floating into her head, when Renée Zellweger says to Tom Cruise, "You had me at hello."

She saw when he drew near that he'd cut himself shaving; a fleck of dried blood marked the spot on his chin. "I'm sorry about your mother," he said, nodding toward Liz before fixing his gaze on Anna. His eyes were faintly bloodshot and she thought he looked haggard. She felt herself grow weak. Had he come all this way just to offer his condolences?

"Thanks." Anna didn't know what else to say.

"I've got to run." Liz cast her a meaningful look. "Nice seeing you, Marc. Sorry I can't stay and chat." She ducked into her Miata, backing out so fast she nearly finished the job Finch had started when she'd clipped the mailbox while learning to drive.

Anna brought her gaze back to Marc. "You're a little late," she said. "Everyone else has left."

He regarded her gravely. "Actually, I was hoping we'd have a moment alone."

She felt her heart climb up into her throat, but was quick to squash the hope that rose with it. Did he think he could just pick up where he'd left off? What about what *she* wanted?

Inside, he sat down on the sofa, looking more like the bearer of bad news than someone who'd come to console her. "Can I get you something to eat?" she asked. "I have enough leftovers to open a soup kitchen."

He shook his head. "Maybe later."

She sank into the chair opposite him.

"Why is it that when someone dies, people descend on you with more food than you could eat in a year?"

"I suppose it's because they don't know what else to do." He eyed a plastic cup Laura and Finch had missed. "Were there a lot of people?"

"More than I thought there'd be." Most had been friends of hers and Liz's, with Felicia Campbell and her husband showing up to pay their respects as well.

"I gather it was sudden."

She nodded. "At least she didn't suffer."

He seemed to know she was only echoing the sentiments of others. "I remember when my mother died. People kept saying what a blessing it was that she'd gone so quickly, and maybe that's true, but wish I'd had a chance to say good-bye."

Anna blinked back tears, willing herself not to cry. "It's harder than I thought. I mean, she wasn't even the same person at the end, but I guess that doesn't change how you feel."

"I'm sorry," he said again, only this time she got the feeling it wasn't just about her mother.

"You didn't have to come all this way to

tell me that." She forced herself to meet his gaze. "You could have just called."

"I wanted to see you."

Anger rose in her, as unexpected as the tears she'd shed today when pausing at her sister's grave. Did he have any idea how this was affecting her? What good could he do when his very presence was like salt in an open wound? She'd been holding her own until he'd appeared; now it would be days, possibly weeks, before she could get back to some semblance of normal. Trembling as if with fever, she got up and walked out of the room.

She was standing at the sink, staring sightlessly out the window while the tap ran unheeded when he caught up with her. He reached around her to turn off the faucet, his arm brushing against hers, and she flinched as if scalded. Then she was reaching into her pocket, pulling out a crumpled tissue and holding it jammed against her nose the way she might have plugged a stubborn leak.

"Faith knows," he said softly. "She asked if I was in love with you."

Anna swiveled around to face him. "And

what did you tell her?" Her heart felt as if it'd been squeezed into a too small space.

"The truth."

She stared at him, stunned. Did this mean . . . ?

A wave of cold reason quickly banished the thought: *Nothing's changed except that his wife knows.*

"And that's supposed to make it all okay?" Her voice shook.

"Anna—"

"Because things have changed. *I've* changed. I don't want somebody else's husband. I want my own. And children, if it's not too late. If you're not free to—"

He seized her by the shoulders, roughly almost. "It's over. She's filed for divorce." She saw the pain in his face and knew that he had mixed feelings, that his love for Faith would always be there, like a taproot after the tree's been cut down. "It wasn't just because of you. She'd been wanting to tell me for a while, but didn't know how."

"I think it was incredibly brave." Anna said the first thing that popped into her head.

"Like someone else I know." He brought a hand to her cheek, lightly running his thumb along it. "What I'm trying to say is, I'm yours if you'll have me."

She felt the breath leave her body and for an instant was scarcely aware of her feet touching the floor. "Are you asking me to marry you?" Once upon a time she wouldn't have dreamed of being so bold, but she'd learned that nothing good ever came of holding back.

He cocked his head, smiling. "Yes," he said. "I'm asking you to marry me."

"I don't want to have to quit my job." Despite the joy that swept through her, making her tingle all over as if just in from the cold, a part of her clung to the niche she'd carved out for herself.

"I don't want you to have to, either."

"I could talk to Bob." The idea was taking shape in her mind. Couldn't she work at home and send her column in? "There's just one thing . . ." Her voice trailed off as she sank into a chair at the table, feeling all at once lightheaded.

"What?" He eyed her anxiously.

She stared at the picked-over platters of food, remembering when she'd been fat— before she'd realized that it wasn't what was below her neck that was holding her back, but what was between her ears. Like Dorothy and the ruby slippers, she'd had to find out for herself what the Good Witch could have told her from the start. "I'm wondering whether to rent or sell," she said.

Then Marc was pulling her into his arms, his mouth closing over hers. It wasn't the happily ever after she'd once dreamed of, just the last piece of the puzzle falling into place. He drew back, smiling. "You had me worried there for a second."

She smiled back at him through a shimmer of tears. "You had me at hello."

CHAPTER NINETEEN

The day after school let out, Finch threw herself into the preparations for the party. She helped Ian with the banners and Maude with the canapés she was freezing ahead of time. When Hector needed a hand erecting the tent, she volunteered without waiting to be asked. All the while putting in extra hours at the shop to pick up the slack left by Laura, who was only working part-time these days. Ordinarily Finch might have grumbled, but it was a welcome dis-traction from the moment she'd been dreading for weeks, when she'd have to say good-bye to Lucien.

The afternoon of the party everything was in place. Ian's banners had been hung. Sam's flowers filled every vase and pitcher. A full bar, courtesy of Wes, stood under the tent, complete with white-jacketed waiters. Claire was in the kitchen with Maude, putting the finishing touches on the cake. And Aubrey, who'd been put in charge of entertainment, had sent over a live bluegrass trio that was tuning up on the lawn. But it was the party favors Alice had made—T-shirts with a photo of Laura and Hector at their wedding flanked by Maude and Finch, with the caption AND BABY MAKES FIVE—that looked to be the biggest hit.

Laura looked a little dazed by it all. She'd been up half the night with Essie, who was cutting her first tooth. But she'd been somewhat revived by the huge breakfast Maude had insisted on. Now her main concern was whether or not the overcast sky would clear in time.

The sun broke through the clouds as Anna and Marc were pulling in, a few minutes before four. "Are we the first?" she called out, looking happier than in months.

"I told her we were jumping the gun," Marc said with an easy laugh, an arm about her shoulders as they strolled up the drive. "But she didn't want to miss a minute of it."

Finch was glad he and Anna were back

together. It made Lucien's leaving that much harder somehow, but she'd deal with it when the time came. "You look amazing in that dress," she told Anna. Light blue with spaghetti straps, it fit her like a glove.

"You think so? I wasn't sure how it would turn out. It's been a long time since I sewed anything." Anna flushed with pride as she fiddled with a strap.

"You made it?" Finch was impressed.

"My mom taught me to sew when I was about your age."

"Would you teach me?"

"I'd love to." Anna looked as if nothing would give her more pleasure.

"You have to promise not to tell anyone, though." She had her reputation to think of: being the only student in the history of Portola High to set fire to the Home Ec classroom.

Anna smiled. "Don't worry. It'll be our secret."

Liz arrived minutes later with her little boy. When she let go of his hand, he raced off like a pebble released from a slingshot. Liz ambled over to say hello to Anna and Marc. She seemed happy for them, though Finch couldn't help noting the wistful look she wore—a look that turned to a frozen smile when the Rybacks pulled up in their Jeep. Watching Liz greet them, she understood the weird vibe between David and Liz that she'd caught on more than one occasion. It was funny, she thought, how transparent people were even when they thought no one knew. She wondered if David's wife was as clueless as she seemed.

The thought vanished at the sight of Gerry and Aubrey climbing out of his silver Jag. All eyes turned to Gerry, in a low-cut jersey top and form-fitting black capris. "The fleet's in!" she called merrily as Andie and Justin tumbled from the back seat. Finch smiled. Andie's mother was so different from Laura, who hardly ever bothered with makeup and favored comfort over style. The one thing they had in common was that they were both fun to be around.

Martha Elliston showed up next. Finch had invited her after she'd singled her out at school to thank her for the banana bread. The visit had really perked up her mom, she'd said.

"I'm glad you could make it," Finch told her. Martha looked prettier than usual in a flowered sundress and pink lipstick that brought out the color in her cheeks.

"I almost didn't. Mother's a little under the weather."

"Um, that's too bad," Finch lied. Out of politeness, she'd included the old lady in her invitation but had secretly hoped she wouldn't come. "Nothing serious, I hope."

"Oh no. It's just that she got it into her head to eat an entire jar of sauerkraut and was up all night with the runs," Martha said with a concerned look that didn't quite hide her relief at having the afternoon to herself. "And she doesn't even like sauerkraut."

"I wonder where she got that idea." Finch bit the inside of her cheek to keep from smiling. "Come on," she took Martha's elbow, "I'll introduce you to some of my friends . . ."

Then everyone began arriving at once. Claire's husband Matt and his kids. The Grigsbys with their daughter Natalie. Tom Kemp and his bride-to-be, Ms. Hicks. Olive and Rose Miller in matching lime-green polyester pantsuits and flowered tops. Myrna McBride with a shopping bag full of books on baby care. Dr. Rosario, who'd delivered Jack as well as half the babies in town, accompanied by her husband, a handsome older man with thick wavy hair the same iron gray as hers. And Sister Agnes, bobbing alongside Father Reardon.

Among the last to arrive were Sam's sister, Audrey, and her husband, carting a folding stroller with a huge pink bow tied to it. Audrey, who was nothing like Sam, either in looks or personality, shouted into Uncle Pernell's deaf ear that it was nice to finally have a great-niece to spoil. Which might have stung more than it did if Sam hadn't slipped up alongside Finch at that moment, saying loud enough for everyone to hear, "Isn't it wonderful? Now I have *two* granddaughters."

Anna's lawyer arrived forty minutes late with one of her FAS kids, a shy eight-year-old named Shoshanna who'd been left behind when her mother failed to pick her up from her riding lesson. Rhonda shot Finch a grateful look when she took the little girl in hand, saying, "You like horses? Come on, I'll show you ours."

Shoshanna forgot her shyness soon and was running off to play with the other kids, while Finch lingered in the barn, feeding chunks of carrot to the horses and scolding them like children when they got too greedy and nipped at each other over the tops of their stalls. From the very first day, this was where she'd felt most at home. She loved everything about it: the rich earthy smells, the saddles on their wooden trees like hobby horses, the way the sun slanted through the boards that didn't quite meet. She didn't even mind mucking out stalls, which had once prompted Hector to joke that she must have been born in a stable.

In fact, the only time she'd been on horseback before coming to Carson Springs was a pony ride at a fair. She must have been five or six. All she remembered was the fun of being so high up—and afterward her foster mother treating everyone to cotton candy but her, saying that Finch hadn't thanked her for the ride. But wasn't that the story of her life? Every time something good happened, it was followed by something bad.

"What are you doing in here? I thought this was a party."

She swung around to find Lucien silhouetted in the doorway, loose-limbed and somehow aloof, in jeans and a Tour de France T-shirt. "I guess I'm not in a party mood," she said, feeling as if she'd just swallowed the chunk of carrot in her hand.

He stepped into the sunlight that fell in a wedge over the hay-littered floor. "I came to say good-bye."

"So this is it, huh?" She'd managed to keep it together so far, but now she felt as though she were falling.

"For now, anyway."

I don't want you to go! screamed a voice in her head, but all she said was, "You'll be glad to see your mom, I'll bet."

"Not half as glad as I'll be to see the last of my dad," he said, with a harsh laugh, though she knew he didn't really mean it.

"I just hope he doesn't change his mind about Christmas." His father had agreed to let her go on the trip, and after talking to him, Laura and Hector had given their permission as well.

"He won't." They both knew it wasn't his dad they had to worry about: Six months was a long time and a lot could happen between now and then. "That reminds me . . ." He pulled something from his back pocket. "I have something for you."

It was a CD. She peered at the label and began to laugh. "Christmas carols?"

"That way it won't seem like such a long wait. Hey, it's not that funny." He drew closer, frowning.Tears were streaming down her cheeks—but not from laughter. He pulled her to him, wrapping his arms around her. He smelled clean, like just after a shower.

"I wish . . ." Her throat closed up.

"Me, too." His arms tightened about her. "We'll e-mail each other every day." She nodded, lips clamped together so hard they were quivering. "And if I run up a huge phone bill, maybe she'll decide to send me back. So either way, we can't lose."

"You'll miss my grand debut." She'd be riding Cheyenne in the Fourth of July parade.

"Simon promised to take lots of pictures."

He kissed her gently on the lips. When they drew apart, she saw that his dark eyes were glittering. "I better go. My dad's waiting."

"Okay, then. Bye." Outside the band was playing something lively, and the smell of chicken on the grill drifted across the yard. Lucien was almost out the door when she called after him with a choked laugh, "Hey, how did you know my favorite was 'Chest-nuts roasting on an open fire . . .' "

He flashed her a grin that went through her like a knife. "Lucky guess." Then he was gone, dust motes swirling lazily in the shaft of sunlight where he'd stood. A moment later she heard the sound of a car pulling out of the driveway.

She pressed her cheek to Cheyenne's neck. It wasn't fair. Why did she always end up getting left behind? Starting with her mother, who'd dumped her at a McDonald's when she was five. Was it always going to be like this? Would she spend the rest of her life like Chicken Little, waiting for the sky to fall?

When she finally rejoined the party, she found Andie and Simon teaching the younger kids to toss horseshoes in the sand pit out back. If they noticed she'd been crying they were tactful enough not to say anything, though Andie was extra solic-itous and Simon, for once, didn't crack any of his stupid jokes.

Finch was on her way into the house when she caught sight of Anna and Marc swaying in each other's arms on the makeshift dance floor built out of plywood. Watching them, she'd never felt so alone.

In the kitchen, she found Maude arguing good-naturedly with Claire over how much sugar to put in the lemonade while Sam and Gerry carried platters of food out to the tables under the tent.

Essie was crying somewhere in the back of the house. Finch followed the sound into the nursery, where Laura sat with the baby in the rocking chair, attempting to calm her. "It's all the excitement—she's not used to so many people." Laura raised her voice to be heard over Essie's howls.

"Why don't I take her while you get something to eat," Finch offered.

Laura handed her over and Essie stopped crying at once, looking up at Finch wide-eyed before breaking into a drooly grin. A long-buried image surfaced: a smiling woman in a blue dress bending over her. She had a sudden sense of something tipped over righting itself as she took hold of a fat brown toe, wiggling it as she chanted in a singsong voice, "This little piggy goes to market. . . ."

I love hearing from readers! If you'd like to contact me with any questions or comments, just log on to www.eileengoudge.com